THE WINTER PRINCESS

KEIRA DOMINGUEZ

KLICKITAT CANYON

CONTENTS

For Jane, my lone wolf

1

—·—

Not Nice

FREJA

I can't blame this disaster on Oskar Velasquez.

Opening the notebook and adjusting the microphone, I smile at the assembled guests in The National Museum. A whisper of unease feathers through me, but I note my mortal enemy holding up an entire wall of Dutch Masters. Spite carries me forward.

"Welcome to The Nat," I begin, a little tight. "Thank you for supporting the arts in Sondmark."

The crowd is too large and the event too ostentatious for a lecture to kick off a new exhibit. My speech was supposed to involve a projector screen, folding chairs, and a lectern in a room that might fit twenty. Thanks to the press and their wall-to-wall coverage of my little sister and her national-hero, Navy-officer boyfriend, our mother needed something to disrupt the news cycle.

What better event than a gala with jewels, fashion, and every prince and princess Sondmark could throw at it? Five of us flung like balloons of paint against an Arduino canvas. Splat, splat, splat, splat, splat. I swallow down the frustration and embarrassment of having my own event taken out of my hands and turned into just another royal engagement.

Oskar shifts, folding his arms over his chest, looking bored and, it must be admitted, handsome in a tuxedo, the white of the shirtfront contrasting nicely with his skin. Though he didn't cause this disaster—only bears witness to it—I allow my worries and irritations about the evening to flutter around his head like moths in the light until I can just about convince myself it's his fault.

I jerk my eyes to the page and continue my remarks, entitled *The Heart in the Machine: Romantic Painters and the Industrial Revolution*, a radical reimagining of the presentation I had prepared, its dense footnotes and references starved back to a string of bullet points and an amusing bit about steam engines.

Beyond the crowd, soft-footed catering staff prepare the lavish banquet, and I want to curl up into a ball. It's too much.

"It's any mother's prerogative to help her children be successful," Mama had explained when I'd warned her about this very thing. But Mama is "any mother" the same way Genghis Khan was a noted equestrian. Yes, but mostly no. She couldn't serve middling cheese platters to the prime minister. She couldn't be content with anything less than ice sculptures and a red carpet. My boss, Director Knauss, agreed to it all. *Vede, vede, vede.*

I haul my attention back to the speech, exercising all the hard-won tools I picked up at Swiss comportment school.

Keep it short.

Project your voice.

And breathe, for the love of heaven. Breathe.

I'm rounding the turn on the final page when I glance up to see Oskar checking his watch. A muscle works in his jaw. *Stultes es*, what's his problem? The speech will last less than five minutes, altogether. I've had elevator rides last longer.

"In conclusion," I say. With these words the room reanimates, the promise of free liquor on the horizon. "This exhibit will help us remember one of the most profound lessons of the Sondish Romantics. Even if our world feels as automated as an ironworks or a manufacturing plant, we all feel a deep human need to be seen and to belong."

A smattering of polite applause follows, and I step from the podium. Director Knauss, who has been trying to attach himself to my mother's side all night, leans forward. "Well done, Your Royal Highness. Well done. The exhibit can't possibly fail when it's been sprinkled with your magical princess fairy dust."

Magical princess fairy dust. My smile is meager. I've poured thousands of hours into my job at The Nat without taking a *fennig*—hours spent lining up donors and selecting pieces to be borrowed from collections in America, the U.K., and Vorburg. It took the better part of two years, and he makes it sound like I texted him the details in all caps, adding crown and tiara emojis.

He only agreed because he's an insufferable suck-up when it comes to the royal family, and being funded primarily from a prime minister's grant, this exhibit wouldn't cost him much.

When he takes his leave of me, I glance over the main building, an architectural wonder in 1965, and notice chipped tiles and suspicious stains. Since Director Knauss took over, each area of the museum has been subjected to deep cuts, pitting departments against each other in a battle for precious funds.

My brother and three sisters congratulate me on the speech, and then Mama leans forward and kisses the air beside my cheek. "Beautifully done," she says before drifting into a sea of political figures. Most of my siblings drift, too, but Ella plucks a *frikadeller* from a passing waiter and presses it into my hands. *Eat.*

I pop it into my mouth and chew unobtrusively. The texture is typical party fare left to steam too long in a chafing dish. Rubbery. My stomach grumbles for more but the only people who can afford to be photographed eating are politicians at election time.

Ella tips her head back to see me properly. "You did a brilliant job."

I smile. "You're a good liar."

She acknowledges the compliment with a finger salute. "Some artists work in paint, others in stone…" The salute twirls away. "Sorry about the hatchet job Mama did on your speech. I doubt anyone could tell. Anyway, you look amazing."

This, I believe.

"I'm wearing vintage Sergei San Martin. This flower pattern," I say, lifting the deep blue fabric, "was taken from a painting. The green sash was color matched." I could go on about the long, tight sleeves with tiny puffs of volume at the shoulder, an echo of the fashions of the late 19th century when the painting which inspired it had been commissioned. I could go on about fashion forever.

But Ella's eyes are already glazed over, and she shakes her head. "Not just the dress, Freja. You."

I nod. Sure, sure.

Ella reaches up to kiss my cheek. "Time to circulate. Do you want to come along?" she asks.

Another shake of my head. Ella has been voted Sondmark's favorite princess in *The Daily Missive* reader's poll for six years in a row. I'm not always dead last, but if anyone has magical princess fairy dust, she does. I have my points, too. I can reach anything on the top shelf. I have an interesting cleft in my chin. I can speak about art for five whole minutes. Still, it doesn't serve anyone well to stand near a fraternal twin and invite comparisons. I can almost see them sort us into tiny, constricting boxes—the smart one, the pretty one, the funny one, the thin one.

I look over the gallery and try not to consider the expense of fresh-cut flowers and fairy lights. A massive banner across the gallery entrance reads *The Romantics of Sondmark: Art of the 1800s* and then in smaller script *Coming for Christmas*. It's slightly lopsided which I find strangely reassuring. I take a cleansing breath, feel Mama's gaze on me as I often do—like two fingers over my wrist, checking my pulse—and plunge into the crowd.

Mama commands a circle of government officials and says, as I pass, "Borrowing art pieces from abroad allows us to strengthen our international ties." She then aims a bland expression squarely at the prime minister, whose foreign policy preferences trend toward putting Sondmark in a hermetically sealed bubble.

I stifle a laugh, glancing away to meet the dark gaze of Oskar Velasquez. His presence should be as calming as the lopsided banner, a reassuring if irritating tether to a world I'm familiar with, but the hairs on the back of my neck prickle.

My oldest sister, Alma, is poised to cross his path, and I want to warn her that Oskar, thirty-ish and barely civil, lives in the dungeons and feasts on the bones of all who venture near. That our feud is marked by a thin veneer of professionalism and collegiality is beside the point. Sometimes one knows things that haven't been spelled out in a declaration of war.

I move from group to group, breaking up talk of tariff negotiations, drawing attention to the exhibit banner. A cabinet minister greets me with a look that says, "What are you going on about? Oh, that's right. The art thing." Tight smile. Murmured platitudes. Back to tariffs.

After a decent interval, I melt silently out of the party, making my way through a series of broken concentric circles ringing the main hall. I retreat to the furthermost band where the lights are low and the music is faint, breathing a long, peaceful breath. Behind me, the sound of another set of heels echoes against the tiles.

Ella, knowing my habits, has followed. When we halt, she pivots in place, assessing.

"Quiet, empty, and full of beautiful things. Just your speed. Though," she says, examining the seating Director Knauss installed last year, running a palm across the high sloping surfaces, "the benches were designed by a sadist."

She's not wrong. They're an example of hostile architecture–design meant to keep guests moving, offering no real rest. After a period of discreet trial and error, I've found the knack of perching on them, a leg slightly hitched, the tip of one shoe holding my position.

Ella is considerably shorter, and after several failed attempts to summit the bench, she leans against it, staring at the massive canvas behind me.

"Tell me what I'm looking at," she commands.

I glance over my shoulder. "Oil on canvas by Lars Kette. That's every notable clash in the Battle of Durmstein. If you sort through the mounted knights and Prussian mercenaries slaughtering one another, you'll find the king of Vorburg's head stuck on a pike."

She assumes a Where's-Waldo silence and then blurts, "Ew. The luggage boys are dancing around like it's a maypole. No wonder they hate us."

I train my eyes on a much smaller piece—one with secrets not so easily discovered as the ones in the epic battle scene.

"What are you looking at?" Ella asks, not turning around.

"A scandal," I murmur.

"Hmm?" She cranes her neck and jabs me on the shoulder when I don't answer.

"You remember there were demonstrations when Mama married Père?"

"Demonstrations" is a polite understatement. There were riots. Père's country, Pavieau, had been taken over by a military dictatorship, but due to a long-standing marriage contract, Sondmark was forced to accept a Pavian prince consort. The political cartoons of their imagined wedding night have scarred me for life.

Ella murmurs, and I gesture at the small piece of art. "Copies of that painting were made into posters and carried in counterdemonstrations, pasted on brick walls and in metro tunnels. It was meant to symbolize two cultures blending harmoniously because the painter, Cor Hammersmit, was Sondish but he trained and worked in Pavieau, mixing traditional Sondish folk tales with the more expressive culture of his adopted country."

"What do you mean 'more expressive'? I'm Sondish, and I'm plenty expressive," Ella says, bumping my shoulder with her own.

"That's your Pavian blood showing," I smile, poking my crushed sleeve into shape. "There were calls to send the artwork back to Pavieau or destroy it. There was even a dust-up when it reentered the gallery after Grandpère passed away last year."

She tips her head. "I like it. It's nice."

The Winter Princess is not nice. There are miles of canvas at the museum depicting flaxen-haired children and linen-capped wives, still-lifes of leeks and lutes, but this is something else.

My eyes trace the strong brushwork. The knight's hair is dark and wild, disheveled by the princess's hand. I could recite the informative label from memory, but I am caught, as I always am, by the image of the princess being freed from her icy tomb by love's first kiss.

Most depictions show the fairy tale princess, rigid and blue, with frost crystals on her eyelids, her form obscured in a blanket of snow, passive under the knight's embrace. But Hammersmit depicted a fast-retreating winter and a girl with color already infusing her face and arms. Sparrows, waxwings, and blackcaps—birds who acted as the knight's messengers, carrying words of love to the princess's ears and saving him from being frozen to death when he made his approach—hop interestedly in the foreground, perching on stones and the ends of long stalks of hay.

Even before the princess is fully herself, she grips the knight's breastplate, returning the kiss, her thaw coming from the inside out instead of the other way around.

How did she know he was worth thawing for? The question bothers me.

Ella examines the painting more closely, head swiveling between me and the canvas, back and forth. "She looks like you."

I nod. "No surprise. She was modeled after one of our ancestors, Princess Alice."

"Alice. Queen Magda's Alice? What became of her?"

"The usual. Her mother picked a minor European prince to marry her off to. Parliament approved. A royal wedding followed at Roslav Cathedral."

Ella shudders, and I laugh.

"What's not to love about Roslav Cathedral?" I ask. "When it's our turn, we'll be part of history, along with every royal bride of Sondmark, making the most of that long nave, the route lined with tiaras and sashes. The stained glass and carved pulpit—"

"Shut up about carved pulpits. I'm not a princess," Ella scowls.

My brow arches. "No? Someone should tell our mother and track down every member of the crowd who was outside the Summer Palace when the announcement of our births was affixed to the gates." I touch her arm. "I'll leave it to you to alert our godmothers, three reigning queens, that we're frauds."

Ella's eyes narrow and she wrinkles her nose. "Not frauds, but you're thinking of it the wrong way around. Being a princess is no different from having an online avatar. Princess Ella is only my username when I'm logged into the game. Every second we can steal from all this"—she manages to encompass our gowns, the vintage Rolls Royce we arrived in, and my stilted speech in her gesture—"you can be Freja who works part-time at the museum and wears weird clothes. I can be Ella who watches Asian dramas and has frustrating hair. And we sure as hell don't have to wait patiently to be plunked on some conveyor belt to Roslav Cathedral."

I nod at the Winter Princess. "She's not waiting." The figure's face is intent on the knight, suddenly flesh after decades of ice-bound sleep. "I'd say they're two drinks and a Lars Velmundson album away from a *moetje* wedding." The kind of wedding with disapproving fathers and anticipated vows.

Ella giggles. "It's so hot the snow is melting." She sighs. "If the option is between fiery kisses and Roslav Cathedral, just know that I've already made my choice, no matter how many meters of antique lace Mama tries to bribe me with." She pulls me from the bench, threading her arm in mine as we walk. "Speaking of hot things, what's the story with that man?"

"What man?"

"The one you keep looking at."

The temperature in my body plunges and soars within the space of a heartbeat. *Vede*, who else noticed?

"What do you mean? I wasn't looking at anyone."

She makes a sound in the back of her throat. "You're so bad at lying, I don't know why you bother. Sure, you were looking. He was about this tall." She lifts her hand, slightly above my head. "Quite tan. Too hot to be a politician. He's on the staff of the museum, maybe?"

"Do you mean Oskar?" The name jerks from my mouth, higher and louder than I intend. I recalibrate it with a cough. "I mean, *Neer* Velasquez."

Ella's look is arch. "Is all that looking your way of flirting? Because there are better—"

"That is hilarious," I say.

"Did I say something funny?"

"You don't flirt with Oskar Velasquez. You get out of his way and pray for the lost souls who didn't."

She gives me a long look followed by a tiny shrug. "My hopes are dashed. Haven't you noticed he's an absolute smoke show?"

I've noticed. I've been noticing for three years.

"I wouldn't dare." I fuss with my skirt as though it's caught in a tangle, keeping my face averted.

"No? I could be your wingman. We could probably have this sewn up by the end of the night."

I blink, a flicker of me and Oskar "sewing it up" flashing beneath my eyelids for a fraction of a second.

No.

No. Oskar Velasquez is rude and opinionated and territorial and the opposite of what I want.

"As fascinating as I find that offer," I begin, marching Ella back to the gala. My strides lengthen, and she has to skip to keep up. We're nearing a bend, and I glance back at her. "Our Head of Restoration is a cranky hermit, probably high on paint fumes. He's frankly terrifying."

The words are no sooner spoken than I crash into the wall and reel back. I swallow a yelp and strong hands band my waist.

The wall is Oskar Velasquez.

My palms are pressed against a remarkably firm shirt front, and I whip them off like a child playing a game of "Oskar Velasquez is lava." As regular as the chimes of the palace clock tower, oxygen disappears from my lungs—a frustrating reaction to a man I don't even like.

Gripping his shoulders, I put a gap between his hands and my waist. He releases me, brows lowered.

My neck goes hot and cold. It's not too late to repair our boundaries. "I'm so—"

"Your speech was terrible."

2

— · —

WARM BODY

OSKAR

"Terrible?"

Her hands fall from my shoulders, the weight reminding me that I used to want them there, that I used to imagine kissing Freja—Princess Freja. When she would visit The Nat, fulfilling the duties of her patronage, I couldn't get it out of my mind.

I'm older now. We've known each other too long for stupid fantasies, and it's easy to avoid each other when we try.

We try.

If we didn't try, I'd see Freja every day she comes into The Nat, because we share an office. *Share.* The word is bitter. The very day I was promoted to Head of Restoration, Freja offered to volunteer at the museum part-time. Of course, Director Knauss found space for a princess. I'm an immigrant, often reminded to be thankful I have any place in The Nat at all, so of course, that space was mine. Though we never spoke of it, the frustrations of that day spilled through the administration wing, loud enough for a princess to overhear.

Eventually, I adapted a corner of the restoration studio for clerical work, but she remains in our office, adhering to a sharp boundary that doglegs around her desk and out the door. On one side of the room, there is her clutter—a calendar and a charging station, sticky notes, and books. On the other side—my side—there isn't so much as a misplaced paperclip.

Though we haven't spoken an angry word in three years, I'm as aware as she is that nothing crosses the line.

I trace my eyes along the soft outline of her collarbone to where the base of her throat works a swallow. Freja gives a shadow of a smile, though it doesn't reach her eyes. I have to harden myself against the tug of her lips and the vulnerability it betrays.

"Not terrible, surely. I managed to pronounce the names of two difficult Dutch painters, which must count as a win for our national pride."

Dimly I register that her attitude is an invitation to not take this all so seriously, but I'm trapped here at the museum, it's October 3rd, and I'm supposed to be somewhere else.

"I expected a presentation of a serious paper. Instead, you delivered a few chopped-up generalities hardly rising to the level of a book report." I set my jaw. "Do you know how hard it is to get your foot in the door of The National Museum? Your Royal Highness," I say, well aware that she loathes it when we fail to pretend she's just one of the staff, "this isn't your dollhouse."

Her faint smile disappears. The tendons in her neck tighten and her nostrils flare. The princess is trying very hard not to scream obscenities at me. "*Neer* Velasquez, be reasonable."

I can feel my father's spirit, holding his head with disappointment, but this frustration has been building for years without a release. "Was it reasonable to drag me into work on my day off?"

Her gaze darts to the other princess. The twin. "Go ahead," Freja tells her.

The twin glares at me but she melts away, leaving us alone. Freja takes a deep breath. "You had other plans? There was someone else's night you had to ruin?"

I have every reason to dislike this woman. She comes and goes from The Nat when she wants to. People bow and scrape when she passes. She gets an exhibit approved when no one else has a prayer. Yet still, I can't keep my eyes off her when she walks into a room.

I slip my hands into my pockets and narrow the space between us. "My plans didn't include being a warm body at your party."

Her eyelashes flicker. "Never fear." Her voice is level, like a finger pressing against my chest, pushing me backward. "No one would mistake you for a warm body."

I breathe a humorless laugh, tipping my head back. "You don't want a fight," I say, heedless of the damage she could do if she were serious about starting one. "It's the wrong day."

Her eyes meet mine in a long, lingering study. "Forgive me for running into you," she says, with no mention of wasting my night or the thin contents of her speech. "It will *never* happen again."

"Good," I say, leaning forward, ignoring the Sondish preference for a generous buffer of personal space. "I'm sure the whole experience was...terrifying."

I stride away and hear her sharp intake of breath. I imagine my father chasing me down, fingers pinched together, waving both hands under my nose in eloquent fury. "That a son of mine—a son of mine—would do such a thing!" He would give me a glancing blow up the back of the head and speculate that I was raised among cattle. He might even twist my ear and drag me in front of her to apologize.

A boy in trouble as often as I have been knows how to make a good apology, but my father is not here and, for once, I refuse to hear his ghost.

I reenter the main gallery, carving a path around the dance floor and the cringe-inducing sight of bureaucrats keeping time to the beat. Two hours. Director Knauss demanded I attend for two hours—three if I want a favorable budget review. A waiter offers a glass of champagne and I take it, checking my watch again.

It's too late to make the gathering of more than a dozen other expats in Uncle Timo's ground-floor apartment for Pavian Independence Day, joining an assembly line making freshly rolled *panze* in his too-small kitchen, and toasting King Gilles's health with measures of colorless distilled spirits. The sound—a clink of heavy glasses, liquid splashing over fingers, a swallow, and hearty laughter—returns me to my childhood.

By now, they'll have started singing sentimental songs. "Pavieau, My Home Forever," "Orange Flowers on the Mountain," "Full Nets and Fair Winds." The old ones laugh whenever they hear my Sondish accent and used to tell my father he didn't teach me properly. He used to tell them it disappears when I sing.

The sound of a blaring pop cover erases my ability to hear myself think, and I shift away from the speakers, pacing through the gallery.

Today is just another day in Sondmark. There's no sign that in a tiny country on the Mediterranean coast, flower petals rain down on parades and street parties, celebrating the twin miracles of the nation's founding and the overthrow of a brutal regime.

The gatherings at Uncle Timo's are smaller now that returning to Pavieau is no longer a choice between life and death, and in the past five years, many from our community have been repatriated. My father never spoke of it. He seemed to understand that my home was here in Sondmark instead of in a country I remember only as a series of bright, truncated memories.

For me, the celebration tonight would have been more about my father than about Pavieau. Hearing the clink of glasses was going to signal a pilgrimage, the first gathering I could bring myself to attend since my father passed nine months ago. I wanted to imagine him perched on the end of a sofa, picking a lap harp, accompanying Cousin Emelie's concertina in an off-key rendition of the national anthem.

Instead, I've been compelled to act as an extra in a Sondish royal production without even the satisfaction of being a citizen.

No. I won't ask Princess Freja to forgive me yet.

I take a swallow of champagne and grimace, passing the glass off to a waiter. The movement rustles an envelope in my breast pocket and my lips thin. The Sondish Office of Immigration has one thing going for it. They get scores back promptly.

When I failed the citizenship test this afternoon, a woman named Mies printed off a copy of the results from each of my three failed tests and penciled in an appointment for a final exam on the last day of December which, if I fail once more, will result in deportation to my country of origin.

I haven't lived in Pavieau since I was five.

Mies was wearing purple glasses and likely brands herself as "fun" and "helpful" on employee self-assessment forms, but it's a Potemkin politeness. She can't mask the fact that the rules for citizenship in Sondmark are harsh and draconian. My father was a Provisional Citizen, his refugee status granted during a wave of political purges bloody enough to rally the sympathies of the international community and open Sondmark's fortified borders just wide enough for him and his small family to slip through.

As long as he was alive, I could live and work in Sondmark with few restrictions. I couldn't vote, of course, but I could pay taxes and avail myself of the healthcare system with a small subscription fee.

When I began the citizenship application process, I knew the risks. I would be given the chance to take the test four times as long as I was a productive, employed member of the immigrant community. If I failed each of these, I would be deported. This didn't matter because I would pass. Of course, I would pass. I've lived here since I was five.

Thanks to Prime Minister Torbald, the tests are far harder than they used to be, and though I consider myself culturally Sondish, no one else does. I'm a mere Provisional Resident, even if my home is in Uncle Timo's kitchen with the plastic, flour-dusted tablecloth. It's in my apartment, three stories up from his, with a view of Horst the Invader in the harbor. It's with the tight-knit community of expats gathering their families in the summertime to play *bocce* in the park until dusk.

Familiar anger rises—at the government, at the grueling process to prove I'll be an asset to Sondmark, at my father for dying. It's too much, so I drop my gaze, looking for nearer targets. Let me be angry at the stupid expense of tonight, at the money being spent to massage a royal-sized ego, at the princess with the bright red hair who lifted her chin as I vented my fury.

3

— · —

LONE WOLFFE

FREJA

"My prepared remarks contained a page and a half of citations!"

I want to shout this at Oskar Velasquez's retreating form. I want to run up to the administration wing, print out the original speech, tie him to an office chair, and make him listen as I work over every major event heralding the rise of the industrial era.

Vailys. It's not lost on me that he's probably the first grown man in ten years who hasn't at least dipped his chin in a bow when taking his leave of me. I'm not a stickler for protocol but I take note of the slight.

I take note, too, that he had his hands in his pockets the whole time. I wish—with the heat of a thousand desert suns—that it made him look hunched over and juvenile, like a high schooler waiting for a train on a frigid winter's evening. Instead, he looked the way some men do when they're standing on a tarmac in a full suit while helicopter wash gently lifts the hair from their brows.

Oskar, with his excellent grooming habits and tailored menswear, has always been appealing to me on an aesthetic level. I've had to remind myself again and again over the years that his frustratingly handsome wrapper is like a wasabi throat lozenge passing itself off as green apple hard candy.

"I've been praying for your soul." Ella jostles my elbow, and color floods my face.

I take a deep breath. "I'm going to need it. He heard everything I said about him. The paint fumes, the hermit—"

My sister laughs. "Perfect. He isn't your type, anyway."

"I'm not looking to date him." I scan the party, picking out Oskar easily. He's moving through the crowd, hardly speaking to anyone. "Anyway, I don't have a type."

Yes, I do. I have a type, and I've known it for years. Green apple hard candy. When the medical community masters personality transplants, my love life will be set.

Ella shakes her head. "Your type is someone who gives you personal space and doesn't insist on having your attention."

How can my twin know so much and yet so little about me? I look away from the party, from the back of Oskar's dark head. Even when he doesn't say a word, Oskar insists.

This type Ella imagines I have takes the shape of a British academic who moves at a gentle pace, offers few upsets, and doesn't mind when I ignore him to delve into my own interests. His clothing is rumpled. Maybe he gardens.

"That sounds ideal." I crane my neck, looking over the gallery, and spot him again. Ella goes up on her tiptoes, using me to balance.

"That one is a little, black rain cloud," Ella declares, a line forming between her brows. "How does he manage to frown without moving his face?"

With each breath, I feel myself returning to normal, thankful to focus on my sister and her chatter. "It's his aura. His aura frowns."

"Since when do you believe in auras?"

Since five minutes ago. I rub my thumbs discretely across my fingertips, brushing the faint sensation of electricity away, and glance down. This is the first time we've ever touched, and I wish I had a time machine to whisk me back to the moment before it happened. I don't want to know his touch does this.

"Stay close to me, if you want," Ella says, glancing around. "If I get a chance to knife him in the back, I'll take it, so watch your shoes." She extends her pinky, prepared to make a blood oath.

"The last thing this party needs is a scene," I say, wrapping her pinky in mine and shaking my head.

"Why do you say it like that? A scene is exactly what this party needs."

"I'll be fine," I smile. "I can take care of myself."

It may have been helpful to have a short, curly-haired shield-maiden by my side when I was a teenager, battling scoliosis with a series of braces, surgeries, and physical therapy. Now I can stand on my own, defending my boundaries as fiercely as any border lord.

My gaze drifts toward Oskar, propping up the Dutch Masters again, and I thread my hand through Ella's arm. "Oskar Velasquez is grumpy with everybody. It wasn't personal."

This is a lie. His anger seemed personal. I still feel his chest under my palms, his dark eyes weighing me up, and the way he said *You don't want a fight* like he was spoiling for one.

"That's another lie." Ella narrows her eyes. "The offer still stands." She draws a sharp thumb across the line of her throat—a deadly assassin in blue silk.

"No need. I'll watch where I'm going." I lead her back to the main gallery where the party has grown louder.

I promised Ella I'd watch out for Professor Velasquez, and I do—following the straight set of his shoulders around the room, my eyes landing on his dark head, glancing quickly away. Making certain we never intersect means always having to know where he is.

"Oskar Velasquez is lava," I whisper, scooting between two clusters of guests, arms raised. "Oskar Velasquez is lava."

It's during one of these checks that Marie, a former air hostess, wanders to my side. Director Knauss's long-suffering secretary kisses my cheek and holds me at the tips of her fingers.

"I owned a knock-off of that dress in 1979. Wore it to my second wedding."

"The one to the political longshoreman?"

She sighs with great satisfaction. "He had such a good mustache. No, it was to the novelist who wanted us to live with his mother. I never looked more stunning. I suppose that's the real thing?"

"Every stitch."

"Well, it's perfect. I liked your speech," she says.

"I have it on good authority that it was terrible." I frown into my glass, irritated all over again. "Too short and insubstantial."

"Good authority, nothing. You gave your audience something light and foundational, tailor-made for a crowd that requisitions art by the truckload," she says, tracing the stem of a dahlia up my sleeve with her finger.

I open my mouth to thank her when a high-pitched siren rings over the gallery, filling the space and driving out rational thought. Guests clap their hands over their ears. Only the director keeps moving, rolling his hand high in the air, prodding the musicians to keep at their work. "It's nothing," he giggles, fishing a set of keys from his pocket and making a beeline for a control panel.

Marie narrows her eyes, and a withering descriptor drops from her mouth. "*Vailys.*"

When the alarm cuts off, I sag in relief. Low chatter and loud music pick up almost at once.

I follow Marie's line of sight to Director Knauss's back. "What's he done this time?"

"Nothing new. This is residual anger for spending buckets of money trading out a perfectly adequate security system for one that ensures I couldn't get into the building when I clocked in this morning. Departments are surviving on the backs of donors and volunteers," she says, tipping her glass at me.

The word volunteer conjures someone wearing a lanyard, standing at the door with maps, and directing people to the nearest loo. I put nearly twenty-five hours a week into the museum, beyond the requirements of holding The Nat as one of my royal patronages, but Oskar's words return to me, carrying a sting. *This isn't a dollhouse.*

Suddenly, Marie pivots to my side, pointing up at a Renaissance painting, her hands sketching the lines of the frolicking nude figures. I am bewildered until she tips her head and says in a low whisper, "Freja, love, why does Oskar keep looking at you?"

Is he? I quell the wish to turn and see for myself. "Is he glowering?"

"Just a sec." She taps me on the arm and executes a masterful pivot—nonchalant, innocent. I wonder if the political longshoreman was a spy.

"It could be interpreted as a kind of sexy glower." Her tone is doubtful.

A line forms on my brow. What does a sexy glower look like?

She taps her chin, considering. "It might be sexy thoughtfulness."

"Are you going to call all his looks sexy?"

She waves a hand at the painting, preserving the fiction that we're engaged in a discussion of profound artistic and historical importance.

"I know sexy when I see it."

"I ran into him earlier. Banged right into his chest."

"Lucky girl," she chuckles.

"He wasn't pleased at all." Just thinking of the interaction makes me annoyed all over again. I hate that I agree with him about the substance of my speech. I hate the way I can't stop thinking about being pressed up against him.

Marie's exquisitely plucked brow arches. "Are you sure about that? You look positively delicious in that frock."

Marie has it all wrong. Our interaction was nothing but antagonistic, and somehow, I find the most offensive thing about it was his hands in his pockets and the easy set of his shoulders. Like I was a threat he didn't even have to protect himself against.

I could be a threat if I wanted to, cutting up his peace of mind as surely as he cuts up mine.

The thought erupts in the tiniest laugh. Among my family, I'm known as the Lone Wolffe, for keeping my own council and tending my own garden. Not for me are hot-headed incursions into enemy territory, galloping into the host with lances drawn and arrows nocked. As long as Oskar Velasquez keeps his distance, he has nothing to fear.

Instead of answering Marie, I hail the Head of Curation, a man who can be counted on to become wildly agitated about the topic of mid-70s architecture, to join us.

He gives both of us a small bow. "Your Royal Highness. Marie." Despite the formal title, Roland kisses my cheek like a much-loved uncle. "I like what you've done with the place. *The Romantics of Sondmark* will be the most comprehensive exhibit of its kind in sixty years."

My first impulse is to apologize for taking up desperate resources, but being part of the royal family of Sondmark—an institution that could swallow me without so much as pausing to chew—makes me careful to draw clear boundaries. It's Director Knauss's problem to worry about the fiscal health of The National Museum. Not mine.

So, instead of commiserating with Roland about the broken drinking fountains in the Breughel wing or the constellation of buckets the janitorial staff put out during every rainstorm, I murmur a thank you.

I glance up. Oskar Velasquez has moved. Instead of a comfortable gallery away, he's lingering barely a meter from me, neither speaking to anyone nor joining our circle, his face possibly thoughtful, possibly glowering. When he won't glance away, my mind stutters like the old outboard motors I'd encounter at summer camp. I'm sawing away at the pull cord. Start. Start.

I turn to Roland and begin, hardly knowing what I'm about to say, hoping I'll grope my way to something sensible. "I'm looking forward—"

The commotion of the gallery spikes, and I feel drumming in my ears. Nerves. I dismiss it until Roland's eyes slide past mine and widen in alarm.

"Watch out," he shouts, clamping his hands on Marie, and dragging her backward.

I glance over my shoulder to see several police officers chasing Director Knauss. What? Before I can make sense of it, the director crashes into me, landing between my shoulder blades and shoving me off balance, the pain of it ripping up my spine. The deliberate posture of a princess is abandoned as I flail, hands reaching for anything to stop me. When someone arrests my fall, I clamp onto him, crumpling wool and satin in a death grip, my head landing in the crook of his neck.

Vede. Not him.

For the second time tonight, I crash against Oskar Velasquez and feel his heartbeat thudding under my hand. There's no time to recover before the director crashes into me again, hand curling over the back of my collar, jerking me. Oskar holds tight and I hear an ominous rip, feeling the sudden coolness of air where I shouldn't. Down and down. My dress.

Within the space of half a breath, Oskar folds me tight to him and pivots. I wait for the painful wrench in my spine, but the motion is smooth, and I'm propelled out of the path of destruction, my thoughts stumbling to catch up to the reality of being pressed against a gallery wall by my work nemesis under a massive canvas of Renaissance nudes. The crowd surges, pushing us closer together. If Oskar Velasquez is lava, I have turned to cinder and ash.

Time slows and I register the gallery spotlights as bright blurs. His breath and mine mingle in the narrow cleft between us. Only a second or two passes but I feel unmoored when he straightens, peels off his jacket, and drops it over my shoulders.

I push the lapels aside. "I'm fine," I say, the suffocating proximity of him makes me short.

His jaw hardens and he tugs them closer. "You're not."

My hands drop away, but once the jacket is secure, I shove him back, bringing more to my view than the exposed column of his throat. The crowd pushes me again, but Oskar's hands grip my upper arms, keeping me on my feet. An opening between people gives me a narrow view of two police officers wrestling Director Knauss to the ground.

The director of The National Museum emits a cloud of sweaty, red-faced obscenities, and I hear an officer say what sounds very like, "*somethingsomething* Fraud Act of 19-*garblegarble*. Theft Act of 1989."

Director Knauss whips his head up, the glowing skin of his unnaturally smooth forehead hot with rage. "Take your *flamen* hands off me," he bellows.

"...and three charges of embezzlement," one of the police officers concludes, his breath hitching with exertion.

A wave of shock rolls through me. Roland sinks against one of those awful benches.

The officers lift Director Knauss with brisk efficiency, marching him past the queen and her government. At the threshold, he makes one last dash before he is tackled again. In the ensuing scrum, he loops his foot in the ropes holding the slightly lopsided banner in place.

When it falls, it takes out the prime minister and half the cabinet.

4

AUSTERITY MEASURES

FREJA

The Rolls sweeps through the gates of the Summer Palace, and Mama glances over. "I'll take care of everything."

Since witnessing Director Knauss's arrest, I've been in a state of frozen shock. Now that we're on palace grounds, emotion begins seeping back into me—waves of mortification at how large the gala turned out to be, the adrenaline rush of delivering the speech, the dance along a knife's edge as I contended with Oskar, the electricity of his touch, and the sheer panic of watching the exhibit launch crash to the ground.

Maybe I shouldn't leave the palace for a few days. Maybe I shouldn't leave the palace ever.

In the Grand Hall, Mama directs the others to go ahead, leaving us alone, cocooned in expensive silence. This is when my siblings would be feeling the iron fist of Queen Helena, the subject of correction and critique. Aides would be dragged out of bed and assignments fired off.

Mama kisses my cheek. "I'm sorry it was such a rough night."

There are reasons for this softness. We don't jockey for position as she and Noah do. I don't escape Mama's intensity by hitting all my marks as Alma does. I don't set myself against her as Ella is determined to. I haven't emerged this autumn with power in my own right as Clara has.

Instead, I heard the lullabies of a tired queen as she bent over my hospital bed and had her coax me to take "one more bite" of Pankedruss, the spoon becoming a sword, knighting me for my good behavior. I felt her tears in the dark as her body bent around mine.

Our rare relationship of easy affection and unguarded tenderness means I can afford to be honest.

I straighten my shoulders. "If there's anything to clear up, I'll do it. My work for the Crown and my work for The Nat are separate things. I'd prefer to keep them that way."

Mama's mouth sets. Involving herself in my exhibit has been a distraction—something to manage instead of brooding about how she and Père have been in a chilly standoff for almost a year. Planning a gala helped avert her focus from how she's losing the battle to keep Clara's private life in line.

Losing. I exhale a silent laugh. *Lost.* Clara isn't going to get over Max.

Mama gives me an appraising look. "You're good at that," she says, pride coloring her tone. "Building a wall, one word at a time, keeping people in their place. Very royal."

I smile, "You're not people, Mama." I wouldn't dare try to keep a queen in place.

She returns a smile, too flat to be quite real. "We can't undo what's been done. We can only manage the fallout. When that comes, you'll need my help."

I nod and return to my suite, imagining an alternate evening, one in which I showed up to deliver a lecture to a nearly empty room, a rote press release went out in the morning, Oskar Velasquez didn't have to come if he didn't want to, and everything went according to plan.

In that other world, my hands wouldn't have wound up against his chest.

I rub my palms together, trying to overlay the memory of it, feeling the echoes like a song that won't get out of my head. I place my shoes neatly side by side and reach for the button securing my dress. Oskar's jacket slides from my shoulder, bringing the scent of nutmeg and lemon.

A wash of cool air chills my back and, pulling my hair aside, I turn, inspecting the damage in a full-length mirror. I take a sharp drag of air through my teeth. Much worse than I imagined. The material is ripped from neck to waist, the delicate embroidery hanging in threads. I tug the jacket from my other shoulder, holding the collar loosely in my hand. Not good.

Careful not to do any more damage, I step out of the dress, tracing the thin white scar running from the nape of my neck past my shoulder blades, the sinuous line offset from the trail of my spine. An angry red scratch raised by Director Knauss's rough handling pulses alongside it, and I feel the tender shift of muscle, leaning back for a closer look.

Disaster.

After changing, I switch on a recording of *Nessun Dorma* and roll out my yoga mat, assuming a side plank position. I close my eyes, willing the seconds to pass quickly. My muscles tremble. Exactly halfway through, I switch sides, the new group of muscles getting the same punishing treatment. "Vincerò, vincerò." *I will win. I will win.* The last lyrics fade, and I drop onto my back, breathing with more effort than I'd like.

My eyes narrow on Oskar's jacket and I frown. I'll have to thank him. In a high-stress situation, his quick thinking protected my privacy. As it is, people don't think of me without thinking of my back.

There's not a rope line I walk where I don't meet some teenaged boy bragging that he has more titanium in his spine than I do, or a young girl in a brace holding a "My Princess Has Curves" sign. The fashion press has picked up on the fact that my high-necked retro style keeps my scar hidden from view. They wonder how bad it could be. For longer, weightier pieces, reporters haul out my scoliosis story as an inspiration.

When I finally slip between the sheets, waiting for sleep to claim me, my thoughts take two wildly different paths. I'm thankful to Oskar for shielding my scar and backside from the news-consuming public. Very thankful. Couldn't be more thankful. Give me a sash and a scepter, crown me Miss Gratitude.

But, also, if someone had to see me at my worst, why did it have to be him?

At the breakfast table, I drag a copy of *The Holy Pelican* close. The image on the front page shows me tipping perilously, mouth agape, while Director Knauss's snarling face takes up the other half of the frame. I can't be mad at the picture, considering the one they almost got. I look amazing in that dress, while the director looks like a rabid prisoner escaping wizard jail.

The headline reads "Knauss Caught With His Hand in the Till," and I scan the story, mumbling to myself. "Director Erik Knauss, 57...double life...luxury apartment...diverted funds...worked at an accountancy firm for many years before helming The National Museum and promising to follow the government's lead in implementing austerity measures..."

I snort. Austerity measures. Stealing millions and making The Nat survive on breadcrumbs is one way to get it done.

As soon as my morning commitments are concluded, I race to the museum, following the directions of a lanyard-wearing volunteer to the crowded conference room. I slip into the back to see that the news is playing on the screen at the head of the table, catching the tail end of the segment.

The perky news host furrows her brow. "Prime Minister Torbald, in The National Museum at the time of the arrest, was asked to comment."

The feed cuts to the prime minister's residence, the front door in the full autumn sun, showcasing a livid bruise on his forehead. Shoulders hunched and eyes squinting, the prime minister mumbles his way through a statement in a way only aristocrats can get away with.

"Of course, it's very sad. Very sad. Very, very regrettable. A man in a position of trust to abuse it as he did is a shock to the whole country."

Heads nod around the conference room. For the first time, I feel in complete harmony with the prime minister and a calm reassurance pervades me. Constitutional monarchy is such a sane, reasonable way to run a government.

The prime minister continues. "Unfortunately, my visit to the museum brought home the sad fact that The National Museum has become inaccessible, irrelevant, and wholly unnecessary to Her Majesty's people."

The room erupts in a collective gasp and Marie slaps a hand against the table. "There's more," she says, pointing at the screen. We quiet, staring in fascinated horror as the man goes on.

"...met with key figures in my cabinet to address this worrying situation." With enough command of the facts to communicate that this meeting wasn't had while queuing up for coffee, he outlines admittedly bad attendance figures and large-scale charitable contributions, landing deftly on one damning fact. "By far, the greatest endowments are from the government." He shakes his head sorrowfully and places a hand over his heart. "No one loves art as I do. No one cherishes our cultural heritage more," he says.

I make an inarticulate, outraged snort, reminded of how he spent most of last night in a bovine huddle, holding forth on tariff negotiations, his back turned away from some of the greatest art in the world.

"I'm grieved by this turn of events, and I continue to be shocked. However," he says, eyes suddenly trained into the camera, dropping his man-of-the-people guilelessness, "while Director Knauss might have stolen money from the museum, the museum has sponged far more from the citizens of Sondmark with no return on investment. In the coming days, I will ask Her Majesty's government to turn off the spigot."

When the perky news host pivots in her chair, saying, "Strong words from the prime minister...," all hell breaks loose in the administrative conference room of The National Museum.

Before the enormity of the problem threatens to overwhelm me, I begin building a containment area for my worries, ruthlessly throwing all kinds of things over the wall if they're not my concern: Broken drinking fountains? Over the wall. Funding shortfalls? Wall. The backlog of repairs? New purchases? Storage fees? Wall, wall, wall.

I have to focus on the exhibit. With the prime minister's words, the life I'm carving out on my own—a life that goes beyond the crude shorthand of being a royal princess or battling spinal malformation—is under siege.

I think of the director's office—the opulent carpet, the ornate fittings, the hand-crafted bookshelves lining the walls. All empty. My fingers tighten into a fist. That should have been my first clue. Never trust a man with empty bookshelves.

Though the room is still loud, the noise organizes itself into a familiar pattern. This is the way Sondish people deal out the plain-speaking we're known for the world over. A dozen department heads and assistants shout over each other, each complaint threaded between and through counter-complaints, woven tightly enough to hold water.

"He denied me funding for more audio guide headsets," Agnes huffs. "Such short-sighted *fennig*-pinching. Half the ones we have are broken and the narration so out of date—"

"When do we have enough visitors to use them?" Lynda counters. "It's practically the Cave of Solitude down there."

Rik, our facilities manager who can perform miracles with a pallet jack and a cargo elevator, bangs his fist on the table. "Did you know I've been laundering cleaning rags at home for over a year? If I see one more burned-out lightbulb—"

"We have to make a plan. The prime minister isn't kidding around." Agnes again.

Marie interjects, a calm and steady influence, "Before anything's decided, we have to wait for everyone to arrive."

"*Dominanstid*, just start the meeting," Rik bellows, leaning back in his chair. The tiniest shove and he'd fall out. "If that *Pavi*–"

"Out of line," Marie cuts in, sudden authority hardening her tone.

Pavi. Blood retreats from my face, my hands, and my feet. The word fills the room, making people shift and send me sidelong glances. As a child, I heard my father call himself "a bit of Pavi flotsam" washed ashore in Sondmark. Mama would laugh and correct him, "Pavi treasure."

My family uses it as a term of endearment, but that's too much nuance for Rik. Too often I've seen comments on the internet venting frustrations about the royal family and the quickest, rawest descriptor of Père is Pavi—the word an obvious slur.

Rik hand-waves away the insult. "We tried calling him. If he wanted to be here, he would be here."

"There's a process laid out in the museum bylaws," Lynda insists.

Lynda runs Human Resources and delights in burying volunteer docents under so much red tape that they're mummified when they finally lead their first tour groups. I am not surprised she knows about bylaws.

I slip nearer Marie.

"What's holding us up?"

She lowers her voice. "When a director is removed, a temporary governing committee is formed to choose the next director. The governing committee must be formed from every department head." She gestures around the table.

Lynda breaks in. "Last I checked, the Head of Restoration is a department *head*." She points to her own head to drive the point home.

"Who, in turn, reports to Roland in Curation," shouts Agnes, the Education and Outreach chief, but her comment only sets everyone off again, demanding management flow charts. Roland looks vaguely confused.

"To move forward, you need the Head of Restoration?" I ask Marie quietly.

She nods. "You know Oskar's not fond of staff meetings."

Not fond. Lava ignites my skin.

My worry for the museum shifts, turning outward and distorting. I'm furious, forgetting the jacket landing across my shoulders last night and his hands bracing my arms. I remember only three years' worth of cold words and hard eyes.

"Are his legs broken?" I spit.

Marie lifts a shoulder. "Oskar's not much of a joiner."

Not a joiner? Her mild assessment rips the pin out of my emotional grenade. The fate of my exhibit is hanging in the balance, and some egotistical *vailys* has the nerve to blow off a simple meeting? No.

"I'll get him."

"He's—" Marie starts but I'm already moving out the door and down the hall.

Restoration. Restoration. It's in the basement level somewhere, and I'm already rethinking the decision to blow past the lanyard lady and her helpful directions. I race through the main gallery and shove through an "Authorized Personnel Only" door, skipping down another long flight of stairs.

After running into a few dead ends, my anger is like a heavy metal band trying to find the stage. Let's rock and roll, already. Finally, when I feel hopelessly lost, I see a set of double doors helpfully labeled in large black letters. Restoration.

I bang through them, stopping short.

It's dangerous to allow Oskar to occupy any corner of my mind at all, but when I've allowed him to do so, I've imagined his basement as a dungeon with suspicious liquids boiling on trivets and instruments to summon his associates from the underworld within easy reach. This isn't even a proper basement. The land slopes away at this corner of the museum and two large windows set into a north-facing wall admit a large quantity of natural, indirect light into the room. They frame an expanse of rolling parkland, the trees beyond already turning orange and red. Broad tables are arranged in the center of the space and empty frames hang on simple metal brackets affixed to the walls. In one corner, there's a bank of white cupboards and a sink. Cotton balls—not the severed tongues of his enemies—fill a glass apothecary jar, and flat file cabinets with wide, shallow drawers line another wall.

No wonder he doesn't want to share a measly office with me when he's got the best place in the whole museum.

I continue my inspection and find a simple iron sitting on a shelf. My mind doesn't know what to do with it. This is the puzzle that jerks me back to my mission.

"*Neer* Velasquez," I call.

Silence.

"Oskar Velasquez," I say, louder.

"Read the sign," he growls, his enunciation more correct than a royal princess's.

My eyes dart around, landing on the ripped corner of a framing mat. In thick, black copperplate it reads, "Busy." An arrow points at a notepad and pencil nearby.

"You don't understand," I say, striding forward a few paces. The vision of the exhibit banner falling to the ground and knocking over the prime minister has been replaying in my brain all night. "You're needed for a staff meeting."

"I doubt that. Is the sign illegible?"

I examine the scrap in my hands. It may be the most legible sign in the history of signs. Impossible to misinterpret. The simple act of lending me his jacket in my hour of greatest need was obviously an aberration.

I raise my voice so it carries. "The prime minister is threatening to pull all government funding. There's a meeting to discuss it in the conference room, and you're going to be there if I have to drag you myself."

I hear an irritated plunk of something hitting water, the roll of wheels on a concrete floor, and a muttered oath. Then Oskar appears from behind a large easel set in front of the windows, his face a thundercloud.

I hold his gaze but brace myself against the instinct to retreat. It's not his size I find intimidating. For a Sondish man, he's not tall, and though his shoulders are level and well-proportioned, his build is more like a runner than a rugby player. It's that he carries himself like the lord and ruler of every room he walks into.

I begin a cold-blooded assessment to determine why this is so. Rik called him Pavi, and he has the same lightly tanned skin as my brother and father. His hair is dead black, the color of a 17th-century Sondish merchant's best coat, and his expression resembles some of those competent, hard-eyed, self-made men.

If only I found this combination unappealing. That I don't is a large part of my irritation about him. A reclusive art restorer should have whiskers and be unkempt. He should have elbow patches on his suit coat. He should look like Roland.

Instead of this comfortable image, Oskar wears a white shirt, cuffs rolled up his corded forearms, suit pants, and a close-fitting vest. These are covered by a canvas apron with leather fastenings, daubed down the front with small, tidy dots of paint. Over his heart, a pen and sliding ruler are held in a leather loop, and when he reaches behind his back to undo the ties, I watch the stretch of his muscled shoulders. So neat. So orderly. The man is begging for disarrangement.

He hangs the apron on a hook and takes his sleeves down, buttoning the cuffs one at a time. Then he reaches past me for a tie, pulling it from a hanger.

I lean slightly away and inhale, scenting the nutmeg and lemons of his aftershave chased by the sweet, piney smell of turpentine. What did I tell Ella he smelled of? Paint fumes? Lies.

Flipping up his collar, he lays the tie across the back of his neck.

I never would have let our friction go on so long if he looked like Roland. I would have tried to win him around somehow.

"The department heads need to elect a temporary director," I explain. I take a step back, seceding some ground, but planting myself firmly. This isn't a social call. I'm mad. I must remember I'm mad. "They've been calling. The least you could do is answer."

A dark eyebrow lifts and he opens a drawer, withdrawing his phone. He looks at me as he presses the power button. Then he reaches for his jacket and shrugs it on. The jacket does have elbow patches, but they fail to give him Roland's quality of avuncular coziness. I can't imagine him carrying caramels in his pockets.

Then he tugs the door open for me. "After you, Your Royal Highness," he says, as though he works in the palace and says it every day of his life.

I brush past him, chin high. His pace is unhurried as he follows. All the while he is knotting his tie, the swish of Italian silk whispering down the hall.

5

PERSONAL VENDETTA

OSKAR

People ask about my work. "An art restorer," they repeat, pleased by the novelty, as though I've ticked a box on a scavenger hunt.

They stuff the bare job description with romantic notions about antiquity and Hollywood heist movies. People have the idea that I work in a tuxedo, that I'm a great artist myself, or an egotist, daring to touch works a thousand years old. People assume I must be in a near-constant state of amazement.

People are wrong.

Five minutes ago, I was restoring a Dutch interior. Despite surviving the War of Spanish Succession and the Nazi occupation, the artwork was nearly destroyed during the conscious uncoupling of a pair of 21st-century Sondish socialites. Though the delicate canvas is more than three hundred years old, any sense of enchantment vanished when the work became a series of tasks to be checked off.

Described properly, it's a job like any other, but now I'm following a princess to a tower, and if that's not a line straight out of one of Viggo Faxeborg's folktales, I don't know what is. All it needs is the addition of a clever crone and a golden ball, a mad king and a talking frog.

I straighten the knot of my tie and drag myself back from princesses and other magical things. My life–my work–deals in concrete objects. Solvents. Dutch linen. Miter saws. Staff meetings.

"Why did you turn your phone off?" Princess Freja snaps. "What was so important?"

Her back is straight as she strides up the hall, taking furious steps, and I try not to notice the irritated swing of her hips or remember the thin, pale line stretching the length of her back. I spend more time than I like trying not to notice Freja when she's around.

Making a brisk, unhesitating turn to the left, she heads to the textiles archive and the loading dock.

I wait.

Ten meters later, she pivots, the controlled expression on her face giving no hint that she took the wrong route if her goal is the conference room. She passes me, her blouse brushing my sleeve, and I follow.

"Well?" she prods. "Why couldn't we reach you?"

"I was in the middle of something."

Freja stops, her hair swaying.

She wants the truth, but I was listening to an audiobook of Sondish fairy tales on my tablet so I don't get kicked out of the country. There are too many emotions dammed up behind that bit of information to let it out freely.

Freja's features shift, and I watch the subtle play of skepticism. I notice, too, the way the tightening of her mouth causes a dimple to appear on her left cheek. Marie says that when I'm examining a painting for the first time, I'm like a hawk inspecting a kill—unwavering and sharp-eyed, narrowing my focus to the confines of a canvas to discover the blend of art and science necessary to recover the lost image. I blink, my chin arcing away, and allow my eyes to fasten on the chipped paint of a fire alarm. I've seen all of Freja I need to see.

Sondish people prefer hearty friendliness to any other emotion, and it's evident in their two favorite activities—cleaning house and getting drunk. Foreign-born as I am, I have a wider range.

"I was almost finished when Your Royal Highness erupted into the room and made threats," I tell her.

"I made no threats." Her eyes narrow and I note that the green irises are rimmed in blue.

Vede.

The story from my audiobook comes suddenly alive—of a shepherd and a spellbound meadow, how he was given a warning about a tree heavy-laden with fruit. He could eat all he liked until its shadow stretched across the meadow. Boys in those stories never heed the warnings, never stop filling their bags when they've had enough, and if they do, no one bothers to write stories about them.

For the sin of losing himself to temptation, he was turned into a rock for eternity.

I look away from Freja. "You were going to drag me to the conference room. You sounded like a member of the *audicia*," I say, the Pavian word slipping in while my attention wanders back to the spotty wash of pink on her cheeks. She does not blush gently. "Mafia," I correct, irritated by the lapse. "Should I worry about my kneecaps?"

The pink deepens and her chin lifts. "Don't be ridiculous." She turns toward the stairs, and I follow, unease camping along every nerve. If my job is on the line, so is my shot at citizenship. Though I've worked at the museum for years and the usual rules about seniority should apply, I don't have patience for administration games or yearly fundraising panics. If people are going to lose their positions, I'm at the top of the list.

But why is a princess getting so worked up? It's not her job on the chopping block. Curiosity makes me slip my hands into my pockets and deliberately slow my pace.

When the distance between us is too obvious to ignore, she turns, retracing her steps. The gallery holds nothing more lethal than the paintings in their frames, a mother pushing a stroller, and an elderly man leaning hard on a cane. I'm safe unless she intends to tear me apart with her bare hands.

"Are you coming?" she asks, her hair a bright splash of color across her navy-blue blouse.

When I see Freja—when I watch her from the corner of my eye on the television or at a staff meeting—the quality that strikes me first is how calm she is. Detached. Disengaged. She isn't calm now, and I want to reach for a palette, mixing up the exact shades of red hair and soft, peachy skin, ruby flakes in her cheeks and down her neck, to sketch out the line of her strong jaw and follow it to her chin with its gentle cleft. The artist in me has chosen a strange time to rear his unwanted head.

"After you." My open palm sweeps between us, urging her along. I can't help the smile touching my mouth as she glares and turns. It's satisfying to bait the little *audicia*.

As we near the conference room, she's a step ahead, pausing before we enter. I collide with her back, gripping her arms to steady us both.

My mouth opens to upbraid her, but she pivots, issuing a short, sharp hiss against her teeth. I know that noise. It's a Pavian noise. My father once said it was untranslatable but means roughly *The government men are coming along the shoreline. Shut up and hide the catch.* Who knows what it means coming from a princess?

Freja drags me to the nearest cubicle. She crouches, and when I don't, she reaches for my tie, tugging me down to her level. The workspace is tiny, and bent over, we are almost nose to nose.

"What?" I ask, my voice gruff. She can't see how every millimeter of my skin registers her nearness.

"Did you notice the brainstorming list on the projection screen? *Vede*, I can't believe they started without us."

No, I didn't have a chance to see anything. I was likely too busy checking out Freja's figure. My lip curls and I lift my head.

She jerks the tie again, and so help me, I like it—the assumption of authority, the way the image of the polite, remote princess slips. A shiver works across my shoulders.

No. I can't like it. Pressing my lips into a thin line, I tug the tie out of her hand, smoothing the Italian silk. I ignore the way my blood feels hot.

"Sorry," she whispers, as though damaging a piece of fabric is a crime far worse than destroying my peace of mind. "They've been coming up with cost-saving measures. Did you see the list?"

I know better than to raise my head.

"Three bullet points," she says, lifting one slim finger at a time. "Absorb the Restoration Department, cut significant numbers of staff, and cancel the Romantics Exhibit."

Damn. In this scenario, the Restoration staff would be placed under Roland's management, slimmed down, and no longer in need of a head. I would be out on my ear. I begin to calculate the level of support I can expect from the other staff members. Freja was right. I can't afford to miss this meeting.

Her stomach gurgles, and she clasps a hand over it, frowning at me again.

"It's not my fault."

She blushes. "I forgot to eat anything before I left the palace."

I shake my head. Better to appear dismissive than amused. I can't afford to find a princess endearing. I begin to straighten and Freja releases a breath, hand wrapping around my forearm. Warmth spreads from her touch. Just as it did last night, my chest tightens.

"If you have even a speck of charm, today is the day to summon it." Her eyes are level with mine. "The museum is in danger of losing its main source of funding, and nothing is safe from the chopping block. Not my exhibit. Not your job."

I can't take my eyes off the way each expression chases over her face. "Speck?"

She shakes her head, refusing to be drawn. "Even an idiot can see we both have something to lose in that meeting. So what are you going to say," she asks, "to keep your job?"

My mouth hardens. "I won't beg for something I've earned."

She lifts her eyes as though praying for patience. "That attitude will get you sacked."

"What do you know about being sacked?"

Freja catches her lower lip between her teeth, releasing it in a blink. My job is on the line. My citizenship. I can't afford to go soft on someone who doesn't need it.

I nod my head toward the conference room. "I'm going to say getting rid of the exhibit would be the fastest way to show the prime minister that the museum is tightening its belt." My glance flicks to her hand on my arm. It's supposed to be a show of irritation but my eyes trace over the bones of her wrist and the slim gold watch banding it. I've never been this close to Freja. I was right to keep my distance.

"Throwing my exhibit to the wolves won't earn you any friends," she counters.

"Why are you concerned about me having friends?" My eyes narrow as an impossible idea forms in my mind. "Wait. Are you trying to form an alliance?"

"I don't need an alliance," she says, drawing herself up to her full height. "I just wanted to know."

She's a princess now, and I'm the subject who shouldn't forget it. Only, I'm not her mother's subject. Not yet. I tug her into a crouch. "You need someone's help. The exhibit must mean something to you—all that work with gallery models, curation research, time spent conducting interviews. You won't just abandon it because a politician is working out a personal vendetta against your family."

"How do you know—"

Please. I tip my head. "I know a grudge when I see it."

"You would."

I didn't mean us. Pavian culture is built around the ability to hold a grudge for centuries. It's too late to put her right.

Her eyes flick to the doorway. "I won't abandon the exhibit, but I'm sure I can save it without—"

"Without a no-account Pavi backing you up?"

Her brows snap down and she stops even trying to hide her anger. "I didn't call you that. I would never call you that."

Again, my frustration with my adopted homeland finds an outlet in Freja. "My apologies, princess. You're so proud of your Pavian heritage, the people of Sondmark never hear the end of it."

Her mouth tenses and I resist the bizarre impulse to smooth my thumb across her lip. I shake my head. Of all the people in the world to form an alliance with, Freja—a Sondish princess, I remind my-self—should be my last choice.

"With your family connections, I'm sure you'll do fine without me," I say, shifting my weight.

Her grip tightens and I feel it in my chest.

"*Stultes es*. Can you choke down some of your own medicine?" she asks, jerking her head toward the conference room again. "You don't have friends in there, and no one cares about your department because you've made yourself as pleasant as a case of leprosy. They won't care about the importance of your job here unless you tell them why they have to. You've never been in a rush to do that." She rakes a glance over my face. "If anyone needs an ally, it's you."

During her speech, she's narrowed the distance between us, and I feel an unaccountable thickness in my veins. I shift and her hand falls away. Just because I don't want her to be right, doesn't mean she isn't. Damn.

"No need to beg," I say. "If you need me to, I'll make sure you have time to explain why staging the exhibit in the middle of a financial meltdown is a brilliant idea."

Freja breathes deeply, collecting herself fraction by fraction. "I only wanted to know what you were going to say."

"That's all you wanted?"

Another breath, then she seems to come to a decision. "I want time to make my case. If you make sure I get it, I'll remind the board—with whom I've cultivated good working relationships—that restoration is indispensable. I'll back you up."

I've kept my distance from our princess for three years, and our borders are crumbling in a single morning. I'm a young boy with an arm full of apples and a face full of the setting sun. Greedy. Tempted.

I take her hand and straighten. "We have a deal."

6

Math Facts

FREJA

I don't like his tone, I don't know about an alliance, and I don't love that my ability to breathe evaporates at his touch. I reclaim my hand, dragging my attention from the Head of Restoration so painstakingly that it feels like I'm unweaving a length of cloth, strand by strand.

"Deal," I say, the word drawn out in indecision.

He nods. "Here's to being resentful allies in a time of crisis."

My nod answers his. We don't like each other—that hasn't changed—but the sense of being opposite poles, forever pushing away from connection, has been lost somewhere between me crashing into his chest last night and our hands clasped between us right now. I feel it in my fingertips. We are allies. We.

Our gazes meet and hold, broken only when Rik's strident bellow reaches us in the cubicle. "Let the whole thing fall down around your *flamen* ears, if you like."

Oskar gestures for me to proceed, and I cross the threshold of the conference room to hear Agnes's equally impassioned reply. "I need those relationships with the university. Years of work can't just be tossed aside. No." She bangs the table. "No. The best thing is to trim the fat. Maybe if we stop buying new things." She sends a withering glare to Roland.

Roland looks alarmed to be caught up in the volume of the discussion. "There's no fat to trim. Curation hasn't made a new purchase in three years, and we sold off an extensive collection of bronze statuary last year."

Finally, Rik's glare lands on Oskar. "Will you look at that? Your Most Reverend Excellency has finally condescended to join us." His chair skitters back as he performs an elaborate bow.

Rik's mangled honorifics have managed to insult both the Prince-Bishop of Handsel—a lovely man of the cloth with a harmless passion for miniature landscape painting—and Oskar.

I learned diplomacy from my mother as she forged the North Sea Confederation. She would tell me that every good alliance begins by building trust. Though I have no love for Oskar Velasquez, we've formed a mutual non-aggression pact, and in this hour, we've promised to fight back-to-back.

I lift my chin. "No need for such deference, Rik. You may call me ma'am."

He sputters. "I didn't mean you...ma'am. I meant the—"

My eyes widen with innocence. "Didn't you?" I glance around as though I've misplaced Oskar, as though I didn't threaten to drag him here and he didn't call me a—what was the word? *Audicia.* "*Neer* Velasquez," I touch the back of a chair next to mine, "your place is here."

"Anyway, you're late," Rik growls, striking the table. "We're talking budget cuts, and the way I see it, we furlough the restoration team until we're in the clear again." He gives a low whistle, hands punching through the air as though clearing an obstruction in a drainpipe.

Oskar moves past and my nose chases the scent of fresh pine needles blanketing a forest floor. *Stop it, Freja.* Stop noticing.

This advice sounds simpler than it is because I've never stopped noticing Oskar, first to find him attractive in a remote way—the way you might fancy the male lead on a perfume commercial or a passing stranger with unexpectedly good facial hair—and then, when we decided to loathe one another, I had to notice exactly where he was so I could avoid him efficiently. I've trained myself to mark Oskar's presence when he's around and to search for him when he's not.

It's never too late to begin ignoring him again. Step one: Don't look at him. I shift my gaze as far as his arm where it rests along the edge of the table, giving me a nice view of the worn elbow patch.

"Furloughing the restoration team is a good plan," Oskar answers. "What are you going to do about the bacteria? Are we going to furlough them too?"

I turn a laugh into a cough.

Rik gives a dismissive snort. "A five-hundred-year-old painting isn't going to rot away in a year."

Oskar brushes the side of his thumb along his jaw. "Maybe not. But the money we save by taking a little care now, will—the British have a phrase." He snaps his fingers, the gesture nimble.

"An ounce of prevention is worth a pound of cure," I supply, adding a quick metric-based translation that loses idiomatic richness but gets the point across.

Oskar nods. *Vede.* I'm noticing. I shift my gaze again.

"The roof needs more than a gram of prevention," Rik counters, still three notches too loud.

It's time to fulfill my part of the bargain.

"That's true. But we can't afford to let national treasures succumb to oxidation or mold. The National Museum isn't the building, but the art and artifacts." I lift a hand, gesturing to include the entire museum complex. "We neglect these objects and we run the risk of breaking trust with future generations and losing our cultural heritage."

I am a prizefighter dancing around the ring, punching her gloves. I am loose. I am ready. Bring it, Rik.

I turn to Oskar, hardly conscious that I'm waiting for his, "Thank you so much. I owe you everything. You are the literal wind beneath my literal wings." He's not looking at me but tracing a line of marquetry in slow, easy strokes.

"Rik is right," he says, glancing down the length of the room. "We do need every *fennig* we can get. Marie–" He gestures to the secretary, thumb and index finger touching, the rest of his palm flat and facing up. That's not a Sondish gesture. "You'll sort us out," he says. "Can you get the numbers? Operating costs, planned expenditures, budget…" His hand loses the Pavian shape and Marie slips out of the room. "We can fix the problem only if we know how bad it is."

That's the art restorer in him talking. I've seen the results of his work. I've carefully inspected it when it returns to the gallery, making sure I do so when he isn't looking. I grudgingly admit that Oskar is good at fixing things—world-class. If there wasn't this barrier between us, I would tell him I admire how he works.

Rik snorts, jerking away from the table so that the rolling chair spins into the wall with a crash. If Oskar is proffering an olive branch, Rik has knocked it out of his hands. "You think you're going to be the boss?" He looks around as though taking a poll. "It's not going to be you."

The more tense the room becomes, the more Oskar looks like he doesn't care. His voice is low, dismissive. "Of course, I'm not the boss. Everyone knows it's Marie."

Marie returns, her arms full of packets, and Roland rushes forward to unburden her, passing the materials out.

"I had these ready," Marie says, slightly confused by the attention her entrance caused. "I don't want you to imagine I have magical powers."

Oskar flips through the packet then glances up. "But you do have magical powers."

I blink. He's a different man when he's talking to Marie. His voice is smooth and practiced, his mouth gently amused. She smiles but shakes her head like a woman who's had five husbands and knows about handsome devils. "Don't try that with me, Oskar. I know your tricks."

His mouth turns up, becoming something feline for a second, then he puts away his tricks and begins going over the numbers like a man who studied Battle Accountancy. I give up trying not to notice him as a lost cause. When he's this close, I can't be expected to help it.

Observing him at such close quarters gives me a new insight. I've been watching my mother run every kind of meeting for over a decade and didn't expect to find her equal in this taciturn, reclusive man. Again and again, he defers to Marie, the least polarizing figure in the room, and holds his tongue unless he has something to say, merely inserting succinct questions to prod discussion.

"Page two?" he asks, the command couched as a question.

"Page two," Marie answers, and everyone flips the packet over.

When we dig into the data, we discover that the gap between actual running costs and requested funds is impossibly wide. In each case, department heads haven't been guilty of outlandish demands. Rik, for instance, requested a new roof and got a small pallet of roofing materials instead.

"It's obvious what we have to do," Rik says, after an hour, tossing down his reading glasses.

"What's obvious," I say, "is that furloughing Restoration doesn't get us anywhere near our target." I close the packet, and he gives me a withering smile.

"But sucking up to the prime minister will. He doesn't even like the royal family." He slides me a sidelong glance "That's what the papers say."

Words tremble on my tongue. *The royal family doesn't like him back.*

Rik smirks. "The best bargaining chip we have is offering to cancel the exhibit led by a member of"—he drums his palms on the table, a crescendo of expectation and suspense—"the royal family."

With that Rik throws my exhibit under the treads of his tank, backs over it, and roars off again as the room erupts with crosstalk, department heads and assistants debating the merits. I read the projector. I knew this was coming. It's what tempted me to form an alliance with a grouchy misanthrope in the first place. I exhale, wishing I'd had more time to prepare, but it's no time to begin worrying about the state of your armory when the enemy is at the gates. One must simply pry the rusty broadswords off the wall and wade into battle.

"The exhibit is already half-launched," I begin, my voice drowned out by infighting. "The British art arrived last week. Surely—"

Time stretches as I search the room for signs that someone is listening. Some of the most beautiful and transcendent works of art in human history are down on the gallery floor, but up in the administration offices, we're making sausage. My stomach gurgles again and I frown, clapping a hand over it. Amid the noise of the room, I feel Oskar's gaze, intent, warm. My breath slows.

Stultes es. Stop noticing.

He gives a sharp, low-toned whistle, looking away when silence presses into every corner of the room. "The Romantics is probably the only exhibit we can stage."

My warrior has arrived.

"How can we afford to stage any exhibit?" Agnes asks, holding her copy of the budget report over her head. "We've all seen the numbers. It's a terrible expense."

Oskar's eyes shift to mine, and even though I detect no measurable warmth in his expression, I take heart. "Ma'am," he asks, "how much does The Nat pay you?"

Ma'am. He must be five years older than I am. "I don't draw a salary."

I wouldn't know what to do with the relatively small sum The Nat could scrape together, but I've often wondered if even a nominal amount would regularize my position here, protecting my right to have a voice in a way that doesn't depend so much on respect for the monarchy.

Oskar glances around the table. "The Romantics exhibit is less expensive than anything else we could put on. Far from being a liability, as a member of the royal family, she has connections no one else in this room has. Isn't that so?"

I don't like this line of questioning, but I have to trust him.

"I didn't pull strings as a member of the royal family," I say. Agnes rolls her eyes, but I persevere. "One of my old professors works for The British Museum and convinced them to lend four works. Getting three more paintings from Vorburg was simply a matter of understanding the political situation. They're desperate to put Sondmark in their debt before the upcoming state visit, and I had some letters drafted on behalf of Director Knauss. Vorburg's royal family approved the loans without any connection to my position."

Oskar is impressed, I can see it in the way his brow gently curves ever so slightly above its habitual line, but Lynda leans forward, reading glasses slipping down her nose. "Even if cost projections are low, there's advertising, leaflets, banners, temporary insurance, transportation, installation. It's not an insignificant amount to be spending right now. The financing for this project came from the prime minister's grant. Is that correct?"

Lynda delivers this with a deadly smile. I slide a hand over the hilt of an imaginary broadsword, hardly expecting someone who wears singing Christmas tree earrings for half of November and every day of December to be this good at deductive reasoning.

"Correct," I acknowledge. "The cost represents a tiny fraction of this year's budget, but if you'll turn to the graph on page seven—"

She tosses the packet on the table and it spins. "Every cut we've been talking about represents a fraction of what's needed. Cutting the exhibit, at least, might carry some symbolic weight for the government. Maybe we could get a show of hands?"

"Stop the vote," Oskar whispers.

I shoot him a glare. We're supposed to fight together, and he's left me like the last deserted island in the Sonderlands archipelago. Alone and under disputation.

I cast about for a brilliant, painless plan to satisfy everyone.

Pool our money and win the lottery? No. Too unlikely. Rob the museum and sell art on the black market? Too risky. Find sunken treasure? Clara's got that new boyfriend, but the seas are rough in the autumn. So, again, no.

I stuff my pride into a deep, dark hole and hiss threats to keep it in its place. It's time to make the most of the connections Oskar spoke of and it's going to hurt.

"Her Majesty the Queen has her weekly meeting with Prime Minister Torbald tomorrow, and I'll ask that we make the museum an agenda item. It might prove an opportunity to smooth some feathers."

Roland slaps the table. "Yes. That's it. That's what we need."

Marie looks uneasy. "Are you sure?"

I give a series of tiny nods like it's no big deal that I'm deconstructing the tallest, thickest boundary wall I have in my life.

Oskar slides me a note and I read his precise handwriting. "Call for a vote on temporary leadership. Nominate Marie."

The vote is unanimous, and I have to admire the way Oskar engineered the outcome. Obliquely. Behind the scenes. No one, least of all Rik, Lynda, and Agnes, objected to his plans because they didn't know they were his.

As curators and staff begin to file out, Oskar rises and touches my shoulder. A quickening brushes along my skin and I stand, pushing the chair with the back of my knees.

"Why don't you want to involve your mother?" he asks, leaning against the table, hands in his pockets. This is not the same man who called me ma'am.

I ignore the question. "You were supposed to be my ally."

His answer is mild. "I said you had the only exhibit we could run."

"And abandoned the field when Lynda arrived with her math facts."

"You handled it," he answers, not begging my pardon. "We have to pull every string we can, and no one else in the room could have suggested an audience with the prime minister."

I look at him head-on, taking in the somber silk tie and the precise fit of his suit, how his eyes challenge mine, how they see everything. He doesn't like the royal family—I know it without being told—but he was quick to exploit my royal position when it came to fighting for the museum. He might hate me. We are birds caught in midair, fighting, clinging, falling. We have not defeated nor been defeated nor gone our own way.

"Tell me how it goes with *Neer* Torbald," he says, writing down a number on the corner of his budget packet and ripping it off. "Call me tomorrow."

I glance at the numbers written in a strong hand.

"You'll answer my call?"

"Always." Then comes the sting. "I can't afford to ignore a royal."

7

—·—

Messy Compromises

FREJA

I could hear a pin drop.

My family used to be noisy. When I was a girl, we'd make so much noise that I'd sometimes have to escape to an unused linen closet with a copy of an Adelheid Nede mystery to hear myself think. The girl spy's cross-country bicycling jaunts and Nazi sabotage were a soothing counterpoint to raucous after-dinner games of charades and *Mali*.

I thought I'd be happy when they all finally shut up, but the quietness pervading the room as we wait for our weekly family meeting to begin makes me uneasy, as though I'm standing in an icy stream as swift, unidentifiable currents drag at my ankles. My father and each of my siblings is absorbed in the agenda, but I touch Clara's arm.

"Have you seen Max this week?" I ask, surprised to find myself needing to be soothed by small talk.

Clara smiles and taps the table with the flat of her fingers. "I'm properly meeting his family on Sunday." She wrinkles her nose. "We're having pot roast at his parents' house. I hope they like me."

"What's not to like?"

She gives a mirthless laugh. "There's been a photographer camped out in front of their place for a week. They won't like that."

So that's what it's like being a princess of Sondmark in a public relationship with an ordinary man. Alma's betrothal to the often-absent Hereditary Grand Duke of Himmelstein hasn't prepared me for what it might be like to run the gauntlet of royal courtship without money and titles to cushion each blow. My interest sharpens, and I lean forward.

"His parents won't blame you for that. I'm sure they'll like you," I assure her.

"They'd better. I've memorized the entire ABBA canon." She snaps her fingers and gives me the opening lines of *Fernando*.

I chuckle. "Why?"

"Max says it's best to be prepared for impromptu karaoke."

We laugh, heads bent together, but swallow it back when the door swings open and Mama enters. Clara straightens in her chair. Père's focus narrows to the painting opposite him—on each tiny leaf in the middling landscape. Ella begins playing with her pen, flippant in a way she hadn't bothered to be before Mama was there to see. Alma's dignity billows in response to a queen who bristles with authority. Noah is watchful.

I'm supposed to feel some version of these things, I suppose, but because I have a thirty-five-centimeter scar running down my spine, I don't. I watch them tighten and tense in her presence with a sense of bemusement, wishing they could see the same woman I do.

Mama opens the meeting with no grace notes, reeling off a list of engagements and concerns with a speed and command of the details that keep us all on our toes. Finally, she turns her attention to Clara.

My little sister calmly answers questions about her patronage, showing none of the warmth and laughter of moments before. Their relationship, like so many of Mama's, carries the baggage of high expectations and the weight of royal duty, but my curiosity turns into respect as I watch their interplay. Clara rises to meet Mama's professionalism, not giving our mother any excuse to call her commitment into question. She's carving her own path, figuring out how to accomplish things that matter, loving someone Mama doesn't approve of and determined to protect him.

I glance at Mama. She used to set aside most of her royal manner around our family, but she's keeping a tight rein on her emotions, even here—like she's burned her hand and thinks every surface is likely to mete out a similar punishment. On one level, I hear her asking about expenses and logistics. On another level, I suspect she has the coordinates of Max's cottage prepared if a nuclear strike becomes feasible.

Satisfied, she moves on to Ella. "Jaegerstaff is producing the Jul beer for the palace. You'll be our family representative at the first tasting."

Ella raises a fist. "Yes!"

"You'll be properly clothed. Heels and stockings," Mama continues, as though wearing a polo shirt, lace-ups, and a pair of jeans to a brewery would be the most profound breach of etiquette.

Ella drops her fist on the table. "It's a stupid rule."

"It's my rule," Mama counters.

"Mm," Ella replies. Paired with a saccharine sweet smile, she means, "Your rule is stupid."

Alma whispers, gently rebuking, like a mother tying her child into a life vest, "Ella."

Any other year, this might be an amusing family moment. This year, it all feels so deadly serious that it's hard to remember that we are—were—a successful family. For decades we managed what few royal families do: to be close and loving, to have the same aim. Mama *is* Sondmark. If she was thriving, and we along with her, Sondmark would thrive too.

Then Grandpère died.

Mama asked the prime minister if she could send an official delegation to his funeral in Pavieau, but he withheld consent. Of course he did. Grandpère had been too beholden to the military regime, he said, even if he worked to dismantle the fascist apparatus as soon as Generalissimo Mondegas died—before his corpse even began to smell. As far as the prime minister is concerned, Grandpère wasn't a father or grandfather. He was a diplomatic nightmare.

Père understood all this. What he didn't understand, he shouted across the Grand Hall the last time there was any shouting, was why Mama couldn't be bothered to challenge the decision or push back in the slightest degree. So we are in a kind of hell—a frozen, wind-scoured Nordic hell—where Père stares hard at middling landscapes and Mama's heart is like a cheese rind, growing harder by the day.

These subtexts and conflicts are exhausting, and I feel the importance, yet again, of having a life away from the palace and all its warping influence. A smile touches my mouth as I remember one particularly implausible Adelheid Nede adventure. If The Nat shutters, maybe I could escape to the deepest part of the forest to build my own tree house out of scavenged army surplus and pick wild mushrooms to sell on market days.

When Mama moves on to Noah, I glance at Caroline, Mama's secretary, who tucks a strand of hair behind her ear.

Caroline is my secret agent. When I told the museum staff that I hadn't received any official help securing foreign-owned art for the exhibit, it was strictly true. I did, however, ask Caroline to put the anonymous request in front of my mother because it would have taken years if I'd sent it sailing along normal channels. Is this a silly line to draw? Perhaps. But the important thing was that I didn't sit in front of my mother to plead my case, my hand wandering meaningfully to the scar on my neck. There was no pity or guilt smoothing my path between us. Mama accepted the proposal on its own merits.

The time for such discretion has passed.

I quietly open the messaging app on my phone and tap out a request.

I need to see my mother today, before her PM meeting.

I watch Caroline glance at her phone and pick it up. A small grunt calls my attention to Noah. Looking up from his agenda, he frowns at Mama's inattentive secretary.

Caroline hasn't seen his disapproval and taps a quick reply.

Official business?

I have my answer ready and send it off, wondering if I should warn her about my grumpy brother.

Yes. About the museum funding. I need her help.

Caroline bites her lip, fretting her teeth along the fulness. For a moment, she loses the mask of brisk efficiency. *Are you sure?*

No, but I can't see any other way. *Yes.*

Noah raps his knuckles against the table and Caroline starts, the phone bobbling in her hands. "If *Vrouw* Teile could spare the time from running her social life, perhaps she might be good enough to note the changes."

Caroline sets the phone face down on a side table and takes up a pen. Only the color washing above the high neck of her blouse betrays her embarrassment.

"The days of autocracy are dead, Noah," Mama says, quick to assert her control of the room. "I work this poor girl off her feet. If she takes a text from her boyfriend now and again, I trust she'll repay my time."

"Apologies, ma'am," Caroline murmurs, all business.

Noah nods, a muscle in his jaw shifting. "My apologies, *Vrouw* Teile," he says, not even looking at her, "to you and your boyfriend."

Caroline glances down, busy arranging a sheaf of papers.

I'm puzzled by Père's half-smile, the way Clara is stifling a laugh behind her hand, and how touchy my brother looks about something that shouldn't matter. When the meeting rushes on, I feel the heavy drag of a current I don't understand.

At the conclusion, Caroline draws me aside to put my request to Mama.

"Yes." Mama's eyes narrow and she begins to nod. "Yes. He holds the purse strings. but let's see if we can box Torbald into a corner," she says, rattling off a list of instructions to Caroline as she sweeps from the room. That's the first hurdle cleared.

By mid-afternoon, I'm in Mama's sitting room as Prime Minister Torbald is announced. He's the ninth prime minister of my mother's reign, and though I've never asked her to rank them, most agree that the worst was Prime Minister Miecyslaw, whose personal aide—and mistress—was an actual communist spy. With his overweening narcissism, his barely-veiled attempts to dethrone Mama, and his ever-ready willingness to stab people in the back, I suspect creeping, disheveled Minister Torbald is on the next rung up.

You wouldn't know it to observe her in action. Mama rises when he enters the room, just as she would have for any of them, and extends her hand. He slouches over it and nods to me.

After dispensing with official business—the citizenship proposal he's putting before Parliament, the appointment of a new Work and Pensions Minister—Caroline brings a tray of coffee, moving through the room as quietly as a mouse. I pour out and pass cups and saucers around, listening with half an ear as conversation shifts to the unseasonably fine weather, the harvest festivals, and the prime minister's two young daughters.

"I've long admired what an involved parent you are, *Neer* Torbald. I've brought my daughter today because she's the patron of The National Museum and is concerned about its future. It would be a great favor to me if you heard one another out."

Nicely done, Mama.

"Ah," he says, rubbing a spot behind his ear.

"The press has given you quite a difficult time," I say, carefully laying the groundwork. "Feelings are running high."

Mama has arranged this meeting and given me tips about how best to approach Torbald, but I must do this on my own. The prime minister's decision to cut funding was rash, she told me. He'll want to wriggle out of the worst of the consequences, and I can provide a way for him to do that.

"If I can't take a punch on an editorial page, I don't belong in this business," he says, inhaling a cinnamon cookie and wiping the crumbs from his mouth with a thumb and forefinger. "The Nat is hemorrhaging money, even if you account for Director Knauss's excesses, and I have to consider the needs of my people."

Mama's brow notches and I can almost see a thought bubble forming over her head, spiky with irritation. *My people.*

I set my teacup down, fastening a pleasant smile on my lips. "Perhaps there's a happy solution that might benefit everyone."

Even as these words leave my mouth, I feel how inane they are. As Mama likes to say, there are no elegant answers, only messy compromises. *Neer* Torbald needs to catch a break with the press. I need to restore funding to the museum. There must be some trade-off he'd accept.

"Would you reverse your decision if we raised the percentage of operating costs that comes from charitable donations? From twenty-one percent," I offer, "to, say, twenty-six?"

Neer Torbald barks a laugh. "So more of the rich can park their millions and dodge tax penalties?"

I swallow. This hurdle would be easier to clear if Prime Minister Torbald was a stupid man, but stupidity is not one of his sins. For the sake of The Nat, I try again. "I hope we can find some area of compromise that doesn't involve withdrawing funds from such a well-loved institution."

The prime minister's eyes narrow.

"It's not though, is it?" he answers. "The numbers don't lie. The name over the door says 'The National Museum' but every time I go it's either very empty or full of the very wealthy."

"On the contrary," I counter, scrambling for concrete information to bolster my argument. "Just yesterday I saw a young mother with a stroller. And...there was an older gentleman with a cane. The young and old together, the very breadth and depth of Sondmark."

Mama's thought bubble reads *This is not our finest moment.*

Torbald's eyes gleam. "What specific illustrations."

I do hate it when one's adversaries have a point. Worse, when it's a good one. One of the reasons I love The Nat so much is because, except at the height of tourist season, I can wander for hours without the jostling of crowds.

Neer Torbald strikes his palm against his thigh. "I've absolutely made up my mind. The Nat must justify itself. If people don't come, why bother having a museum at all?"

My eyes meet my mother's, and she tips her head in sympathy. She can't do more than this and what power she holds in Sondmark must be exercised strategically. Though the museum is important to me, it's not high on her agenda. If she spends political capital here, she won't have it to spend on some other project.

I take a breath.

"You say The Nat needs more visitors. What if we improve in that area?"

He gestures for me to proceed, and my mind explodes, spitting out an entire projector screen's worth of brainstorming in less than a second. I quickly strike through several ideas—some of them bad (free tote bags with a verified visit), some of them very bad (compulsory museum attendance for the right to vote in the next election). I light on one that sounds sane.

"I propose a trial period. We don't change the funding until the staff has a chance to get the numbers up."

"Trial period? Numbers?" His mouth splits into a grin. "This isn't my first trip through the Sonderlands, Your Royal Highness. Where are your hard numbers? What's your firm timeline?"

I miss the sensation of Oskar Velasquez at my back, holding my shoulders so I don't fall, but *Neer* Torbald has given me the opening Mama told me to watch for. I have to take it.

"Two hundred thousand visitors," I offer. "By the end of the year."

As soon as the words are out of my mouth, I want to cram them back inside. Two hundred thousand. By New Year's Day. That number is insane.

"Or?" he presses

It hurts to speak. "We cancel the exhibit—"

He shakes his head, a gust of laughter telling me to try again.

"—and we cut a third of the staff," I finish. No, no, no, no. Stop, Freja. This is insane. Insane. "I'll make The Nat the most popular destination in Sondmark, or you'll get to make serious cuts without taking a political hit for it."

A calculating light leaps into his eye and he reaches out. "Two hundred thousand."

He clasps my hand in his, shaking it hard. I try not to throw up on his shoes.

8

LESS CRANKY

OSKAR

I'm working at the hot table when I get a text from Princess Freja.

Talked to the PM. Good and bad news.

My brows gather. I told her she could call. I never tell anyone they can call. Why did she text?

I pull up the tiny typing screen and painstakingly tap out a reply, fumbling over the keys.

I am working on a tricky painting. I will be here until 9 or 10. Come to tell me the news when you're free.

Send.

I turn off the phone, lay out the webbing, and slide the canvas into position. Pulling a layer of mylar over the face of the work, I begin taping it down to create a vacuum seal, beginning the process to reactivate the glue in the canvas, stabilizing flakes of paint, and flattening out ripples. It's not really tricky, but I refuse to do that thing where we volley texts back and forth for the next hour. Does she think I have nothing else to occupy my time? If I have to use money with her mother's face on it, the least she could do is call.

She arrives after dusk, and my first thought is that a text thread would have been better for my concentration. Freja is wearing an old-fashioned cashmere coat, the kind every woman in mid-century pictures wore to a party or as a going-away outfit on her wedding day. It's draped over a long gown, and the sequins around her hem catch the low light as she walks across the workroom. She holds paper bags with Chinese characters printed on the side.

"What's that?" I ask, clearing my throat.

"You didn't answer my texts, so I got a little of everything," she says, looking around at the surfaces. She pivots toward my desk—government-issue from the early years of the Cold War—and sweeps behind it, setting out white boxes and cellophane-wrapped fortune cookies. To keep from watching her, I turn on my phone and hastily scroll through a string of messages delivered over the course of the past hours.

I have an evening event.

Velasquez?

Is this Oskar Velasquez of The National Museum?

Okay, I'll come after. 8-ish.

Do you like Chinese food? I do.

Do you have nut allergies? I don't.

Have you ever wondered how much less cranky you'd be if you just picked up your phone?

I got the Pecan Chicken. Don't expect me to send flowers if it kills you. *vomit face, headstone, skull*

I exhale a silent, grudging laugh. Who would have guessed she uses emojis? It's cute. No, I amend, with anyone else I'd think it was cute.

"You didn't have to do this," I say, setting aside solvent and heading to the sink. As I lather up my hands, I realize it's not true. I'm ravenous.

"Fine. More for me," she answers, ripping the package of a pair of bamboo chopsticks, tapping the paper off, and pulling the ends apart. But she digs into the bag for a couple of bowls and holds them in her open palm. Her brow lifts with an expression that says, "Don't be silly."

Fine.

I take one, about to explain that I'll accept a little to tide me over, but she's already scooping the contents of the take-out containers into her bowl, filling it generously. I watch her, and she catches me.

"Galas are culinary wastelands. I get very grumpy when I'm starving," she says, filling the silence.

"What does very grumpy look like?" I ask, inspecting the contents of the remaining boxes.

My question must have been more friendly than I intended, because she gives a small laugh and her cheek tucks in a smile. "There was a non-negligible chance I would bite your head off if I didn't stop for take-out."

My hand hovers over a box. Our alliance is one thing, but I don't want to like her. I don't want to like anything about her.

"Did they starve you?" I ask, dragging my eyes away by digging into the fried rice, spilling a quantity into my bowl.

"I had a square of chocolate, half a glass of champagne, and a tepid sausage roll."

We eat in companionable silence. I could tell her my last meal was thinly sliced ham, olives, and crusty bread at mid-morning, consumed in front of the computer while I was preparing a restoration proposal for a modernist still life. I don't.

There are no forks or spoons, and my ability to use chopsticks is poor. I gobble down a piece of chicken, angling my head under the unsteady utensils like I'm drinking from an outdoor spigot. The chicken falls into my mouth, and I see her trying not to smile as she deftly manages a similar bite.

I shift so I'm not looking right at her and lean back, the legs of my chair tilting with me. "Tell me how it went."

She swallows and wipes her lips with a paper napkin. It doesn't smudge her lipstick, a rich shade of cherry red deepening into currant at the center. "Good and bad. I got him to agree to a concession, but what I had to promise to get it is...not great."

She leans back, skirts draping the utilitarian lines of my office chair, and reminds me of portraits from the late years of Queen Magda's reign. The style was expensive, designed to flatter the sitters, making them tall goddesses playing lawn tennis or contracting loveless marriages.

Princess Freja already looks like a tall goddess, her gaze direct and disconcerting. Her appearance doesn't need any flattering touches, and I get a little lost tracing the curve of her neck.

"The prime minister promised to reinstate the funding if we could get two hundred thousand visitors by the end of the year."

I tip forward, the legs of the chair crashing onto the floor. "Two hundred thousand?" I cough through a mouthful of Pecan Chicken and put a fist to my lips, swallowing. "Or else what?"

She takes a breath and looks away. "Staff cuts. We could expect up to a third."

"We?" I drop the bowl, rattling a tray of brushes. *Stultes es.* My mouth hardens. "There's no 'we.' No one fires a princess."

She shoves her chopsticks deep into the bowl of noodles and rises, leaning across the desk. "Why do you have to be such a—?"

"Should I thank you for making me collateral damage in a war between your family and the prime minister?" I make a frustrated noise at the back of my throat. "Did you think twice about gambling with my career?" I stand, braced against the desk, and lean across, jabbing a finger at the take-out boxes. "Was this a bribe?"

Her eyes almost roll out of her head, and suddenly I have regrets.

"I could think of a better bribe," she grits out, pounding the desk with each word. "The other option was to make cuts today. At least now we have a chance to restore our funding. I bought us time."

"You bought us a fairytale." I release a furious breath and spin away. I look back. "Two hundred thousand, Freja," I say, her name slipping out along with my frustration.

I look away. My father's ghost crouches at my side and looks up from his game of *tanque*, puzzled and amused. Imagine calling this creature by her given name, he thinks. Imagine saying it to her face with the ease of a lover. Imagine your lungs and lips waving it through the gates like a liberator. Imagine fighting when you could be kissing.

I shake my head and his laughing spirit disappears.

"I have enough to do in the next few months without worrying about my job," I say, trying to cling to my righteous frustration, though the hottest fires have burned themselves out.

For her, too. Freja subsides into the chair, props her chin in her hand, picks up her chopsticks, and stabs into a take-out box. I watch a tidy collection of noodles travel to her mouth. The cherry and currant lips purse as she chews.

Frustration, I remind myself, brushing a hand through the air. Freja makes me feel frustrated. "There's not a prayer we'll get a hundred thousand, let alone two."

She looks down, and her eyelashes settle against her cheeks. She holds the tip of her tongue between her teeth until she looks up, resolute. "I'm sorry about that. I should have thought up a more reasonable number."

She says this with the bravery of a French aristocrat mounting a tumbrel. I'm a sucker for brave apologies.

"He wouldn't have settled on a reasonable number," I concede.

Freja's lips twitch. "Are we agreeing? Do we agree on something?"

I push my fingers through my hair. "Three months?"

Her slight smile vanishes. "Three months. I won't go down without a fight."

I think of the women in Sondish fairy tales. Viking maidens with braided hair down to their feet, woven girdles resting on their hips. Unafraid. Often armed with a weapon. Freja looks like one of these, and I wonder where she might be hiding the dagger. I blink the image away. I don't believe in fairy tales.

I return to the sink and wash up. Perching on a tall rolling chair, I pick up a razor-sharp scalpel and begin separating the edges of a canvas patch from the back of a painting. The gentle scrape of my work goes on. Freja moves from the desk chair to a battered sofa I've pushed up against a wall.

It's better to occupy my hands with this simple task than think about the way she sinks into the sofa and crosses her legs.

I switch the scalpel for a simple cotton swab, working in tiny concentric circles with a weak solvent. The glue isn't reversible. It won't ever come completely off, I think, switching the cotton swab for the pad of my thumb, the friction of the skin on the canvas doing a delicate job of removing waste and residue.

This is a simple, straightforward task. I know which steps come next and how to shift with each new obstacle. I don't even know where to begin getting two hundred thousand visitors through the museum doors.

I glance up. Freja is watching me. An electrical charge races through my veins, and I have to consciously tell myself how deeply to breathe, how slowly.

After a moment, I say, "We'll have to tell the other department heads tomorrow." I return to the canvas with eyes that hold her image—an image too strong for my simple studio. I shake my head.

"Rik is going to have a stroke."

I hide my smile. "Agnes is going to blame you for destroying the entire museum."

"Do you blame me?"

My hands pause. We've been at odds—and maybe we will be again—but something in me recognizes the uncertainty, the vulnerability, in her. "You saw a way forward and took it. Since *Neer* Torbald made that deal, we have to make him wish he hadn't."

Brave words. Steady employment and a successful citizenship test go hand in hand. I should start looking for apartments in Pavieau now.

"He was right about one thing, though," she says. From the corner of my eye, I register her stretching, the lithe form filling out the gown, twinkling lights dancing on the edge of my vision.

I pick up the cotton swab again, every nerve alive to each fiber in my hand. "What's that?"

"The museum is always empty. If its purpose is to preserve cultural heritage and artifacts, we're not really accomplishing anything if people never come to see it."

I grunt. "He's still a *vailys*."

9

— · —

Low-grade Euphoria

FREJA

"*Vailys* or not, if we take the prime minister's definition, The Nat isn't a great museum."

Though the studio is dim, a task light illuminates the side of Oskar's face. He grins, I can see the edge of it even as he keeps his head bent over his work. At least we're not fighting. We can't afford to fight.

"Give me an example of one that's great," he says, brushing his thumb on his apron.

My lips part, and I press them together against the strange sensation of words flooding my mouth, sentences piling up like canvases in the workroom. I am a quiet person. In the event the monarchy does implode, I could have a successful second career in a medieval-style nunnery, copying out illuminated manuscripts. Keeping the vow of silence would be a piece of cake. Oskar makes me want to talk.

"The Victoria & Albert Museum is spectacular," I answer, careful to release only a few of my words. He glances up with dark eyes. I release a few more. "I attended Cambridge and spent every weekend I could down in London."

I watch his shoulders shift as he works, observing the control he wields over his tools.

"You liked England?" he asks. He's only making conversation.

"Yes. The art and literature, the history, the food—"

"Food?" He surprises me with a laugh, and I feel satisfaction at the sound. I've made grumpy Oskar Velasquez laugh. What else can I make him do? "The British aren't known for food."

Even with a belly full of Chinese noodles, I tip my head back, smiling at a happy memory. "You haven't had a Christmas sandwich from Waitrose—turkey, stuffing, bacon, cranberry sauce."

He looks up and his eyes are bright. Maybe with scorn, maybe with amusement. I can't quite tell. He returns to his work.

"You'd wander around the V&A with a sandwich in your satchel and look for...?"

I lift a shoulder. "Everything. Anything. Miniature dollhouses. Home-sewn stuffed elephants. A room of jewels. I like being surprised, and the V&A is good at that. The Nat could use a few surprises. The last time the art in the main gallery was rearranged was in the 70s." I grab a fortune cookie.

Snapping it open, I pull out the paper and munch on the crisp, sugary offering.

"What does it say?" he asks, head bent over his task.

I read the fortune. "You must wade into the river to catch a fish...in a tiara."

"Hm?" he grunts.

"My sisters and I tack 'in a tiara' at the end. Like, 'You'll go on a long journey...in a tiara' or 'You'll meet your future spouse...in a tiara.' That actually happened to Alma. She met her fiancé Pietor at a Ragnar Prize banquet."

"Ah." He lapses into silence and then asks, "What's my fortune?"

Surprised, I reach into the bag again, tear the wrapper, and snap the cookie in half. I hold it out, but he lifts his hands with the scalpel and centuries-old dust. He opens his mouth, and I lean across the table to drop it in. I almost miss and have to chase it. It ends with my fingers pressed against his lips, his breath warming my skin.

I feel a tingling sensation all the way up my arm. Withdrawing, I watch the column of his neck as he swallows. My words evaporate, and I drop my eyes to the paper.

"Hang in there, little kumquat," I read, forcing the words through my throat.

"In a tiara," he adds.

He returns to his scraping. I retreat to the sofa, breathing slowly and quietly, willing the pace of my heart to slow. The rhythm of the work relaxes me—the way he bends over the old canvas. Dark hair falls over his forehead. He shakes it back, but it slips, strand by strand, to brush lightly against his skin until a sweep of his wrist banishes it, only to have it fall again.

To prevent myself from crossing the room to rake it into place, I close my eyes. My ears pick out the difference between the scratch of a dull blade, the low rasp of his thumb, and the brush of a cheap bristle brush sweeping away the debris.

Two hundred thousand visitors. Oskar is right to be outraged. The terms of our alliance are that I will stand with him to protect the Restoration department and he will help me secure the exhibit. It sounds like an even trade, but my mind pivots around the hardest fact. Two hundred thousand visitors. I don't know how it'll be possible to achieve such a staggering number of guests when the effort of staging an exhibit will eat up so much energy.

I think of my plans, the carefully curated art, the research. My stomach twists in a way that has nothing to do with Chinese food. The museum is in too much danger. The thought begins like a small seed and grows as large as a magic beanstalk. When I climb it, I can see what I don't want to see. I have to cancel the exhibit. *Vede.* I bite my lip and want to cry. All that work. I have to let it go.

To keep a growing sense of dread at bay, I train my ear to Oskar's movements. *Scratch, scratch.* The sounds he makes are like the whispering videos Ella turned me on to.

"You like quietness, Freja," she explained after a particularly overcrowded event that left my nerves shaking like a plucked string. "That's what these creators specialize in. They upload a video of themselves unwrapping a piece of candy and whisper about the process."

"That's weird," I declared a few minutes later as I watched a surgical dissection of a globe of chocolate on her phone. "That guy sounds like a doctor with a hangover. *You're going to feel a little pinch,*" I finished in a tight whisper.

I laughed but Ella was right. Now I put the videos on whenever I need a specific kind of relaxation. Based on the massive number of views, I'm not the only one who finds them appealing.

I shift slightly, kicking my heels off, and curl my legs under my skirts, imagining Oskar's husky whisper. He would be brilliant at those kinds of videos.

"What kind of videos would I be brilliant at?" he asks.

My eyes snap open. Speaking my thoughts out loud is a sign of being too relaxed.

No need to panic. I was thinking very business-y thoughts. "Have you ever heard of ASMR?"

He shakes his head, dislodging a few locks of dark hair. I ball my hand into a fist and bury it in my skirts.

"Some people get a low-grade euphoric response when they hear whispering or the bristles of a brush moving over a surface. Tapping fingernails, things like that. There's a whole cottage industry of people who make those kinds of videos."

"I could give someone low-grade euphoria?" he asks, looping his thumbs around the bib of his apron. He holds his chin slightly up-tilted.

My eyes narrow, trying to read him. I've noticed that he lifts his chin when he's trying not to smile but, like a light in a house, it doesn't matter that he's closed every door and shuttered every window. It finds its way through tiny cracks.

Part of me files the knowledge away. The other part is awash in light. My cheeks warm.

"No," I yelp. "Maybe. I don't know. While you were working just now, it occurred to me that art restoration would make for amazing content."

My nose wrinkles at the word. Content. That's definitely something I heard from Ella. My YouTube viewing history is limited to live opera recordings, "jazz cafe in a rainstorm," and ASMR videos.

Oskar grunts and returns to his work. It's no longer relaxing me. I collect our leftovers, popping them inside a small refrigerator near his desk with a spare set of chopsticks, and stack the trash into a tidy pile for the cleaning crew.

"Don't go," Oskar says. At his words, my hand stills and my stomach dips.

"What—"

His answer is businesslike. "The security system will lock the whole place down if someone exits improperly. Give me a few minutes to finish up, and I'll walk you out."

What did I think he was going to say? Not that.

I resume my place on the sofa, sitting primly with my hands resting around my knees, deeply annoyed to find the air simmering with energy. My air, anyway. His air looks as placid as a millpond.

It is a relief when he pulls off his apron, dons his coat, grabs his keys, and escorts me through the darkened halls of the museum. The seeds of another idea have been planted in my brain, and I mull it over, hating the way it could change this place I love.

"What's your favorite museum?" I ask when my thoughts become too attuned to the way he walks and the precise number of centimeters separating us.

"Greybull Museum."

My forehead furrows. "I've never heard of it."

"Oh, well, if *you've* never heard of it…"

I knock a hand against his, the contact sparking an unwelcome reaction. "Stop being difficult."

He opens a door and guides me through, hand gently on my back. Sparks where he touches. Sparks where he doesn't. I was right to avoid him for three years. I should have made it ten.

"The Greybull, Wyoming community museum is housed in one room."

I halt. "I painted a sincere picture for you of an art-starved college student, knapsack loaded with delicious sandwiches, wandering the V&A for hours. The least you could do is give me your real answer."

He puts his hands in his pockets and leans lightly against a column. "Greybull is my real answer. It doesn't have a prime minister's endowment or wealthy patrons. It's got rocks and quilts, stuffed bison busts, and panoramic graduation photos. That kind of thing."

"Your favorite museum has rocks?"

He lifts a shoulder. "It has enthusiasm." There goes that chin again. He wants to smile. "Someone had enough passion to gather it together."

"Passion? Does it even have a gift shop?"

He thinks. "There was a t-shirt stand."

"You got one, I hope."

His eyes light. Warmth spirals through me. "I was a poor student on a foreign exchange trip. The *markke* was down against the dollar."

"A missed opportunity," I add, softly.

He bumps away from the column, taking my arm as he goes. Pulling away would be an acknowledgment that it means something. It doesn't, so I leave it in his gentle grip and suffer the storm of tiny lightning bolts in silence.

"That was the most precious souvenir, after all," he begins, sounding like the parting lines of a children's tale. "The lesson that, if I want something bad enough, I shouldn't let it slip through my fingers." He punches a complicated code into a touchpad, and I hear a click. Pushing the door open on the chilly autumn night, we follow a path to the staff parking lot where I suspect my security officer has been watching a Dragon's game on his phone. Freddie hops out of the car and opens the door before I've even reached the bottom of the steps.

"This is *Neer* Velasquez," I tell him. "He wanted to walk me down."

"Good thing he did, too, ma'am," he chides, as though anarchists and assassins are waiting behind every bush. My security needs are light, my routine visits to The Nat needing no extraordinary precautions, but I'm supposed to text Freddie when I'm ready to leave. He would've met me at the door.

I look at Oskar and turn the collar up on my soft cashmere coat. "Think about what can be done to get people in the doors of the museum, will you? I'll announce the deal with the prime minister at the staff meeting tomorrow, and I hate to think of springing it on them without something already in mind."

"You didn't hate springing it on me," he says, hands in pockets.

"You're different."

I am a person of pauses, of silences that stretch until someone says, "Well?" like the honk of a horn at a traffic signal to get me moving. Those words spilled out of me, but they are no less true because they haven't been weighed and measured. He *is* different.

Instead of trying to figure out how, I allow Freddie to tuck me into the car. He closes the door with a snap, and I look at Oskar through the glass. He can't hear the sound of my breath, loud in my ears. When the Mercedes pulls away, he's frowning.

The trip to the Summer Palace is swift, and on my way to my suite, I halt outside my sister's door, rapping the wood with my knuckle.

"Ella," I call.

No answer.

I pull out my phone and text her.

Need to talk.

A mechanized lock slides open, and I push through the door, making my way to her office, a room with tasteful furnishings hidden somewhere underneath the mass of cords and technology.

My twin flips back one of her headphones, her curly red hair bunching on one side. "You look fancy," she says, swiveling around in her complicated office chair.

"Vintage Dialli," I murmur. "What's this?" I take in Ella's monitors. Various lines of code—I know that much—fill several screens, and a ReadHe thread is open on another. The last is playing a K-pop music video featuring exploding angel wings. I haven't the faintest idea what she's working on, but I'm sure it's impressive.

"Just a side project," she says. "What brings you to my kingdom?"

"I need your help."

She peels the headphones away and pushes off the desk, wheeling herself and the chair across the room.

"You never need my help. You never need anyone's help. What's the trouble? Man or beast?"

"Both."

"Oh?"

I shake my head. Ella is going to get ideas.

"Neither. I meant neither," I correct. "It's to do with the museum."

Ella sighs. "It's not like I don't appreciate your interests, little sister, but you need to broaden your horizons. The world is bigger than the grounds of The Nat." She sweeps an arm out.

"Yes," I nod, gazing over the room, my tone dry. "The thrilling expanse of an airless office with an excellent internet connection is a perfect illustration of your point." I shake myself out of my coat and slip into a chair. "I really do need your help. Tech help," I add, hopefully.

Ella grins. "You're speaking my language."

"I'm looking for ways to drum up interest in the museum, and when I dropped by the museum tonight, it occurred to me that restoration work would make good ASMR videos—it's lots of scraping and brushing."

Her mouth makes a perfect *O*. "Yes, and it's more specialized than fiddling with candy wrappers, so the audience you did find would stick with you. Over the long haul, it would generate interest."

"What about the short haul?

"How short are we talking?"

I grimace. "New Year's Eve."

She laces her fingers behind her head and exhales, finally answering with a shake of her head. "Absolutely do ASMR vids when you're more established—it's a genius idea—but you'll need an aggressive, multi-pronged strategy if you want to drive people to act. Lots of diverse content, lots of flashing lights."

"Like what?"

She considers. "You could do a bunch of BTS content. Behind the scenes," she explains when I look confused. "You have the resources. Maybe interview some of the curators. You'd want long-form interviews for YouTube and shorter clips for social media."

I tap my lip. "Our curators aren't public figures. Would people be willing to watch Roland become completely unglued about pre-Lutheran reliquaries?"

She lifts a brow. "You underestimate how thirsty the internet is for people becoming unglued about things viewers don't understand. If you're lucky, the comment sections will become a battleground of warring factions, brother fighting against brother over provenance and"—she spins her hand, searching her mind for something obscure and art-related—"carbon dating."

"I'm worried there won't be two hundred thousand people who'll take a train out to the museum on a rainy, autumn weekday. Not in Sondmark." I cup the back of my neck, rubbing the tendons. "Still, we could do it with a pretty small budget."

"You could cut to the chase and hang more naked art."

I push her chair with the tip of my toe, admonishing. "Sondish painters really liked a kirtle," I say, referring to the exterior petticoat necessary in a chilly northern climate. "Cleavage we have. Nudity, not so much. Other ideas?"

She swivels around and rolls to her desk. "You know you have a Pixy account, right?"

I do know it. One of Caroline's secretarial underlings manages it, and I hear there are appropriate posts under my name.

"Honestly, the biggest tool for bringing more visitors to the museum is in your own pocket." While delivering this scold, her fingers are dancing over the keyboard. I speak the language of technology like it's a second tongue, grudgingly learned, but Ella is a native, the kind of native who works in the UN automatic translation booth while simultaneously reading Tolstoy from the original.

"Let's take a look at what other museums are doing. Ah." She tilts the screen. "Here's a hashtag campaign called #MuseumTwinning."

For a second I think I'm looking at a lavish painting from the Rococo period, but then I look closer. It's a photograph of an actual person, in their actual bathroom. "Are those toilet paper rolls?"

"Clever, right? Patrons are encouraged to send in recreations of the art they see on the walls. This is Madame du Pompadour by @srsly-historical, her elaborate wig rendered in toilet paper rolls, her gown a budget shower curtain."

I'm impressed but I grimace. "There's not much dignity in bathroom products."

Ella rolls her eyes at me. "Knock it off, okay? This Vestal Virgin of The Nat talk, this 'Oh, no, the *poors* might be having fun with our precious heritage' business—" She snaps her fingers under my nose. "You want visitors, you get rid of that face. You want to get a whole new crowd into the museum? Be prepared to hustle for them." She points at her computer monitor. "It's unexpected and a bit mad, but people like things that are surprising and full of passion."

Surprising like the V&A. Passion like Greybull.

I scoot closer to my sister. Search after search yields more ideas, and I hastily jot them down on a scrap of paper, wondering what Oskar will think.

"I'm sending links to your email, Freja," she says. "Lay off the notes. You should get help from that art restorer, the hot one who hates you. Audiences would eat him up."

I shift in my seat, irritated. "You only think he's hot compared to the rest of the museum staff."

She hunches over her keyboard, tapping out a staccato of doom. Several research papers and a profile picture pop up. Evidence.

The picture is just his staff photo, and the photographer did nothing to flatter him, but even with utilitarian lighting and no effort to smile for the camera, Oskar looks a lot hot and a little grumpy.

Ella leans in and reads aloud. "Oskar Velasquez, 32, born in Pavieau—" She gasps, really shocked. "Oh, sister, I thought Clara was playing with fire, falling for a decorated Sondish Naval officer. That's amateur hour compared to falling for someone from Pavieau."

"It's not a problem because I won't be falling for him. He's just a coworker."

She looks skeptical but holds her palms up, a wise sage's final pronouncement. "I'll tell you this—put his face in the frame and those videos will go viral. It won't matter what he's talking about."

10

LIGHTNING STRIKE

OSKAR

I register Rik's squinty glare from my peripheral vision and take my seat at the foot of the conference table. He wants me gone and probably feels my position should go to someone Sondish. Who's really happy to be working with a Pavi? Marie. Others tolerate it. Still others make few distinctions between families who fled the dictatorship and ones who ran it for decades.

Marie claps her hands several times, silencing the room. "We've got an update and then a short presentation," she says, calm and trustworthy, taking on the persona of a flight attendant explaining what to do in the event of a catastrophic water landing. She looks to Freja. "Ma'am?"

I've been trying very hard not to look at Freja, having spent the night fending off memories of the way she consumes Chinese noodles, but turning off my attention is not as easy as turning off my phone.

She's wearing another of her vintage princess costumes—a blue dress with a soft collar, buttons from neck to knee, and a belted sash. Professional but particular. The Sondish preference is for women to wear dark unisex pantsuits or, if they fancy themselves creative, leather clogs, layers of linen, and wooden jewelry. A hollow forms in her neck when she takes a breath, and I look away, inspecting the grain of the wood paneling on the wall.

"Prime Minister Torbald was good enough to meet with me yesterday," she begins. Freja presents a cool, confident pose but looking more closely, I notice the fingers smoothing her notes and hear the tiny catch of hesitancy in her voice.

"...and he agreed," she wraps up. "If we increase visitors, we keep our funding." Freja catches my gaze. Here it comes. I give her a small nod and she takes a short breath, leaping. "Two hundred thousand by the end of the year."

Half the room—Rik, Agnes, and a dozen other staff members—erupts in a burst of anger and noise.

"Two hundred thousand?!"

"How on earth—"

"I just bought a boat," Agnes shouts, a hair's breadth away from calling for pitchforks and rough justice.

My gaze swings to Freja, alone at the head of the table, and her eyes lock on mine. She's not asking for help, but her color is uneven. I catch the moment her chin tightens. This is how the royals get you. It's hard to watch dignity brought low. I tuck my lip against my teeth and give a sharp whistle. The noise drops like a bird in mid-flight.

"No amount of shouting will change the facts," I say, my voice low and civilized. "What Her Royal Highness—"

"Freja," she corrects, cheeks a shade paler than they should be.

She's granting me the right to use her name. This is how the royals get you. "What Freja did is lay down a marker Prime Minister Torbald can't wiggle out of," I say, glancing across the room. "Two hundred thousand is a hard number, but he has to respect it. He's tied to it now." I meet Freja's bright eyes.

"We'll have to make sure he chokes on it," she says.

My lips twitch. I can't imagine any other circumstance in which I would get an honest opinion from a princess about her mother's prime minister. Maybe it's a once-in-a-lifetime occurrence, like a comet or chicken pox.

"You have some ideas to meet that figure?" I ask. Together we are acting out a pantomime, that I'm absorbing this shock for the first time along with everyone else, that I'm not feeding her lines.

"I do." She slips over to her computer, and Marie flicks the lights off. As the first slide illuminates the room, Freja glances over and catches me watching her.

"Thank you," she mouths. The sudden wish to hold my arms open and have her walk into them hits me like a left hook to the chin. I shift my gaze, crossing my arms over my chest, the text on the slide blurring before me. Freja has only to walk into a room for people to fall all over themselves for her. I'm not one of them. My eyes are open. I won't be one of them.

I blink, and the words snap into focus. I need her plans to work just as much as she does. More, even.

The slide reads: *Cancel Romantics Exhibit, Art Twinning, Curator's Corner, Pixy (Informative Slides and Quizzes), Live Events, Social Media Backdrops, Behind the Scenes, ASMR videos.*

"What's this about the Romantics exhibit?" The words jerk out of me. The exhibit was the only thing she cared about.

Her lips are dry, and she wets them. "It's asking too much of the museum to stage an exhibit at this time. Agnes was right," she says. I recognize one of my tactics. Agree with your biggest critic. Knock them back on their heels. "The numbers aren't great, and the attention it's going to require will be too much, don't you agree?"

She sounds certain and calm, like she's not losing anything that matters. It mattered enough to make an ally out of an enemy.

"Now," she says, turning to the screen, "if we want to get patrons into the museum and spend very little money doing it, social media is the best tool we have. I've been trawling through the online presence of every major museum in the world, and this is a list of some of their most effective campaigns. No matter how silly some of them sound, we aren't in a position to pass up any opportunity to get bodies through the door."

"Curator's Corner," Roland says in his guileless, *Would you like to look at this Mesopotamian coinage I found jangling in my pocket?* way. "That's from The British Museum, isn't it? Videos of Irving Finkel going on about cuneiform? Riveting stuff. Are you suggesting we try something like that?"

"Yes," Freja answers. "The idea is that every person who works at the museum has a different answer to the question, 'What's your favorite thing?' Hopefully, your excitement and animation about the contents of the museum will spark a desire for more people to visit."

Freja scrolls through several slides, explaining the basic ideas in simple terms. "Two hundred thousand patrons in the middle of a cold Sondish autumn is a lot to hope for but, as you can see, we're not without resources."

I look around, gauging the effect of her speech. Lynda has been taking copious notes. She's practically bouncing off her seat.

I catch Freja's eye and bump my chin at Lynda.

Freja smiles. "Does anyone have more ideas to add?"

Lynda's hand shoots up. "Oooooohhh. I have one." She swallows a deep breath. "Every time I walk through the jewel galleries, I feel—" Her hands adjust the seasonal charm necklace draped over her chest, each leaf and raindrop glittering in the low light. "I want to take to my bed and clutch the smelling salts. It's so depressing." She looks around, whipping up agreement. I find myself nodding. "I don't even care when it's art or medieval weaponry locked in a case. It's fine. But jewels are meant to be worn, and seeing them behind glass is murdering my soul. Literal murder."

My brows lift slightly. Freja asked for animation. She's getting it.

"What I want—what I've always wanted—is to introduce a lottery where patrons can win a chance to be photographed with a featured piece. If you come to the museum, your name is entered. We'd have to choose the most structurally sound pieces, but if we do a drawing once a week—"

"We'd get repeat business," Agnes finishes. I try to read her expression. It isn't that she hates the idea. It's more that she hates herself for not hating the idea.

Freja doesn't hate the idea either. "Can I enter for the Wheatrose tiara?" she asks of the silver and sapphire headpiece, one of the largest in Europe. I hate how easy it is to imagine her wearing it.

She tucks away a slight smile. She's relieved that the shouting has stopped. "Any other ideas?"

"I have one." My eyes shift away as soon as she lifts her face to mine. "We could take advantage of the upcoming Christmas season by traveling to the scenes and settings of our Christmas and winter-themed art."

"For instance?"

I shrug like this is coming off the cuff. "The hill in *The Baron and His Hunting Dogs* is an actual hill south of Vaado. Not much of the village remains anymore but it would be an interesting contrast. That particular piece has a lot of detail. If we show some of it, people might come to see the rest."

She nods. "Can you compile a list of appropriate pieces?"

Once we've agreed on several short-term projects, Marie breaks us up into leadership teams. Was this part of her air hostess training?

What To Do In Case of a Crash: Assign a team to collect firewood, another to build a shelter, and another to make a distress signal. Keep us busy and feeling like we're doing something to stave off anarchy and cannibalism.

"Oskar, Freja, let's put together a calendar of events." Assign one team to dole out the rations. As the room begins humming with ideas and collaboration, I join Freja. She looks up, and I brace myself while Marie slaps a calendar between us. The theme: a felted otter family positioned in a 70s-inspired dollhouse.

"Marie—"

She sniffs. "I apologize for nothing."

I smile and inadvertently catch Freja smiling, too. For a half second, I'm overcome by brilliant light jolting through my limbs and leaving me weak. I put the smile away.

For the next hour, we start filling the boxes in with dates and events, taking notes about whom to call in favors from and which teams will assume which tasks. From time to time, Freja touches my arm to clarify a point or bring something to my attention. I could shift away but leave my arm where it is, precisely within her reach. I'm a fool in an open field holding a copper rod, waiting for a lightning strike, every nerve prickling.

She pulled her exhibit, sacrificing the thing she wanted most for the good of the museum. For my good. I didn't think she was capable of that. The thought clashes with all my ideas of what a princess of Sondmark is like.

As we near the end of the planning session, one of the interns flops into a nearby chair, sharp elbows digging into the armrests as he squirms upright.

"I've got an issue," he says. "There's a fine line, right? Between 'I threw this together. Come see how relatable and breezy we are' and

'I don't care about this because it's garbage.' Our branding should be as tight as possible. Same colors, same filters, same fonts on all these posts. Like, there should be, like, a last edit before anything goes out the door."

I exchange a look with Freja, and she lifts her shoulders. We're new to this.

"Are you volunteering?" Freja asks.

"I mean, I'm just saying."

"Congratulations. You're hired," I tell him.

We finish our calendaring, and Marie promises to send out color-coded copies to each department. If we're on a deserted island with a flaming wreckage, at least it finally feels like someone salvaged the snack trolley.

"Here's the thing," Rik says, leaning back in his chair. "We don't have a snowflake's chance in a bonfire if we don't tell people what we need. Two hundred thousand of them, through those doors, by New Year's Eve," he says, pointing in the direction of the museum entrance. "It's no time to play coy."

I nod. "Rik is right," I say, enjoying some satisfaction that the man is confused about sharing any common ground with me. "The weather will get worse, and we'll be fighting the shops and Christmas Markets for people's attention. No matter how good the programs are, they'll push off their visits, planning to wait until after the New Year. But if they know what we need and why, people will be invested. Let them know how close we are to our goal...like a telethon," I say, recalling the variety shows of my childhood.

"With one of those money thermometers?" Freja laughs, and I feel the vibration of it along my skin. I brush a hand down my sleeve.

She continues. "Social media is weird, I'm told, and the more slap-dash something is, the more authentic it appears."

"Honest," the intern corrects.

"Yes, honest. So let's tape some printer paper together and use a marker to show our progress."

What were the words Lynda used earlier? Murdering my soul. I cross my arms, thumb rubbing the material of my jacket. The heart of my work is a commitment to meticulous craftsmanship. Tape and printer paper. I just—

Freja touches my back twice. Pat, pat. *There, there.*

I freeze and force myself to speak. "The sooner we make our pitch to the public, the better. Do we have any volunteers?"

No eager rush of raised hands greets my question. For all our planning and brainstorming, this is where the shore meets the sea. Our faces will appear on camera.

"I'm too pig-ugly," says Rik, which isn't true. He's good-looking in a large, obvious way. With his lint-fair hair and Sondish frame, he could be in Viking dramas, a medieval warrior leading a raid against an ill-prepared abbey. But I'm unconvinced his fans would be natural art lovers.

It can't be Agnes. There's something censorious in her eyes that makes people worry that they haven't flossed. I lift my eyes to Roland with his bushy beard and stammering excitement. Sondmark would love him.

"I won't do it," Roland says before I can open my mouth. "I'm too liable to lose my train of thought—start out on the museum and end up in the Punic Wars, as always. No, Oskar's the one." He assesses me as mercilessly as I assessed Agnes, and I feel the weight of every pair of eyes in the room. "You're telegenic. Isn't he telegenic?"

"Every maiden's dream," Marie laughs, adding dryly, "I'm no maiden, of course."

Sondmark wouldn't love me. The words lodge in my throat, and a churning panic invades my chest.

"Freja has the largest social media reach," I say, tapping my phone and bringing up the official Pixy account of HRH Princess Freja, Duchess of Piskmont. It's not her making the posts. I figured that out last night when I scrolled through her feed. They don't sound like her, but she has 3.2 million followers, and most of them are bound to be from Sondmark.

She goes on her tiptoes and looks over my shoulder. I point to the number. Her breath, gently brushing my ear, catches.

"That's an official account, nothing to do with The Nat beyond the boundaries of my patronage."

"You said this was important to you," I remind her, turning my head. We're suddenly close, our conversation low and private. I hold a finger up to say *We need a moment to settle this*, and the rest of the room rumbles comfortably with talk. "You've got to be the public face of this."

"Roland's idea was a good one," she counters, dropping into a whisper. "The camera would love you."

Does she realize that she gave me a compliment?

"I'm an immigrant, and this is The Nat—the bastion of Sondish culture. But you've got 3.2 million followers. We'll set up in the main gallery, and you can have a few minutes to make some bullet points," I say, as though we've decided. I have to be ruthless.

"Marie is glamorous. She should be the one—"

"Marie is running the whole museum," I say, "and she's not a globally recognized figure, beloved by all."

Freja's glance sharpens. Her lips purse slightly, and I want to run my thumb along them, just to see.

"Are you mocking me?"

I drag my attention in line. "I would never mock a member of a cherished national institution. We need you." Leaning forward, my mouth is just centimeters from her ear. "Enough standing on the shore, ordering everyone about. You have to wade into the river to catch a fish."

She clicks her tongue, drawing back far enough to look me in the face. We're too close, and I feel the tightness of my tie.

"I will if you will."

11

— · —

STEADYING GRIP

What have I done? What have I done?

The golden rule of the royal family is discretion. Don't commit hastily. Don't be impulsive. Promise nothing if it hasn't been run past the privy council and prime minister.

If I regret my bargain—and I do—it's too late. Oskar takes my hand and tugs me toward the door. Shock keeps me from breaking the grip. It must be shock.

"It'll be over in a few minutes," he says. I feel the scrapes and calluses on his palm and knuckles and stare blankly at our clasped hands as we walk at a brisk pace.

He's ruthless when he really wants something. The success of this campaign means his job, and I see how determined he is to keep it. His intensity has nothing to do with me, personally, but my fingers burn, nonetheless.

The intern shuffles behind, eyes on his phone.

"What's your name?" Oskar asks.

"Erik," the intern mumbles, not lifting his head.

"Erik," Oskar repeats, "we're going to save the museum."

Erik grunts.

In the central gallery, rain beats on the skylights, bathing the space in soft, blue light. Ella explained to me all about light last night, how direct sunshine isn't ideal for these kinds of things. I'd hoped to be passing that information along to someone else who would be doing this.

"Where do you want to do it?" Erik asks, glancing up.

Oskar doesn't relinquish my hand as he turns. "Let's position ourselves in front of a favorite piece of art. What's yours?"

"*The Winter Princess*." I must have answered too quickly. His brows lift. "The painting by Cor Hammersmit on the outer ring. It's got—"

He nods, impatient. "I know it. I did some restoration work on the canvas before it returned to the gallery."

"The light won't be any good there," I say, as though I've known these facts longer than twelve hours. I glance around the gallery. "I like this Beyerling, too."

Oskar tilts his head, taking in the depiction of the final judgment featuring a surprising number of soberly clad Sondish merchants and their wives, draped in jewel-toned velvets, collecting their heavenly rewards. "That'll do."

I shake my hand free of Oskar's. He looks gently surprised, as though he'd forgotten he was holding on to it and can't understand why I bothered to let him loose.

He pulls a notebook from his pocket. "We need an introduction," he says, jotting. "You can say, 'We're standing in front of the historic' etc., etc. I'll say something about the work the museum does to preserve the cultural legacy of Sondmark, and then you'll finish up with something like, 'Come on down to The Nat. Bring the wife and kids.' Are we good?"

Good? No. This is not good. "That's all we have? A few scribbles on a page?"

He rips the paper and tucks it under one of Erik's fingers so that we'll see it when we look at the camera. His gaze darts to the skylight and along the row of spotlights. He touches my arm, and I shift a few centimeters, earning a grunt of approval. "You were the one who said it's better to be slapdash."

He doesn't understand.

"I don't speak in public."

His face arranges into the universal sign of "Are you trying to sell me a piece of the Oiwevest Bridge?"

"Not extemporaneously," I clarify. "My speeches are written weeks in advance. They marinate long enough for me to discover whether I'm offending the dairy farming constituency or inadvertently starting a third Motovian war." Rising panic threatens to close my throat. "I hate this."

He touches my arm and bumps his chin at the intern. "We'll hate it together." Then to Erik, "We're ready."

No, we're not.

Erik, gripped by delusions of grandeur, nods and silently counts down with his fingers. *Three, two, one.* A finger sweeps forward. *Go.*

"Greetings, Sondmark," I say, immediately wishing for a do-over. "I'm–I'm–"

I feel Oskar take my hand, gently stroking his thumb across the back of it. I meet his eyes.

Take a breath.

Any port in a storm. I twist my fingers, tangling them in his. I breathe.

"I'm Princess Freja, coming to you from The National Museum." The rest of the introduction is a blur, but I manage to get it out. Finally, I look over my shoulder. "Did you know that Beyerling's canvas was so massive it had to be sliced in half to be installed in its original home?"

"And I thought my stairway was narrow," Oskar laughs, not sounding at all like he hates this. His amusement warms the gallery on this chilly day. "I'm lucky enough to walk by this painting on my way to work." He looks at the camera, directly addressing the people on the other side of the lens. "But you can't get a sense of the scale of it if you're watching this on a tiny screen." He slides a conspiratorial glance at me, as though we really are allies. "Don't you think they'd better come to see it in person?"

I take up the narrative, returning his volley while Erik hunches over his rectangle, standing on the edge of my vision. Oskar's presence steadies my charging pulse, and I begin to mirror his easy authority. If I had pockets, I might even consider putting my hand in one.

"What do you love so much about coming to The Nat?" he asks, pressing my fingers. It's my turn.

"Hm. I love that when I walk through the doors, I'm sure to find something fresh and inspiring each time. Even when I gravitate to favorite pieces, I do so with new ears."

His short laugh is spontaneous. "Ears? Not eyes?"

"Those too," I shake his hand reprovingly. "But when I'm standing in front of a thousand-year-old wedding portrait or a baby rattle that was buried in a tidal estuary for a few centuries, I can almost hear the sitters and the owners and the makers speaking to me." My free hand comes up to my ear, opening and closing slightly—a little mouth whispering secrets.

The smallest smile in the history of Sondmark brushes his lips. "Princess Freja hears voices at The Nat."

It's the smile. I almost stop breathing, losing myself in a moment of perfect stillness. He shakes my hand slightly and I blink, feeling the scrambling sensation of a small animal toppling into a pond and paddling to regain the edge. I tear my eyes away, encountering the unblinking eye of the camera again. "And I love that the art and artifacts of The Nat have the power to put whatever concerns I'm carrying around into perspective."

"That's true whether you're a royal princess," he says, tipping his free hand at me, "or someone who holds a Provisional Residency card." Oskar places the tips of his fingers lightly against his chest.

"The Nat is for all of Sondmark," I say, "which brings us to our announcement." I launch into my pitch for more visitors, framing the prime minister's ultimatum with as much neutrality as possible. Two hundred thousand visitors. Before New Year's Day.

"The prime minister challenged us to find new ways to bring art to the people—and to bring people to the art," I say, attempting to sound appreciative. "In the coming days, we'll be rolling out a series of events and social media activities to make you welcome."

"Come and see what The Nat holds for you," Oskar finishes. He nods at Erik who presses his phone and drops it. Oskar and I look at each other.

I exhale. "At least we didn't end up in the Punic Wars."

"That last bit. I sounded like I was inviting Sondmark for a river cruise," he says, frowning.

"No, no." Yes, yes.

"Okay," Erik interrupts, hunching over his phone. "I'll edit the ends and add some captions. I'll upload it within the hour and tag you," he says, bucking his chin at me. "You should share it to your Pixy stories right after. Maybe your family..." The exertion of full sentences seems to overtax him, and he shuffles off.

I turn to Oskar and look down at our hands, shaking out of his grip to rub my frozen knuckles against my palm.

"I've never strung so many unplanned phrases together at one time. I don't know how you people do it. It's exhausting."

Oskar leans up against a pillar, hands in his pockets. I'm winded and he looks annoyingly comfortable. "You people?"

"See what I mean? It's too easy to say the wrong thing," I say, rubbing my hands up and down my arms

He bumps away from the wall. "Cold?"

"It's the adrenaline. If this was kindergarten, they'd give me a blanket cocoon and a cookie."

"Come." He takes my hand again. This time I have the presence of mind to look startled. Is this a Pavian thing? Pavians have passions and emotions we approach with a sharp stick in these northern latitudes. Of course, I've been clinging to him for the last quarter hour. He releases me, impatience bracketing his mouth.

"I don't bite," he says, ushering me through the staff doors and down to his studio, giving me a pointed amount of personal space as we make our way. As we enter, I hear muted conversation and the scrape of chairs and equipment in the adjoining rooms. He reaches for a soft blanket draped across the back of a sofa and drops it into my arms. "Here's a cocoon."

I can't afford to refuse the offer. My teeth are almost chattering. Sinking onto the sofa, I pull the blanket over my knees. Oskar reaches into his desk drawer and drops a Righteous Bar in my lap. "And here's a cookie."

I peel back the wrapper and hold the bar up for inspection. "Liar."

He crouches in front of me and tucks the blanket more securely with impersonal, economic gestures. He doesn't bite. His brown eyes dart up to mine. "Liar?"

I cough away the sudden dryness in my throat. "This is nuts and grains lightly dusted in cocoa powder."

"I suppose you want a tin of *Kyriekager*," he says, pacing to the table.

I can breathe and be amused and feel normal things. I am a woman of many parts. I contain multitudes. "The soft kind with the brittle layer of frosting instead of those crispy abominations. You don't happen to have—"

"No luck."

I've made him smile again, all the more rewarding because he doesn't want to do it. My eyes follow him as he shrugs out of his jacket and drapes it over his office chair. He sits, beginning to unbutton his cuffs, and I watch his tanned forearms twist this way and that as he rolls the cuffs to his elbows. I could write a dissertation on those arms, complete with citations and cross-references to famous forearms of antiquity.

"You canceled the exhibit," he says. "Why? They would've backed you up." When he looks at me, my eyes blink to his face. I reach for his work apron and toss it to him. He catches it.

"Because I'm a princess?" He makes no response, and I feel the sudden wish to prove him wrong. "Do you think being royal means always getting your way? Because I've got news—"

He shrugs. "Forget it."

I adjust the blanket. "Erik should start filming for your behind-the-scenes posts tomorrow. Make some notes about what you want—"

"Not Erik," Oskar grunts, tying the apron strings behind his back. "If I'm going to do this, it's going to be with someone who doesn't make me want to roll up a magazine and hit him upside the head."

I stifle a laugh and try to look disapproving. "I thought you promised to wade into the river to catch some fish."

"I promised to wade with *you*, not with Erik." He picks up a scalpel and begins the gentle scraping, head bent low. "Let him edit all he wants, but I don't want anyone else in here."

"Why are you being ridiculous?" I smile since he can't see me anyway. "I barely know how to operate my own Pixy account. I can't—"

He looks up, and I whisk my smile out of sight.

"You'll learn." He returns to his work. "I'm not letting anyone else down here."

What else can I do? I nod.

I'm on my way back to the Summer Palace when the museum's social media account tags me in a new video.

Like Ella showed me, I tap the like button and share it to my page. My phone vibrates happily, and I glance at the screen, taking a closer look at the image Erik selected.

"Oh, *vede*," I groan.

"What's that?" asks Freddie, eyes on the road.

He navigates through a turn, and I describe the cover image, snapped after we'd finished. "I'm looking up at *Neer* Velasquez like he's the best thing since designated bicycle lanes. The title of the video is 'Breaking News.'"

Freddie's brows launch up his forehead. "Do you have something to tell me?"

"Only that I'm about to commit a murder," I say, finding Erik's number in the staff directory. What on earth possessed the *flamen* idiot to use *that* picture?

The catastrophic intern answers.

"Just a sec—" Erik raises his voice, addressing someone else. "A *høj* pumpkin spice coffee, one-and-a-half pumps of caramel syrup...*and a half,*" he enunciates, sounding as beleaguered as a general running perilously low on ammunition in the face of an advancing enemy. His voice switches suddenly. "Okay. Erik, here. Why is this a call?"

It takes me a beat before I realize he's speaking to me.

"This is Freja," I say, enunciating with similar clarity. I wish to use my title. *This is Her Royal Highness, Princess Freja, Duchess of Piskmont, and you had better start groveling.* "You have got to take that cover photo down."

"What?" he draws the word out, pitching up at the end. "Why?" The words are glacial, dropping from his mouth like cold treacle.

"Because, Erik, it either looks like I've just announced my engagement or I'm going to start making out with someone on the internet."

"Ooh," he drags, shuffling through the sound like he's scraping gum off his shoe. "Yeah. I mean, I guess. Just a sec."

I pull the phone from my ear and stare at it in unblinking consternation. My ancestors didn't have to put up with "Just a sec." They would have chained Erik to a mooring ring at low tide and waited for the merciless onslaught of nature to finish him off, a cautionary tale, celebrated in epic poetry for generations.

"Yeah, but here's the thing," Erik says, when he returns. "It's viral."

Freddie lifts a shoulder and whispers, "Good viral or bad viral?"

I speak into the phone. "Is that good?"

"I mean…" Erik's vowels stretch. "Some comments are all, 'This is clickbait. Shame on you,' and others are like, 'What kind of foreign is he?' which, gross, for one thing. But most people are just, 'Torbald is the literal worst' and 'Freja snagged a hottie. Let's go to The Nat.' So."

Though his words only have a glancing relationship to The Queen's Sondish, I think I've worked it out. Oskar and I have managed to go viral, and whatever other complications his post has wrought, viral is going to help our cause. "Okay. Thank you. Get permission for pictures you grab when the videos have ended, next time."

"For sure. Consent is key," Erik says, repeating a recent ad slogan from the Ministry of Health. Minister Bendixen will be thrilled Erik has absorbed it, but by the time I arrive at the Summer Palace, I've concluded that I'll never let him near Oskar. We can't afford to lose our Head of Restoration to a charge of senseless violence. To that end, I stand outside my sister's door, texting.

I need to talk.

When the lock slides, I follow the noises into her office. This time she's busy with a video game, one in which all the characters seem to be having seizures. "What's this called?"

She hits pause. "It translates to something like 'Lightning Bang Family Clash,'" she says, stretching her arms and ruffling her curls. "Having a battle royale in an ancient cemetery calms me down after a long day of being polite."

I know that we shared the same womb. Her hair is the exact color as mine. I do not understand my twin.

"You didn't have an engagement today. What do you need to calm down about?" I ask.

"Nothing. Mama's sending me to that expo dressed like a schoolgirl. Button-down shirt, jumper, slacks..."

"Slacks are a win," I cheer, having no interest in slacks.

"Stockings. Heels."

It sounds like a lovely outfit. My own taste would dictate vintage jewelry and a patterned blouse, but I attempt to commiserate about a hoop I have no difficulty jumping through.

"Sorry," I say.

Ella suddenly grins. "I saw your introductory video on Pixy. Oh, my goodness, that man is so hot."

I try to look confused, but Ella has a nerdy, *I'm thinking in Excel spreadsheets* look on her face. "He's not like Guns and Abs Action Hero Martial-Arts-ing His Way to His Dying Girlfriend hot. He's more like Tuxedo-Wearing International Spy and Thief of My Heart hot."

My eyes drift out of focus. Like a distant mirage, I see it. I would pay for that movie. I would crowd-source the funding to produce it.

"Were you holding hands? Please tell me yes." She grips my hands. "I am begging you, with tears in my eyes, to tell me yes."

"Why do you think—?"

She wiggles our hands. "It was just out of frame, but his arm moved and then your arm moved. It's like they were connected."

I do not pretend to not know what she is talking about. As Ella has pointed out, I'm a bad liar, and her question is too direct to evade. "I had some nerves. He gave me a steadying grip." I've parceled the explanation up, stamped and addressed it. All she has to do is sign off on the delivery.

Ella emits a squeak. "Steadying grip. Is that what the kids are calling it these days? You guys were fire." Her fingers wiggle upwards like a tiny flame. "Who was filming?"

I make a noise of disgust at the back of my throat, relieved to have come around to the point of my visit. "Erik, the Social Media Team. He isn't going to survive two minutes with Oskar." Ella's brow notches at the sound of this name. A correction will only goad her further. "I need some tips on how to film the Head of Restoration effectively."

"Shirtless," she declares.

I press my lips into a tight line. Such a sight might cause a stampede of single women to the museum. Two hundred thousand all in one afternoon. They'd have to call the police, cordon off the area, and helicopter him out.

I shake my head, and the mental image dissipates. "I need real tips."

"My family has got to learn how to use a search engine," she sighs, swiveling in her chair. She taps a few keys and finds several basic YouTube videos of sufficient length. "These'll get you started. Mostly it's about having a clean lens and not aiming toward the windows. People will forgive a lot if you can be interesting. I saw that video. You're going to be very interesting."

She bends over, rummaging through a box—an actual cardboard box in the middle of a royal palace—and tosses me something that looks like an alien mothership component.

"That's a cell phone stand with a built-in ring light. It'll keep your phone steady but it's better to use natural light when you can. The best thing is to watch videos and practice with that," she says, pointing at the contraption in my hands. "Start with short snippets, focus on one thing, don't try to do it all, and, for the love of Erasmus's cap, use the gift you have."

"Which is?"

Ella looks skyward, as though calling upon the heavens to strike me down for the crime of stupidity. "Chemistry."

12

Cinnamon Siren

OSKAR

"You were holding her hand," Uncle Timo says, spooning the thick stew into his mouth and chewing around a large potato. He shakes a finger at me, a gesture which would give him away as a foreigner even before he spoke one word. "When will I meet her?"

"She's not a girlfriend, uncle." My mind soberly nods in agreement. The frisson of electricity coursing through my body does not. "Princess Freja and I only work together."

He taps the front page of The Holy Pelican with its sedate headline. *Prime Minister Challenges The National Museum.* The article mentions my residency status, casually pairing the fact with the prime minister's immigration plan. The photograph below the text is meant to sell papers, the work of Erik the Intern who should hire himself out for royal wedding announcements.

"Then why are you holding her hand? Is this harassment?" He picks up the paper and gives the photo a close inspection. "Are you harassing her?"

I chop at a carrot with the edge of my spoon, mincing it into tiny pieces. "Neither of us wanted to do that video. We were just trying to get through it."

Uncle Timo smacks the paper with the back of his hand and snorts. "You liked it."

I liked it. I allow the raw-boned truth to slip out of the shadows and into the forefront of my thoughts. Being filmed for the impromptu announcement hadn't been comfortable, but holding Freja's hand had conjured a primal reaction. I rub a thumb over my palm. I liked it.

I frown into my stew. Rain lashes the windows of the ground floor apartment and Uncle Timo's small garden, making the skeletal outlines of his potted plants shiver. I've spent more than twenty-five years building a life here. People like me don't get second chances in Sondmark, and I can't afford to be distracted now when citizenship is on the line.

I carry this reminder with me into work the next morning, punching my keycode into the security system, repeating the pattern several times until the door clicks and I tug it open.

"Wait for me," comes a voice. Freja skips up the steps buttoned into a wool coat and carrying some dry cleaning, a drinks container, and a paper bag. She scoots past, bringing the smell of autumn, cold temperatures, and freshly baked goods.

I sniff, and she holds up the bag from La Baiser Chaleureux—The Warm Kiss—an expensive bakery in the heart of Handsel, thrusting it into my hands. "I'll carry our coffee," she says, tilting her head at the insulated cups.

"You don't have to bring me food," I say, peeling the dry cleaning out of her grip. I'm being wise, sternly setting a boundary between me and my distraction.

"My sisters have this theory that I'm nicer if they feed me first. Maybe you are, too." She strides ahead, unaware she's left me tumbling like a bird in a high wind.

"Are you? Nicer?" My boundary loses a few stones with this question, and I'll have to build it back again. After she gives me her answer.

She bumps my arm with her elbow. "We already established this over Chinese food. Everyone's nicer when they're not hungry."

"We should be getting to work," I say, but when we pass through an exhibit of Viking pottery shards and Early Iron Age implements, I can no longer restrain myself. Unwrapping the top of the bag, I push my nose in, inhaling the smell of fat, braided cinnamon bread. I'm seized by a cinnamon siren who's wrapped her hands around my head, sucking me into the pastry vortex with her sweet and fragrant blend. Maybe this is how Freja's ancestors claimed the throne. Conquest by gluten.

"The food doesn't care if you're in a bad mood," Freja says. "It would be a wicked thing to waste it."

She makes a good point.

In the studio, she hangs her coat up on my only hook and takes the pastries. I hang the dry cleaning over a door jamb, examining the folded-over paper stapled to the plastic.

"This is my suit jacket?"

"Yes," she says, setting the breakfast things out on my desk in the same configuration we used when it was Chinese takeout. Her hands still. "I didn't thank you, before, for lending it to me. My back—thank you." She clears her throat. "I had it dry cleaned."

I nod. There'll be nothing left of her on the material, no lingering scent.

"There was a paper in your pocket so they—"

"I see it."

I fold my coat over the back of the sofa. The toffee glaze on the cinnamon bun is glistening in the morning light. I fight the pull of it—and her—moving to the hot table, peeling tape, and taking up the mylar. The painting beneath it is in good shape. I shift it to a spot between some weighted boards until it acclimatizes. I wish I could accustom myself to Freja as easily.

I push a smoothing hand across the surface of the boards using careful movements. Too careful. I recalibrate. Casual. My gaze is neither shifting nor intent. My breath is measured. The distance between me and the desk is safely within conversational bounds but not close. The effort it's been to find this spot is making me sweat.

She tears off a hunk of the bun and pops it into her mouth. "After a few minutes, you'll forget I'm here," she says. She lifts the paper plate, tilting it towards me. "This is really good."

I deliberately add another weight to the boards, dimly aware of some battle going on within. A mocking grunt rises from my chest. A battle about breakfast. I surrender.

"Do you buy everybody off with baked goods?" I ask, taking a chair and rolling back my cuffs.

"It's an innocent pastry, *Neer* Velasquez," she says, removing the lid from her cup of coffee and blowing on it, vanilla-scented steam wafting off the liquid. My hand clenches, and I notice more than I want to. The deep green of her dress and the small navy-blue dots scattered over it. The careless bow at the high neck. The tiny beauty mark under her lips. These colors make me want to reach for a brush not merely to sweep away the decaying genius of dead masters but to make something of my own.

I want to sketch her.

I watch her in carefully timed glances. Freja doesn't eat like I imagined a princess would, by daintily picking up her pastry with the protective tissue paper. She tears long strips of it, chewing with obvious contentment, licks the pad of her thumb, and tears off another hunk, nibbling around the ragged edges.

I demolish a bun quickly, giving her less time to notice my enjoyment. "What's on the agenda this morning?" I ask, tipping my head back and looking at the ceiling.

"The good news is that you won't have to work with Erik. I practiced taking short clips with my phone last night and watched a lot of videos. If we start small—maybe begin with an introduction—I can work my way up to other things."

"I don't need an introduction."

She licks her thumb before frowning and scrubbing it with a napkin and tossing it into a wastebasket. "Don't be silly."

I head to the sink. "Sondmark isn't going to be interested," I say, knocking the faucet on with my elbow and plunging my sticky hands under the stream. I want distance between me and Freja, but she joins me, crowding the sink, shoulder, hip, and hands brushing mine. By some miracle, I don't run. Instead, I pump the soap. She swipes it, palm sliding across mine, lathering up her own hands.

"What?" she says. I've frozen.

Swallowing, I pump the soap again. "You don't need to introduce me. We're supposed to highlight the art."

She grabs a towel, hands it over for me to dry, and grabs another for herself. "*Neer* Velasquez—"

"Oskar," I correct.

She nods. "Oskar."

Vede.

I was building a wall.

She holds my gaze. "The point of all this is to get people into the museum. Have you seen the numbers on our post yesterday?"

"More than 700,000 views," comes a voice at the door, breaking our concentration. "It was *insane* exposure."

The intern.

My eyes narrow. "How many of those came from Sondmark? How many will visit The Nat?"

"The takeaway here is that they liked you guys and I was, like, processing it," Erik's splayed hands rotate around his head, "when I realized we have to keep our focus narrow." One of the hands splays at us. "You were giving us a whole Thora and Bjarke mood. We would be crazy not to use that."

What?

Freja shifts. "Erik—"

Erik ignores her. "So I'm thinking that the other staff can do content, or whatever, but you guys should be, like, the hosts. My marketing professor calls it *delivering a narrative through-line*."

I cough away a laugh and catch Freja's eye. "I have no idea what he's talking about."

Freja doesn't share my confusion. "Do you remember those coffee commercials from when we were kids?" she asks. "The woman runs out of coffee, so she has to ask her neighbor, who happens to be a sexy middle-aged man. The next commercial would be him coming back from walking his dog when the woman comes to return what she borrowed. You know," she drops her voice into a husky alto, "*Coffee and company turn friends into lovers*."

Erik joins in, his laugh like the bark of a seal. "We studied this in class. Her hair was amazing."

They look at me expectantly.

This happens. It's a reminder that my childhood was spent reading comic books and watching VHS tapes shipped from Pavieau as my father tried to keep the ties to his homeland stronger than the ones of his host country. He succeeded. And failed. My identity exists in the cracks somewhere.

"I have work," I remind them, returning to the desk, and picking up the coffee. "I don't have any time to become fluent in—" I wave a hand indicating social media, Unspeakable Interns, and princesses.

"For sure," Erik drawls. "That's my job. You just give me content."

"I'll be in charge of collecting that," Freja breaks in. I look away, my mouth captive to a fleeting smile. She's shielding me.

"Whatever," Erik says, walking backward, "just send me the raw video. I'll text you a list of assignments I've worked out with Marie."

He bangs through the door, and Freja and I are alone. The silence between us prickles with electricity.

"I don't understand why I need to be more than a cursory part of this," I say, blowing on the coffee, inching away from her without it being obvious.

She makes the distance vanish by striding across the studio and slipping into my desk chair, crossing her legs at the knee. She laces her fingers and the chair bounces slightly as she considers me.

I look away.

"Did you see the comments from people who hold Provisional Residency Cards?" she asks. I mean to replace the coffee lid, but my hand stills. "Most of them talked about how exciting it was to have one of their own inviting them to The National Museum."

In my mind's eye, I can see a series of countless football pitches and hear the shout of *Hej, Pa-vi!* I'm in a classroom, shrugging when my surname is mangled so that the teacher will stop trying to get it right and move on to another Larsen or Sorensen or Christensen. I'm being interviewed for my first job and asked to account for why I speak Sondish so well. I remember why it became easier and easier to narrow my circle down to those who gather at Uncle Timo's.

I secure the lid, careful to set it all the way around. Freja is playing dirty.

"How many comments told me to go back to where I came from?" I ask, taking a swallow of coffee.

I frown into the cup. *Stultes es.* This is excellent.

When I look at Freja, she holds my gaze.

"About one in twenty. Too many." Her gaze flicks away but returns. At least she doesn't lie and tell me there were none. "Have you ever thought of trying for citizenship?"

I was beginning to think this strange creature and I were starting to understand one another. I thought we'd reached some unspoken truce so that we wouldn't mind appearing on camera together and it wouldn't be inconceivable to touch her hand again.

This happens.

"Do you know when the Battle of Podense was fought?" I ask, and she straightens, her mouth pulling in confusion. She doesn't know what to make of this shift.

"Yes. Sixteenth century," she answers.

"The exact date?"

"Let's see." She runs a finger gently along her lower lip. *Vede.*

"The Battle of Podense was a lesser skirmish in the War of the Amber Cross, sparked off by an incident involving a stolen pig, if I recall correctly."

Of course she knows. Her ancestor probably stole the pig. "When?"

"1546?"

"Wrong. May 9, 1556. It rained in the morning, giving the archers from the Duchy of Lowenwald a strategic advantage. Can you tell me what industries flourished at the neck of the Aunslev Valley between 750 AD and 850 AD?"

She shakes her head, playing with the bow at her neck, fingers winding around the fabric. "The Aunslev Valley produced pottery. One of my engagements last year was visiting the excavation sites."

"Is your answer pottery?"

Her eyes narrow in irritation. "Why do you sound like the host of *Raining Millions*?"

"Is it?" I press.

She drags out her answer. "Yeeeeeees."

"Wrong. The valley experienced a brief period of tin smelting."

"Sondmark has tin?"

"*Had* tin. Your forefathers smelted it all. Ready for a third round?"

She gusts out a breath and lifts her palms, not understanding the game but playing along.

"What's the annual average rainfall in the Sonderlands, to the nearest ten millimeters?"

"Five hundred?"

"Five hundred and fourteen," I say, crossing the room, and tearing off the paper stapled to my dry cleaning bag. I thrust it into her hands. "Congratulations, Your Royal Highness. You're on your way to failing your first citizenship test. The opportunity to attempt a final test is conditional on a clean criminal record and steady employment. Be sure to grab a resettlement flier on your way out."

I take a painting from where it's leaning against the wall and lay it right-side down on a table while she absorbs the bare information of my previous test results.

"You weren't even close that first time," she says, voice tight. "57%. How is that possible?"

"I'm an ignorant Pavi," I answer, running my fingers along the frame.

She gives me such a look as I have only seen on canvas. Valkyries riding the storm. "Were those real questions you asked me?"

I nod. "Her Majesty's government is good enough to give applicants a few areas of emphasis to focus on for each test cycle. December will feature obscure Sondish fairy tales. I have three months to turn myself into an expert."

Freja releases a breath. "That sounds easier than ancient metallurgy."

"How easy will it be for people who didn't grow up hearing them? How easy is it if there aren't fairy tale translations into an applicant's native language? These tests are meant to fail us."

There's a whole minefield between Princess Freja and me, unnavigable and dangerous. I don't want her to offer a facile apology. I don't know what I want.

She dips her head and I set my tools out in precise lines, bracing myself for a general prostration. Her jaw works. She knows what her challenge with the prime minister might cost me now. I wanted her to know. I expected to feel satisfied. I don't.

She clears her throat. "We didn't get 700,000 views because of me. We got them because we appeared on camera together, and it would be crazy to dismiss that kind of success." Her eyes light and she lifts her hands, pressing the air. "We're giving them Thora and Bjarke."

I grunt, half amused. "Who are Thora and Bjarke?"

Her humor checks. "You did the restoration work on them last year, remember? The Winter Princess and her knight."

Ah.

The silence stretches and she leans forward, arms resting on the desk. "I can't undo what's happened, but I can work as hard as I can to meet the prime minister's goal. We should start filming your behind-the-scenes now."

"What do you need, Thora?"

Her smile returns. "Cooperation, Bjarke," she says, lifting a bag.

While she moves quietly around the studio, I meet with members of the restoration team, quickly taking their reports. One has to dye some fabric to patch a moth hole. Another is cleaning a piece of Germanic statuary. When they return to their workrooms, I return to the table where Freja has laid out her supplies and loop the apron over my head.

"May I start?" she asks.

"Mm."

Turning the camera, she begins, "Hello, I'm visiting the restoration studio at The Nat with the Head of Restoration, Oskar Velasquez. Say *hi*, Oskar." She tips the camera at me.

"Mm."

She laughs. "What are you doing today?" she asks, training the camera on me.

This is my job. I have to keep it. My hands are busy as I answer. "I'm removing the frame."

"Is that the first step?" Her voice lulls me into thinking it's just her here. Not half a million unblinking eyes.

"No, I've already examined it under a UV light. That shows me areas of discoloration and retouching. It has to come out of the frame before I know what else it needs." I glance up into her face and glance down again before I lose my train of thought. "This painting was backed in paper by a previous restorer which—"

Freja must see my face because she finishes, "You don't recommend doing."

"We know better now." I reach for a wooden-handled tool. The metal is flat and gently pronged, and I cut the paper away.

"*Stultes es,*" I mutter.

She looks up from her cell phone. "What?"

"Copper staples," I point an accusing finger at the canvas, "driven in with a pneumatic staple gun."

"Should I be upset?"

"The whole country should be upset. Look. Look," I say, levering the canvas out of the frame. "Forty staples on this side when a third as many tacks would do."

"But it's secure," she offers, as though that's any excuse for this lazy and destructive job. I tip the frame higher. Can't she see?

She mounts the camera on a stand, coming around the table to get a closer inspection.

"Just watch what happens when I try to remove one." I wiggle the tool under the corner of the staple and, feeling the purchase, I ease the whole thing up. As expected, the staple bar rips through the material, leaving a precise rectangle of destruction.

I make a sound of disgust and toss the knife on the table.

"What's that?" she asks, hovering a gentle finger over the rip. Our heads bend over it together and when we look up, I'm reminded of Uncle Timo's words. *You liked it.*

I frown my thoughts away.

"That brilliant green there," she prods.

"It's copper," I answer, pushing through the roughness in my voice. There's a refuge in pedantry and science, and I take it. "It oxidizes as it ages. If the previous restorer had used an acid solvent, he could hardly have made a worse choice."

"It means more work."

I shake my head. The work isn't the thing.

"It means that the restorer had something rare and priceless in front of him, and he was too stupid to know it."

13

─ · ─

ATTACHMENT SENT

FREJA

"Go ahead and work," I tell him. "I'll ask you questions occasionally and then have Erik piece the footage together."

His glance shifts to my mouth, and I rub the corner, expecting to encounter a crust of sugar. Nothing.

I adjust the camera so he's in the center of the frame and drag a stool near enough to observe, setting up my laptop. As he pries out the tacks, I search "Sondmark citizenship practice tests" and find an archive. An introductory paragraph reads, "Before Prime Minister Torbald's premiership, citizenship test pass rates approached 42%, however, these tests aren't useful in training current students. Below are accurate facsimiles of tests administered during his time in office."

I click on the first test.

Question one: Name the reigning monarchs of the sixteenth century. I do the rhyme, nailing the list. Still, it's a trick question. Frederich and Frederick have almost the same spelling.

Question two: Which king forbade his wife from using thread-wrapped buttons?

My brow wrinkles. Pre-Renaissance, surely? I take a stab. Malthe II. The screen flashes red, and the correct answer pops up. Malthe III.

After I get the next four questions wrong, I receive a notification that I've failed. "Follow this link to Dragon Test Prep, your trusted partner in citizenship for over 50 years. We have a 17% pass rate!"

17% is something to boast about?

I'm a princess of Sondmark. These questions were about my own family tree. Maybe I'll do better after the cinnamon bun has had a chance to settle. I turn to my phone, inspecting the settings.

I spent hours last night attempting to get to know it as well as I know my books and music, trying to understand the quick, bite-sized nature of content required to be successful on most social media platforms. I invested hours watching glossy blonde women hold cosmetics in front of their faces, palms situated behind a tube of revolutionary foundation/lipstick/mascara/primer, all talking fast.

"I've got the LUX Lune Eyeshadow palette on this side of my face and the Moongoop palette on this side," they'd say, hands sweeping left and right. "It's a total dupe."

I'm a quick learner and realized quickly that The Nat has to have slower branding. Our strengths are gorgeous visuals and knowledgeable authorities. Oskar grunts for what seems like the millionth time, and I hide a smile. He's furious and it's adorable.

Lifting the camera from its base, I take shots of the growing pile of staples, of the once-rigid canvas peeling from the weathered stretcher, and the grime accumulating on Oskar's finely boned hands.

"What are you doing?" he asks, looking over his shoulder.

"Nothing." I scurry back to my seat. No. Not scurry. Scurry implies something to be scurried from. I return to my seat with royal dignity and agreeable swiftness. I cast about for something improving to think about. The videos. This noble work. How Oskar is going to lose his job, fail his last test, be deported to Pavieau, wind up homeless, and how it's all my fault.

He has every reason to hate me.

The knowledge gets into my head like a pungent smell, the combination of low tide and summer. I was fine when I knew he didn't like me—we've spent years having to be civil to one another as seldom as possible—and I've never been bothered by the fact. I realize that it's because I could tell the story about how I was the injured party or, at least, about how I wasn't making such a bother about half an office. I can't tell that story now.

His hair brushes forward as he bends over his work.

I can't fix the last three years. I can't even fix the last three days, but I can do the right thing now. I text Erik.

"Our first video will be about copper staples. Trust me."

I plug the camera into my computer and find my handwritten notes detailing Ella's instructions about files and windows. I breathe deeply, consider the mysteries of eternity, and address the computer gods like a supplicant in the middle of a long drought. Within minutes, I send a massive video file to Erik, watching the loading bar with fingers secretly crossed underneath the table.

Attachment sent.

I lift Ella's list and kiss it. It's not enough. I want to run around the room with the flag of Sondmark draped over my shoulders. I want *Neer* Hjefdal to thrust a microphone into my tear-stained and panting face and ask me how I did it. I want to thank my mother, my coaches, and every citizen for their unflagging support.

"What's next?" Oskar asks, dumping a pile of staples in the trash.

He braces his arms wide against the edge of the work table, and I pinch my lips together.

"What's next for this painting?" I manage. It's heroic how I manage. Those forearms should qualify for a royal warrant.

"Try to control yourself," he says, voice low and teasing, "but I'm about to brush accumulated dust and residue from the back."

My lips close tighter than a mousetrap until I'm able to push my slipping control firmly back on the shelf. "Riveting. What tools do you use?"

He drags over a long, soft-bristled brush and a smaller one that looks like it came from a hardware store. "Come here," he tilts his head. "This is something I can teach you to do."

"Me?"

"We're supposed to be creating a narrative through-line, so come here."

He pulls me into the frame with him and addresses the camera. "Her Royal Highness is good enough to be my assistant today," he says, sounding like a chef on a morning show. "The painting has been removed from its stretcher, and we have to prepare it for any structural repairs. The first step is to remove the gunk—"

"Gunk." I peer over his shoulder. "Is that a professional term?"

One of his brows notches up. "I'm a professional, and I'm using the term. Here," he says, offering me the long brush. "We don't want to stress or stretch the canvas, so we'll make short, gentle sweeps in one direction and then sort of scoop it up over the barricades with the other brush."

"Sort of scoop it?" I make a face. "You don't sound trustworthy, and this is hundreds of years old. You're making me very nervous."

"Don't be nervous," he decrees.

"Oh, that's fine, then. I'm completely sorted."

A slow smile touches his mouth. "I wouldn't let you anywhere near this canvas if I thought you'd punch a hole in it."

My face spasms. "Don't say *punch a hole*. You're going to make me punch a hole."

"You're not going to punch a hole," he repeats, stepping behind me and wrapping his hand over mine, guiding it down to the canvas at a forty-five-degree angle. His breath stirs the hair at the nape of my neck.

My brain goes completely dark, but when the lights begin to flicker on again, all I can think about is how hot I am. The task he's set before me is simple, and eventually I find my rhythm, sweeping the debris into one corner.

In an attempt to be brisk and businesslike, I put the brush down. "Let me get a close-up of that gunk," I say, reaching across the table for the camera. My toes lift off the ground and I panic, imagining all the damage I might do. But he puts a hand at the small of my back, keeping me from toppling onto the canvas. I overcorrect and land, camera in hand, too close, tipping into his space. He holds my waist, steadying me.

"There you go," he says. It's what he would say to a child who had fallen off a slide, and it feels forced, as though my breathlessness and his hands are a byproduct of gravity. He lets me go and I lift the camera. Order has been reestablished and I should be grateful for it, not investigating the riot of feelings running wild in my head.

"This whole process is strange," Oskar muses as I train the lens on a pile of dust and deteriorating canvas. He's stepped back a pace, and out of the corner of my eye, I see his hand clench.

"We have to give the people what they want," I reply.

I note the time stamp on the screen and put the camera down, giving myself space. I like space. My sisters call me Lone Wolffe for a reason. It's a small wonder I should feel flushed and sensitive after an entire morning spent in close proximity to a man I...a man I...

"Let us say," my subconscious allows me, her voice as regal as my mother's, "I have spent the morning with a man I am unsettled by."

"Could we stop here?" I ask, already folding the camera stand away. The activity occupies me. "I have an evening event and have to run up to the admin offices first."

"Sure," he says, turning away with the carelessness of a person who might use copper staples to secure a canvas. "Do you want me to leave this painting at this point so we can pick up where we left off?"

"Narrative throughline," I nod. "Good idea."

I collect my bag and coat, leaving him hunched over another piece with a pair of tweezers, and find my way out of the labyrinthine tunnels easily now that I've visited several times. I repeatedly open and shut my hands, trying to force blood back into my fingers. I lift the hair at the back of my neck and let the air cool me. At the stairs, I climb towards a strange sound, swinging through the "Staff Only" doors into a crowded gallery space.

"Oh, beg pardon."

A woman jostles me, and I hastily step out of her path. Her eyes widen in recognition, and she dips an awkward curtsey in the confined area. I nod and keep moving, squeezing through the crowd before it happens again. In seconds, I've reached the administrative wing, bumping through the doors with relief, and find Roland at a one-way window overlooking the gallery. His smile is swallowed up in his beard.

"Is this really happening?" I ask. "Are we breaking any fire codes?"

"I'm not about to look them up," he laughs.

"How many visitors have there been since we opened?"

"Three thousand, with more trickling in every minute. You know, I think we might be able to do it."

For a few seconds, I sail on an ocean of optimism. These numbers will have to be sustained.

"What else has been going on today?"

"Rik installed the lottery boxes—painted them out with gold lettering and everything—in the jewelry gallery. That's been a surprising draw," he informs me. "Lynda's idea was a good one. Agnes has been calling schools all morning, trying to get them to stage Christmas concerts at the museum."

"That won't add up to more than a few hundred guests, surely."

He holds up a hand and ticks off his fingers. "Children plus parents, plus grandparents, plus godparents, plus siblings." He scratches his beard thoughtfully. "I wish Sondmark had a higher birth rate."

"I'll bring that up with Her Majesty," I laugh. "I've been in the basement working with Oskar." I pause before saying his name every time, needing a kind of spur to take the leap. And each time I do it, the sound sends my mind spinning off onto strange tangents.

The tangent I am spinning on now is that I can't remember the last man who kissed me. Cambridge grad night but I can't recall his name. Something about the dim memory tastes bland and anonymous, but my personal life has never absorbed me much. When the time comes, Mama will present me with a list of acceptable matches. I'll pick one.

"Come see the Guests Visited thermometer," Roland says, tugging me down the hall. We fetch up in front of four pieces of printer paper stuck together with tape. The pages aren't even, and the marker ran out of ink coming down the final stretch. I tamp down the wish to reconfigure it, spacing each 10,000 visitors hashmark with more precision. Perfection isn't important, I remind myself. Because of all those lovely citizens in the lobby, we're filling in that intimidating expanse of white.

Erik appears at my elbow, his blond hair flopping over on one side. "I uploaded a teaser, using only the images in the actual video."

"Nicely done, Erik."

"This one's going viral too."

Viral without the suggestion of a royal romance? This is progress. I navigate to The Nat page, pressing the phone almost against my nose, and spreading my fingers to magnify the image. I groan. "Erik, for the love of Erasmus's cap, can you stop making it look like we're about to make out?"

Erik leans over my shoulder, resting his chin on it. "You told me to take a frame from the video. If you didn't want to look that way, you shouldn't have looked at *him* that way."

I do not like his logic. I thought I was looking at Oskar with the benign friendliness of a cooking partner on a morning news show. Instead, I look like a teenage fangirl about to squeeze his bicep. *Show me how you fold in the cheese, Oskar. You do it so well.*

He's looking at me like I'm a Waitrose Christmas sandwich.

My stomach growls.

"There's nothing to be ashamed of," Erik reassures me. "Physical attraction is healthy."

I tap the video and groan again. Erik did one hell of a job teasing this video.

"I thought you were going to edit me out," I say.

Erik leans over my shoulder again. "Your faces are right next to each other. You looked like this the whole time. What am I? A warlock?"

14

— · —

GOBLIN LOVER

FREJA

When I return to the Summer Palace, I head straight to my suite, a set of rooms reminiscent of a British manor house library with tall mahogany bookshelves and a crackling fire. Even though the weather outside is furious and rain lashes the windows, I can take refuge here. More importantly, I can take tea, settle into a deep chair to read a book, and listen to overwrought operatic sopranos going to their graves, singing of doomed love.

This recipe never fails to soothe me.

It fails today.

An entire pot of tea has been unable to quench the restlessness kicked up in the wake of my hours at The Nat. My hours with Oskar. After opening and closing several books, I give inner tranquility up as a lost cause and begin preparing myself for this evening's event. After doing my hair and make-up, I slip into a close-fitting velvet sheath, the high collar topped with a tiny ruffle, and step into the hall.

"I like that," Clara says, sure-footed, even in impossibly high stilettos. To balance out the shoes, she's wearing a basic cocktail dress in light blue. "I never think to wear black to these things, but you look…" She searches for a word. "Sexy."

I catch a glimpse of myself in a tall mirror as we pass, seeing the over-large mouth, the interesting nose, and the jawline that means business. My sisters say I have the looks of a woodland fairy, but this is a kindness. I bear a striking resemblance to sculptures of Magda the Great who was famous for the fact that all her bad parts combined to make something striking.

There are worse things. I laugh. "I've been spending too much time drinking at the fetid trough of social media to believe that. Anyway, I haven't had a date in over a year," I remind Clara.

"That's only because you live in a walled castle." My sister slips a hand into the crook of my elbow.

"You manage to date, and you live in a walled castle."

"Max is a one-man siege engine." My sister pauses, grins quite stupidly, then jostles my arm. "You look like a goddess who won't put up with anything short of being worshiped. That's always sexy."

We're still arguing the point when we join the others in a small anteroom. Mama, going over some notes with Caroline, lifts her head, does a quick perusal of me and Clara, and, giving a brisk nod, returns to her whispered conference.

On the other end of the room, Père, Noah, and Ella cluster near the mantel, loudly discussing the last Dragons match and employing a lot of hand gestures.

Clara makes a beeline to join them, but my gaze lands on Alma, standing in front of a flower arrangement and staring down at her phone with an unnaturally rigid set to her shoulders. It's my habit to be private and to leave others their privacy, but this business with the museum has forced me out of my customary reserve, involving me in problems beyond my scope. I see Alma's distress. I can't unsee it.

I search my mind for any relevant details, ashamed to recall so little about what's going on in my sister's life. Her fiancé, Pietor, has been rowing across the Atlantic for some charitable, awareness-raising cause but the couple is supposed to be meeting Parliament this week to begin hearings about their forthcoming marriage—a formality, but a necessary one for a Sondish royal bride. No one in Parliament is going to object to Alma's advantageous alliance.

I glance around the room. Isn't Pietor supposed to be here?

"What's up?" I ask, pitching my voice low.

Alma looks at me, bewildered, but I persevere. *I'm trying something new here.*

She tips the phone showing me a Pixy post from Pietor's account, @HereditaryGrandDuke_Himmelstein. He's taken a selfie on a tropical beach, the curve of white sand behind him dotted with sunbathers and elegantly bowing palm trees. I'm offended by his straw hat, which has the tiniest brim all the way around, and by the way the camera is strategically angled to capture his bare shoulder and tanned upper chest.

The caption reads, "Inspired. Resolved. Fighting for change. #no-plastics."

I stifle an eye roll. Nothing says "fighting for change" like standing your fiancée up on the most important week of her life. I hope Pietor spends the next month picking sand out of his dense mat of chest hair.

"Did he miss his flight?"

Alma lifts a rigid shoulder. "Plans changed. He says in the comments that he's flying back next week."

Communication via pretentious Pixy post? No.

The thought is sharp, unequivocal, and cold with fury. I haven't spent any time ThumTac-ing the perfect wedding, but I know with sudden clarity that I will not take this garbage when it's my turn to beg Parliament for the privilege of marrying the titled man of my mother's choosing.

"He's not rowing back to save on fossil fuels?"

Alma snorts a laugh, and when it's time to line up for our entrance to the gala, her chin is up.

The event tonight is going to highlight the contributions of Sondmark's immigrant communities, and Père, Sondmark's most famous immigrant, takes his place a step behind Mama. "I like this event, Helena," I hear him murmur. "Torbald's protectionism needs one of your famous rebukes."

I hold my breath, wondering if I'm watching a thaw. Please. Please.

Mama's response comes straight from the blast chiller. "The Crown doesn't do politics."

Vede.

The doors swing wide, we are announced, and I'm swept into the formalities. Social situations are difficult, but being an attentive listener smooths the worst of my path. I join a group and begin asking questions, my stomach in a high state of "desperate for a cookie."

A quarter of an hour in, I glance across the crowded room and choke, turning the sound into a polite cough.

Oskar Velasquez. Oskar Velasquez in evening clothes. I lift my eyes to a row of mirrors and spot him again, calculating angles and distances, dredging up all I know of geometry. He looks up and catches me staring. His chin bumps a greeting and I blink, swinging my attention back to Hafsa, who's telling me in excellent but accented Sondish about her first year in the country and how she and her husband saved up enough to open a small convenience store. How the business has grown into a mini empire.

"Sixteen-hour days, but it was worth it to send my daughter to one of the best schools in Europe."

Another woman in the circle laughs. "No time to study for the citizenship test, even if you had a hope of passing." The sound of her amusement echoes around the circle, as though she's said one of the few things no one could possibly argue with:

There is no hope of passing the citizenship test.

Sondmark will never win the Eurovision contest.

Oskar Velasquez is mouth-watering in evening clothes.

The topic is taken up by the group, and soon they're trading stories of near-misses and outright failure.

Hafsa's husband shakes his head. "One question about the domestic policy of Jeroen van Vliet and—" He buzzes his tongue between his lips and slaps his hands against each other. "A question about a prime minister who served over a hundred years ago. I wonder how you would do," he laughs, shaking his finger at me.

"I spent the afternoon taking practice citizenship tests."

A thread of tense curiosity cinches the edges of our circle, drawing us all close. "And?" he prods.

"Three attempts." I mimic him, slapping my hands together.

"There you go," Hafsa says, adjusting the ends of her headscarf. "It's not just me. You were brought up here with as good an education in the history, culture, and geography of Sondmark as anyone, and you still failed." Her eyes shift over my shoulder, and I hear the voice I have been expecting. Dreading.

"Is that what you were doing while you were working me so hard?"

Oskar. His voice vibrates in my ear and along the tendons of my neck. It's unsettling and invasive, like a seasonal allergy when the itch gets into my brain.

When I look at him properly, my bones turn to liquid. *Stultes es,* only six hours ago I was in his studio behaving like a mostly rational human being even when his forearms were uncovered. I paste a blank expression on my face, acknowledging a sudden tightness in my chest, another symptom of a sickness I don't care to diagnose.

"*Neer* Velasquez."

"I told you to call me Oskar."

"Mm."

Hafsa gasps. "You're the man in the video." She jiggles her husband's arm. "He's that man. The one with the PRC, Amin."

Her smile lights up her face. "I must have watched it a dozen times. My daughter's school is planning a field trip in a few weeks, and I messaged the teacher right away because I have to come."

Her eyes flick from Oskar to me and back again. In every culture, in every language, these are matchmaking eyes.

Oskar draws a card from his pocket and hands it to Hafsa. "Message me when you plan to come through. I could bring the class into the restoration studio for a look at what goes on behind the scenes, if they promise to keep their hands to themselves." He gives a warm smile, which Hafsa returns.

I blink in surprise, smoothing it away as the circle breaks up and the guests move on to other clusters.

"What was that look?" Oskar says.

Our backs are to the room, and we're facing one of several massive fireplaces. To anyone else, it will look like I'm explaining the history of the mantelpiece. The noise in the ballroom, steady and animated, has receded, enveloping us in a sense of intimacy.

My eyes trace the scrollwork on the frieze as I wait for my heartbeat to settle.

"I'm attempting to reconcile the man handing out his cell phone number to a stranger with the irritated art restorer I've been working with all week."

"Irritated?" He sounds amused.

"I thought you didn't tolerate distractions."

"You're a distraction." His gaze swings down to mine. "I tolerate you."

I should be moving on to another circle farther up the room, doling out polite interest and royal glamor. These events aren't social occasions. Mama runs a family business, and it's all hands on deck for the dinner rush. *Table Six has a drinks order. Hurry, hurry. Mop the spill in the corner booth.* There's no time to chat up the delivery boy in the alley even if I want to.

I return my gaze to the mantelpiece, cheating my duty for another minute. "I didn't know you would be here."

He gives a light grunt. "There was no 'Notify Freja' box to check on my invitation."

"You might have told me this morning."

"I was busy cursing pneumatic staple guns. It didn't cross my mind."

I didn't cross his mind.

I catch a reflection of him in a mirror and my pulse jumps again. A tablet of Acrivastine would clear these symptoms up. I'm sure of it.

My lashes flicker as I surreptitiously glance over the room. Which of these women is his plus one?

"I'm with Uncle Timo," he says, tipping his glass. "Come meet him."

I cross the banquet hall, my nerves on fire where his fingers rest lightly under my elbow. It's an elbow, I remind myself with impatience. An elbow. But it's on fire and I worry there's not an over-the-counter medication for that.

"Uncle," he says, "meet Freja."

I reach a hand out towards a gentleman who looks to be in his seventies. He bows at the waist and says with a touching courtliness, "*Bom niute*, Princess Freja."

I respond in Pavian, the vowels furring delightfully on my tongue. "*Bom niute, Sehor–*"

"Fornasari."

His eyes twinkle, and he lets loose a torrent of words until I hold my hands up laughing. "Slowly, slowly, Sehor. My broken ear must be mended," I say, using the flowery Pavian phrases Père taught me.

He returns the floweriness, calling me beautiful, magnificent, a goddess. When I encounter Oskar's raised brow, I fight off a blush.

"Have you met my father, the prince consort?" I ask the old gentleman, reverting to my native tongue.

"Met him?" *Sehor* Fornasari bursts. "We're old friends."

A booming laugh echoes over the room, and before I have a chance to look for Père, my father reaches past me to pull the other man into a full embrace.

"I would have known that laugh in the darkest dungeon," he says. The greeting is effusive, drawing eyes as they kiss three times on the cheek, right-left-right.

I bump backward into Oskar, and he tugs me out of the way. I glance up. "Did you know about this?"

"I didn't know it was true."

My eyes dart to my elbow, and he lets me go.

"Well," he says, "I won't keep you." He drifts off in the opposite direction.

For more than an hour, I keep my distance, performing my job with an exhausting level of focus. It feels like constantly correcting an articulated lorry that wants to veer off into the Ditch of How Good Oskar Looks Tonight or the Perilous Embankment of Wondering What His Hair Feels Like. In desperation, I glance at an ornate French clock near the exit. Almost a quarter to nine. Almost done.

Relief turns into awareness as I sense the presence of someone behind me. Oskar. I know it without turning around.

He leans forward, stirring the hair at my neck. "You're starving."

My stomach gurgles in agreement. I frown. "How do you know?"

He touches the champagne flute in my hands. "For one thing, the level hasn't changed in more than an hour. Why hold it if you don't drink it?"

He was watching? "This is easier to do if I've got a prop."

He grunts, looking around the room, hands in his pockets. "You were right about these things. No good food." His attention swings back to me. "Your father asked Uncle Timo to stay for a nightcap. If you come out with me, I'll feed you."

A plate of beef sandwiches is only a phone call away, ready to be whipped up in the palace kitchens the moment I need a night feast. I could tell him this, but I don't. I stuff the words so far back in my throat that they'll need a pickaxe and crampons to see the light of day.

"Will I need to change?"

He gives me a long look and I thank heaven for Swiss comportment school.

"No need."

When the party concludes, I return to my suite, doubling back to meet him in the Grand Hall. He's conferring with Nils Helmut, our head of palace security, standing under a blazing chandelier in a dark coat and scarf, a shoe softly scuffing the checkerboard tiles.

"A team will follow your car," Nils says, giving me a brief smile before continuing through the doors. When Oskar sees me, his foot pauses. He straightens.

We live in the Summer Palace for most of the year since the invention of modern heating and cooling systems. Ella speaks of it as though we're a middle-class family who lives above the shop, but few of the customers ever venture into the family quarters, as it were, calling on the daughters of the house. My manner with them—polite, interested, willing to be amused by the driest anecdote—is entirely useless when presented with a lone man of extreme attractiveness.

Oskar reaches for the wrap I have slung over my arm. It takes some doing, but he finds the top and holds it up for me, head tilted.

"That's a very judgemental face," I say, standing perfectly still while he drapes it over my shoulders.

"It's a cape."

"It's a cloak," I correct, "and it's got pockets for lip balm."

I take his arm as we descend the exterior stairs, delighted by the gust of wind swirling the cloak in dramatic waves around my dress. The practicality of pockets has nothing to do with my choice. I can't pass up any chance to look like I'm running away from an enchanted ball with my goblin lover.

"Is this your car?" I ask when he tucks me into a low-slung, black vintage Mazorh. I run my eyes over the sinuous wood of the dashboard. My mother's fleet of Bentleys and Rolls Royces are more expensive, but this bucket seat is cradling me like packing material around a china teacup. And it is sexy.

"It was my father's," he answers, sliding into the driver's seat.

"It suits you."

He gives me an inquiring look and color rises in my cheeks. "I only meant—" I clear my throat. "*Are* you an international spy?"

He turns the key, and the motor turns over, growling. His eyes narrow and his voice drops. "If I told you, I'd have to kill you."

On the expressway, he shifts the car into fourth gear and accelerates, turning east and winding into the rural foothills above Handsel. The lights of the security car shine in the side mirror, keeping pace.

"Where are you taking me?" I ask when the heavens break overhead, pounding the windscreen and the road beyond. There are few signs of civilization, and I'm already wondering if I could sleep in the bucket seats in the event of a catastrophic stranding.

Not next to him, I couldn't.

"We're going to an inn, but it isn't far, and the road is good the whole way. We'll have an excellent view of the city lights and nourishing food. Surely we can set aside being mortal enemies for a single meal?"

I nod. Mortal enemies? I said as much last week, railing to Ella about the recluse in Restoration, but it's hard to hate someone up close. I've spent my days since leaning over his shoulder, the scent of his cologne in my lungs.

For the first time, I wonder what it would've been like to meet for the first time in the ballroom of the Summer Palace, trading introductions as an art restorer and an art enthusiast. Would I have cornered him the whole night? Would he have handed over his card and invited me to tour his studio? What would it be like without the entire future of the museum riding on our efforts to work together?

"There won't be a crowd at this hour," he assures me, and there isn't. He parks near the entrance and tells me to stay put, charging into the rain and jogging around. He swings the passenger door open and holds his wool coat over my head.

"We'll dash for it," he says, and I lift my skirts, scurrying along like a woodland creature under his protective canopy.

We stop in the lighted entry, laughing as I shake diamonds of rain from my skirts. In a flurry of movement, he hangs his coat and my cloak on a pair of hooks and turns to me. We're well-matched, and it takes only the slightest incline of my head to look him in the eye, absorbing the expression on his face. I can't read it. I haven't learned his language yet. My broken ear must be mended, as they say. He's not as simple as a Lars Kette canvas, with clashing knights and mounted riders, that I can see once and understand it in whole.

I look so long that when my brain catches up, I jerk into action, brushing my hands over his shoulders, wicking away the raindrops.

"Freja."

My hands still, my fractured breaths loud in the silence. We are frozen in a pool of soft amber light, and he reaches up, wrapping both of my wrists in his hands, thumbs over the beating pulse.

"Ach, Oskar," booms a voice from the great room. "You always come when no one else dares. You want a booth?"

Oskar drops our hands, sliding one of his into one of mine, and leads the way forward. "Konrad, what's on offer today?"

The innkeeper points to the booth with the flat of his hand. When he sees me properly, he gives a bow, and I answer with an unself-conscious nod, sliding onto the bench. Oskar settles across from me, shaking his head at the byplay.

"The missus made a tenderloin, apple, and sausage stew, fresh crusty bread, and lemon torte for after. Will you stay for a bit of everything?"

My stomach gurgles again. Oskar looks at me and I clutch his hand. *Don't you dare take me away.*

"We'll stay," he says.

Konrad whisks out of sight and returns with a bottle of Socrè Barbaresco and a basket of cheese straws, chatting briefly about the weather. Oskar asks him about his son, the doctor, and his daughter, the legal clerk, before he whisks away again.

I pick up a cheese straw and begin to nibble. "How did you find this place?" I ask, vowing to return. If the smells coming from the kitchen are any indication, I won't get the chance. I'll die happy tonight, doing what I loved most.

Oskar leans against the high back of the booth, tugging his necktie loose and unbuttoning the top button of his shirt. I try to make the way my gaze drifts to the column of his throat appear casual, accidental.

"Giana, Konrad's wife, is Pavian. She comes into town for dinner at Uncle Timo's from time to time." He rolls the tie and tucks it into his breast pocket, nodding to the windows. "In the spring and summer, you can sit out on the patio with a view of the entire valley."

In the mellow atmosphere of a restaurant booth with rain plinking against the window glass, fire popping in the hearth, and the taste of Italian wine on my tongue, my mind drifts from one image to another. Oskar wearing an open-necked shirt and a pair of sunglasses. The wind sweeping up the hills tosses his hair, his expression unguarded. He invites me into the walled garden. He leans over and kisses my mouth.

I bolt upright.

15

THE BASICS

OSKAR

I stretch across the table, settling my fingertips on Freja's arm.

"What is it?" I ask.

"A crow landed on my shoulder," she tells me, explaining away the thunderstruck look in her eyes as nothing more than a sudden, inexplicable shiver.

I withdraw and she rubs the spot, reaching for another cheese straw. "I enjoyed meeting your uncle. How did *Señor* Fornasari wind up in Sondmark? Does he come from your mother's side?" she asks.

I pour two glasses of wine, mine half as much as Freja's to account for the drive back to Handsel, my nose filling with the scent of dried cherries, anise, and vanilla. Words seem to spill from her lips. She seems nervous but what would she have to feel nervous about?

"He's not actually my uncle." The bottle thumps when I set it down. "He's not any kind of relation even if he's been shoving his nose in wherever he likes for as long as I can remember. Pavians call everyone uncle or auntie or cousin. We all know each other's business."

She smiles, her chin angling away as she tries to keep her amusement to herself. We share words. We share wine. A few smiles. Not many.

I want to make her smile.

The thought arrives in my consciousness fully formed, having incubated inside me, in the dark, unexamined corners of my mind for heaven knows how long. I don't want to know. It's the first ordinary wish I've had in almost a year, I think, attempting to shrink the thought down into something I can wrestle with and win.

It's a nice smile. It would be good to see more of them.

It's not working. The more I try to make this nothing, the more it saturates my lungs and brain and heart, a spreading poison I haven't found the antidote to.

"What?" she asks, sipping her wine.

I wipe the puzzled look from my face and make a deal with myself. Nothing that goes on here has to spill into the rest of my life. I can drive back to Handsel, and it'll be as though this has never happened.

I grunt past the tightness in my throat.

"Uncle Timo was part of the security detail sent for the royal wedding."

"My parents' royal wedding?"

I nod. "Your Pavian grandfather insisted that his son be able to bring his own security team for a year."

"To prevent his new bride from an assassination attempt?" Freja breathes a laugh.

The sound shakes me, and I have sudden sympathy for a pork cutlet being pounded flat under the steady drum of a tenderizing mallet. Another grunt. "My father also formed part of that detail."

"Didn't they return to Pavieau after their year was up?" Her brow wrinkles. *Vede.* I want to see more of those expressions, too. "You were born there."

I nod. "Uncle Timo returned almost fluent in Sondish. My father," I say, old stories flooding me, "returned to the girl he'd left behind to start a family. When the political situation got worse, Uncle Timo was able to get out. Because he spoke the language, Sondmark took him in."

"And you?"

"My father forgot every bit of Sondish he'd learned, and we had to wait five years for Uncle Timo to find a way to sponsor us. You should have seen us on the train platform—"

I'm grinning and then I halt. There's a way I tell this story to fellow Pavians and a way I tell it to people from Sondmark. Freja is getting the Pavian version, I realize. I gather the details close, inspecting each to figure out which ones to share and which to keep hidden.

I think of the tablecloth. It's a simple thing to slice out an amusing part of my story and share it, scooping the other pieces to one side.

"We set off from Pavieau warm enough, but as the train traveled north, we encountered a storm. My mother had to add more layers, finally wrapping me in her best tablecloth, bright white with tiny blue flowers stitched onto a border. When we arrived, the snow was falling so hard that we couldn't see from one end of the platform to the other. If I'd wandered off, they wouldn't have found me until the spring thaw."

I finish the anecdote with a laugh, remembering my father shivering at the stationmaster's window in his best suit and my mother's pink nose. I glance up.

Freja's fingers stop tracing the stem of her glass. Her mouth pinches on one side. "You didn't have a winter coat?"

Damn. I feel the sensation of being shoved off a ledge, air leaving my lungs, twisting as I fall. I gave her a funny story. She was supposed to laugh at the blizzard and the blue flowers. She wasn't supposed to see anything else.

My mouth opens to keep her from seeing the kid who came to school with a few words of Sondish and strange-smelling food, who learned quickly to stand between his parents and the laundry kiosk, to read the fundamentals of a rental agreement and argue with landlords about deposits. *Stultes es.*

Konrad rescues me, bringing out bowls of deceptively simple soup. I make room for the bread and spend more time arranging the salt and pepper near Freja's setting than is necessary, the act moving us further and further from her question.

Vapor rises from her bowl, and Freja's eyes light before closing. She inhales the aroma. "Now I get why we drove so far." She blows on her spoon and takes a swallow. I can't look away.

I smile into my bowl, stirring the contents. Giana is a Pavian witch, managing to turn even the simplest fare into something that tastes like it pays Sondish taxes but winters on the Mediterranean coast. I dig into the bowl, tearing off hunks of bread to dip in the hearty stew, our conversation kept well clear of anything deeper than the weather. When we finish, Giana comes to clear the table setting, kissing me on both cheeks for good measure. I pass over a plate and check my watch.

"We'll have to head back soon," I tell her in Pavian.

Giana's eyes shift to Freja, and she says in halting Sondish, "Not before Her Royal Highness has had my coffee and torte."

I nod and settle back to find myself the object of Freja's interested gaze.

"What?" I say, wiping the edges of my mouth with a cloth.

She tilts her head in the direction of the kitchens. "It's interesting watching you obey someone so meekly. Do you have a chance to speak Pavian very often?"

"Not as much as I'd like, now that my parents are gone. It's a beautiful language, though," I concede, "so is Sondish, in its way."

She begins singing the second verse of her national anthem, her voice low:

Even our fair princesses will drag
Every Vorburgian corpse
To the Borderlands—
Picking the flesh from their Swords and
Raking the blood from our Soil

Her tongue does its poor best to soften the stabby-sounding threats, but it's impossible to turn the language into something it's not.

I grimace. "I think we've located the source of the low birthrate. How did your ancestors manage to populate the Sondish peninsula in the first place?" I lightly pound the table with a fist, my accent reminiscent of a Viking raider. "*Carry my shield.*" Grunt.

Her eyes narrow, and she props her chin on her hand, bright hair sliding off her shoulder. "What if I say *I love you?*" she whispers and my breath is gone. "*Don't go. Stay with me forever.*" The burrs of the language now make me want to lean forward, listening to the throaty stops and breaks. Not lyrical. Not beautiful. It's intense and undomesticated, wild and wind-scoured.

"My ancestors managed just fine," she laughs.

I breathe again, swallowing past a hard knot in my throat. The Sondish people will never go extinct.

"For all the bloodthirsty things you can say in Sondish, it's easy to tell someone you love them," she declares. "I'm sure you've done it."

I've never told a Sondish girl I loved her. I've never wanted to.

Giana brings coffee, lemon torte, and an unwelcome observation about how I'll get fat if I work in a studio all day.

I dig into the torte with the edge of my fork. "We've covered Sondmark. How well do you speak Pavian?"

She looks into her cup, her eyes crinkling at the corners.

"Noah is almost fluent, but I think Père gave up trying to fight the tide, because by the time my sister and I arrived, he was only covering the basics."

"The basics?"

She clears her throat and holds up one finger, saying in elegant Pavian, "Pardon, *sehora*, do you sell roast chicken?" She holds two fingers up. "Pardon, where might I find the nearest lavatory?" A third finger. "No, *sehor*, I do not care to be kissed."

I choke, and she attempts to give me a quelling, teacher-ish look. Her mouth betrays her.

"Tomorrow, when we are mortal enemies again, you will forget that."

"We'll forget all of this tomorrow," I vow.

She lifts a shoulder and I follow the line of it. "I'd like to be more proficient in Pavian. There aren't many people for me to use it with."

Not her grandparents? A question forms in my mouth, but I can guess the truth. They say that when young Prince Matteo came to Sondmark, he left his whole life behind—the father who placated the military regime until Generalissimo Mondegas died and the mother who refused to come to his wedding and the christening of each of his children if her husband, King Zeren, could not attend. The Sondish parliament never relented on that point.

These are details well-known and often repeated around Uncle Timo's table when the *anau* is flowing. I point at her with my fork.

"Well, your accent is excellent," I say. "No one would think you were ordering boiled peas instead of roast chicken."

When we finish, I return her to the car, the air cool and wet, the security detail following close after us. The drive back to Handsel is quick, and while I navigate through the darkened streets, she asks,

"Your father and Uncle Timo were military men. How did you end up at The Nat, working in art restoration?" she asks.

"You're asking a lot of questions."

She doesn't apologize. "I am," she says, brow furrowed. Have I confused her as much as she's confusing me?

"My mother was an artist. She trained in Hamburg before the civil war."

Her head tilts. "You wanted to be an artist, too."

She's done it again, seeing more than the careful slivers of information I dole out.

"Well," I say, declarative, final. "I'm not enough of a genius to be a successful one, but restoration is more science than art, and it gives me steady employment," I say, brushing past the details around the provisional residency which made a dependable paycheck necessary. "I began at The Nat under Roland, and when he moved to Curation, I took over as head of the department." There it is. The whole story. No need for follow-up questions.

She tilts her head. "Do you like it?"

Damn her. Damn her.

"I like knowing how to work through a problem. I like making things better rather than worse."

Her hands smooth the fabric over her knees. "Yes, but you planned to be an artist. The ideal thing is that a restorer expresses nothing of himself but always thinks of the artist and what he intended. Don't you find it constricting?"

My heart hammers. I don't want to be unwrapped like a Christmas present in front of anyone, least of all Freja. I don't want to be trapped in the close, intimate confines of a car while she does it.

"I find it necessary. Not all of us live in a palace." My tone is clipped.

She withdraws, picking up her phone, the glow of the screen lighting her face.

"Huh," she says, after a few moments.

"What huh?"

"Erik the Up-Talker is running The Nat's Pixy page. He's doing quizzes. He's got a picture of a metal device and then one of those quiz stickers below it." She reads the text. "Is this a labor and delivery tool or a blood-drawing device?" A pause. "*Stultes es*. I got that wrong. Here's another." Now that I've stopped at a light, she holds the screen up. "Is this a pattern from a men's waistcoat or a queen's coronation robe?"

"Waistcoat," I say, "but I'm cheating. *Vrouw* Larsen in textile restoration worked on it last year."

"This is really clever. Ella told me that quizzes and questions excite the algorithm. It's going to increase engagement with our posts."

I grunt. The rain has all but stopped, and there are wide puddles across the road. I slow, navigating the turn into the gates of the Summer Palace. My appetite is satisfied, there's plenty of gas in the tank, and I'll have time to read a few chapters of a Luftslottet thriller when I return home. I shouldn't be feeling this gnawing unrest in my stomach.

I halt by a guardhouse, rolling the window down, unprepared when Freja leans across to exchange a few words with the security officer, hand braced on the edge of the door. Breathe. But don't breathe hard. Inhale. But don't inhale the scent of her hair.

"That way," she points, shifting into her seat, leaving me almost gasping, thankful for the dark. "I'll take you in the side door. *Señor* Fornasari isn't far."

She guides me to an illuminated path, and we walk quietly together, stopping outside an insignificant door where she punches a code in a keypad. The door swings open, pouring us directly into a passageway lacking a grand entry or high ceiling. There are only a few sconce lamps casting pools of light down the hall and a whiteboard affixed to the wall with a message reading, "The next sister who takes my car without asking is going to get beheaded. Alma." She's included a doodle of a guillotine, a basket, a severed head, and seeping blood. There's a row of key hooks underneath, and hers is missing.

Freja turns, her posture polite and official. Our interlude is finished. Tomorrow we'll have the width of a worktable between us, the dark eye of a camera recording each word.

I look around, tracing every line of molding, the precise fall of the carpet runner, and the path between Freja's throat and lips and eyes like I have a hundred times tonight. A son of Pavieau has entered the palace, as soft-footed as any mouse, and likely as welcome. The thought makes me want to engage in a little insurrection.

"Thanks for dinner," she says.

Before I think better of it, I ask in Pavian, "May I kiss you?" My tone is threaded through with a challenge.

She'll laugh. She'll trot out one of her father's essential phrases and thank me for giving her the chance to use the words in actual practice. She'll say that Pavian boys are just like he said. Instead, her eyes narrow and blood roars in my ears. Thud, thud, thud. Then she lifts her chin, almost daring me to kiss her. Her eyelashes drift down.

Dominanstid.

I try to hang on to self-control only to find it's been burned away like a stubble of hay in a field, the earth rich and black, the soil dense with potential. There's so much I don't know yet—how she'll feel under my hands and how she'll take this—but I rest my fingers lightly on her waist, each point of contact like the strike of a match against a coarse surface.

I lean forward and time slows, compresses. She's going to stop this with a laugh and a hand on my chest. She'll see how much I want this, even if I can't understand it all. Terror forks through my body, blinding and hot. She'll see me.

She'll think I'm getting above myself or that I'm a fool. Then I inhale her scent.

So I'm a fool, I think, brushing my lips against hers, waiting for regret to catch up, pulling us apart. I wait and wait and wait.

I taste lemon amidst the shock of discovering I want to kiss Freja forever.

I can't want that. This is nothing but a dare. Nothing. But Freja's hands fist the fabric of my sleeves, and I mold my palm to match the narrow point of her waist, deepening the kiss with the next breath.

The current is strong and already beginning to twist out of control. In another moment, we'll lift our heads and step back. We'll retreat. We'll remember ourselves. *Vede*, how? I can't remember my name. Or I could pull her into my arms and admit I want something from this.

I feel the still, weightless moment, balanced perfectly between two choices. Not flying, not falling.

She takes a small breath and her fingers curl around my lapel. My hands shift to her back.

A noise crashes into my concentration. A whirr and a click. The sound of the door.

16

SONDISH ICICLE

FREJA

Oskar takes a hard breath and leans against the opposite wall.

When he crosses his arms over his chest the boundaries between us, momentarily blurry, harden. No need to freak out. It was a kiss, not a thermonuclear weapon. I haven't exploded, though I crush the impulse to pat myself down for missing parts and check my vitals. I have kissed and been kissed before.

I'm almost sure I have.

A lava-hot blush washes over my cheeks, and I struggle to compose my features. On the other side of the hall, Oskar looks nonchalant, as though he'd done little more than bump around a fellow commuter. I'm torn between wanting to slip back into his arms and wanting to throw something at his head, but I lean against the opposite wall, maximally calm. The current World Record Holder of Unconcern.

The door swings back to reveal Ella at her most grubby, with headphones and a hoodie hiding her distinctive curls, and massive fogged-up glasses speckled with rain. She's got a reusable shopping bag in her hand and jumps slightly when she sees us, slipping Alma's keys onto the hook.

"Oh, hello." She wipes her glasses and slides them back on, eyes darting from one side of the hall to the other. She gives me a narrow look. "Am I interrupting something?"

Not the time, I say, in a silent language she understands–semaphore with eyebrows. *Really, not the time.*

What is this? Her eyes widen and widen some more. *Were you about to kiss? I mean, holy crap, Freja.*

"This is *Neer* Velasquez," I gesture, "the man I'm doing the Pixy campaign with." How did Erik's infernal upspeak get in my mouth? "He's come to collect his uncle, who knows Père. He's Pavian. They're both Pavian."

Ella shakes her head, a half-smile tickling the dimple on her cheek. *You sound ridiculous. I'm here for it.*

Death. I wish you suffering and death.

Ella grins cheerily at *Neer* Velasquez—at Oskar, I correct. I can't use a formal title for a man...who hardly kissed me at all.

"*Neer* Velasquez," Ella repeats, pursing her lips in a prim, innocent smile. "It's nice to meet you when you're not bawling my sister out. I've seen your Pixy videos."

She darts a look at me, and my semaphore flags are snapping. *Leif Sobelsen, galloping through the East Gate with three thousand mounted cavalry, thundering into Vorburgian forces and tearing them limb from limb, did not long for the blood of his enemies as I do now.*

Ella's smile scrunches her nose. *You're adorable.*

Oskar straightens and gives a brief, correct bow. "You've been help-ing her with the tech, I hear. Thanks for that."

He's never bowed to me.

"Mm." Ella clasps her hands the way we have been taught to do on official engagements when we must communicate diplomacy and interest, hypnotizing the public into docility and trust. "Are you dating? Is this a date?"

"What?" I smack her on the elbow, jarring her magic hands loose. She rubs the spot, and words bubble out of me like logs floating down a waterway, jamming in the narrows, piling up, crashing. "No. We would never—why would you—? He's a coworker. Honestly, Ella, what a thing to say."

Oskar tips his head around my sister. "Will someone tell my uncle I'm waiting?" He sounds bored and slightly impatient. *Vede.* What if he feels the same way about our kiss? Humiliation slides into my stomach, settling hard against the lemon torte.

"I'll do it," I say.

Ella. "No, I'll—"

I race away before my sister can call me back. The cloak billows dramatically, and I whip it off, tossing it over an arm. No more goblin lovers for you, Freja. No more letting your imagination get complete-ly out of control. No more thermonuclear detonations in a narrow palace hallway.

"*Vede. Vede, vede, vede.*" I repeat the words in an intense, furious whisper. I've been so careful, since the inception of my volunteer work, not to overstep any boundaries, particularly my boundaries with him. I've been so careful to be professional. I'm no navigational expert, but even I know that Oskar Velasquez's lips are on the wrong side of professional boundaries.

"May I kiss you?" he asked, and like a dummy, I didn't trot out one of my stock phrases or ask him to clarify his meaning. I roll my eyes half out of my head as I walk. I didn't even pretend not to understand. Instead, I just leaned in, daring him like I was totally down for it.

I *was* totally down for it.

I have never been down for anything more in my whole life.

Handing off my cloak to a footman, I race down another corridor, trading elegance for speed. The sooner I can get that man out of my palace, the better my sleep will be.

I fetch up before my father's rooms, knocking lightly before hearing the low answer bidding me to enter. When I step across the threshold, I feel myself entering a foreign country. Though, as elsewhere in the palace, there are French furnishings dating back several hundred years, the room also contains vibrant Pavian textiles scattered on the floor and sofa. Instead of quiet Sondish interiors or idyllic fields of grain, each piece of artwork over the mantel and lining every wall celebrates the blinding contrast of sun and shadow.

Père is settled near the fire, a tumbler of Scotch resting on his knee. His necktie is loosened, and his jacket has been tossed over a chair. He must have finished some hilarious anecdote because *Señor* Fornasari is laughing, tears in his eyes.

Père laughs too, but then he spots me.

"Not already, *donnina*," he says, using his old nickname, little woman. *Can this be my sweet donnina?* he would ask, finding me at the back of a closet with a book perched on my knobby knees and hauling me into his arms to carry me off to dinner. I haven't heard it in ages.

"How can you be back so soon?" Père groans. "A true son of Pavieau would've had my daughter out for half the night." Once again, my color rises.

Oskar's Uncle Timo shifts to the edge of his seat and shakes his head. "That boy's blood travels through his veins like water dripping off a Sondish icicle." His hands make a series of parallel boxes in the air. "Everything in its time and place, each item in its pigeonhole. I pray he may find some Pavian girl who will blow his ordered life into disarray," he says.

A chill races between my shoulders. *I don't pray for such a girl.*

The thought shocks me enough that I have to mentally print it off and feed it into an imaginary shredder.

"Had he stayed in Pavieau, in a rundown apartment in Gransoleil with a pretty girl across the airshaft to get into trouble with, he would be another man, not so—" *Sehor* Fornasari gives an exaggerated shiver.

Père laughs.

My face feels hot, and I shift slightly at this unrecognizable description of a man who seemed to know exactly how to get into trouble. Oskar's manner is not warm. His speech is not flowery. These things he has learned from Sondish culture, perhaps. But Sondmark didn't teach him everything.

"He is waiting for you, sir," I say, smiling at *Sehor* Fornasari. "Shall I have a footman bring him here or—"

With a clap of his hands on his thighs, he rises. "It's time I go."

"You'll come again," Père says, surprising me. This is the most content I have seen him in a long time. Since before his father passed away and his relationship with Mama became a rock, the cracks and fissures growing deeper with each freeze. Every day I can almost hear the rock groaning, straining to cleave in two or hold together. A true son of Pavieau would prefer fire to ice. Maybe they should have done more shouting.

The men clasp both forearms in a hearty farewell. "Yes, tell me when and I will come," Uncle Timo says, taking and receiving the three kisses.

I escort him from the room, and when he offers his arm I take it.

"I hope you had an enjoyable evening," I murmur as we walk.

He slices across the air with his hand. "You're the girl in the Pixy videos with Oskar. What? Have I surprised you? I follow my grandchildren on Pixy."

I laugh. "Yes. He hates being in front of a camera, but he's a natural. Whenever he talks about his work, it makes me want to listen."

Uncle Timo lifts his brows.

"It—it makes the whole country want to listen," I finish, thankful that one of Noah's cost-saving schemes has been to dim the lights in the common areas of the palace when there are no official functions. Uncle Timo can't see my blushes. Thank you, Noah.

On the other hand, these measures produce the wrong atmosphere for sobriety and clear-headedness. If the side entry had been glaringly bright, I wouldn't have leaned into Oskar's kiss like he was the last drops of iced coffee at the bottom of my straw. Thanks a lot, Noah.

I pause at the head of the last hallway. "I wish you a lovely night," I say.

Uncle Timo chuckles. "Thank you for entertaining poor Oskar," he says, loud enough that poor Oskar can hear him. The Head of Restoration is a forbidding figure next to Ella and looks impatient to be gone.

Señor Fornasari shakes his head and wags a thick finger, calling, "Another princess and you don't know what to do with that one either. You are hopeless, *adano*."

Adano. My boy.

"You'll embarrass Their Royal Highnesses with such talk," Oskar counters, his face in a scowl.

Ella looks like she'd like to drag up a chair and a bag of crisps to watch the drama play out.

The old man sighs when he turns to me. "I'll give you the kiss he should have given."

He lifts my hand, bows, and places a courtly kiss against my knuckles. It's delightful and gallant and nothing like Oskar's.

When they depart, Ella jogs up the hall with a little squeal.

I hold up a hand, forestalling her effusions. I can't do it. "Not now," I warn her. "Not now."

She takes a deep breath. We're twins with a lifetime of practice in adapting to each other's particularities—learning to be devoted, even when our characters are so different—so she puts out her pinky and I wrap it with my own.

"Later." That's the promise.

I nod. "Later."

By the time morning arrives, I've worked out a plan. No matter how fascinating last night's kiss was, I have to return Oskar to his place and me to mine. He is a private resident. I am a public figure. He is a goblin. I am a princess. He is Pavieau. I am Sondmark.

The country still hasn't forgiven my parents for fulfilling the marriage contract. The populace certainly won't be docile if one of their princesses gets serious about a Pavian.

There, I huff, pushing through the doors of the restoration studio. We have that sorted. I'll tell him he has to work with Erik. I'll be cool and quelling and so nonchalant they'll have to invent a new word for it.

My eyes light on Oskar, who sits before a massive canvas of St Sebastian, the holy body riddled with arrows. A rectangular frame rests beneath the loose painting, and Oskar tugs the canvas in position, reaches for a handful of tacks, and tosses them in his mouth like peanuts.

The surprise of it jerks me into action. "Are you insane?" I ask, darting forward, and dumping my things on the sofa. "Are you trying to kill yourself?"

He glances my way, his cheek barely bulging, and brings his hammer up until it's just kissing his lips. The surface comes away with a tack on the end, held lightly by a magnetic connection. In a quick, precise motion, Oskar flips the hammer around, taps to set the tack, flips the hammer again, and taps the tack into position.

He's on the fourth or fifth one when I say, "I'm filming this."

He doesn't smile or stop but grunts briefly.

I dig into my bag and set up my equipment, capturing the moment when he refills his store of tacks and the way he drags his upholstery pliers down with his free hand to get a good stretch on the canvas. I'm close but careful not to interrupt his rhythm.

He scoots away from the table when he's finished and deposits the few remaining tacks onto a folded-over paper towel. When he looks up, my blood starts to race.

"Good morning," he says.

I have to say something, anything. I look through the camera screen and train the lens on him, grateful for this small measure of breathing room. I ask, my voice sounding like newsreader Tor Hjefdal asking a guest to explain her position on monetary policy and looming infla-tion, "What was that you were doing with the tacks?"

He goes to the sink and washes his hands, drying them on a towel. When he turns, he braces his hands against the counter. Has he read the comments from our videos? Sondmark loves it when his shirt stretches across his chest like that.

Not just Sondmark, Freja.

His answer is spare but engaging. "It's called spitting tacks, an old upholstery trick."

I adjust the focus. "Do you work faster than if you hold them in your hand?"

"Yes, but the frame is old and dry. If I nailed the steel tacks in there, as is, they'd slip right out. Because they're a little wet, the wood swells slightly and grips them. Why are you making that face?"

"It's spit."

His head tilts back and away as he tries to keep himself from smiling. "It's a legitimate trick of the trade."

That's a good end to a video that will be both informative and unnecessarily hot.

I nod and set the camera aside.

Now that there's nothing to distract me, my thoughts come crowding back. Oskar kissed me last night, and it can't mean anything. It can't. I think of the list my mother will one day present to me, full of barons, grand dukes, and princes whose titles originate with the Holy Roman Empire. I think of my well-ordered life and the sanctuary of my palace suite. I think of how Oskar and I come from different worlds.

I remember the way his hair slips forward and the strong hand which sweeps it back. He's sweeping it now.

It's time. I have to clear the air. I start wrapping my charging cord around my hand. I unwrap it. I have to tell him not to get any ideas about us.

"It wasn't a big deal," he says, brown eyes hooded.

17

SEXY TOWN

OSKAR

The lie slips from my lips, sharp as a steel tack. Freja's shoulders stiffen. I could see, the moment she walked in this morning, that she was planning to have words with me.

We're grown adults—

Don't assume—

I didn't mean anything by—

She doesn't need to say them. I've been imagining her words all night.

No. Not all night.

I was thinking of other things, too. I drove Uncle Timo back to our apartment building, where he returned to his ground-floor flat and I returned to my walk-up. I changed for bed. I brushed my teeth, gripping the sides of the pedestal sink, and looked hard into the bathroom mirror.

No. No. No.

The self-administered lecture was precisely as complex as it needed to be. No, you will not do that again. No, you will not develop feelings for a *flamen* princess. No, you will not think of that kiss all night.

It has not improved my mood to see her looking fresh, her hair smooth and bright. There's a green blouse with a silky bow at her neck, which ought to remind me of grandmother but reminds me, inexplicably, of the lyrics of a 70s song.

My girl's built the right way

Earthquake won't knock her down

She's got the finest house

In Sexy Town

I clear my throat and cross to the canvas.

"Why did you do it?" she asks, a little pale.

I focus on the painting and run my tongue along my bottom lip. I kissed her because I wanted to—because I wanted to for years.

"I wasn't thinking that hard." I'm not going to put myself at her mercy simply because she's curious.

"Right. As you say, it wasn't a big deal. We're on the same page."

I scowl at the St. Sebastian painting and hold it up to examine the fit of the canvas on the stretcher, setting it down flat when I'm satisfied.

"Is there anything else?" I ask, taking a small palate knife and scraping some fill over an area of flaking. I remove the excess with a small cotton swab, appearing absorbed in my task.

"Erik will be recording interviews this week from a selection of the curators and department heads, to be edited and rolled out over the next month. The topic is easy—just pick your favorite object in the museum—but I need a time frame for when you want to do yours." She's already moved on, her tone brisk and professional.

"There are plenty of other people to choose from."

"Your videos are the most popular," she says.

I frown, locating another area of flaking. "Why's that?" *Dominanstid*, I've been reduced to fishing for compliments.

She's silent and I put down my tools, glancing over. When she blushes, she looks like something out of the Renaissance, a vulnerable red flush over the high ridge of her cheekbones. She looks delicate. Priceless. Last night I kissed her.

She takes a breath when she decides to answer. "The camera loves you." She swallows. "You obviously know a great deal about your subject and—" Her color deepens.

"And?" I prompt.

"You're not Sondish." Freja's eyes drift to the windows and back again. "That's part of it."

I breathe a mirthless laugh. "At least you're honest."

"Does it bother you?"

I'll be honest, too. "A little."

"Why?"

I weigh the risk of giving her more honesty, and the seconds tick by. Finally, I reach over and grab a piece of durable washi kozo paper and pull a pencil from the front of my apron. "I'm happy that people like Hafsa can see someone on a national platform whose ancestors didn't come from here, but I'm not kidding myself. I'm a curiosity. Most people who watch these videos," I say, drawing a series of short, dark strokes on a corner of the paper, "don't think I belong here."

Freja's eyes flash. "Of course, you belong here. When you pass your citizenship test—"

"When?" Her optimism is touching. "You think passing a citizenship test has anything to do with belonging?"

Her hands juggle the air. "Doesn't it?"

I finish my drawing and sketch a wide circle around it. Except for the lack of birds, it could be a representation of The Winter Princess.

"Here's what it means to belong in Sondmark," I say, pointing to the center of the circle. I've reproduced a likeness of Freja in a few strokes. The cleft in her chin. The eyes that seem to take in everything. I'm shocked at how easy it was to capture her on the page. "Imagine a field and you're in the middle. You're a citizen of Sondmark. A native speaker. A princess. There's no one more in the center of Sondmark than you."

I look up to see if she understands. She nods.

"This," I say, tapping the circle, "is a wall. It's invisible, and on one side you're Sondish and on the other side you're not." I glance up. Her bright eyes are trained on the paper. "You've never bumped into this wall. You've probably never seen it, though your father is as Pavian as mine. Your title and position put you right in the center of Sondmark. You belong. There's a whole verse in the national anthem about it." I lift the pencil in the air, sketching an encompassing gesture with the tip of the eraser. "You can recite the history of Sondmark and take its odd quirks for granted. *Vede*, you probably even like Pankedruss," I grimace.

"Guilty." She gives me a smile, and it warms me like a burning piece of coal placed in a pocket warmer. She touches a soft finger to the paper. "Where does Oskar Velasquez belong?"

I draw a dark X over the perimeter of the circle. "On the edge. So it doesn't matter that I still have my striped waistcoat and cloth cap from the year our class did folk dancing on Saint Wyten's Day, that I root for the Dragons no matter who they're up against, or that I grab my ice skates when the canals freeze over. I still have people"—Her. It matters that it's her—"remind me I'm not Sondish. Even if I become a citizen, I'll still be touching the wall."

I thought these feelings were dead, decomposing somewhere, but the battery of failed citizenship tests, the strange fact of Freja's princessness, and the nothing kiss we shared are digging them up.

"Touching the wall?"

"It means being in a staff meeting when my ideas are passed over because forty generations of ancestors aren't buried in this soil. It's translating for my father at the grocery store, realizing the clerk thinks he's stupid, and trying to keep him from finding out." The words rush out in a hot torrent. "It's not knowing the name of a native dish because my mother didn't cook like that, and then it's forcing myself to remember and not make that mistake next time. When you belong, you never have to think about the wall, but people on the edge can't afford to take their eyes off it."

The words reverberate through the room.

I reach for scissors, snipping away the drawing, collecting myself one gesture at a time. Better to use basic lined paper the next time I explain cultural alienation to a member of the royal family. Washi kozo is too valuable to waste.

"Are you going to throw that away?" she asks.

Only then do I realize I was going to keep it. Why?

I nod.

She tugs the restoration paper out of my hands, smoothing the surface with her thumbs. "Are you ever in the center of the field?"

My brows furrow.

She points to the line. "This represents citizenship, but there must be times in your life when you're at the center. Places you're perfectly at home."

My mind finds an answer faster than I can stop it. For one weightless second, I was at home in the hall of the Summer Palace with her hands on my arms and my lips on hers. The thought won't be forced out with a laugh. A lie won't come as easily as a tack.

"What do you need for the interview?" I ask, impatiently, picking the canvas up and placing it on an easel. This painting is one I've been working on for some time. It's been stabilized, cleaned, and re-stretched. Now I need to retouch the areas that have been lost. I'll try to imagine what might have disappeared in the flat and empty places and attempt to make a bridge the eye can wander over without realizing what's missing.

Freja looks down at the paper, and when she looks up, her face has taken on its usual composed expression again.

"Anything you love best. You know, I used to think your work was rote, but every time I come, you have some new process you're employing. It's interesting," she says, turning on the ball of one foot. She moves so smoothly—her posture is that of a princess—but the thin, winding scar is longer than anyone could guess. I wonder if I'll ever be able to forget the soft curve of her back, the surprise of seeing the human side of a royal princess, and the quickening of desire for this specific princess.

I blink. "Often the work *is* rote. You can't be that interested in cotton swabs and mulberry paper."

She lifts the scrap of washi kozo, mischief lighting her eyes. "I've been reliably informed that I belong at the heart of Sondmark. Doesn't that mean I should be the one telling you what the country is interested in?"

She has me there.

I take my seat behind the canvas and reach for my palette and reversible restoration paints, blending a peachy hue with a tiny brush. I smile into the face of St Sebastian. Freja can't see me, so it doesn't matter.

"Since you haven't given me a time, I'll let Erik know he can start to collect footage tomorrow," she calls.

I frown—I feel safer when I frown—and lean around the canvas.

"No," I answer. "I've already told you. It's you or no one."

18

Both of Us

FREJA

I bury myself in our shared office for the rest of the morning, going over the calendar of events and social media releases for the coming season, carefully shifting my seat, the stapler, and a rolling pen away from the invisible boundary that divides the room into my domain and Oskar's. I am adept at staying on my side, but such skill requires me to think about him.

After a couple of hours, I sit back, rubbing my temples. It was one kiss, Freja. It was one deeply unsatisfying kiss, and he didn't even really want it. It didn't mean anything. There's not a prayer a Pavian non-citizen and a princess—my throat hurts and I swallow. It's good that we both know better than to take it seriously.

I rub the heel of my hand over my heart and grimace, frowning at the empty expanse of his side of the office. Finally, I push away from the desk, looking for a distraction and finding it in front of the museum attendance temperature gauge hanging in the common area. Whoever is adding to it isn't even bothering to use the same color marker, so each day's totals look like sedimentary rock stripes. Up and up, one day at a time. We're making slow and steady progress.

"Forgot yesterday," Erik says, reaching past me to scrawl another strip, the tip of his tongue sticking out the side of his mouth.

All night and all morning I've been fighting the bizarre sensation that if I don't talk to someone I'll explode. I can't talk to Oskar. He's the root of this mess. My family is too close. They'll remember things and follow up and worry. Erik won't worry. His attention span resets every time someone new enters the room.

"Erik," I say, drawing his name out in the event I think better of this madness. "I have a question."

"Hit me."

"What does it mean," I ask, "when someone tells you that something didn't mean anything, but you're almost sure it did mean something...to them?"

He taps the marker against his lips. "Oh," he brightens, "like gaslighting?"

"What?"

"Gaslighting." The word sounds like a question and carries a whole raft of judgmental surprise. "It means that someone is trying to get you to go insane and ignore what's in front of your face. Like, there was this one time my friend was all, 'Hey, wanna go get kebabs?' and I was all, 'Yeah, sure. I'll cancel all my plans.' So I did but then he was like, 'I never said that. You're dumb and I hate you. It's your own fault you're destined to own a million cats and die alone.'" He spins his hand out, as though this explains all. "You know. Gaslighting."

My brow furrows as I remember the kiss, trying to find the moment when Oskar acted like it didn't matter. Maybe when he tossed off his Pavian phrase. Not when his breath caught. Not when his gaze drifted to my lips.

I close my eyes and it's there, playing against my eyelids. His hand at my waist was light and the contact of our lips too brief, but it made me feel like the first time I took a bite of Minty's warm salted caramel custard—delighted something so delicious exists. Desperate for more.

"Restoration wants me to film the interview this week," I tell Erik. Restoration. Like that's his name. Like his job title will keep us at a distance. "Let me know what the specs need to be."

"Your phone is good enough, only give me at least an hour of footage. We can edit out the boring parts."

I quash a sudden flare of irritation. Despite all expectations to the contrary, Erik the Kebab Enthusiast is going to save us all.

After lunch, I head over to the jewelry raffle to draw a winner on Pixy Live. I miss Oskar's steadying hand, but I smile into the camera as I read the slip of paper. "Agneta Rasmussen from Aarlo. She'll be photographed wearing the Nedeweiss Peridot Necklace, 1832. It was gifted to the young Queen Magda's chaperone on the occasion of her charge's marriage."

Based on the size of the stones, I wonder if the young queen had been tying bedsheets together and trying to rappel down the palace walls. It must have been quite a lot of work keeping Magda out of her lover's arms until the wedding night. One doesn't give jewels like that for embroidering handkerchiefs and sleeping on a truckle bed.

At the end of the day, I return to the palace, crunching through autumn leaves littering the path. I hang my keys upon the hook by the door and pause, reaching toward the wall where Oskar leaned. I snap my hand back, frowning.

"Really," I admonish. It was the same hand that curled around his coat lapel.

A noise at the door signals the arrival of my sisters, and I whip my hands behind my back.

"Were you walking without me?" I ask, on the principle that the best defense is a cracking offense.

"Clara and I went out to visit Lady Greta. We played Fast Blintz and listened to old records." Ella's eyes gleam, her nose pink with the cold. "Are you going to forgive me?" she asks, bumping my arm.

"What are you going to forgive her for?" Clara asks, shaking out her strawberry blonde hair. I like that forgiveness is a foregone conclusion. I wish our parents felt the same.

"Nothing. There's nothing to forgive."

Ella wiggles her brows. "I interrupted Freja and her boyfriend while they were making out."

I gasp but Clara squeaks. Clara is in love. She wants everyone to be making out. Clara is an idiot.

Ella goes up on her tiptoes and throws an arm around my shoulders like I'm a sideshow attraction. She has to entice the crowds to spend their money with a salacious story. "Imagine it. The art guy she swore she didn't like—disheveled, tie undone, igniting the very air with his hotness—was propping up this very wall, sexy-breathing and looking at our sister from under hooded eyelids ."

Clara nods. "I see it."

I see it.

I shake Ella's arm off and turn down the hall. "Do grow up."

Ella yanks Clara's wrist and follows in my wake, still the carnival barker. "Freja was plastered against the other wall like a fugitive of justice."

We pass the library and Alma pokes her head out. "Who's a fugitive?"

"We're talking about Freja's secret snog. Get in, princess," Ella says, grabbing Alma and sweeping her up with us.

"Snog?" Alma says. "But Freja's not dating anyone."

"How would you even know if she were?" Clara asks, breathlessly trotting behind. "Sonnets? Freja, would you write him a sonnet?"

"Keep focused, Clara," Ella admonishes. "The point is that when I walked in on Freja and Oskar *Fuego* plastered on opposite sides of the hall, she looked like she would as soon murder me as give me an introduction."

"I have a low murder threshold," I say, ascending the stairs. "By the way, Alma, Ella took your car last night."

Alma emits an outraged noise and reaches for the thief, giving her hair a yank. Ella squeaks but takes the punishment as only fair. She rubs her head and continues harassing me. "So I'm thinking that this situation calls for the proper etiquette—"

I snort.

"Perhaps we need a signal when we're planning to make out anywhere in the Summer Palace. A sock on the door handle?"

"A colorful Hermès scarf," Clara supplies. "They're brighter and hard to miss." We collectively stop and give her a look. "What? I've given this thought."

I continue, almost to my suite. I see the doors and double my pace.

"Point of order, darlings," Clara says, huffing now. "Why does Freja's boyfriend get to come to the palace if Max is still He-Whose-Abs-Must-Not-Be-Mentioned? Is Oskar *Fuego* a prince of someplace?"

I'm at the door and I wheel. "His name is not Oskar *Fuego*."

Ella pushes past me, uninvited. "The committee denies your motion."

My other sisters scoot through the gap. Alma is the only one with the grace to wear an apologetic smile.

There is little point barring the door now that the cows are all in, but I shut it with a firm snap. "He's not a prince and he's not my boyfriend. I would tell you if we were."

The others turn to Ella who delivers her verdict. "She's not lying."

Clara nods, mollified. This is a sore subject for my little sister. Mama is praying that Clara's infatuation with Max will burn itself out, but she'd be better off praying for a hard snow on Queen's Day. Max isn't going anywhere. I can see that much.

Ella rings for coffee and a snack to be brought up. The 'later' I promised her has arrived. I touch a match to the fire and nurse the flame gently as Clara peels back more layers and kicks off her boots.

"I love your suite in autumn," she says, sinking into a club chair. "It makes me want to paint over my pastel walls and drag in all this gorgeous English leather."

Alma nestles into another chair covered in tapestry fabric woven with a hidden design of harp seals and dragons. Ella sits cross-legged on a pillow near the hearth.

"Alright. Oskar. He's not a prince and he's not your boyfriend," Ella acknowledges. Then, glancing at the others asks, "Did you hear her deny they were kissing?"

Alma lifts a brow. "I did not, sister."

"A notable omission," Clara says, smiling at the maid who brings the tray. For a few moments, we are occupied, pouring out and passing around coffee and tiny cakes.

This isn't a full meal. It's a little tide-you-over. A few morsels. Perhaps my sisters will be content with an equally modest slice of information.

"He's an art restorer at the museum. The one in the video."

"The one she was holding hands with?" Alma asks.

Ella, with a mouth full of spice cake, nods.

"And, yes, he kissed me."

Spice cake crumbs fly out of Ella's mouth, and she leans forward, coughing. She swallows, grimacing. "Shut. Up. Are you being serious with me right now?"

"You said you knew we were kissing," I counter.

"I was teasing!" She looks shocked, as though someone cut her Wi-Fi in the middle of a boss battle. "You looked like you were about to throw up."

"Ladies, ladies," Alma shouts, mimicking our British nanny, the profoundly plain but enormously loveable Poppy Fforde-Hughes. "A polite princess is a pleasant princess."

Ella subsides against the carved pilaster. "My honor as a Girl Tracker," she says, holding her hand up in the shape of a long-eared dog–the tracker sign, "I didn't know. I wouldn't have teased you quite so hard about it. My deepest apologies."

I can't help the smile which tucks my cheek. The thing I like best about Ella is that she always says sorry.

"It was hardly a kiss," I say, ready to brush the whole thing away. It's not too late to laugh it off. "It was more like a dare."

"Did he dare you to kiss him? Or did you dare him to kiss you?" Clara asks. "I just want to understand the logistics."

I shoot her a glare. "The logistics don't matter. The point is that we exchanged a brief kiss."

"How did you even have time to meet up last night? We had the gala all evening. Weren't you tired?"

I give Clara a level look. She spent the summer conducting a late-night clandestine romance with a man who lives in the back of beyond.

"He was already at the palace for the gala. You meet Max after events."

"Yes, pet, but I love Max." She places her elbows on the arm of the chair and tucks her hands under her chin. "Do you have anything to share with us?"

I share a throw pillow, launched from across the room. It dislodges her arms, and she smacks herself in the face.

"Enough of that," Alma admonishes. "I don't think I saw him."

Ella scratches Smit between the ears. His purr is low in his throat. "The short version is that he's Pavian, so he's an absolute smoke show."

"Speak Sondish, please," Alma says.

"It means he's so hot there's a danger Sondmark's last ancient forest will be burned to the ground."

I stifle a laugh and shake my head. "It was only a kiss. Not even a very good kiss." Much too short, for one thing.

"It doesn't have to be a good kiss," Clara interjects.

"Hm?"

"I mean, if you like him, it takes very little in the technical department to get the job done."

Ella scoots Clara's chair with the tip of her foot. "You're telling us Max is a bad kisser?"

Clara smiles a feline smile. "I am not telling you that."

Ella, Alma, and I share the kind of look that must pass between fellow hostages.

Ella clears her throat. "The question, Freja, is do you want it to happen again?"

Vede. Yes. So much. My subconscious answers lightning fast, the rest of my body rushing along at blistering speed.

I place a hand over my stomach and flicker my eyes closed, trying to reorient myself.

"The point, Ella," I say, "is that we're not dating and we're not going to date. It's not like you and Max," I say, tipping my cup at Clara.

"Soulmates?" she supplies, grinning stupidly. She is very difficult to take.

"Or you and Pietor." I hastily add Alma and her hereditary grand duke.

"Cellmates?" Alma laughs, giving her coffee a bitter stare.

The answer is worrying and we quiet, each of us shifting our attention.

"You're navigating the parliamentary process okay?" Clara asks. Of course, she's interested in what it's like having a royal marriage approved by the government. She's thinking of a future with Max. It's real to her.

The coffee must be absorbing because Alma regards it for a long while. "Sure."

When my sisters disperse to get ready for their evening assignments, I pick up my purse and turn the light on in my office. It's filled with more bookshelves and a heavy desk, electrical cords tucked neatly out of sight. There's a small, tasteful bulletin board in one corner, and I fish the paper out of my bag, smoothing the rumpled edges. I'm in the center, my likeness drawn in a few quick lines, and there's Oskar's X, bang over the perimeter wall. The edge and the center. The wall and the field.

I trace the circle. What's the moral of this fairy tale he spun for me? The story he wanted me to take is that we're different. There's an unbridgeable distance between us, wider than the width of the palace hallway, and I have no hope of really understanding him. I shouldn't even try.

But fairytales are rarely as clear-cut as they seem.

If the question is not who belongs in Sondmark but, rather, who has an ordinary life, he's near the center of the field and I'm perched against the wall.

When I want to run an errand and have to bring along a security detail to prevent someone from shoving a knife between my ribs, I touch a wall. When I spent months in physical therapy and chose clothes that will hide my scar, I touch a wall. When I speak my few phrases of Pavian and get no further because it's not politically expedient to know about my father's homeland, I touch a wall.

Oskar's simple story makes it easier to understand that I'm blind to his walls and he to mine—that seeing them will stretch our imagination. It's easier to see why I should take care not to speak about Sondmark like it's a place that belongs to me instead of a place that belongs to both of us.

Both of us. The unconscious phrasing slips into my head, whirling like a seed falling from a tree. He taught me something about how to understand him and I don't like thinking of him being able to travel that bridge in the opposite direction.

I tack the paper onto the corkboard and step back. From this distance, we look like an electron and a nucleus–orbiting around one another in an endless dance. Two parts of a single thing.

19

STUPID QUESTION

OSKAR

I'm drawing again.

It started with that scrap of paper. The image seemed to spool out of the tip of my pencil on its own, unleashing a flood of sketches—a wall sconce, a tin of cookies, an office chair. And Frejas. Dozens of Frejas.

Not the whole of her. I trace the pattern of her blouse or the careless fall of a bow. A scribble becomes the divot in her chin, and I add the lower lip in a stroke both deft and familiar. I know that spot. I've touched it.

A flick of the pencil reproduces the arch of her brow. On a strip of paper, I paint square blocks of color that resemble paving stones, the rigid shape keeping me in check. This block is the color of her hair in sunlight. The one next to it is her hair in shadow. Here is the shade of her lips. The tone of her skin. Her eyes.

It's been years since I drew for myself, but this is nothing—a way to work off steam as I study for my test and meet the demands of the Restoration department, all while The Nat rocks precariously on the edge of a cliff. I tuck the paper into my wallet because it doesn't matter.

I see her each working day, aware that I'm waiting until she comes, aware that I'm thinking of her when she goes. I draw at home to focus my mind while listening to fairy tales in the background–stories of knights and dragons. Someday I'll come to the end of drawing her. I'll exhaust my interest.

The drawings keep coming.

Today, I sketch the shape of an earring, an oblong twist of gold with a blue-green jewel on the end, just the shade of her eyes. I hear the door and crumple the paper, tossing it into a wastebasket.

My duties include repairing a small L-shaped rip on *Child with Beads and Rinkelbel, 1622* and I move in front of it, brushing a hand over my arm, automatically smoothing the raised hairs.

"What is it?" I ask, my tone level and unhurried. When I look up there'll be new things to see and catch my artist's eye. I will want to convince myself that the list is getting smaller, that the material is winding down.

For some artists, the fascination with one subject is endless. They find novelty in how their muse changes with each season and condition. There's Oppeger the Elder and his goddesses that look suspiciously like the wife of a prosperous tallow merchant. For Botticelli, the memory of Simonetta followed him for much of his life. He was buried at her feet.

I had opinions about that, once.

But here we are now.

"I'm filming your interview today," she says, slipping into my office chair which has become her office chair, and unpacking her bag on my desk which has become her desk. "You got my email?"

She's wearing a fitted black turtleneck and camel-colored skirt with a heavy seam down the front. A pair of gold chains loop around her neck. Her shoes have slim straps banding her ankle, and I fend off the impulse to tell her to sit for me so I can pick up a pencil and get each detail just right.

I run a finger over the canvas, checking for bumps. "I'll give you ten minutes."

"I'll take all day," she counters. When I look up, she smiles. "Erik wanted lots of footage."

I rest my arms on the table, sending a forbidding gaze into the weave of the canvas. I don't need a whole day of Freja, of that almost imperceptible smile, of her direct gaze, of being reminded that an immigrant can be a guest at the palace but he can't be at home there.

Freja braces her own arms against the table. "We need to attract guests to the museum and these videos are drawing far more of them than your current program of—let me check my notes," she says, glancing around the room, "scowling at a canvas in a basement."

Vede. I like her even when she's insulting. "I said I'd do it."

"Then try not to look like I've dragged in an iron maiden and the branding irons. I'll film while you expound—"

"Expound?"

"Stop being difficult, Oskar."

I scowl harder. "You're being very familiar."

She chokes on a laugh. "We're not mortal enemies."

"No?" My hands are heavy.

"We can't be. You've been disagreeable since the moment I walked through the door, and I didn't think once to pitch you out a window."

I shift the canvas, absorbing myself in meticulousness. "Nice to see the monarchy turning over a new leaf," I answer, not smiling. I won't smile. "It's never too late to kick the defenestration habit."

Her eyes narrow. "It was the *one* time. King Victor went on a pilgrimage after. It's sorted."

"I know I'm inspired." I check another smile.

She shakes her head. "Anyway, we're not enemies."

"Then what are we?" This is a stupid question. I regret it. I would go on pilgrimage to wash away the foolishness of it, put up stone conciliation crosses, and wear a hairshirt against my skin.

"Friends," she declares, more and far less than I want. Her smile peeks out. "We have a common enemy."

"Prime Minister Torbald?" In the last weeks, he's rolled out his immigration reform bill with a slate of interviews and vague, menacing statistics. Newspapers report that he's cracking down on members of his own party for being insufficiently enthusiastic about slowing the trickle of new citizens.

She laughs. "I thought you were going to say Erik the Walking Quiff."

I can't stop the whole smile. "Quiff?"

"That fluff of hair he has. You know—" She reaches across *Child with Beads and Rinkelbel, 1622*, lacing her fingers through my hair and tufting up the front. I reach up to smooth it. Our fingers touch, and I feel each point of contact at a microscopic level. I feel it in my elbows and the backs of my knees.

Her hand contracts. Then she takes a breath and holds it out again.

I look at it and back to her face. *Vede.* More expressions I want to paint.

"What's this?"

"We have to shake on it," she prods. "To seal the friendship."

I look at the hand. An actual friendship with a princess of Sondmark? Maybe this is safer than our uneasy alliance. I know I'm attracted to her, even if I try not to examine it. Like steam coming off a pot, I don't have to lift the lid to know what's boiling inside.

No, this is good. Friendship is the right path. I could see myself running, running headlong into love, but now that the lid is lifted, the steam can dissipate into something less stupid. Appreciation, for instance. Friendly appreciation of her talents and gifts. These feelings boiling away will have a healthy, non-humiliating outlet, and I can return to room temperature in peace.

I take her hand in a firm, collegial grip. "A handshake? Erasmus's cap, where did you grow up? A palace?"

She laughs, the sound dry and unimpressed. "You're hilarious. Never change. Now," she says, turning to her equipment, "We need to make more progress out there. Visits are up, and you have nothing more important to do today than tell me about something you love."

I frown. Friendship. I love friendship. "I don't have anything to talk about."

"I gave you more than a week to select an art piece. Can't you narrow it down? We keep getting emails from Roland. *Can I do the Loes chess set? No, Friggand's bear. How about King Malthe III's murder ring?* We can't shut the man up. Don't worry about needing to include everything you're passionate about. This is a series."

"Narrowing it down is not the problem." I shrug. "There's just nothing that jumps out."

Her look lingers, eyes narrowing as she tries to understand. I shift, remembering again the night I saw the thin, white scar running down the length of her back. This is like that. I feel as transparent as glass. Exposed.

"The best art in the world passes through your studio, and there's not one thing that's your favorite. Are you a freak of nature?"

I give Freja a look, and she lifts a placating finger. "Withdrawn." Still, she regards me, one eye squinting, as though I'm disordered. "Isn't there something in the whole museum you like best?"

"I'm not Roland. I can't whip up enthusiasm for pieces I see through a critical lens." I point, in rapid succession, to a few canvases near at hand. "Ripped. Flaking. Discolored. Warped. Moldy. These are problems. I fix problems."

Freja emits a shocked, high-pitched noise, and her jaw drops so far it'll be a miracle if she doesn't have to have her food cut into tiny, pre-chewed pieces. I walk around the table and press a finger under her chin, closing it. Her eyes are as big as the moon, her skin as soft as a round-tipped paintbrush, and my heart pounds.

My neck is warm. I drop her hand, stepping back to put space between us. Retrieving a sharp pair of scissors from a drawer, I return to the painting with a scrap of fabric. I shove my mind full of the task, punching the details into every corner, pushing everything else out. I slice along the frayed end and tiny strings fall to my worktable. I adjust the line and smaller strings fall. And again still smaller.

Freja gives a gust of a sigh. "We should go back to being mortal enemies."

I grunt and pick up tweezers. "Too late. I'll text you what I'm wearing tomorrow, and we can twin." I look forward to how this new state of affairs will release some steam. I wait to feel the pressure ease. I wait. I wait. I wait.

"I have a twin. We dress nothing alike. Now, we still need content. What are you going to let me film you about?"

"Anything you suggest," I say, sorting the fibers by length into piles.

"Do you know what Rik wanted to talk about? Assyrians. That's it." She lowers her voice into a grunt. "*Assyrians.*" My new friend is regrettably adorable. "Assyrians is an A-plus choice. Oskar," she says, the sound of my name crowding out my task for one wild, uncontrollable moment, "we have to find something you really love."

I pick up a strand of fiber with a pair of tweezers, holding it up. "I love Belgian linen."

She sighs. Aggravated. "All right. Today you can tell me about Belgian linen, but it doesn't count for your Artifact Interview."

"Deal."

She sets up two cameras, one trained on the rip and one taking a wider angle, each with a red blinking eye. "You're now free to explain the majesty of Belgian linen."

"Come here," I coax. Picking up a tiny brush, I load it with conservation adhesive and place it in her hand. Our fingers touch. Again, I feel it behind my knees. "We're going to dab the glue a little bit at a time and then place different lengths of thread perpendicular to the tear. That's it," I say, correcting her placement.

"Why don't we paste a whole piece over the rip?" she asks, intensely focused on setting the string just so. The tip of her tongue is captured between her teeth.

I clear my throat. "The shape of it would show through to the other side. We want our work to be invisible."

"The same reason to alternate lengths of string?"

I smile, conscious of the camera. "Are you sure you've never done this before? You'd make a good apprentice if being a princess doesn't work out."

She nudges me with her hip. I'm like a tuning fork, vibrating to her particular frequency, and I place my palm flat on the table to still the reaction. It'll go away in a second.

"Belgian linen is three times stronger than cotton. It's durable, breathable, and resists friction," I say, rattling off the facts. "Now cover all the threads in more adhesive."

She follows my instructions and looks up when she's done. She's too close, but I don't shift. The camera would catch that.

Instead, I look over the work and offer praise. "There. You built a bridge."

20

SHIPPING YOU

FREJA

I deliver the raw footage to Erik, and he scrolls through a digital calendar tool.

"I'm sorry it's about Belgian linen. Restoration wasn't cooperative."

He shrugs. "Doesn't matter what he talks about."

"When is it scheduled to post?" I ask.

He points to his computer screen full of hot pink highlights at the beginning of each week. "Museum Mondays for behind-the-scenes stuff. That's where most of Velasquez's posts will be."

"*Neer* Velasquez."

He shrugs.

"Orange is...?"

"Feature Fridays. Roland is this week. Agnes is next week. You and Oskar are the week after that, if you can get the artifact interview to me. These things take time to edit," he says. If he were a spinster librarian, he would be delivering a pointed look over the top of his reading glasses.

I lean forward, examining the rest of the boxes. "Trinket Tuesdays is when you post about the jewel lotteries."

"Um-hm, either the drawings or the photographs. Marie used one of her ex-husbands, a photographer named," Erik consults his spreadsheet, "*Neer* Hom to shoot them."

"Hom? Asger Hom?" I squeak. "*The* Asger Hom? As in the man who wired the first photos of Lars and Bianca's wedding to the world?"

Erik grimaces, his face squishing into his neck, hands flailing, creating an invisible barrier between us. "I don't know what you're saying."

"Asger Hom is a 70s icon, and he's a legend for getting that shot. Marie is a legend for nabbing him. The scandals would melt your eyes."

I glance at the paper thermostat. The top has more white space than the cover of a book about disappointed French people and the sedimentary layers representing each day's guests are getting progressively thinner. I look at Erik's screen again and swallow back my panic. He's got social media posts scheduled every day. It's something.

"Have you forgotten to add new updates to the visitor count?" I ask, crossing my fingers.

"Nope. That's it," Erik says, leaning back in his chair like a grizzled veteran of many wars. He has seen much. He deals only in cold facts. He is resolute.

Vede.

"Any new ideas for how to reverse that trend?"

"Now that you mention..." Erik taps his finger on an electric blue strip highlighting something called On-Site Saturdays.

He leans forward and he is a slouchy young man again. "So, like, going live on social media is hot."

"Hotter than well-considered posts that provide context?"

"Way hotter. People want authenticity."

"Forgive me, Erik, but people want to watch a train wreck so they can slow down and rubberneck for gore."

He bobbles his head. *Isn't that what I just said?*

"Velasquez suggested visiting places in person which tie in with art in the gallery. He even made a list," he says, tapping a second screen. "I want you to set aside a few Saturdays to go out on excursions with him."

I lean in and scan the list. I've got a lot more latitude than my siblings when it comes to royal engagements, and I'm going to need it. Erik has scheduled me out every Saturday for eight weeks, the last just before Christmas Eve.

How is Oskar supposed to study for his test if we keep eating up his free time? "I could go alone."

Erik swivels in his chair and nods, clapping his hands on his knees. "Let me be real with you, Freja. The numbers look bad. Like, a zeppelin crashing into the ground in a fiery conflagration bad." His voice pitches into a quiet panic. "The humanities! The humanities!"

"Humanity, Erik."

"Yeah. A lot of people came out that first week to support the museum, but most of our base has dried up. They made their visit. So."

I cannot overstate how profoundly I hate this habit he has of only expressing half a thought.

"So...?"

"So yours are the only videos catching serious fire—the ones with you and Velasquez. If you do this, I won't even make you come up with an artifact interview."

"I just gave you a segment on Belgian linen. I'm thinking of taping one on mulberry paper and another on hot tables. It's not as riveting as—"

Erik's hand floats in front of my face. "I could literally not care what you guys talk about. Sondmark doesn't care. They like and share and chirp your videos because you're pretty to look at, no offense, and you could cut the sexual tension with a knife."

Color creeps up my cheeks. "We talk about conservation adhesives."

"I know. Should be a snooze-fest. Doesn't matter. People are shipping you."

"What?"

"Oh, Freja." The *you poor thing* is implied. "Shipping. They want you to be a couple."

"We're not a couple," I insist. We're friends. We shook on it.

"Okay. Sure. Whatever." Erik presses his fingers to his chest. "But I just want to say that there's an unacknowledged complexity here. When you're on, the fire emojis flow like water, and when we get you in front of the camera, we harness that power." I stare, trying to sort him out. "It's like solar panels."

"Hm." A brisk nod and I move on, knocking on the doorframe of what was once Director Knauss's office. In the weeks since his criminality was uncovered, Marie has worked a change, filling the shelves and bringing in comfortable furniture, turning the sterile showpiece into the hub of the administration wing. She looks up from her desk.

"Darling, you'll give yourself wrinkles if you keep looking like that."

I smile, probably creating more wrinkles. "You were married to Asger Hom. You never said."

"You never asked."

"I'll ask now. Why did you break up?"

"He had an eye for beauty." She tips her head and looks exceedingly wise. "He comes for Christmas Eve dinner each year and brings nut loaf."

I slip into a ruby-red Saarinen chair, curling up like I've landed in a basket of pillows. "I saw Erik's spreadsheet," I say. "My mother's going to have words with you about taking so much time to be with the goblin in the dungeon every weekend."

There's a movement at the door, and I turn to find Oskar regarding me with a cold, dark stare. A zip of apprehension travels down my fused spine.

"Erik called down and said you wanted to talk about doing some traveling," he says. My heart drops. We are cursed.

He enters the room and leans against a console. I'd have to twist around to get a good look.

"Am I not doing art restoration anymore?" His tone is testy.

Marie waves. "Calm yourself, Oskar. We're in an unusual circumstance, at least until Christmas. All hands are required to dig us out of this hole. Even princess hands," she says, giving me a smile.

"Especially princess hands," Oskar replies.

My back stiffens, and I no longer feel the delightful contours of the chair.

Marie frowns. "We'll have you start this week in the gallery, walking through some of the less visited exhibits and introducing the new series."

"I'm going to be busy over the next few months."

How high his walls are. He doesn't tell her why he needs the time. He doesn't share anything more than he strictly has to. Marie would understand about the citizenship test, but he doesn't lay his neck open in case she doesn't.

Marie shakes her head. "Whatever it is will have to wait until after the new year. This is more urgent. Sondmark is counting on us."

I sneak a look. Oskar's hands are curled over the edge of the console, gripping hard, but Marie gets us to agree to meet on Saturday.

My next few days are absorbed in duties for the Crown. I'm unsettled by the way Oskar and I left things. I attend the launch of a new orthopedic surgery wing at Arnhuis Hospital and lead a roundtable discussion of Women in the Arts. These events require research into personalities and issues. Royal secretaries spend hours stitching me into a cocoon of knowledge so thorough that nothing has been left to chance.

Not so when I return to the museum. Oskar greets me with withering professionalism, briskly suggesting our route down the gallery and various topics we might touch upon. Where is this much vaunted sexual tension Erik spoke of? Though Oskar's wearing a brown herringbone three-piece suit like a man with many pheasants to shoot, I can hardly appreciate it. My mind is full of all the things I could say, all the things that could go wrong as I wander into the wilderness, live, without a script. I feel how thin the ice is.

He's still irritated about the goblin crack. It's too late to explain that I find goblins sexy, that I have an imaginary goblin lover who drags me off into the forest and likes it when my long skirts swirl around my ankles. That at this moment the goblin is smooth and civilized in brown tweed.

He checks his watch, tugging his sleeve back slightly. "It's time."

"Now?" I breathe, twisting my hands. There's a non-negligible chance that I'll throw up on a live Pixy feed. I really might.

He takes my phone and lifts it into position, not glancing at me as he takes my hand in a firm grip. We've done this before, and it will be fine. It will.

He hits the red button.

"Welcome to The Nat," he says, doing a wide, slow sweep of the gallery space with coats of armor and ghostly outlines of war horses sheathed in protective metal. Banners hang from the ceiling. Unlike the modern main wing, this was once a palace mews, the stone and timbers a fitting backdrop to medieval pageantry.

Oskar's manner doesn't significantly alter now that he's on camera. He enunciates more clearly when speaking to an audience, but his energy level doesn't skyrocket. He doesn't act like a showman. His way on screen is an accurate reflection of who he is. Authenticity, Erik called it.

He squeezes my hand slightly and I shift into action, holding up Erik's sketchy thermometer sign, pointing to progress made and the progress yet to be made. "If you came once, thank you so much. Luckily," I say, "The Nat has an inexhaustible number of delights, enough to fill days and days of visits. Perhaps you didn't poke your head inside the Medieval armory."

As Oskar guides us down the main gallery, my grip on his hand is murderously tight. He stops, prompting me to introduce the topic of shield designs.

"You can see the brilliant azure of the Counts of Herrenmendt who ruled and protected the southern border for five hundred years. A student of heraldic symbols has lots of material here to explore."

"Wait a minute," he says, brow arching. I can feel him going off our outline and my hand squeezes harder. His only response is a smile. "Princess Freja is a heraldic expert. Shall we quiz her?" he asks his camera.

A cloud of fire emojis bloom on his screen. Now he chooses to be a showman? He tugs me and points a finger at the case. "This orange one with the bear. What does that mean?"

"You've heard the phrase 'mama bear'? It means the warrior is fierce and merciless to protect the ones he loves."

He gives the camera, not me, a nod to show he's impressed. "And the cat?"

I'm too busy thinking of the answer to be nervous. Oskar has found a way to loosen me up. Maybe this isn't so bad. "It's a northern lynx, actually, signifying vigilance and courage. If my own cat is any indication, it also means that the warrior liked to be rubbed behind his ears."

Oskar's gaze narrows on the screen. "You have a cat?"

We have strayed off topic and I smile into the camera, pretending the public has asked the question. Not him. "His name is Smit."

He draws a quick breath and looks down and back up. "Here's a question coming in," he says. "User @balledout15 asks, 'My History of Sondmark teacher will give us extra credit if we follow this account and ask questions. So: Why is history supposed to matter to me?'"

"I love your teacher," I say, and the screen receives another of Oskar's quick smiles. I'm not above throwing him under the bus. "Perhaps *Neer* Velasquez has a good answer for this."

His lips pull in thought. "I think it's because we like to think we're different from those who came before us, smarter, as though it's terribly clever of us not to die of the plague or childbed fever, wise enough to be born in a time of indoor plumbing. We can convince ourselves that we'd have the good sense to be on the right side of every historical question. I, for instance, would have freed the serfs."

I laugh and follow his lead. "I would have talked my way into being the first lady-apprentice of Oppager the Younger."

He looks into the camera, interested. "Do you paint?"

I wave a hand. "I don't need your negativity."

He coughs a laugh. "History teaches us to be modest about our virtues and more generous about the motivations of others. It forces us to see that people are people, whether they live across the continent or come from another century."

Is this a truce? I squeeze our clasped hands. "This particular room shows us how medieval people used symbols on family crests, in religious rites, or in fairy tales, whether it be a dove on a triptych, a bear on a shield, or the poisoned thimble in the story of Thora and Bjarke." More fire emojis. I stumble on. "We still use them. Consider a Dragon's jersey, a brand insignia, or the violets handed out on Queen's Day. Symbols are storytelling devices and when you learn to read that language, a whole world opens up."

Oskar crowds into my frame, his head bending to mine. "Don't let her fool you into thinking you have to know anything special to enjoy this," he breaks in, obviously flirting with Sondmark. "Here comes a group of schoolchildren to illustrate our point. Let's listen in."

Oskar taps a button with his thumb and the camera flips, framing a young woman herding nine-year-old boys in suit coats and ties, shouting in a sing-song voice to manage them. "Don't lick the glass," she warns.

Several of the youngsters bunch up in front of a case exhibiting a suit of armor made for Horst the Invader and begin shoving each other, laughing. Oskar moves closer, but the image of what's on the other side of the glass pops into my brain. Too late, I reach for Oskar's elbow, scrambling after him to prevent disaster.

Cut the feed. Cut the feed!

The teacher notices the unruly boys and, loud enough to mobilize an army, bellows, "Of course, the armor looks like that. If you were a king in charge of the succession, you'd want to protect *all* your bits. But especially that one." The boys erupt in laughter, but her exhausted monologue continues as she shepherds them away. "Yes, yes, I *know* it's prodigious, but don't get excited. Come on, come on. Don't dawdle."

Oskar lifts the camera to my shocked face.

"Your Royal Highness?" Oskar says, voice as mild as a spring day. "Would you care to comment on...the succession?"

I drag him into the frame with me. "Of course, we can't show you what they were looking at. You'll have to come to the museum and see for yourself."

"We'll see you soon," he says, eyes twinkling.

The screen goes blank, and I release his gorgeous tweed sleeve. "That was live. That was *live*. Did we really capture children of Sondmark eyeballing a medieval king's..." Words fail. "...succession bits?"

He breathes a laugh. "We only got the backs of their heads. That's a ridiculous piece of armor." He leans toward the glass, looking over the plus-sized armor with the massive codpiece. "Riding full-tilt at another knight, wielding a long pointy stick and thinking this tin can would offer protection." He shakes his head. "It's a miracle you were born."

Adrenaline has burned its way through me, and I'm feeling exhausted. "I need a cookie," I say.

He grips my hand. "I've got one in the dungeon."

21

SWEET DREAMS

OSKAR

The goblin in the dungeon. I shake my head as I make my way to the studio. I want to say I don't care what Princess Freja thinks of me, but that's a lie so bald even my subconscious grunts derisively.

I look down at our joined hands and release hers, dragging the drawer of my desk open with a hollow metal *thunk*. It used to contain stationery supplies, but over these last weeks, I've accumulated an assortment of snack foods, some of which I don't even like. When was that decision made? In the check-out lane of the grocery store? The decision to take on the care and feeding of Princess Freja seems too momentous to be an impulse.

I stir the contents of the drawer with my hand. "How do you feel about oatmeal and raisins?"

She wrinkles her nose. "Raisins are the devil's fruit."

I file the fact away. For what? I don't need to know this about her. She's not a piece of art under my hands that I'm preparing for an exhibition. Still, each time I discover a new facet of her, I add it to my mental collection—a collection that has become a fat file of notes and histories with tags and addendums spiking out of the edges. It's taking up the whole desk.

"Do you like nuts and chocolate?" I ask, holding up a tin.

"Like them? I want to give them a knighthood and a pension," she says, reaching for the cookie and taking a huge bite. She closes her eyes and tips her head back, her face blissful. "I hate doing this so much."

Of course, she does. I forgot. Goblin.

"It's not easy," I say, moving away, giving myself space. I pick up a whisk broom and begin brushing the worktable even though there's nothing to clean. I can feel her watching me, and I spool out the activity as long as I can. But the longer I work, the more she sees.

"I meant having to be on camera." She watches me closely.

I sweep a few nothings into a dustpan. "You're on camera all the time."

"You know what I'm worried about? That I'll laugh at a joke I'm going to have to apologize for or that I'll make the wrong simile and torpedo government talks. *That brushwork is as bad as the pickled herring Vorburg keeps trying to pass off as food.*" She takes another bite of the cookie. "Worrying about every possible implication of everything that enters my head wears me out."

"You weigh all your words?" Damn.

She sits up and takes a breath, holding her cookie like a silver tennis trophy. "No, I don't. I'm sorry about what I said in Marie's office," she says. I glance up.

"The goblin crack." There. It's out.

She nods. "The goblin crack."

"It wasn't a big deal." As soon as the words leave my mouth I want to feed them into an incinerator. I told her our kiss wasn't a big deal. My designated snack drawer is making a very good case that it was.

"It's a big deal if I ruin our working relationship."

Is that what she's worried about? "We don't have to love each other to work together. We just completed a successful Pixy Live without fighting."

She frowns. "We accidentally highlighted a medieval codpiece, and you didn't look me in the eye."

Stultes es. It's harder hiding a thing she's already noticed. "No one is giving me directions. I'm an art restorer. I can scrape rabbit skin glue for eight hours straight. I don't know anything about being telegenic."

"You know," she mutters.

I carry on, hardly hearing. "If I forgot to look at you, I'll do so next time."

"You know it's more than forgetting to look at me." She takes another bite of cookie and leans against the table at my side. She breaks off a piece and I take it unthinkingly, tossing it into my mouth, chasing the crumbs with the back of my wrist.

Yeah. I know.

"I hurt your feelings and I'm trying to say sorry. The least you could do is let me."

I steal another piece of the cookie so that she's left with a small bit, pinched between her thumb and forefinger. "I'm a grown man. I'm too old to feel hurt when people call me names."

"Is anyone too old for that?" The last bite disappears, and when she swallows, she tips her head.

"Why goblin?"

She looks away, her cheeks pink. "Oh, you know. There was that row with the janitorial staff a couple of years ago and names got tossed around the staff meetings."

I don't see Rik calling me a goblin.

I open my mouth to follow up, but she says, "What was it about? The row, I mean."

"Rik discarded a stack of old canvas scraps, thinking they were junk, but they're priceless for conservation work. I spent an hour in the dumpster unearthing them again. We might have exchanged some words when I banned them from cleaning the restoration studio."

She breathes a laugh. "I'm sorry for calling you names, especially when you're making it easier for me to be in front of a camera." She chews her lip. "I'll do it without mangling your hand next time. You'll lose a finger."

I hold my hand up. Intact. "It's fine if you need to hold my hand." How careful I've been with my words.

Her expression shifts so slightly that few people would see it as the smile it is. "Thank you. It helps."

"We can't have you passing out in the galleries."

Her lips twitch, an acknowledgment that we aren't fighting anymore. "Until the end of the year, let's go all in on being in front of the camera, on working out the details of our posts, on doing whatever song and dance Erik the Boy Wonder—"

An unwilling laugh breaks from me.

"—tells us to do. They've signed us up for a lot of traveling, but we can be a team. We travel together. We make this work. And you'll promise to stop frowning at me every time I walk through the door, and I promise I won't call you a goblin. I promise you—I promise you on the *Herzollen*—that I won't ask you for another thing after New Year's Eve. You won't have to hold my hand again. You won't have to see me in your studio, not even when I'm desperate for a cookie. Do we have a deal?"

Stultes es. I clasp her hand, liking, as I always do, how it feels in mine.

"*Herzollen*?" I ask, clearing my throat.

"Oh. The Wolffe family heart crypt."

Our hands are still clasped, and I'm not going to be the first to break contact. I like it too much. "That clears up nothing."

"You've never been? It's the church where my ancestor's hearts are interred. You can get in free, though they suggest a few *markke* as a donation," she says, sounding like a tour guide. "There are about four hundred years' worth." I must be making a face because she follows up with, "We don't do it anymore."

"I work in a museum housing the severed toe of St. Leofdag, but you've won a very strange competition. That's the weirdest thing I've ever heard of."

"Surely not," she answers, reclaiming her hand and turning for the door. I miss it. My fingers curl over and run along my cooling palm while I try to think up more bargains we can strike. Freja turns, walking backward a few paces. "Handsel hosts a stark-naked winter solstice swim, but a few hearts are weird?"

"A few?" I sense a rhetorical weasel. "How many?"

She looks down and taps out a tiny rhythm on a table, murmuring, "Fifty-seven."

"What?"

"Fifty-seven," she repeats, louder.

"Stacked? I want a visual."

"Lined up on risers like a school concert, if you must know. Some big urns, most of them small. It's not that weird."

"It's the implication," I say to her retreating back, allowing myself to appreciate the way she fills out a skirt since she can't watch me watching her. "Someone had to stand by with a knife, have a bowl to transport the thing, plop it into the jar. Good heavens, the plop. I'll be up all night," I call.

"Sweet dreams, courtesy of The House of Wolffe." Her low laugh echoes down the hall.

The door closes with a sigh, and I stare dumbly. Right. Then I bang my head repeatedly against the nearest post. "A little past Christmas," I whisper. I just need to make it past Christmas.

I return to my flat at the end of the night, tossing my keys onto the table in the hall. A note from Uncle Timo tells me he left a dish of baked *pescillini* warming in the oven.

I sort my mail, tossing aside a new issue of *Conservator's Journal*, noting an article on German solvents I want to check out. Then I come to an envelope with the national seal on the face addressed to *Neer* Oskar Velasquez. I rip it open, the cellophane window flexing noisily.

It's just a friendly reminder of my looming citizenship test, the location, and time.

22

—·—

HUMOR ME

FREJA

Smit curls into the crook of my knees, dislodging my book. I right them both and reach for a bracing swallow of coffee. I've been thinking of Oskar. It happens when I'm not paying attention–like a car with the alignment out of whack, drifting over the line into oncoming traffic.

Smit lifts his head, and I scratch him behind the ears, a purr rumbling deep in his throat. "He has no business being that good at kissing, not when he doesn't mean it."

Never mind what I told my sisters. Oskar's kiss was good.

Smit arches his back, pink tongue curling from his mouth, and allows me to work undisturbed until I hear the chimes of my mantel clock. Tonight is a Wolffe family dinner.

There's no special dress code when we gather in the old apartments that used to house all of us together before we began moving out—Noah to Lily Cottage and the rest of us to our private suites. It's rare that we're all together without any official duties. Before Mama and Papa began keeping separate quarters, it was a time to relax.

Noah walks in through the French doors wearing an old Army sweatshirt and a pair of jeans, hardly recognizable as the suited and shaved heir to the crown. He chafes his hands together, warming them with his breath.

"Your ears are pink," Ella points out.

He hooks his arm over her shoulders and kisses her head. She shakes out of his embrace in protest. "You're freezing," she protests.

Noah grabs her in a bear hug, rubbing his cold, scratchy face across her cheeks, and Mama commands him to stop tormenting his sister in the same tone he ignored when he was a teenager. Papa throws a pillow. My sisters shout advice to the captive. For a moment, my face hurts from smiling.

Then Noah's laugh breaks off and he releases Ella abruptly, his expression shifting. It's not my brother there but the Crown Prince of Sondmark. Ella rubs her face and looks around in confusion–we all do–but it's only Caroline, hovering a few centimeters inside the door. Her jacket and handbag are over an arm, and her posture is stiff.

I move to her side. "You need something?"

"Just a quick word with Her Majesty, if I'm not interrupting. I have a message from His Majesty King Otto."

The monarch of Vorburg may not be an old friend, but he's an important one.

"You're not interrupting," I assure her. "Come in."

"I'll wait here, if you please."

A line forms on my brow. "Don't be silly."

The moment is resolved when Mama crosses the room with her favorite aperitif, Dubonnet and gin, drawing Caroline aside in a smooth motion.

"That was weird," I say under my breath.

Noah hears me. "What's weird?"

"Caroline, just now. She was hesitant."

"This is a private family dinner. She won't want to intrude."

"Intrude? She should have been off work an hour ago, and she'd never have come unless it was urgent. She's around us so much, it's almost as if she's one of the family."

"Not my family," Noah declares.

I frown. "Rude."

His stern face softens. "Tell me about your museum," he says, escorting me to the other end of the room and filling a small glass with dry vermouth and a thin slice of orange—one of the Pavian customs we've carried on.

Caroline is gone before I've taken my first sip.

"We aren't supposed to talk shop over dinner."

Noah's gaze is on the open door. His jaw flexes. "Humor me."

I follow his eyes, wishing I understood more than I do. This is what comes of being so much on my own. I take another sip of my drink. "I'm a social media influencer now."

"Really? Our bookish *donnina*?"

Mama's housekeeper, Una, announces dinner, and Noah escorts me into the small private dining room. "Where's your wide-brimmed hat and aspirational selfies?"

Thanks to these last weeks of research, I understand his joke, even if it's a few years out of date.

"Are you describing your last girlfriend?" I shoot back. He laughs even though such a girl doesn't exist. I can't remember the last time he saw any *one* girlfriend.

We bow our heads for Père's brief Pavian prayer. My ear picks out each word, and I feel a sudden wish to go beyond these rote phrases. I touch the wall. I think of Oskar.

When Père concludes, I reach for my serviette, draping it across my lap. "I'm mostly appearing on live broadcasts and doing short videos about art restoration."

"They're good, too. Freja's been holding out on us," Ella pipes up from the other side of the table. She serves herself the asparagus and prosciutto before reaching for the next dish. "Ooh, scallops."

"These will be the last of the season if we don't want to start another war with Vorburg," Noah warns.

There was something in the news recently. I try to remember what it was, but the truth is that tensions between the two countries are always at a rolling boil. There's no matter too trivial to trigger a diplomatic skirmish.

"It wasn't a war," Ella counters, spearing a quarter of a scallop and popping it into her mouth.

"Max told me," Clara chimes in. Mama's mouth tightens. Clara halts but pushes forward. "Max told me it was more heated than it appeared in the newspapers. Nearly forty Vorburg vessels surrounded five Sondish boats, throwing nets into their propellers, attempting to ram them. They had to deploy a rescue craft. It got tense."

Mama dabs at her lips. "I read the reports."

It's Alma to the rescue. She coughs lightly and pins me with a look. "The social media campaign," she says, taking a sip of wine. "Is it having any success?"

If Alma wants allies, I'm game.

"Some. I'll be making regular trips out to historic sites in the coming weeks. We'll be at the Blessing of the Horses," I say, hoping to distract my family from a line of questions I don't want to answer.

Noah glances at me. "We?"

Questions like that.

Ella chortles. "You haven't seen him?" She reaches into her back pocket, retrieves her phone—expressly against the mealtime rules—and leans into Noah. "He's this absolute dream of a Pavian art restorer. I wouldn't let him near the crown jewels," she says, her voice matter of fact, "unless we wanted them melted down."

I cast my eyes to the ceiling.

"Pavian?" Mama says, the word destroying the delicate atmosphere.

Père sets his fork down with deliberation. "It isn't a condition one can catch, madam." He turns to me. "This isn't the young friend of *Sehor* Fornasari, is it? What was his name?"

"*Neer* Velasquez," I answer.

"His Christian name," he prods.

"Oskar." Saying the name aloud in front of my mother feels like pushing all my chips onto a roulette square, placing a bet knowing the house always wins. The idea makes me feel overly warm and I wish we could crack a window.

Mama slices through a spear of asparagus. "I trust you will take care, Freja."

I glance over, and Clara is biting the inside of her cheek—a habit she's trying to break. Mama is offering me the mildest warning against upsetting an entire political applecart by being linked, even professionally, with a Pavian, while Clara was practically banished for dating a decorated navy officer. It's not fair. I know it's not fair.

I glance at my father, whose hand rests on the table, fork held comfortably in his grip, a slice of carrot speared on the end. His face is a mask of indifference, but the waters are churning hard between one end of the table and the other.

Have they ever come to terms with what it meant to cut my father off so completely from his homeland? But what could Mama have done?

My gaze darts from one to the other. Maybe the seeds of this unraveling were always there. Maybe it was too much to ask a young queen of Sondmark to bend her ways to a proud young prince of Pavieau.

I stare at my plate, trying to remember when it was different.

It was different.

My parents used to have a secret language, the kind which developed between me and Ella naturally. We would be at the Hunting Lodge, and I'd be hiding with a book in the music gallery overlooking the ballroom. Uncle Georg would be talking Mama's ear off about cracking down on union demonstrations at the Handsel industrial ports, and she would lift her eyes to Père. I would almost laugh at his expression. A lifted brow. His inflated appearance of self-regard. *Do you want me? Of course, you do.* He'd walk over so slowly that it used to drive her wild, and when he finally got there, he'd slide his arm around her waist, receiving a wifely nip on the elbow for his tardiness.

I remember feeling such deep, settled contentment when I'd return to my book. No matter how remote Mama had to be in public, I knew how they really felt.

I thought I did until everything froze over

"Speaking of...people," Ella says, doing her part to diffuse the situation. She looks to Alma. "I thought Pietor had to be with you for, you know, running the dreaded gauntlet of official approval while the government examines his finances and associations through an electron microscope."

Usually, Ella would rather swallow a fork than talk about Pietor but such is our desperation to get back to some kind of family feeling.

Mama leans forward, touching Alma on the hand. "It's only a formality. The entire country knows Pietor is perfectly acceptable."

Alma toys with her knife. "He decided to stay over in Lijuela for a series of beach clean-ups."

"How admirable," Mama says.

The conversation shifts, but Alma's face is pale.

23

REALLY DETERMINED

OSKAR

Another on-site Saturday. The horses at the Royal Mews are massive, large-boned animals with midnight coats and thick, plaited manes. I'm a city kid with a newfound respect for personal space.

"They won't hurt you," Freja assures me, guiding me closer, bare hand around my arm. "Friesians are known for their strength, intelligence, and calm temperament." She glances up and a brow notches. "We haven't had anyone crushed under their steely hooves in weeks. I think there's even one of those 'We've had no workplace crushings in 43 days' signs somewhere."

"It's not funny," I glower. "They're huge. One careless step, and I'm a forgotten stain on the stable stones."

"Not forgotten, Oskar." Her mouth tucks with a smile. "I'd put up a plaque with your name on it and bring you flowers every year on this day."

"My birthday, too."

Her smile is prim. "Noted."

The weather is bitterly cold, turning her smooth peachy cheeks a brighter pink. I file the detail away, promising myself the chance to mix just that shade. She's wearing a green wool coat with the collar tilted up, and tiny flecks of snow sprinkle her hair and the ground at our feet.

"Come meet them." Freja steps onto a stool and leans over the stable door. An enormous beast glances up from his feedbox and ambles over, nuzzling her cupped hands.

"Greedy beggar," she says, rubbing a sure hand up the bridge of the nose. She's at home here, with the gilded carvings on each door and the ornate columns flanking each box.

I think of my childhood spent in a Handsel flat with trips to the ocean for picnics, of changing into dry clothes behind a clump of tall dune grass and feeling the stinging points prick my skin. I think of school trips to local farms where we picked fresh apples, shined against our shirt fronts, to carry on the bus back to the city. I try to remind myself that Princess Freja and I are nothing alike.

I forget our differences when she turns, tugging me closer to the great animal she handles so deftly. "Hold your hand like this," she says, cupping my palm in hers. I catch Freddie watching us from across the courtyard, wearing an expression both knowing and amused.

"Like this?" I repeat, perfectly still.

"Mmm," Freja murmurs, her voice dropping into a whisper. "His name is Bone Breaker."

I shake her hand away. The massive beast nods, and I scramble back. "You are a sadist."

She dimples, and my breath catches. It's the cold air, sticking in my lungs, sending needles of sensation throughout my chest, sharp as dune grass.

I want to tell her about the memory. I want to tell her all the memories.

"Only a little," she counters, hopping down. Freja has sensibly worn boots, and she strides into the stable yard, well away from the forming procession of horses decked in bells strung along red velvet ribbon and grooms in the royal livery. "Are you ready to do this?"

I've been immersed in fairy tales for the last month. My information about the Christmas horses wouldn't amount to a decent Group-Source article. We'll have to lean on her knowledge this time. "What points do you want to hit?"

Freja may not like doing these live feeds, but they've been successful. Thanks to a piece of medieval armor and a trending hashtag—#ItsProdigious—there's been a 36% rise in visitors over the last week. And local news shows have caught on to the fact that The Nat is a visually rich environment with free content and a desperate backstory. Marie stuck Roland with the job of giving interviews, and he's delighting a demographic of women interested in feeding aging bachelors nourishing meals. He's practically a sex symbol.

Freja's brow puckers. "I have a story about the history of the Christmas horses—the rescue, of course, and why Ellsbach did a painting of it. Maybe you could add something about the physical properties of the painting itself?"

I nod. That's easy enough. "I'm ready when you are."

I slip a glove off my hand, stuffing it into a pocket, and hold the phone at an arm's distance. I leave the hand between us free. I wait. She slips hers into mine. My heart tightens, but I press the record button.

"Welcome to the Royal Mews," Freja begins, launching into a short, colorful summary of the night the Sondish royal family was trapped on a high mountain pass in a sudden storm. "They had become separated from their outriders and servants due to an unfortunate landslide. My great-great-great-grandmother wrote that they had to survive on their wits, the remains of a roast chicken, and the dubious entertainments to be wrung from an elderly, ill-tuned piano."

"How long were they cast adrift from civilization?" I ask, making sure to actually look at her. A mistake. Her lips are berry-red and mere centimeters from my own.

"Sixteen harrowing hours."

Once upon a time, I would have shaken my head or rolled my eyes, but these are Freja's people, and it's impossible not to find the story as adorable as she is. My lips twitch.

"What?" she says. "They'd never even buckled their own shoes." She turns to the camera. "They were completely at sea, and no matter who we are, we all have a story about being in that position."

Leave it to Freja to make people wearing brocade and panniers relatable. "Now you've done it. I'm rooting for them. How did they get out?"

"Well," she begins, as though she, me, and the entire country are in a tight-knit group at a lunch table. "There they were, huddled up for warmth, everyone piling more and more blankets on little Crown Prince Alfonse who, I am sorry to say, did not repay the consideration of his family by living a long and healthy life."

"No?"

"No. He allowed himself to be carried to his eternal rewards just ten short years later by an expertly aimed bullet, taken in a duel for the affections of a lady who, it pains me to relate, was not the crown princess, his wife."

"I'm shocked."

"They didn't call him Alfonse the Ever-Ready for nothing."

I cough. Erik is a genius. Getting Freja in front of a live audience is magic. She'll end the year with the whole country in love with her. I clear my throat. "As interesting as this rabbit hole is, we have to return to our tale with the sickly, not-yet-lost-to-virtue crown prince and his entire family, huddled together for warmth."

"After that long, cold night, dawn arrived and the queen went to a window, seeing a long line of Friesian horses coming down a trail over the hill. The firsthand account says they looked like woolly black sheep from a distance, and in her memory, the Royal Mews likes to give them sheep-appropriate names."

Freja smiles, and a stable worker, dressed in the fancy livery required for this event, leads over the largest land mammal I've ever seen up close.

A massive dark head dips between Freja and me, nosing our joined hands and pushing my shoulder. I grip her tightly. "What's this one named?"

Freja laughs. "Lamb."

She reaches up with her free hand and rubs the horse's head, planting a kiss on the soft cheek. "Ellsbach painted *Christmas Rescue* more than a hundred years later. By the mid-1800s, when the Industrial Revolution was upending society, the tradition of marching the animals into Handsel's central square operated as a romanticized, rural memory for newly industrialized citizens. Change had arrived, and Ellsbach's painting struck a chord."

It hits me that this could have been part of her speech—the one at the exhibit launch. The one I called terrible.

Freja pats the horse, and it moves away. She looks up at me with apples in her cheeks and tiny crystals of snow dotting her woolen collar. She wets her lip and squeezes my hand hard.

My turn.

"Did you know," I begin, clanging into action, "that it was painted on the heartwood of a lime tree?"

A furrow lines her brow. "Is that good or bad?"

"Heartwood is wood at the center of a tree. There's less moisture there, so the boards tend to be relatively stable. They won't warp like a wet piece of wood will. One of the things you'll see when you come into the museum this week is how the back of the board is discolored."

Her brows lift. "I've never looked at the back."

I glance into the camera. "Here, you can use this to impress your date. Tell them it's because of garlic juice."

Freja squeezes in close. "*Is* it garlic juice, or are we peddling disinformation?"

I look at her. Again, a mistake, but the nation is watching. "Paintings and carvings on wood were susceptible to insect infestations, but some clever medieval cook came up with the idea of spreading garlic juice on the back to keep them away."

Her eyes crinkle around the edges. "Oh, it's like loading up on garlic bread and onion rings if you don't want to be kissed."

I frown into the middle distance. "That's not going to put off someone really determined."

Our glances meet, holding a shade too long. I tug my gaze away just as the bells grow louder. I hear shouts and whistles as the Friesians begin to move. Fire emojis erupt from the margins. We need to get the eyes of the nation away from our faces.

I tap the screen, flipping the camera. "Let's watch for a while."

24

FOLLOW ME

FREJA

The temperature gets colder and the nights get longer. Lynda starts wearing her singing Christmas tree earrings. Oskar and I broadcast from a Christmas market, and I watch his eyes light up while we eat hot stroopwafels. The fickle gods of social media giveth and taketh away. One day the museum is packed. The next day is a Dragons game or a massive weather event or it's Tuesday and no one wants to go to the museum on a Tuesday.

Progress toward our goal is made in frustrating stops and starts.

Père and I receive an invitation to dine with *Sehor* Fornasari. Since Père has prior commitments, he sends me with half a dozen bottles of barrel-aged '57 *anau*, his best wishes, and Freddie, who watches me from the curb.

I turn to the door, pressing a finger against an ornate doorbell next to the nameplate reading "Fornasari." Though the night is wet and dark and the street is quiet, music is playing from one of the flats. The bell emits a harsh buzz and I step back, shifting slightly to adjust the weight of the bottles. The door swings open, sending a shaft of light across my skirt.

"Good evening, *Sehor* Fornasari."

"Uncle Timo," he corrects, kissing my cheeks while reaching for the box. "Come in, come in. Your man—"

"My security detail. He'll wait outside."

He takes my coat and leads me through the modest tiled lobby down a narrow hall toward the source of the music.

Dinner, he told my father when the invitation was made. I chose a plaid wool skirt and crisp white blouse with the expectation that *dinner* could mean anything from a formal occasion with courses and candlelight to a plate balanced on my knees in front of a fireplace with an electric heater set in the grate. From the energetic sounds emanating from the apartment, it'll have the numbers of a union strike. I smooth a hand over the wool and hope it's up to the job.

Uncle Timo propels me through his tiny entryway and into a moderate-sized sitting room, where I find clusters of people on the sofa and chairs, another group on the floor cutting up tissue, and more standing in the center, arguing loudly over what my bad Pavian ear translates as *boneless lamps*. Other guests scurry in and out of the kitchen, halting in the hall. I don't see a table.

He whistles for silence and gets it. Even in Sondish, his speech is flowery. "It is my profound honor to introduce a sister of Pavieau, Her Royal Highness, Princess Freja."

I lift a hand. "Just Freja," I smile. There is a general murmur of welcome before the noise kicks up again. I haven't been made a fuss over. That's good.

Uncle Timo holds my elbow. "Oskar should be here," he says, looking around with lowered brows as though doing so will conjure him. Only then do I admit that I've been looking for him too, every time the kitchen door swung back.

"Where is he, anyway?" This from a girl sitting with her legs crossed on the carpet. She's wearing high-waisted slacks and a slouchy sweater, dark hair spilling over her shoulder. Her Sondish is perfect, casual in a way only a native speaker can achieve. A Uni student is my guess. Second generation. She would be indistinguishable from her Sondish classmates except for the faintly olive skin. Her slightly narrowed eyes rake over my face and clothes. She's interested in Oskar, and I wonder how I could be so precisely attuned to that.

Uncle Timo waves his hand. "Help your cousin set out the cutlery, Adeline. Freja," he presses my arm, "go see if you can coax Oskar down from his tower. We won't eat for a while. You have plenty of time."

Adeline scoots past with a sharp smile, eyes level with mine, holding them too long for friendliness. "Does she even know where he lives?"

Uncle Timo shakes his head. He points a finger to the ceiling. "Number Six."

I follow Uncle Timo's directions up three flights to the topmost floor. Tissue paper Christmas buntings—a Pavian tradition Père has passed down to us—crisscross the open stairwell as I climb up and up. Reaching the top, I'm slightly winded as I rap on a deep green door with a gleaming brass number six.

"Come in," a voice calls, muffled but unmistakable. The sound sets off reverberations through my nerves, the price that must be paid for spending any time around Oskar. I push open the door, as silent as a scout entering a foreign kingdom.

It's a nice kingdom. The floors are bright Scandinavian pine, and the rug running down the hall, faded in a pleasing way, has a graphic Pavian print. Other than the faint music of the party, the only sound is the heavy wash of rain against the roof.

I see no one to interrupt my rank curiosity so I tiptoe down the hall to where it opens onto a sitting room with a massive bookshelf on one side and a perpendicular bank of windows. From these I see golden lights sweep along the contours of the harbor and the brilliance of the Summer Palace high on the headland.

Mentally I orient the building along the points of a compass and a smile touches my mouth. The windows are north-facing—good for painting. Perhaps this is a coincidence. Perhaps Oskar's a better liar than I am. He claims to be no artist, but there's a drafting table set in one corner. Grimly I measure the distance between me and it. Six meters of Scandinavian pine. I weigh up the desperate need to discover what he's been working on and balance it against the mortification of being caught snooping. I can almost hear the metallic clang of the second option banging to the ground. *Vede*.

From the relative safety of my position, I note more prosaic details. The furniture is old but sturdy. Good bones. There isn't an overabundance of it, and there aren't any Christmas trimmings. Oskar's flat is comfortable but spare, as though he's on a short-term lease and hasn't decided to stay or go.

"I told you, uncle. I'm busy," his voice calls. I jump slightly, my heart hammering in my chest. Three long, silent strides take me back to the kitchen door. I shake feeling back into my hands and push the door open to find Oskar sitting at a small table with a pile of notes and a textbook perched against a stack of others. A cup of coffee rests on a coaster.

He's wearing a blue button-up and a dark sweater with leather elbow patches, hair falling forward over his forehead. I take a breath before speaking, trying to find a frequency that sounds normal.

"Too busy for Saint Luz's Day?"

His head snaps up, and the book clatters to the floor. He rises, picks up the book, closes it, and dusts the cover.

"What are you doing here?"

I swallow. Even though I've been walking into his studio for weeks, coming into his home is more intimate.

"*Señor* Fornasari invited me for dinner. He wondered where you were." I look over the neat lines of the kitchen with its vintage tiles in black, cream, and ochre. I look at anything but the way his sweater stretches over his shoulders.

"I'm working."

Taking a few steps into the room, I crouch and run a finger along the spines of his books. *Freud and the Fairy Tale, A Thousand Stories: Folk Tales of Sondmark, The Secret Meaning of Goblins, Gorgons, and Golden Balls.*

I straighten and glance around his kitchen. It's more modern than my taste but there are touches here and there which feel chosen with an artistic eye–a rustic jar holding a collection of wooden spoons, the hand-painted salt and pepper shakers resembling Pavian pottery.

"You haven't decorated for Christmas."

"No time."

"You're too busy for Christmas?"

He lifts an uncertain hand, finally pushing it through his hair, a gesture unlike the purposeful, deliberate movements he uses in his restoration studio. When I take a step into the room, he inches back, the action almost imperceptible.

He straightens his stack of books. "I didn't do the decorations."

I give a short nod. "You and your father lived here?" I ask.

"Mm."

Oskar leans against the counter, and for once, his hands aren't in his pockets. His arms are folded over his chest, and he wishes I would stop asking questions. I can't. I want to inspect him the same way I want to poke around his flat, turning over letters and pulling books from the shelves.

"I didn't realize you lived in the same building as Uncle Timo."

"He's Uncle Timo now?"

"He won't let me be formal."

"He owns the building. Everyone's Pavian."

I'm not. I touch a wall he may not even realize exists, but I smile. "That's why he can play music so loud. He knows you won't call the police." Oskar's expression lightens. "This was your family home?"

"Mm."

If we're playing a game of snakes and ladders, I've slid back to square one.

I'm struck by all the things I don't see. Family photos cluttering a side table, piles of old magazines, faded art prints left on the walls too long, signs of the life this flat had before Oskar's father died—the anchor of memories.

"Come down to dinner," I invite. "Uncle Timo wants you. A cute Uni student wants you—" I say this with a laugh, but I watch his reaction closely. He has no idea what I mean. I feel relief—like I've been crossing a stream on my tiptoes, almost going under, and coming out of it on the other side.

"I'm busy." He nods to the stack of books.

My brow furrows. "You wouldn't have to live like a monastic scribe if you could study while you work."

"You don't say." He offers this with a flashing smile.

"I could help." These words must have caused a disturbance in the ether because I can almost hear Ella in my head. *Oh, sweet summer child. If he plopped you on square one, go find another game board.* "It's only fair since I'll be monopolizing your weekends for the next month."

I don't want another board. I like *this* board.

He tips his head. "You would quiz me while I scrape conservation adhesives? Hit the books while we drive to our on-site locations?"

"This I so vow." I make the sign my mother did when taking the coronation oath as I repeat her words. "All you have to do is come down for dinner."

He lifts his chin, trying to avoid the smile taking hold of his lips. "I like it when you strike bargains." He bumps away from the counter and crosses his arms, tugging his sweater over his head and crowding me against the door. I can't breathe.

"What are you doing?" I ask—I can't help but ask, staring at the line of his shoulders.

He drops the sweater onto a chair. "It's going to get hot."

Swiss comportment school never covered what to do if I turned into a hyperventilating nitwit. My mother should be entitled to a refund.

"On a night like this?" I glance at the window and the pounding rain.

"Especially on a night like this."

I didn't want to be on square one with him, but I didn't imagine climbing a ladder up to the last row on the very next move. He grabs my wrist. I know what to do. I lift my chin, and my eyes drift—

He pushes through the door, tugging me to the hall. What?

"There'll be dancing later and talking all night," he says. "You'll be warm."

What? Did he know what I was expecting? I rearrange my face.

We descend hand in hand, all three levels, with him pretending to help me down the stairs, me pretending I need it, nerves dancing with electricity—the feel of it arcing between us like tissue paper bunting across a stairwell. Only when we reach Uncle Timo's door do we let one another go.

Our eyes don't meet. He coughs. I exhale. His fingertips rest lightly on my lower back as he guides me through the threshold. Adeline bounces to Oskar's side, puts a hand through the crook of his arm, and leads him away. Giana, from the inn, waves from the kitchen, and I fix a bright smile on my face, already determined to spend the next twenty minutes asking her about the ingredients of a sauce or a stew.

Dinner is laid out in a buffet, and Giana's husband Konrad piles my plate with food, explaining each item. I sit on the arm of the sofa, nibbling on knotted sweet bread and honeyed lamb, talking to a succession of people with ties to my father's homeland.

Adeline follows Oskar from group to group—never my group—finally coaxing Uncle Timo to put on some music for dancing. Sofas are pushed to the walls, and the carpet is rolled up. In moments, there's a postage-sized dance floor, and I'm pulled into an old-fashioned, brisk-paced dance. I do my best to keep up.

Someone opens a window to alleviate the heat, but it does little to change the atmosphere which is warm and close and loud, and soon my face is shining from exertion. What would my sisters think to see me, moving from partner to partner, trying out a growing number of Pavian phrases—shouting them, almost?

When the heat becomes almost unbearable, someone dims the lights and old women, who have been content to watch, coax old men to the floor. I laugh in the arms of a middle-aged plumber.

One song ends and another begins, markedly slower than the others, a sort of foxtrot if any room could be had to execute it. My hand is enfolded, and even before I turn, I feel tiny sparks travel up my veins. I don't have to look. Oskar.

I laugh as I have been laughing with handymen and students and house painters all night. "I'm not very good."

The music is still too loud, and he angles his head. "I'm not very good," I repeat. I've been battling my awareness of him all night, from the moment I set off from the palace with bottles of *anau* clinking gently in their crate, and I'm thankful for the refuge of the crowd, the volume of my voice which hides any other feelings.

He whispers against my ear. "Follow me."

25

CIVILIZED SILHOUETTES

OSKAR

This has been the longest night of my life.

From across the room, I watched Freja nibble on a wedge of zucchini and feta pie, scarf down fried bacon and polenta patties, sniff an almond shortbread cookie, taste it, delight wrinkling her nose, and lick away the powdered sugar on her lips. I swear, if you feed the girl, she'll love you.

My mind wanders when it can least afford to. While scraping off a delicate lining or preparing a painting for the hot table, I've been running mental simulations of Princess Freja being in my ordinary life. In the grocery store pushing a trolley of cat food tins. At a seaside picnic on a public beach. At a Pavian night with Uncle Timo.

Eventually, she'd gather a crowd and I would be shouldered out of her orbit.

See? You don't fit together.

But tonight isn't going as I imagined. She talked, laughed, and danced with anyone who asked, crushed in the embrace of a warm Pavian welcome. She hates crowds but no one can tell.

When I can't stand it anymore, I slip a young cousin five *markke* and tell him to hit the lights and change the music. I watch Freja take a few turns about the room before making a move.

She thinks this—how I've slipped my hand casually into hers—is happenstance. Only I know how much maneuvering it took. Being deaf when Cousin Addie asked about my Christmas plans, cleaving my way through the crowd at just the right time, and giving Uncle Paolo a warning look when he tried to move in.

In the low light, her skin shines from the heat and press of bodies. She places a hand on my shoulder. I slide mine around her waist. We look anywhere but at one another. It's hardly dancing. There are no steps to match, no room for them, but we move to the music in a tight coil, jostling into other couples. The ballad is Pavian, a throwback to the glamorous 1950s, and I wonder if she understands the lyrics.

If you want me
Don't ask my Mama or my Papa
Don't ask Cousin Cecilia
Who wants you for her own.
Now that I'm grown, and you're grown too,
Ask me, ask me, ask me...

I shift Freja away from a collision, hand against her lower back, pressing her against me. Her grip tightens, and I steer her through the hall, bumping backward through the swinging door to the kitchen. It's cooler here. That's my excuse. It's cooler. We'll have more room. But even so, we fall out of the rhythm of the music—a little at first and then more and more, until we're barely moving between the sink and the table. Somewhere in all this, her hand slides up my shoulder and rests against my neck.

We stop swaying, locked together like a painting. I memorize the line of her cheek, willing her to look up. When she does, I would only have to lean forward a fraction, release her hand, and lift her against me, to cover her mouth with mine. My gaze shifts over her eyes and mouth, taking in the flush in her cheeks. My heart beats painfully as I look for signs.

She lifts her chin a millimeter. I swear it.

I take a breath.

"You're overheated?" Uncle Timo bangs through the door, bringing a waft of warm air, and we break apart. Freja nods over and over and over. Too much. He'll see. My hand lifts to take one of hers but she clasps them together.

"A bit. Next time I'll wear lighter clothes, maybe even something with an elastic waistband. The food and…and everything, it's been so lovely. I really should be going." Her words spill out, climbing over each other like the tiny crab Sondish children catch along the jetties. Freja manages to shake Uncle Timo's hand and make it into the hall at the same time. I follow, not content with a handshake.

She felt what I felt.

"I'll walk you out," I say, reaching for Freja's coat and taking it from her hands. I don't look at Uncle Timo or give Freja an opportunity to refuse. I find the lapels and hold it out like I'm impatient, and she tucks herself in, pivoting away from me and quickly doing up the buttons.

Timo kisses her warmly and tells her not to be a stranger.

"Freja is going," he calls into the crowded room.

Up rises a chorus of *Antio ya*. She smiles and waves. "*Antio tu.*"

She's done well.

We proceed through the darkened lobby, our steps softly echoing on the tiles. If she wants small talk, she's out of luck. My silence will be one more piece of evidence that I'm a taciturn monster, but I can't afford to divide my attention from the litany in my brain.

Keep your hands to yourself. Keep your hands to yourself. Keep your hands to yourself.

"Freddie's waiting?" I ask, holding the exterior door for her. When she passes, I release the door and plunge my hands into my pockets, looking up and down the pavement. Snow falls, muffling the sounds of the city, the flakes dissolving on the concrete.

Her phone screen lights her face as she taps out a message. "He has to circle around to get closer." She looks down the block for Freddie's tail lights, and a shiver skitters over my shoulders.

"You're cold," she says.

Freezing. But I wouldn't move if there was a blizzard howling around me. "Not really."

She glances away with a heavenward lift to her eyes, gives an exhale, and shakes her head slightly. What did I do?

She tugs her scarf off and goes up on her toes, winding it around my neck. Once, twice, tucking the ends in, fingers brushing my bare collarbones, the warmth and scent of her lingering. Her lips are close, and I take a deep breath, feeling the chill in my lungs. My hand covers hers, stilling it against my chest.

My brain forgot its litany and no longer cares what I do. "What did you think?" I ask, bumping a chin towards the party. "Was it too much? Too loud?"

Freja drops back onto her heels. "I recognized a lot of my father in there, his habits and mannerisms." She pauses, her lips tightening. "Adeline seemed very interested in you."

"I babysat her. She used to kick." I look up, expecting to see the headlights of Freja's car any second, frustrated that she's wasting our time. I hold her hand more firmly. Let her think I'm warming it. "Your collection of Pavian phrases is growing."

She laughs, the sound close in the falling snow. "I'll be faster on my feet the next time someone asks to kiss me."

Snowflakes settle against her hair and melt on her skin. A rough whisper escapes me. "That would be a shame."

Her eyes widen. We're on the edge of something, skating right on the border, with one foot over the line. Puffs of breath meet in the space between us, suspended, mixing. I lean forward, closing the distance slowly, fighting a raging battle with my better judgment, wrestling it into submission. Playing dirty.

It can't be serious. Freja is a princess, and I don't even know if I have a future in Sondmark.

It can't be serious. It's the last concession wrung from me before surrender.

Our fingers lace together. My lips meet hers, cold at first but quickly warming. Is it different from last time when the sheer chance of it made it feel like finding a hundred-*markke* note on the ground? Is this chance too? No. No chance, I think, gathering her close. I've spent half the night burning off reservoirs of hope, the other half stoking wildfires—looking for a way to kiss her from the moment she poked her head around my kitchen door, from the moment I crowded her into it, wondering what she'd do if I got close.

Look. That's what she did. She looked.

She's been looking for hours, glancing across the room, careful to maintain speed and trajectory across her target. Putting something halfway between us in her line of sight so that I'm always on the periphery of her vision. I know those tricks. I've been doing them too, lending half an ear to a conversation about Torbald's immigration cuts and half an ear to Freja saying in halting, ungrammatical Pavian, "Good time dance now."

I hold her waist, frustrated by the stiff wool under my hand but unwilling to let her go–going mad as her fingers explore the nape of my neck, hand shifting forward to touch my jaw, to place a finger in the soft spot under my ear.

I want her. I want this. I'm shocked by how much. It's like coming to the edge of the water and realizing it's not a puddle to be stepped over but a vast ocean to drown in. If this goes on, I'll be lost. She's a princess who lives in a palace and I'm an art restorer in a pre-war walk-up. None of these details mean anything. The truth, if I can bear to look at it in the light, is that we fit.

I close my eyes tighter. We can't fit.

Finally, I lift my head and take a shaking breath, resting my forehead against hers.

What am I supposed to do now? If I keep kissing her, maybe I'll find out. Maybe I'll drown. I take a breath, but headlights flash against my eyes. We break apart, arranging ourselves into separate, civilized silhouettes.

We watch her car approach. I lean over and brush my lips against her cheek, not strictly necessary but it's the right side of the border, this time. Freja glances away.

"Freddie," she calls with a wave. When she looks at me again, she's completely in command of herself. Maybe she goes around kissing every immigrant in Sondmark.

"Thanks for coming down to the party," she says, very much the princess. My body is humming with frustration.

"Thanks for agreeing to study with me."

She gives me a tiny smile and settles into the black Mercedes. Freddie shuts the door with a snap. I should be putting more distance between us.

Instead, I stand on the curb watching the red lights until I can't see them anymore.

26

TOP BUTTON

FREJA

For the last several days, palace workers have been winding garlands around newel posts and erecting evergreen trees in the Grand Hall, threading them with thousands of fairy lights. It doesn't matter how cost-conscious Noah wishes we could be, the Summer Palace is flooded with light from Saint Luz's Day until the new year.

All this light means that I can't avoid my reflection as I make my way along the halls. I know what I look like. Flushed and vulnerable and also, somehow, like I've started both halves of a football game, scored three goals, and need a shower. I rake my fingers through my hair and fan my cheeks before entering Ella's suite.

She taps on her keyboard and swivels in her chair. "What do you want?"

"Hello to you, too."

Ella closes a laptop, dismissing several screens. "All right. I'll take a break," she says, leading the way to her sitting room. She slips into a low-slung hammock chair, her bare foot resting on a knitted pouf, keeping her from swinging. I sink into the sofa opposite her, kicking my heels off and curling my feet underneath me. I've always liked this room. The bohemian atmosphere is a counterpoint to the formality and elegance of mine.

"Paige, play Rainy Day Coffee Shop," she says, reaching for her tumbler of Vestfyn and taking a pull from the metal straw.

The virtual assistant responds by cueing up exactly what she asked for: rain, the faint murmur of patrons, the clink of cutlery, and a lazy piano picking out a tune. My twin and I are different, but this is an area where our taste overlaps. We gestated during a nuclear warhead crisis, and the joke in the family is that it made us high-strung.

Another joke is that Ella always has her headphones on, her hoodie up, and a gaming controller attached to her hand. The truth is that she always comes through for us. Even better, she knows me like no one else does. She doesn't hurry me along or make me feel slow and silent. Instead, she nurses her Vestfyn, the bitter bubbles tickling her nose, until I'm ready to speak.

Does she already know how I feel about Oskar? My fingers brush the velvet nap of the sofa this way and that, creating contrasting patterns, erasing them. Does she know how much I want him to kiss me again? Does she hear it when I say his name?

I sort through a series of scenarios where I tell her about my...crush seems the wrong word. I could see Clara using it in the early days with Max. But things are not going anywhere with Oskar. A relationship won't develop. We're not a thing. I only want to kiss him senseless for an unfixed amount of time.

Attraction. It's an attraction. The word sounds like window shopping, passing an impractical red number with a plunging neckline on a mannequin and thinking, "That's nice. Lovely color. Wonder if it comes in my size." But eventually, my plan is to move along to the simple, mutually-beneficial arrangement of Mama's choosing: the classic sheath dress of royal relationships. Mama could use a win, these days. There's no reason to spill my guts to Ella.

"I need some technical help."

She puts her tumbler down. "The doctor is in."

"I made a promise to help someone with their studies in exchange for their cooperation with the social media campaign."

She snorts. "You got tangled up with that intern, didn't you?" For weeks it's been easier to describe Erik's eccentricities than talk about Oskar. "Better you than me."

What luck, a misunderstanding. I infuse my words with exasperation. "If it were up to me, I'd do it the way the Lord intended—flashcards and sharpies—but we're tight on time and I want to have him prepared before—" The truth. Here it comes.

"The semester ends," Ella finishes.

My stomach dips and bounces back. Is this what gamblers feel like when the ace turns up at the right time? "I was thinking about that computer thing you drew up—"

"App. It's called an app, and I wrote it."

"Yes, the one where you took the biographies of world leaders and made a quiz to help us memorize them. I want something similar, and I don't know if this is something you can do—"

She raises her hands like a mid-century unionist on a South American balcony. "Let's assume I can."

"I wondered if I could give you some textbooks and then your software could, you know..." I make motions as though I'm pulling apart raw wool. This is the zenith of my technical expertise.

She watches my hands with tented brows. "I'm horrified by how you talk about computers." I open my mouth, but she holds up a finger. "Horrified. The short answer is that I can't do books, not in your timeframe and not without a team."

She rests her hand on her chin, tapping the pinky against her lower lip. "If you wanted to glean the info from GroupSource articles where it's parceled out in more formulaic ways, I could use a lot of the same code as the World Leaders quiz. Even so, it's going to spit out some strange questions."

I nod. "I could probably weed those out."

"I'm an artist. This chop shop stuff hurts my soul." Ella shakes her head. "Anything else?"

I wish I could talk about Oskar, but he doesn't fit neatly inside a formula. Boyfriend. Co-worker. Citizen. Friend.

"No. That's it."

I head to my own suite, quickly shower, and change for bed. It's time to sleep. The illuminated clock emits a soft glow, and I turn the face around. Sleep. I need sleep. Or I could think about what happened with Oskar, going over every facet of the night like a Belgian diamond merchant.

Good idea. I snuggle into the bedding, listen to the sound of the storm outside, and think about the banked excitement of getting the invitation and the wild hope I'd see one particular Pavian, the tiny flame of triumph when I coaxed him to come to the party. Touching him.

Maybe he thought he was taking me by surprise, leaning in to kiss me. As if I needed that much help down some stairs. As if his neck could possibly be that cold. As if I could forget my hand was resting on his chest, feeling his heartbeat through the thin material of his dress shirt.

Maybe he thinks he came up with the idea to kiss me all on his own.

Clara says that technique has nothing to do with it, but it must make some difference. Oskar didn't even try the first time and he was interrupted the second time. Even so, both times left me shattered.

I narrow my eyes at the dark ceiling. Twice is nothing. If we were conducting an experiment, we wouldn't even have enough information to know what qualifies as an outlier. We need more data points. Sometime around 3:00 a.m., I resolve to ask him on a date. No harm in that. Princesses go on dates. Our brother asks out a succession of models, and none of it seems to mean anything.

Whatever's happening between Oskar and me has to find an ordinary, pedestrian outlet. A date, with all the awkward fumbling of two people who have to figure out how to split a check, will clear my head, bringing my attraction out of the clouds.

On Monday morning, I walk into the museum to find the Education and Outreach staff practicing a coordinated dance number in the statue gallery.

"Pixy is all about dances right now," Erik informs me, his voice rising above a looping clip of a Sondish girl group.

My face spasms. He wants us to dance? "*Neer* Velasquez would never—"

Erik holds a hand up. "Please. Give me some credit. Oskar's brand is barely restrained hotness, not coordinated hip snapping." Erik glances over at me and narrows his eyes. Perhaps he sees something in the way my fingers won't stop doing and undoing my coat button. "Oskar," he repeats.

Erik sucks in a startled breath. "There. You did it again. When I said 'Oskar' you tensed. Did you fight or something? You look nervous."

"I'm not nervous. I mean, I am, actually. We've only got a few weeks, and that *flamen* thermometer hasn't budged in days."

He turns and claps. "TWO, THREE, FOUR! To the left, Lynda!" and then pivots back to me. "The visitor count is totally dire, and whatever this is," he says, his palm doing a loose figure eight from my shoulder to my hem, "we can't afford it. Our main couple has to be rock solid, so do whatever you do to put him in a good mood. Buy him a restoration adhesive or, I don't know, breathe on him, and be ready to go live in the silversmithing gallery at noon."

I make my way to the restoration studio, trying to stop my fidgeting fingers, but when I brush through the doors, he's nowhere to be found.

"Oskar?" I call.

"In the storage room." The voice is muffled, and I follow it, entering a high narrow space with a series of large shelves painted dead black, holding row after row of boxes and canvases, a whole cubby of stretcher bars, and rolls of bubble wrap. A black curtain is hung against the back wall and an easel set in front of it holds one of those over-heated Rococo images of young French lovers hiding in shrubbery and getting away with all kinds of nonsense while their chaperones, on the other side of the shrubbery, scratch their heads in bewilderment.

I tsk. "Who do you sympathize with?" I ask.

Oskar straightens from adjusting the lighting equipment.

I nod at the painting. "The lovers or the chaperones?"

He grunts. "I sympathize with the restorer who has to see what he's up against. Have you come to film me again?"

Ah. So we're not going to talk about the kiss. The tension, winding more tightly as the weekend went on, releases in a rush. I could use a cookie and a sit, but he'd probably want to know why.

"I haven't been in the storage room before. It would make a good subject—something quick. We'll do it live." He grunts again, and I swap out disappointment for irritation. Let Adeline have him if she wants. Let them be happy together. Let them choke on it. Asking him on a date was a fever dream. Madness. "What are you doing here?"

"Get your camera out. I'm not going to repeat myself."

My brows lift, and he makes a conciliatory gesture with his hands. "I haven't been sleeping. I'm sorry."

Digging into my purse, I retrieve my camera. "Neither have I, but I haven't taken anyone's head off."

His hands still. "Tell me why you haven't been sleeping."

Over my dead body. "You first."

We are in a tense, cold standoff until he nods. "Fair enough," he whispers. "Ready?"

I hit the record button, and we introduce ourselves. Oskar explains the basics of UV photography and light absorption.

"What's the upshot of what you're trying to accomplish?" I ask, feeding him a question.

"Some problems hide, but that doesn't mean they're not there. If I don't drag them into the light, I can't sort them out." I blink, my smile fixed, but he continues. "When I inspect a piece for restoration—when I look at it with a raking light or under a microscope or in a UV photo—I try to see things from as many different angles as I can, to really get to know it, so that when I'm working, the only surprises are good ones."

He lifts his eyes to mine. In this dark, confined space, it's difficult to remember that my phone is a window to the entire nation. He bumps his chin. "Are you ready to turn the lights off?"

Oh, Oskar. Someone in Sondmark is already turning his words into a meme. He has an enthusiastic fanbase, and they haven't spared themselves, shouting their love of him from the wastelands of ReadHe threads to YouTube edits of our most romantically ambiguous moments set to power ballads to the heights of royals fanfic. Girls wearing Team Oskar t-shirts have started coming to my royal engagements. Words like these will launch a thousand Pixy shorts.

"Freja," he prompts, then strides towards me, reaches past my shoulder, and flicks the switch. The room plunges into darkness, but the camera's still on. The country caught all of that.

"As you can see," he says, voice too rough to miss. He clears his throat. "We'll have to turn off your phone to get a good image. Even that light will contaminate the final photograph."

I cast about for enough breath to speak, gleaning for tiny grains in a field already harvested and bare. He is close, so close, and I'm clutching my phone in my hands between us. "But this is what it looks like when it happens?"

"Yes."

"All right." I don't dare step away, as dark and unfamiliar and full of priceless art as this space is. "When we return, I'll show you the picture *Neer Velasquez* took."

I rub my thumb along the outside of the phone case until I find the power button. In seconds, the little light we had is extinguished. I can hear my breath, the shortness of it. I hear a click.

"That's the camera," he says. He must have a remote because I can feel the warmth coming from his body, hear the drag of his lungs. He hasn't moved a centimeter.

"Is it over?"

"These projects need a long exposure time."

I don't know a thing about photography. He could tell me a long exposure is forty-five minutes and I'd have to stand here, nerves screaming the whole time.

The pitch-black presses against my eyelids, and I find myself beginning to worry about knocking into him or losing my sense of orientation and overbalancing against his chest. That's a mistake. Don't think of his chest. I take a yoga breath. I am a statue. I am marble. I am a *flamen* paleolithic carving. I could do this all day.

"The sleep…" he says. "Is it because of the kiss?"

I actually yelp, and he reaches out to steady me, hands wrapping securely around my arms. He probably has goblin night vision.

"Is it?"

What am I supposed to say? "I have other things that keep me awake. The visitor count, the state dinner with Vorburg next year, Pixy algorithms, back pain, anthropogenic climate change…"

He gives my arm the tiniest shake.

"Is it?"

I stuff as much offended incredulity into my "No" as possible.

He's silent and then, "You're a bad liar." He says it like he's adding to a list of problems that have been exposed in the light. Dark varnish layer, lifted colors, 7mm tear, bad liar. How dare he know me as well as Ella.

"There's a lot going on right now," he says, "with the museum and my test. Let's focus on that."

How tidily he's sorted us out. My face is on fire. "Is the picture done now?"

He releases a breath, and I feel him reach past me as he gropes around for the switch, feel the press of his chest and inhale the scent of his cologne. My lips are almost on his neck. Click. I blink against the light, unable to meet his eyes.

"How soon can I record the image?" I ask, stepping clear of him and backing toward the door. As my phone turns on, it pings with missed messages. A few texts from Ella.

Why is #OskarsTopButton trending? Also, #WhatHappenedInTheDarkFreja?

My eyes fly to Oskar's shirt and I tap my own clavicle. "Your button," I squeak. *Vede.* "When you reached for the light, you brushed me. The camera was right there." It's just horror after horror today.

He looks down, no more than mildly interested that the contours of his collarbones are exposed to the entire world, given out for free like lollipops at the bank. He pinches the fabric and button, fiddling with the placement and inadvertently showing more of his throat as well as, surprisingly, a thin gold chain following the sinuous line of muscle. My eyes trace the line until it disappears.

His hands stop, and he draws a circle on his skin, looping the chain with his forefinger, displaying a small gold medallion on his palm. "It's a Pavian saint."

I flinch, training my eyes on the over-heated Rococo. No. I focus on the black curtain behind it.

"You seemed interested." He's laughing at me. "Santo Laurenzi. Saint of greatest need." He tips the medal into place and does up his button, taking the camera from its stand and striding into the studio.

I slump against the wall and check my phone again. Ella has followed her text with screenshots of various chirps.

@King_of_Fromage: Four minutes and counting. Get the Summer Palace on the line. Lone Wolffe on the loose! #WhatHappenedInTheDarkFreja

@hairy_dragonslayer: #OskarVelasquezsTopButton be like, "Judge, I was an innocent bystander in this conflagration of sexiness..."

@RoyalWeddingRiot: Will someone please get married!?!? #KingOskar #OskarsTopButton

*@trashpandaprincess: Five minutes!! #WhatHappenedInTheDarkFreja *GIF of popcorn-eating pop star**

"Are you coming?" Oskar calls. "The picture is ready."

I straighten, press cold fingers to my warm cheeks, and clear my throat. Only when I am absolutely certain my voice won't betray me do I answer. "Coming."

27

— • —

WINTER WEDDING

OSKAR

It's murder working with Freja—the accidental brush of her shoulder in the close confines of a car, the false sense of ease we have to convey in front of the camera, or the way her eyes shift away as soon as I look at her. The attraction between us is like a boulder crushing me into bedrock. With every move of my body, with every desperate attempt to wiggle free, it squeezes me more.

We can't have a relationship. I decided that in the few days and sleepless nights between kissing her and meeting her again in my studio. There are too many things at stake—a precariousness to my life in Sondmark she couldn't possibly understand. In these last weeks, Prime Minister Torbald has raised the temperature for immigrants. He argues on every podcast and news show, baiting the country with stories about people who look like me.

I try to take lessons from the fairy tales that play endlessly in my ears each day, reminding me that the world is dark and dangerous for those who venture into the forest or scale a castle's heights. Hugo Littleshins can't play with a family of giants unless he wants to end up as a smear of blood and bone. The Incessant Farmer wards off a wicked enchantment by maintaining his acre of land each day—no more, no less. A starving cobbler keeps himself from eating the bread that arrives on his doorstep each morning or must see his daughter devoured by a wolf.

I look at the royal seal affixed to the letterhead of my citizenship correspondence. The rampant dragon and the harp seal. That is Freja. I try to merge them in my head, but she resists me. She taps the paper off her chopsticks or brings me a chocolate letter on Piet's Day or feels perfect in my arms. She laughs.

We see each other constantly—an hour or two each day and longer stretches on Saturdays when we're out on assignment. I till my little plot of land and try not to want too much.

Today, I tell the reflection in my bathroom mirror it will be short. No car. I've told her to meet at my place and we can walk over.

There's a sharp chill in the air when she arrives. Her nose is red, and she's dressed more simply than usual—black trousers and a loose black sweater tucked in the waistband. But Freja—my Freja, comes a voice at the back of my head. I don't fight it—my Freja can't be that sedate, so she's wearing a bright marigold coat with a turned-up collar.

I have to make some justification for my close inspection. "Need gloves?"

She fishes a pair from a pocket—leather and fur-lined—and stuffs them back in.

"You don't have a scarf," she says when I reach for the door handle. "I'm—"

"You still have my scarf. It has to be here somewhere. If I know ancient churches," she says like she's the world's foremost expert, "it'll be like an ice box in there."

I fall back into the flat, and she follows me up the hall, perching on the arm of the sofa when I open a closet.

"Still no Christmas decorations?" she asks, looking around.

I grunt, pushing hangers out of the way.

"What's that?" she asks, making me flinch at her closeness. Now she's looking over my shoulder. "The white thing."

I push the hangers back. "This?" I touch the garment, hanging in a dry-cleaning bag. "My mother's Pavian dress." I reach up high.

"May I see?" she asks. I nod and she ducks under my arm and carries it off, peeling back the plastic layer while I continue my search.

"This is amazing," she says, laying the dress out on the sofa and peering into the neck.

I lose myself a little in the way fascination chases over her face. How was it possible that I used to think of her as little more than a spoiled princess?

I clear my throat. "How?"

"Let's set aside the fact that the embroidery is world-class. These are all French seams," she exclaims, tipping the shoulder out like I should know what she's talking about.

"Mm. My grandmother made it."

"Then your grandmother was a wizard." She waves me over. "See?" She holds an opening wide. "This garment was made to be lovely no matter where you look. These ribbons make the bodice adjustable."

"Isn't it better to have something fitted to the body?"

Freja shakes her head. "Your mother would've been able to wear this even if she gained twenty kilos and had a baby." She emits a blissful sigh. "Folk dresses are so genius."

I smile.

She smooths her hair, self-conscious. "Why are you looking at me?"

"You're very excited."

She pokes me with an elbow. "You're not excited enough. This dress tells a whole story—of your grandmother, who bothered to make those seams so pretty when no one would see them. Of your mother, who added the petticoats—"

My brows come together. "How would you know that?"

"Feel this," she says, dropping the fabric into my hands. "You wouldn't need skirts so heavy in Pavieau. You'd be boiling. She must have sewn them in when she came north. You can tell because she left a clue." Freja runs a finger along a seam. "These are wide basting stitches—easy to unpick if she returned home."

A knot forms in my throat. My mother never settled here.

"She was married in that dress," I say, nodding and chewing on the inside of my lip. Walking briskly to the closet, I dive into my search with more purpose and find Freja's scarf where it had slipped from a hanger onto the floor. I wrap it around my neck, noticing the way her scent has lingered.

On our walk, we review the salient points of *The Winter Wedding, 1854* by Frederick Olsen. We agree to start in the forecourt and move inside the church where we'll speak briefly with the pastor. I've called ahead, and he knows to keep an eye out for us.

We arrive at the small chapel jammed up against the Vorburg ambassador's residence, and as we come around the corner, a sharp wind bites into our faces, sending us dashing for the weak sunlight. It's hardly better there.

I hold the phone out and we squint.

"No good," Freja says. "The sun will wash us out. We have to broadcast from the shade."

The shade looks bitterly cold, and I have a sudden wish to be on a beach in Pavieau, soaking up nutrients integral to sustaining human life.

"I don't belong here," I answer, clamping my jaw tight to prevent my teeth from chattering. "My people were meant to dive bare-chested into the sea with knives clenched between their teeth. We were never meant to wear so many layers."

She laughs. "There's no such thing as bad weather, only insufficient clothing," she says, reciting one of Sondmark's most loved maxims. "I'll block the worst of the wind."

I glower. As if I would let her.

"There's a seat carved into the porch," I point, already marching her toward it. By heaven's grace, it gives us a picturesque backdrop and puts us in close proximity since I have to wrap my arm around her waist to fit.

"Hello, Sondmark," she says, "We're at The Stranger's Parish today, the pocket-sized Lutheran church set on the grounds of Vorburg House." She lifts her face to mine. "Did you know that for diplomatic purposes, we're not actually in Sondmark?"

"No," I breathe, feigning incredulity. My teeth chatter, and I clamp my lips together.

She dimples. "Yes. It's a provision from one of the oldest treaties in northern Europe. Once we entered the forecourt, we were as much in Vorburg as someone standing in their capital, Djolny, right in the heart of Liberation Square. The treaty, drawn up the first and only time a Vorbugian princess married a Sondish king, stipulates that the church must always be open for weddings, day and night."

Freja touches my arm, and I begin to describe the composition of *The Winter Wedding*—an image of the young bride in a dark, full skirt, the sunlight shafting across her red hair as her new husband signs his part of the registry, free hands entwined awkwardly, cheeks almost touching.

"The velvet fabric, the bright red and green of holly winding up the column behind them, his thumb touching the soft center of her palm. It's not an image you might expect of the mid-1800s."

She nods. "Agree. Queen Magda's reign has a reputation for emotional repression and layers of formality—"

I choke on a laugh. "She had eleven children. How formal could it be?"

Freja lifts a finger, almost touching my nose. "Do not get me into trouble, *Neer* Velasquez."

"I would not dream of it, Your Royal Highness," I reply, wanting to do nothing more.

She turns back to the camera, shifting in the seat. My hand slips to her hip and I lose the signal to my brain for a second. When I lift my hand, I grip the back of the bench.

"As...as I was saying," she continues, "The Stranger's Parish has a colorful, some may say scandalous, history of elopements and quickie weddings, the most famous of which was that of international superstar Lars Velmundson and his fitness guru wife Bianca."

"How scandalous was it?" I don't even care. I only want to stay here until I die, frozen next to her.

"Word got out before they arrived." Her tone isn't suited for a princess delivering an on-camera lecture. We could be talking together over a steaming dish of *xiao long bao* as we were last night. "The bride wore a bell-bottomed pantsuit and a massive hat. The groom had one of those powder-blue, frilled tuxedo shirts unbuttoned to his waist. Fans crowded at the door, catcalling Lars like he was giving a concert. Police were called in. It was almost a riot."

"Did it stick? The marriage?" My lungs burn with the cold and the memory of Freja's smile when I gave her the last dumpling.

"Contrary to all prejudices one would have against a powder-blue suit, yes."

Our gazes hold for a second. I let a shiver work through my shoulder.

"Are you ready to meet the pastor?" I ask, lifting her to her feet.

A bloom of fire emojis appears on the screen, and we enter the small octagonal church, chilly as she promised it would be but a refuge from the wind. The aisle is carpeted in deep blue and flanked by three rows of pews with room enough for a dozen people. Holly boughs wind up the columns. The ceiling is vaulted in a series of arches creating a star pattern, meeting over the altarpiece. Instead of the more typical explosion of craftsmanship, the altar was carved in spare, peaceful lines. Light streams in from three high windows. Tall, ornamental candle stands flank the altar, providing light at night.

"Are you here to be married?" The pastor enters from a door to our left.

I freeze, feeling the Oskar Does Social Media mask slip from my face—the pleasant, informative mask. *Vede.* I don't dare look at Freja.

"You're a lovely couple. I have some time now if you're ready," the pastor continues, hands clasped together, his face wearing an eager, open expression. His hand darts between me and the princess. Me and Freja.

Then he claps. "And that's how it's done." He's smiling widely now. The show is over. "Heavens, you should see your faces." He gives Freja a brief bow. "Your Royal Highness. And you must be *Neer* Velasquez," he says, extending a hand and gesturing to a pew.

We're fortunate that Reverend Kjar is an engaging speaker, pulling a few amusing stories from his memory, quick to respond to questions.

"There's something I've never understood," Freja says as we prepare to wrap up. "Frederick Olsen was a respectable painter with a thriving career. The bride's family was far less prosperous and would have welcomed the match gladly. Why do you think he chose to be married so quickly? Why this chapel?"

The reverend's eyes arc over the ceiling as he thinks. "People will say that this is nothing but a church for *moetje* weddings—for stern-faced fathers and guilty young lovers—or a place to make slapdash vows, quickly repented of." He lifts a shoulder. "Frederick Olsen didn't count time like a sensible person. He didn't save up for a ring or pick a strategic date to work around his schedule. He met Elsa eight days before they married. As soon as he became alive to what she was to him—the one person to whom he could open his heart—he was ready to make every promise he knew how to make. It was as simple as that."

It isn't meant to be a sermon, but I feel the same tense wonder as when I was a child and first heard the story of Noah gathering his animals from the storm. A refugee on a train wasn't so different from an elephant on an ark, in my five-year-old mind. The story wasn't about me, but it was mine, nevertheless.

Reverend Kjar thumps the back of the pew. "It's the most romantic chapel in Handsel, and if it were up to me, everyone would be married here," he laughs, gesturing at Freja. "Not you, ma'am, of course. We can't hope to compete with the grandeur of Roslav Cathedral when it's your turn."

Freja's turn at Roslav Cathedral. The thought chokes me.

I turn the camera around and Freja concludes the live. I murmur something coherent. We soon find ourselves standing in the wind and the weak sunshine. I want to kiss her again. I always want to kiss her.

"Can Freddie and I drop you off?" she asks, nodding at the Mercedes.

"No. I'll be studying. I could use the walk." I shove my hands deep in my pockets and burrow my neck in the scarf, ignoring the bitter cold as I make short work of the walk to my building and up the stairs.

I sit on the couch and unwind the scarf. I hold it in my hands, elbows on my knees. I glance up, my focus going to the window, to where the ocean curves into a headland, to the palace.

The breath eddies and flows from my body without sound.

I can't let myself think.

I can't let myself think.

I can't think about how, when the Reverend Kjar asked if we were there to be married, I almost said yes.

28

Don't Snore

OSKAR

"We'll have to stop there," Freja says. "My battery is almost zero."

I glance up from my work.

She texted around dinner, four hours ago, asking if I had time to study. She also asked for my desired spice level out of five flame emojis.

I sent back five and she brought me aromatic yellow rice and Thai stuffed chicken wings, sticky, delicious, and hot enough to make our eyes water, afterward quizzing me on Sondish fairy tales as I prepared a painting for a new varnish layer. This isn't the first time I've stayed at work hoping for a text. It isn't the first time she's sent one. Even within the careful confines of the studio, with the width of a worktable between us and an activity absorbing our focus, my hands shake.

When will I learn to keep my distance?

Not yet.

"I have a—" Charger. But before I can finish, a piercing peal rings through the studio and Freja claps her hands over her ears. I set aside my tools.

"Maybe there's a thief," she shouts.

If this were the first time the *flamen* alarm went off, I'd be worried. "Not funny."

I shrug on my jacket, she collects her coat and bag, and we rush upstairs to the staff door. If anything, the alarm is louder here. I punch in my code while Freja ducks her head, the noise like an ice pick to the brain. When the door doesn't click open, I punch the code again, careful to wait for each vibration under my thumb.

I push the door, shoving it hard with my shoulder, but it doesn't budge. Freja shrinks against the noise. I pull her against my chest, adding my hand against the one covering her ear. "Five minutes," I say. "It's almost over."

She nods.

When the alarm silences, Freja sags against me. "It's going to start off again," she reminds me, gulping her breath.

The ringing is still in my ears, and I punch in the code again, trying the door. Still, nothing. We've got a couple of minutes until the cycle repeats. I'm racing against the clock.

"Call security," she suggests, straightening away from me and tapping a number under the alarm.

I ring the guardhouse. "We're at the employee entrance near the parking lot," I explain too loudly. "The door won't open."

The line is quiet for so long that I wonder if I've gone deaf. Finally, "We were wondering if this was possible. Weren't we wondering, Jan?" the voice asks in a thick regional accent. "It was theoretical before. Now we know."

"Know what?" I ask.

"No need to get uppish," he says. "No one can get in, so the national treasures are fine. Thing is," a laugh, "you can't get out."

I must have heard wrong. The ringing. "What do you mean we can't get out?"

Freja grabs my arm in a desperate death grip. "We can't get out?"

She's too close. I hold my thumb over the microphone. "Maybe. I don't know."

The voice comes back. "Each wing is sealed off, and we can't reset the system for…" He stretches out the word as though he's consulting an owner's manual. "Let's see… Seven hours, sir. That puts us at five in the morning. Good luck finding somewhere to pass the night. Those benches won't do you any good."

Freja tips her head close as she listens in. The scent of her perfume is in my lungs, and she presses against my back. There would be nothing more natural than putting my arm around her waist and drawing her close. Pass the night. Like this?

I aim a ferocious look at the phone. "There's *got* to be something you can do."

"If we rip the hinges off the door and something really does get stolen, it's my head, not yours. We weren't the geniuses who installed such a stupid system, beg your pardon."

"Is there anyone else here?"

"Our cameras pick up the galleries and hallways. There's no one else in the place. You're it. If there's an emergency, we'll have a crowbar ready. Otherwise, we'll have guards patrol the perimeter. Oh, and don't vandalize anything."

I hang up, hardly daring to turn around. "Seven hours. What will your mother do?" It's easy to imagine a lorry driven by the queen blasting through plate glass gallery walls.

Freja strides away, and I watch her silhouette outlined in shifting moonlight. She holds a low-voiced conference with her own security, delivering explanations in abbreviated detail.

"Do they think I've kidnapped you?"

She shakes her head. "Freddie knows I'm in safe hands."

Safe hands. I'm not safe hands. But for six hours and fifty-three minutes, I have to be.

"Does your mother know?"

She laughs. "Are you kidding? Never call Mama unless you're ready for a tactical police unit." She shakes her head. "I'm inconvenienced, not in any danger. I'm thinking of those reporters they assign to listen to the police frequency. If it gets out that we're stuck, it'll be all over the papers."

As we talk, our steps take us through a tour of the gallery in no particular pattern. We have seven hours. There's no hurry. She removes her coat and slings it over an arm. I take it from her.

"Seven hours?" she confirms.

"Mm."

She puts her hand on my elbow, bending down to remove her heels. When her hair falls to the side, I see a white flash of the old scar. "At least it's not interfering with the operating hours."

"Mm." I take the shoes out of her hand, hooking them from my fingers.

"Have you seen Erik's thermometer?"

I nod. There's a scant week until Christmas, and visits have slowed—little wonder since the weather hasn't been trustworthy. All of Sondmark is busy with preparations for the holiday season, buying apple garlands for their doors or twists of caramels and straw to put in children's shoes.

"We might make it," she says.

Freja looks hopeful, like she trusts every day will be sunny and every wind fresh. I wonder what it's like to expect miracles.

"I hope you're right."

She nudges me with a laugh. "We've got the whole night to fill. What do you want to do?"

Maybe locking the doors to the museum has sucked all the air out of the building. I can't breathe. "What do you have in mind?"

She pivots and walks backward. I imagine her taking me by the hand and winding up in some storage closet somewhere, squashed up next to paper products and cleaning supplies, kissing where no security cameras can see.

"Do you want to play 'This Like That'?" At my look of confusion, she explains. "It's that parlor game where one of us says a word and the next person has to find another word that relates in some way, but we could do it with art."

"You mean 'Marry the Pair,'" I correct. "It's a Pavian game."

"Sondish," she insists.

"Pavian."

She bites the smile on her lips. "You start."

We rove the gallery for the next hour, bouncing from an icon of Mary to a contemporary painting of a sparrow by Mary Nenin, to the sparrows in *The Winter Princess*, to a woodcut carved in the same village Cor Hammersmit was born, to a reliquary containing the jawbone of the saint the village was named after. It keeps us busy and distracted. We're keeping it light.

"You win," Freja says, peering into a glass case at a carving of an amber bear, a talisman from a long-dead hunter-gatherer found in a car park excavation.

"What's my prize?"

Freja blushes but she laughs. "The warm satisfaction of knowing you can recall an exhaustive store of information at will?"

I shake my head. We're firefighters tonight, I decide, both of us holding back the heat of our attraction. "I was hoping for a knighthood."

Freja drifts to one of the high, sloping benches and leans against it, stretching her back.

"Ah," she says, closing her eyes. "That's nice." Her head tips up, eyelashes resting against her cheeks.

I was wrong. I'm a firefighter. Freja is an arsonist.

"We should try to sleep," I say. "It will pass the time."

However, the restoration studio is no refuge. I'm too conscious that there aren't working security cameras in this space. Too conscious that the quiet she loves so well envelops us as the doors whisper shut.

I banish it with a flurry of activity, preparing the sofa by tossing the throw pillows to one side and laying out a long blanket, tucking it into the cushions.

"Where do I sleep?" she asks.

"This is yours." I survey the room for more useful things and drag over a chair to act as a side table. Keep busy, I think. Be as stern and Protestant as a Sondishman, born and bred. "I don't keep toothpaste in the studio, but I have some of those peppermint flossers in my desk."

Freja begins her own inspection, opening and closing several drawers, and I hear a cry of surprise. She reaches into my snack horde, drawing out an aluminum tin. "What's this?"

I swallow, remembering her words like she's saying them for the first time. *Kyriekager. The soft kind with the brittle layer of frosting instead of those crispy abominations.*

You can't buy them anywhere. I know. You have to ask Giana if she has a recipe. You have to run up to the inn one Sunday morning and act as her assistant. You have to be willing to receive her broad, amused smiles and overhear her telling Konrad about my newfound love of baking. You have to admit to yourself that Freja matters and that if you can't have her in your life, maybe it's enough to give her cookies and watch her face light up.

It's not enough. Her face lights up and my heart constricts, a painful pressure growing in my chest.

"It's just some *Kyriekager*. Have them if you want." I replace the throw pillows, punching them into shape. "Your bed's ready."

She sighs. "Thank you."

It's the sigh. I put the width of a worktable between us and watch her gobble down a spice cookie.

My father's spirit leans against my desk, hands in his pockets, shaking his head. *Kiss her.*

I glance away, focusing on the painting in front of me, fully cleaned and patched. Areas of damage have been mended and filled, hidden behind the clever application of paint. The restoration process is complete, but the surface is dull and lifeless.

"Now you have time to finish the painting," she says, cradling her tin of cookies and leaning against the table.

"We should wait until we can film this. It's the best part of restoration. The country would love it." I remind her of our audience, inviting them to crowd into the studio with us, praying they save me from myself. But the eyes of Sondmark aren't on us now. Every pair has turned away and we're as isolated as the darkest corner of Elsum Forest.

"*I* would love it." She smiles and tips her head coaxingly.

My hand tightens on the brush.

I dip a wide brush into a container of varnish and begin to lay down a layer in long overlapping stripes, the soft scratch of the bristles the only sound. As I go, details emerge—the intricacy of lace, a loop of beads, the individuality of each curl. In the lamplight, the painting begins to shine, the colors leaping into vibrancy as it transforms. It's the same painting as when I began but something has shifted.

She whispers, "Are you magic?"

I inspect the painting from every angle and set the materials aside. Then I stack my chin on my fists and look at Freja, unconsciously matching my breathing to hers. I know I appear calm. I'm fighting every nerve to maintain the illusion. "You should get some sleep."

She nods, replacing the lid on the tin. In the dim light, she moves swiftly to get a drink and takes a position on the floor.

After a minute of watching, I crouch next to her. "What is this?"

She lets out a labored breath. "Side plank. What does it look like?"

"Is it to correct the curve?" I have no right to ask.

She exhales through gritted teeth and switches position. "Surgery corrected the curve. This is because I can't afford to be weak. Do I look silly? No one watches me do this."

"No. Do you want privacy?"

She laughs, the sound of it is breathy and tired. "It's too late for that."

"Because I've already seen your back?"

She collapses to the floor. "Because you're hard to keep secrets from."

I feel the reaction in my stomach—all roaring adrenaline. The worst of it is that I know what she means. Even when we're not confessing anything with words, I can hardly keep myself from her, either. When the entire world is looking the other way, her eyes are looking at me.

"Help?" she asks, waving her hand. I pull her to her feet, and she doesn't step away or give me space. The worktable is at my back.

She regards me for a long while. Then she leans forward and kisses my cheek, the texture of our skin a study in contrasts. Our hands touch, and I'm disoriented by the simple, glancing contact. I'm falling through a lightning storm. "You didn't get your prize," she explains.

I lift a hand to my cheek, tracing the spot.

"I know, I know," she says, amusement coloring her tone, "it doesn't matter. We've got a lot of other things to worry about right now."

I swear if she comes closer, I'll light on fire.

She yawns, turning slightly and covering her mouth with the back of her hand. "Where will you sleep?"

"I can sleep anywhere," I answer through a yawn.

She narrows her eyes at me. "Just because you can doesn't mean you should. If I get the couch, you get half."

Bad idea. Very bad. What about spontaneous combustion? Sitting next to Freja all night, I could burn through the studio and half our national heritage. *Vede.* She's still too close.

"I—"

"If you don't take it, I won't either. Think of my back after a night in an office chair. You'd probably have to wheel me out of here. My mother might toss you out of the country with her own two hands."

I move away just to put some distance between us and cast myself onto the sofa. Sinking as deeply as I can, I cross my arms and ankles. I close my eyes and say with as much boredom as I can plausibly feign, "I hope you don't snore."

Freja settles on the other end with a light laugh that brushes over my skin. From time to time, she murmurs a few words until she finally drops into sleep. She shifts and turns, swallowing up more and more of the neutral zone until she's leaning awkwardly on my shoulder. I tilt a small lamp away from her face and let my mask fall as I watch her slow, easy breathing.

Nothing has changed. She's still a Sondish princess, I'm still a Pavian immigrant. No matter how much I wish these facts didn't exist, they do. I'm not Freja who can look at the world and trust in miracles.

Nothing's changed.

I have to believe that. If not...My breath catches. If not, I have to admit that everything *has*. Finally, I fold a coat in my lap, and carefully—as careful as I am with priceless things—I shift her sleeping form so that she's stretched out.

"Mm," she murmurs, her hand slipping into mine. I move a lock of hair away from her face. My hand shakes.

Everything has changed.

I love her.

A miracle.

29

SNOWBALL

FREJA

My eyes jerk open and I take a deep breath, inhaling the scent of nutmeg and lemon. Oskar. His arms tighten around me, and I slowly orient myself in space. That's right. We're in the studio on the sofa. I lift my head, and hazy consciousness sharpens into white, hot focus. I'm facing the back of the sofa, curled up against Oskar, my arms wrapped around him.

His face is relaxed and his eyes are closed, but when I stir, his hand cups the back of my head and he settles me against his chest again. I'm all for that. I tighten my hold on him and my eyes drift closed.

There's a jab on the back of my shoulder and I bolt upright, scrambling to the other end of the sofa. Oskar inhales hugely and sits up, washing his face with his hands.

"You guys," Erik says, leaning over us and biting his lip to contain the smile. "This is a place of business."

"If you poke me one more time, you'll lose a finger," I warn.

Oskar breathes a laugh. "*Audicia.*"

For Erik's safety, I get to my feet and rake the hair out of my face, explaining about the alarm, awash in mortification and fumbling for my things. Unhurried, Oskar feeds me my bag and coat. He sets my heels side by side on the floor in front of me, not even emitting a grunt when I lean on his shoulder for balance.

I bend to finish the job, but he brushes my hands away and fastens each tiny buckle around my ankles. The desire to sink back onto the sofa nestles next to an equally strong desire to stuff Erik into a cannon and fire him across the city.

"That looked super uncomfy," Erik says with a bland smile.

"Um," I answer.

Oskar pushes a hand through his hair, stretching his arms wide, his top button straining. That button deserves a medal for showing extraordinary valor in the face of enormous odds. "I have to work," he says. "Take the intern?"

Gladly. I grab Erik's arm and drag him from the room.

"Look at this," Erik says as we jog along the corridor. He lifts his phone, showing an image of me and Oskar wrapped up together, sleeping.

My cheeks pale. Photographic evidence. What does Mama always say about photographic evidence? Burn down the building and bury the bodies.

I skid to a halt. "Erik, you didn't upload it to—"

He snatches the phone back and shakes his head, offended. "I *took* the picture. I didn't *post* the picture." He taps the screen. "There, I sent it to you. I won't share it with another human soul."

I glare at him, but my phone vibrates, and I click to open the attachment. This is not an image of a man suffering another's presence, happy with being friends, fine if he never kisses me again. It's Oskar holding onto me like he's the wreckage of a car I'll need the jaws of life to escape from.

"Invite me to the wedding," Erik sings as he skips down the hall, throwing imaginary rose petals in my path.

I return to the palace for a shower and spend the rest of the day helping my sister. Ella ropes me into putting up a small white Christmas tree in her suite and listening to holiday music as we snack on cookies.

"There are more than forty trees scattered all over the palace," I laugh. "Do you need another?"

"Those aren't Christmas trees. They're designated public servants. Here," she says, plopping a package into my lap. "Help unbox my ornaments."

"I'm sure the palace has extra. You didn't need to buy—" I halt. "What's this?" I hold up a handful of tiny army men.

"The main characters from *Ancestors of the Moon.*"

"One of your Asian dramas?"

She answers around the peppermint in her cheek, smiling at me. "It's been a hard year in the palace. I apologize for nothing."

Further inspection of her packages reveals a dizzying, mismatched assortment of ornaments including a pink octopus, a shopping cart with a tiny old woman in it, a nine-tailed fox, and a miniature claw machine.

I hold up a garland of cable ties. "Do we need to talk?"

She looks up from her task—plunging a full-sized glowing blue sword through the tree while adjusting the angle. "That was a very good show," she smiles.

I toss her a cookie. "I like you."

"I like you, too."

I hold her gaze and the atmosphere shifts. "Mama had Una put up the family tree in her apartment, just like always."

Ella's voice is clipped. "I'm an adult. I wanted to do my own thing."

"It's more than that." She hasn't said so. This is twin intuition leading me.

Ella is as ugly as I am when I cry. Blotchy skin and red eyes. We fight hard to keep from doing it. She clears her throat, fighting now, and I see how angry she is.

"It was fine when we had to act out there," she points beyond the palace gates, "to perform a role and say our lines. It was fine because in here we got to be real people. That was the deal. We knew it could work because it was working for our parents. Well, it's not working for them. It's not working for any of us. We could pretend before Mama and Père—" Her voice is shaking, and she fights for control again.

She smiles, half grimacing, and steps away from the deepest well of emotion with a gusty exhale. "Maybe this is silly," she says, touching the hilt of the sword. "Maybe it's not something any other princess would do, but it makes me laugh and heaven knows we could use a laugh." Her mouth hardens.

"And?"

"And it's a reminder not to be sucked into the machine. I don't have to serve up my life's happiness as an agenda item to be discussed around a conference table."

Her words play on a loop in my head all night. I haven't been fighting against the royal way because the royal way bent easily around my wishes. It's not bending now. I wish for Oskar. The road divides. I choose.

When I make my way to the museum, I find Erik in the admin wing making a face at his computer screen.

"He is the literal worst," he says.

Prime Minister Torbald is taking questions from parliament, and the crawling text beneath his video feed reads, "In Wake of Seong Crisis, PM Pushes Targeted Immigration Caps."

"What's this?" My brother's closest friend is half-Seongan and flew out for relief work. Most of Ella's dramas originate from Seongan studios and she made a sizable, anonymous charitable donation from her personal fortune.

"I can't even." Erik shakes his head and rolls his eyes, clicking away from the news and pulling up a work document. He reaches for his iced Americano. "Do you need something?"

I smile. "I need a favor."

"Shoot."

"I need to change the art and destination for Saturday. And I need you to not tell anyone that I asked."

Erik swings around and pops a straw in his mouth, one of his brows lifting into the stratosphere. "Why do you want to change it, Freja? Why?"

I clear my throat and feel a hot blush wash over my cheeks. "It's a small change. We're swapping out a trip to Luteborg Abbey for a domestic scene of Christmas. It'll be easier to coordinate, and we won't have to make a big trip if the weather gets bad."

"Easier to coordinate. Let's see about that." Erik swivels in his chair and pulls up the art I scoured The Nat database for. The artist is L.S. Thord, and his marionette-like figures have been painted in a quiet room, lit by candles clipped to the tips of a freshly harvested tree. It's titled, simply, *Christmas Eve at Home, 1912.*

"This isn't a super exciting location," Erik says.

I clear my throat. "*Neer* Velasquez has a flat that looks something like that."

"*Neer* Velasquez." His mouth gropes for the straw, and he takes a long pull, his eyes never leaving mine. "We're calling him *Neer* Velasquez? M'kay."

"Knock it off, Erik."

He blinks. "My wedding invitation should include my full name. Erik Gjermund Tørres—"

"Erik."

He begins to tick his fingers. "You'll invite me because, first, I am trustworthy. Second, I have dignity." At my look of skepticism, he bristles. "I was in a brass quartet with a uniform. I wasn't one of these second-rate trombone buskers. Third, I would tell you if your veil was crooked or if there was *fefferfisch* in your teeth."

"I'm horrified that you think I would eat *fefferfisch* before walking down the aisle of Roslav Cathedral under the glare of an international press," I say, suddenly breathless. It's Oskar. I'm imagining Oskar waiting for me at the altar.

The image is clear until I begin to imagine the parliamentary approval process and the endless interviews with the press, the investigation into his family and their ties to the government. In my head, I'm still walking down the aisle, but Oskar disappears, replaced by some faceless groom. My stomach slithers, and I pull myself up short. I've chosen my path. I don't know if there's a future for us, but I've decided to water this little sprout and see if it'll grow.

A gust of wind buffets against the museum, rattling the windows. What kind of gardener decides to grow things in the middle of winter?

"I just want to switch out the art."

Erik taps the changes into the spreadsheet, all the while giving me a knowing glance.

When I've printed out the changes, I bang through the doors of the restoration studio. "Our trip to Luteborg Abbey is off," I say, attempting to sound exasperated. *These interns and their spreadsheets, amirite?* "Something about the logistics."

Oskar glances up from his laptop. It's the first time I've seen him since scrambling off his lap, and my pulse quickens. I feel the memory of his hands at my ankles, fingers brushing over my stockings.

"I thought you'd quiz me on the drive over."

I fuss with my handbag. Finding Creative Ways to Not Look at Oskar Velasquez While I Attempt to Lie is a new hobby I have to get good at fast. "I'm still going to quiz you but on our way to another place."

"Hm?"

"The art was switched out," I say, absentmindedly passing over an informational packet about the new piece as I continue to dig into my bag. My cover story, if asked, is that I'm looking for mints. Darn elusive mints.

He flips back one of the pages and looks up. "This is domestic. Where are we going to film? The artist's residence?"

A curtain of hair hides the red of my cheeks. "No. They thought we could find someplace and decorate it like in the picture." Who is 'they'? I pray this question does not occur to Oskar. "The palace—"

"This isn't a palace."

"*Vede*, you're right."

He lifts his head. I can sense this rather than see his close observation. I'm keeping my hands busy. The silence stretches, and I shift into the second phase of Exasperated, But Quite Plausible, Mint Search by taking each item from my handbag and sorting it on a worktable. Cell phone, wallet, eReader, spare paperback in case my eReader dies, lip balm, each line of my figure hopefully communicating that I've only got half a mind on our conversation.

Another page flips back. "This looks like my flat."

I glance over at his papers which he tips toward me. "Ah."

Phase Three. I turn my handbag upside down and shake. A tin of mints tumbles out and I sigh. A happy end to a desperate search.

I don't like his slightly drawn brows. He's thinking. I don't want him thinking. I flip the tin open and offer him one. He shakes his head.

"We could use my place," he says.

I drop a soft mint onto my tongue, sucking slightly on the lozenge. "Oh?" I say, as though the thought was an island so remote that I was the first seafarer to set foot on it. "We'll have to cut the tree ourselves and find trimmings." I begin to reassemble my purse under his heavy regard.

"I have lights and ornaments if you don't mind some Pavian touches."

"I don't mind."

On Saturday afternoon we meet at The Nat. Oskar puts his head around the door of our office, hand gripping the door jamb. "Ready?" He pauses. "You look..."

"Like a lumberjack?" I laugh, scooping my hair to the side. I'm dressed for the weather. Though I prefer wide-legged slacks, I'm wearing a pair of high-waisted wool pants and lace-up boots. I've topped this off with a 1940s-style cropped sweater jacket and a soft scarf.

"You look like you. I wondered how you would, in snow clothes."

"You were expecting a crocheted poncho and balaclava?"

"I wasn't expecting—"

He looks at the door, at his watch, and at the bookshelves. He does that whenever he's tempted to kiss me, I think. Every time. Like my lips are a tractor beam and he's in danger of being caught.

He's not wrong. I do plan to catch him.

On our way out, we pass the thermometer. The ends have curled up from being frequently handled, and it looks more authentic than ever. The nearer we get to Christmas, the thinner the lines are. We need almost 30,000 more, and there isn't enough time. I haven't said so out loud. None of us have.

"We need something big," Oskar says, catching my glance.

"Bigger than a 1400-year-old Viking ship?" Roland's latest enthusiasm.

"Come," he says, breaking me from a reverie in which I'm single-handedly responsible for the shuttering of The Nat and countless artifacts crumbling into obscurity, plunging the world into a new dark age.

He leads me to a sturdy, all-wheel drive car. "I borrowed it from Cousin Tomas." He looks around. "No security?"

I shake my head. "There's lots of coming and going at the palace this week—lots of guests. Security is stretched thin."

"I wasn't planning to abduct a princess, but the time seems auspicious." He adjusts the rearview mirror. "By the way, I brought a saw."

I choke on a laugh. "Driving into the deep woods with a man carrying a saw. I can't wait to debrief with the security team."

We pull onto the ring road, and soon we settle into our customary pattern. I fire off question after question with the aid of my sister's app. "What was the year Viggo Faxeborg published his first collection of folk tales?"

"1835."

I nod. "The name?"

"*Fantastical Stories for Young Minds.*"

"Your favorite?"

He looks over from the road, brown eyes amused. "Is that going to be on the test?"

I point guilelessly at the phone. "I just read the questions."

He smiles without actually smiling. "'The Steadfast Plowman.'"

I wrinkle my brow, recalling the plot. A young man is promised riches beyond imagining by a witch who tells him to plant a yearly harvest, reap the grain and weave the last sheaf into a cross, storing up reserves. He grows rich and old and fat, passing away in his bed after having the best slice of Christmas pudding he's ever had in his life.

I shake my head at Oskar. "'The Steadfast Plowman' isn't anyone's favorite."

Oskar follows the GPS toward the Elsum Forest Reserve. As we gain in elevation, the snow becomes deeper on the plowed edges of the road and into the woods.

"Wouldn't the Citizenship Board be happy to hear that an immigrant already loves such prized national virtues as thrift and hard work?" he returns.

I don't love this, the way he has of detaching himself from Sondmark, holding us at arm's length. "Give me your real answer."

"Will you get back to quizzing me if I do?"

I make a signal in the air between us. "Promise."

We are silent until the road bends, crossing a narrow river. Droplets of spray have frozen on the rocks below, turning them into downy pillows. The silence doesn't make me fidget or shift. He'll answer when he's ready.

He releases a breath as though confessing to a petty crime that covers him in no honor. "'The Boy and the Nykur Horse.'"

Green and white flash past the windows as I recall the story. A lost boy befriends a nykur horse—a creature with the terrible power to trap a person with its sticky hide and barrel roll them into the depths of the sea. Because the little boy loves and trusts him, the horse betrays his nature and carries the boy away on adventures.

"Where did the horse take you," I ask, "in your imagination?"

"Pavieau...at first." He turns a rueful smile at me. "I could hear the thunder of his hooves pounding down the cobblestones of Gransoleil, and I'd bounce along on his back like a sack of potatoes."

I smile and the car, so spacious when we began our journey, narrows. I see the child who wanted to go home. I see the little boy who must have whooped and laughed before he discovered how to brace himself for the worst of his adopted land.

The hum of the engine fills the space. If he loved and trusted me, I would betray my nature—the nature of a woman who likes to be alone—and take him on adventures.

I clear my throat. "Name the five enchanted trials of 'The Woodsman's Daughter.'"

The road narrows and becomes more winding until, eventually, Oskar steers the car into a layby and cuts the engine. We could be teenagers. I open my mouth to say so, snapping it shut when I remember that you can't make a kissing joke to a man you want to actually kiss. Not if kissing hasn't been nailed down as an itinerary item.

He shifts and my breath catches.

Click. His seatbelt unfastens, and he steps out of the car leaving me feeling as though I've been nearly swept off a cliff, pushed back onto the grass by a chance gust of wind. I breathe deliberately and step into the snow, tugging on my knitted cap.

Oskar, handling his saw, halts.

"What?"

He's silent for too long, but I know how to wait. He tugs the end of my scarf. "I like this."

Turning, he leads us into the woods where the ground is uneven. Pockets of snow camouflage hidden holes, and it takes a half-hour of scrambling over tree trunks and boulders before we find a likely candidate—a Nordmann fir, one-and-a-half meters high.

"Perfect," I say, charmed by the tiny scale of it when contrasted against the tree in the Great Hall of the Summer Palace which almost brushes the ceiling.

I unfold a tripod and set the camera up, framing Oskar and the tree. "Ready?"

He nods, putting his back into getting the tree down as I introduce our subject. Soon, I hear the crack of the trunk and a glistening Oskar fetches up at my side, holding the tree at the top.

"In Lothar Thord's day," he begins, "he didn't have to buy a permit to cut down a Christmas tree. Families would load into sleds…"

Oskar seems distracted, losing himself in minute details of the period and art style. This is not why people watch us. I smile at the camera, stepping away and bending over a feathery pile of snow. Shucking off the mittens, I press snow with frozen but dexterous hands while he continues, too conscious of his duties in front of the camera to look around.

"…when Thord found fulfillment in domestic life, he became—"

In a Christmas miracle, I achieve the perfect aim, and my snowball bursts against Oskar's neck. He whips around, brushing it away, but more than half slides into his collar.

"Freja!" he shouts.

I laugh, taking over the narration.

"So that's the feeling Lothar Thord was trying to get at. He—" I duck the snowball flying at my head, my words squeezed off in a yelp.

There's no help for it. I continue the informational presentation in a crouch, grubbing for more snow, packing five balls, and dodging his volleys before being knocked square in the middle of my back. I fall onto my knees, wheezing.

"He was a day laborer but led a happy home life," I sputter at the camera, firing off a snowball and clipping Oskar's shoulder. "Some believe this tension elucidates—"

"Woman. Did you really say 'elucidates' in the middle of a snowball fight?" he calls, nailing me in the side.

I scoop the remaining ammunition into my arms and square off against my foe. Instead of standing his ground, he advances quickly, and we fight over what's left, a tug of war I'm determined to win until I lose my footing. Grabbing out, I clutch him, and we fall together. He twists, and we land in a thick drift.

Whomp.

He's underneath me, taking the brunt, our lips a hair's breadth away, cold air swirling between us, thickening into a fog. I wanted today to end this way, but not yet. Not on screen. Oskar's eyes are closed, hands wrapped around my waist.

"Let me loose," I whisper.

He doesn't stir. He's so gorgeous, and I feel the impact of it in my solar plexus—a blow that has knocked the wind from my lungs and the sense from my head.

We're still on camera. I pat his cheek, going up on all fours. "I can't have killed you in the middle of a live broadcast. The country would revolt."

His brow quirks up, even as his eyes remain closed. "Broken," he groans, lifting his head, closing the distance between us, his cold lips almost brushing mine. I jerk away and he flops back, arm outflung.

"Oskar?" I say, a tiny bit worried. I inspect his face, limbs, and torso more closely. He flinches away from my touch. I lean in to hear his breathing when he moves in a motion so fluid, I can hardly break apart the pieces—the lifting of my collar, the tightening of his abs under my hand, the sweep of his arm, and the ice-cold snow washing down my back.

I yelp and scramble off him, shaking the snow further down my back. "You traitor," I cry. "You goblin. I was checking for vitals."

He brushes the snow from himself and reaches for the tree. Then he gives a wolfish smile. "Shall we return to our guests?"

Dirty trick, using all of Sondmark as his shield. I give him a withering side-eye and turn to the camera.

"Thank you for joining us for Part One of Lothar Thord's *Christmas Eve at Home, 1912*. We'll be back in a few hours for Part Two, *Let's Bury Oskar Velasquez in the Woods*."

30

It's Tradition

OSKAR

"Next question," I prompt, guiding the car through late afternoon traffic. The weak winter sun has slipped below the horizon, and the city is ablaze with light. Evergreen boughs hang above the streets, the swags threaded with fairy lights and ornamental stars. White lights wrap up the trunks and branches of nearly every tree we pass.

When we crawl through an intersection, I catch sight of hatted and gloved dancers in an open square and hear the strains of a brass band. The scent of sausages sizzling on a brazier is carried on the night air. My roots are shallow in this country, reaching across the topsoil, braced against the constant buffets of unbelonging, but sometimes I send down a taproot, winding around bedrock, drinking deeply of elemental waters, anchoring me to this place. There is nothing like Christmas in Sondmark.

"Who was The Stone Princess promised to in marriage?" Freja asks.

I frown. Any talk of princesses and contractual marriages is as liable to give me indigestion as the sausages. I pray this specific irritation passes.

"The Lord of Starlight," I say, pulling the answer from my store of knowledge, ignoring the way I want to reach for her hand, threading her fingers in mine, brushing my thumb over them.

When we pull onto my street, I spy an empty spot near the block of flats, just large enough. Lining up the wheels of the car, I reach behind Freja's headrest, turning my head to gauge my angles. Spinning the wheel, I slot the car into position quickly.

"Show off," she taunts before I have a chance to subside back in my seat. I grip the steering wheel, conscious of how close Freja is, her profile rimmed in the glow of a streetlight.

I've lost the capacity to take things lightly in the last hours—when I chose between keeping my feet and letting Freja fall or holding her close and falling together. It's as though I've finally been dragged to the well of self-reflection, the enormity of my feelings for her like a remorseless hand on my neck, plunging my face into the water and making me drink. This isn't a game. I'm not going to get over her. I can't fight it anymore. I'm ruined.

I put my hands on the steering wheel. Ten and two.

I know how to repair things that are ruined, I think, my mind slipping into the mode of an art restorer. Stabilize the piece. Clean it up. Patch the tears. Disguise the damage.

That's the answer. Do my work so skillfully in the next few hours that my feelings will be invisible. Whether we win or lose the prime minister's challenge, this is the last time we have to meet like this.

I breathe, turning the car off.

"I'll get the box," she says. "Do you need help with the tree?"

I grunt a negative, undoing the twine. Pulling the tree from the roof of the car, I tap the trunk against the pavement to rid it of misty droplets and fir needles insufficiently committed to making the trek to my flat.

As we climb the stairs, her phone pings and vibrates.

"How can you put up with that?" I ask, unlocking the door, and leading her down the hall. I've examined the question from every angle, deeming it safe before I allow it into the wild to pollinate Freja's possible answers.

"Oh, sorry," she breathes, unwrapping herself from the coat and scarf, folding them over a chair, and pushing the sleeves of a soft white sweater to her elbows. "It's my sister."

"Alma?" I ask. Alma is the one in the news, with the fiancé who hasn't returned from Lijuela. The one asking parliament for permission to marry a man everyone knows her mother picked out for her. The one whose wedding is spoken of endlessly.

Freja shakes her head.

I will never tire of the way her hair picks up the light. I frown at the thought. My plan to disguise my feelings is off to a poor start.

"It's Ella. She keeps me up on things." Holding her phone out, she bounces it lightly in her fingers. *Take it. See.*

I do, scrolling down the list of messages.

@Morrissey_is_Murder: Freja is the new Clara. #ThinkAboutIt #TabloidFodder #TeamFrejaGetsSome

@JelloBlogger/GovWatcher: FYI, Torbald's policy would push Oskar Velasquez out of the country. #NationalTreasure #ReformImmigrationNow #HotPaviansofSondmark

@SamuraiMamacita: What do we think, fam? Is this a staged romance or an innocent fall? Why was it off-screen when the whole snowball thing was front and center? Why are they teasing us? Why is the Queen allowing it? #questions #ReformImmigrationNow

@trashpandaprincess: If our skies were full of drones, we would have that out-of-frame footage already. #TheCaseforUniversalSurveillance #ReformImmigrationNow

The last has a screenshot of the toppled tree, an expanse of snow, and our boots tangled together. It's a suggestive image, and I lift my head to see Freja regarding me closely. Disguise. It's best to set her back on her feet and me on mine.

I hand the phone over. "Is this a problem?"

Freja laughs. "All publicity is good publicity, right?"

We've both been playing games, dancing right on the edge of outright flirtation, knowing in the back of our minds that it increases our visitors. I don't know what she means anymore. Worse, I know exactly what I mean.

"Mm. We should get started."

Soon, we are at our self-designated tasks, taking a few still pictures and short video clips as we set the scene up.

"Paige, play Christmas carols," she says, making herself at home. She peels off her boots and pads around the flat in wool socks, moving to and from the kitchen with a charcuterie board and mugs of *Glogg*.

"You look like you know what you're doing," she says, assessing my progress.

"My father didn't want to be the expert," I reply, wrestling the tree into a stand.

Freja is untangling a string of lights. She doesn't answer or indicate that she's waiting for me to finish the thought. Nevertheless, she's listening with her whole body.

Unexpected emotion lodges in my throat. "When I cleared Christmas away, just after he passed, I dumped everything into boxes and shoved them in a closet. I'm sure things are broken."

I nod, returning my attention to the tree—to get it as level as my father would have liked. I turn the tree so a snapped branch is to the back.

"Our trees have always been big," she says, plugging a string of lights into an outlet, testing them. "I'd get tired before we finished trimming it and run away to read."

I like imagining Freja as a young girl, with two bright braids running down her back, resisting group activities.

"Help?" she says, and we pass the bundle of lights around the tree, our hands brushing as it goes back and forth. There's no witty banter. We're not even flirting. But the simple rhythm of our work makes me finely attuned to her.

"What am I doing wrong?" I ask. She didn't even have to say anything for me to see that she's been trying to steer my hands with her eyeballs.

"That branch is bald," she accuses with a laugh. "I like to light a Christmas tree as though it's the only thing standing in the way of me and seasonal depression."

She likes her own turn of phrase, and her lips twitch in amusement.

I want to toss the lights aside and push her back into the rug, covering her mouth with mine, discovering the finer points of how she likes to be kissed. We haven't had enough time to find out—no slow, unpromised hours to explore the question. We don't have it now.

So I unclench my fist and beckon for the lights. "Is that how mental health works?"

We finish with the tree, set it in the middle of the room, and consult the painting several times. We scoot the sofa back and rest a tray of food on a nearby ottoman.

"Ready?" I ask. She nods and I press the button.

Unlike our romp in the snow, we deliver this video in a controlled fashion.

I lean towards the screen to read the comment feed. "User *@højpumpkinspicecoffee* asks, 'Aren't you going to hold hands and sing around the tree?'" I look to Freja. "It's tradition. How's your singing?"

She smiles. "You know how the Sleeping Princess was given the gifts of Beauty and Song by her fairy godmothers?"

I nod.

"Yes, well in my case, I was gifted with Ordering at Restaurants and Finding Quiet Places to Read."

"Those are really good gifts."

"The best," she laughs.

Vede. She's easy to love. My feelings are all over my face for the whole *flamen* country to see. I swallow them back. "Don't you sing at Christmas?"

"Always."

I turn to the camera. "I do too. All right, Sondmark, what would you like?"

Suggestions pour in ranging from old folk songs to modern pop classics. I read them out. "'Piglets Will Warm Our Grandma,' 'Gentle Queen Agnetha,' 'An Orange to Keep from Starving'—that's a little dark—'When There's No Snow There's No Christmas,' 'Poisoned By a Mistletoe Kiss,' 'The Dead Return as Sparrows'…. For the love of heaven, what is wrong with you people?"

"We enjoy the bleak, the grim, the faint possibility of imminent death." Freja smiles. "Do you know any Pavian carols?"

"I know all the Pavian carols. 'Basket of Plenty,' 'Bebe Jesu on the Sea,' 'Cinnamon Churias'…"

"I know that one." She explains for the benefit of our audience, "It imagines a fourth pilgrim who brought his treasure of fried dough to the Christ child. We make *churias* at the palace on Christmas Eve, along with traditional Sondish *oliebollen,* and sing the song. I think I can manage it if you don't laugh at my accent," she says, holding her hands out.

The Sondish tradition is to have a larger group making a complete circle around the tree. We simply clasp hands and I allow my thumb the indulgence of brushing against her knuckles. Not too much.

"Hm, hm," she intones, finding a pitch. "Start us off?"

I lift my chin, and as I nod, we begin.

Soft and sweet

I travel the weary road alone…

It's a slow and simple song. Freja meets my eyes and swings my hands gently. As she promised, her voice is thin, but her accent is good. Like mine, it's better when we sing. My heart tightens painfully. This is a Pavian song folded into a Sondish tradition. As our voices trail off, I clear my throat, wanting no traces of emotion when I speak to an audience. Freja tightens her fingers.

"*Joieau Natal,*" I say, voice thick with memories of my parents. "As you know, we—we—" I swallow, pressure building behind my eyes. *Dominanstid,* I'm going to cry in front of a national audience. My hand shakes and my jaw sets as I wait for it to pass. I wait.

Freja slides her arm around my waist.

"We still need more visitors to The Nat to reach our goal. Come see Lothar Thord's *Christmas Eve at Home* in the Magda Wing and make your holidays a little brighter. From our home to yours, Merry Christmas!" She waves, bends over the phone, and cuts the feed.

31

ANOTHER PROMISE

FREJA

I know what it looks like when I say, "From our home to yours," with my arm around his waist. My emotions don't allow for a palatable edit—for striking a red pencil through the words, replacing them with banalities. *For everyone out there...*

Ella's eyes have probably melted out of their sockets. It's just as well I silenced my phone.

I thought I was so clever, finding a way to help Oskar decorate his flat for Christmas, getting a date in the bargain. I didn't anticipate being completely undone by the sudden tightening of his chin, my ordinary "trying not to panic as I livestream in front of Sondmark" feelings shoved aside, replaced with a ferocious, ungovernable desire to protect.

I exhale a short laugh. I've never belonged to anyone but myself. Ella would say it's my brand, honed to a fine edge—the Lone Wolffe, the one with her nose in a book, the one who is sought out, not seeking—but I'm not wholly my own anymore.

So this is love.

I give Oskar a tiny shake.

"Hug," I say, unsure if I'm offering or asking but Oskar pulls me into his arms anyway, our heads angling to fit one another more closely.

I like how we match, his height not dwarfing me, his frame not swallowing me up. Instead, we hold and are held, and the knowledge of it falls onto the mountain of things I love about him. *Plink.* Another grain of rice has been added to a pile a thousand miles high. Where did the mountain come from? How did it accumulate without my knowledge? I imagine a parade of ants, each carrying a tiny grain past my busy feet, dropping their burden into a cavity until it became so big that even I—who cannot perceive anything beyond a book held at the end of my arm—can see the immensity of it.

He smells of evergreen trees and mulled wine. *Plink, plink.* I grip the collar of his shirt and breathe it in.

"I don't know what that was," he says, hand running down my back, fingers skimming the scars, the rods, the spine hauled into obedience. I ought to feel exposed. Instead, I shiver with newfound strength.

"Hm?" My question is muffled against his shoulder.

"Losing it on a live video feed."

I rub my cheek over the soft fibers of his sweater. "It's the first year. Of course, it's hard."

"Mm," he acknowledges, hands continuing their lazy way up and down my back.

"Did your father hate *Glögg*?"

He laughs and the rumble vibrates down to my toes. I nestle closer.

"*Vede*, yes. How did you guess?"

"Père says it tastes like pie filling. It must be their Pavian tongues."

Another laugh and he tightens his arms. "Thanks."

I'm not certain I can speak without my mountain of rice spilling into the light. I hold my breath until it hurts under my jaw and behind my eyes. "Mm?"

"For stepping in for me when—" I am held fractionally closer. "And for making me decorate for Christmas, too."

I lift my head. "You cut down the tree. You hauled it up here."

He nods, but there is a smile. "We would have gone to the abbey instead. Why—"

Does he know I arranged all this? I shift back a few millimeters, blood drumming in my ears. Is he about to bring this into the light while he's studying for his citizenship test? *Stultes es*, we're failing to meet the prime minister's deadline. We can't do this. We can't.

"I liked the Thord painting better," I say, untangling myself from his arms. He holds on for a moment—the space of a breath—then his arms go slack.

He nods, bending to pick up one of the food trays, eyes shifting away from mine. When he disappears into the kitchen, I wander to the window, looking out on the dark city. It's clear and cold. I hear the water running and the clink of dishes as he washes up. Glancing along the bookshelf, I come to the drafting table. It's messier than on Saint Luz's Day. There's a box of pens, tips with various thicknesses, and an array of brushes stacked on a flat surface. A traditional Pavian mug with paint stains around the rim sits next to a tray of watercolors.

I run my finger around the edge. Oskar keeps his restoration studio neat as a pin, and this is positively untidy. There's even a series of papers stacked on the table as though he hastily tipped out a box.

Unlike Adelheid Nede, I would make a terrible spy, but the sound of the sink settles the nerves in my stomach and I perform a closer inspection. Clipped to the edge of the table is a series of preliminary sketches–the fall of a bow, the curve of a brow, the pattern of a blouse.

My eyes narrow. I recognize that pattern. Vintage van Brandt. Below these pages is a list, written out with red ink and black ink and pencil in various modes of Oskar's hand. "Mid-length skirts, blouses with bows, *The Winter Princess*, fortune cookies, any cookies, sparkling water, scarf weather, baked goods, the V&A museum, *Kyriekager*..."

The sound of my breathing is loud in the lonely room. I unfold a rectangle of paper to see a series of painted squares and a few scribbles alongside. "Freja, Studio, Autumn."

Freja? My heart beats out a deep, resonant rhythm. The noise from the kitchen gets louder and I glance up, mouth going dry. Hurry. Hurry.

I lift the last paper and clap a hand over my open mouth, pinching off a gasp.

It's me.

It's other things too—a portrait, the head and torso circumscribed by a frame in gold leaf, the style marrying Sondish folk art and the delicacy of an old-fashioned miniature. But it's me, and somehow I knew it would be.

My mind splinters, half of it sounding like static and looking like the empty vacuum of space, the other half absorbing every facet of the painting before time is chased down a drain. I take in that the ornate wallpaper behind my figure hides tiny details–a dumpling and pair of chopsticks, a small but detailed reproduction of *The Winter Princess*, the earrings I wear most often, a looping river of words, *You must wade into the river to catch a fish...in a tiara*.

The water stops, and it takes a second to register the silence. I dive toward the ornament box, busying my hands by flattening and stacking large tissue paper squares. My flaming cheeks are the only sign I'm not just another industrious Lutheran, filling every idle hour.

Oskar halts at the head of the hall, observing. There isn't a whisper of suspicion in his eyes. Still, my heart is charging in my chest, banging on the walls so loudly it's a miracle he can't hear.

"You don't need to help me clean up," he says, rolling his sleeves down.

Don't do that. Don't hide them away. Perhaps I could send up a prayer to Santo Laurenzi? Yes. The good Lord created forearms. Oskar's hands still, he pushes his sleeves up again, leaning against the back of the sofa.

Maybe someone with a better grasp of physics would understand the way time is bending and folding within this small flat on the west end of Handsel. Perhaps they would have an answer to the questions blinking in my mind. Have Oskar and I known each other for three years? Or only properly for three months? How long does it take to know someone well enough to stake your life on it?

Frederick knew Elsa for eight days.

My eyes flick to the drafting table, and he clears his throat. "We did a good job," he says. A distraction. What would he do if I asked him about the illustration? Lie. I know this because I know him. He'll tell me it's a Christmas gift, something he tossed together in an afternoon. Or he'll say it's an exercise, a way to keep his hand in, fingers nimble for restoration work. But I know what I saw—weeks of painstaking work and a man with an intimate knowledge of his subject. I saw the effort of someone who took the time to watch and know. I saw his heart.

I try to press a piece of tissue paper smooth, my clammy hands fouling it up as astonishment squeezes the air out of my lungs. I want to excuse myself, barricading myself in the dark, close confines of his coat closet to come to terms with the fact that my entire future has been blasted to pieces and I'm not even mad. I thought I could follow Mama's plan for us all because I was someone who wouldn't care very much either way if a husband was found for me or if I found one on my own. Six of one, half a dozen of the other, as the British say.

No more. I bite the inside of my cheek as Clara does. My Swiss school has a lot to answer for. My training does a poor job of cooling my skin and steadying my heartbeat.

"This is the last Saturday feature before Christmas," he says.

"Right," I answer, brisk like a Sondish housewife sweeping her threshold. We have to stay focused on The Nat. "I'll see you at the museum?"

He nods, his gaze shifting away. Why hadn't I seen it before—the extraordinary care he takes to hide himself from me? A line of ants, each scurrying a burden of rice in the other direction, adding grains to another pile. Now that I've seen them, it's impossible *not* to see them, and I want to follow the parade, discovering what's at the journey's end.

"We should schedule a time to study," I say.

"After Christmas," he answers. "You deserve a break." He rolls his forearm and checks his watch.

Of course. It's been a difficult day for him. I pick up my phone and type out a text. "Freddie is waiting to pick me up," I say, hopping to my feet. I fumble for my scarf and coat.

He takes the coat and holds it out, hands gripping the collar. I walk into it, and he clears his throat.

"What?"

"Nothing. I like this on you," he allows.

I think of the illustration, the careful notes. I wonder if he'll make a study of this. Freja in a Winter Coat. We could hang it in The Nat and charge a few *markke* to see it. I might finally get satisfaction when the entire world reads the words we can't speak, filling column inches of newsprint, torrents of digital commentary, to repeat the truth that Freja loves Oskar and Oskar loves Freja.

I struggle with the zipper and want to laugh. There's nothing short of spending my life loving Oskar that will give me satisfaction. My hands freeze and the realization lands with all the subtlety of a nuclear warhead. *Vede.* My tastes have always been specific, but not wanting anything more in this life than a taciturn Pavian art restorer in a dress shirt on a Saturday is more than specific.

I tug the zipper and feel it catch on the fabric, only adding to my frustration. Loving him is one thing. Being ruined for anyone else is another. Ruined after, what, two kisses? He hasn't even asked me on a date. What if it doesn't work between us? What's the answer then? Cats? Am I going to have to get a lot more cats?

I tug harder, anxious to be gone.

He puts his hand over mine, stilling them. "Let me do it."

My throat is closing, and I plan to cry down three flights of stairs. "Freddie's waiting. I have to go."

Oskar doesn't step back, only bends his head over his task to free the small metal tab at my waist. I could touch his hair and he might not even know.

Then he says, his voice low, the words forced from him, "I hate it when you go."

He looks up and his hands tighten. The noise of the day skitters past like a puppy on a hardwood floor—the snowball splash of midday, the frozen breathlessness of being nose-to-nose, the cautious tightrope walk of speaking on camera. But, here, within the circle we form together, it's perfectly quiet.

"Freja." It's a breath of sound. Expressions chase across his face, hope and hopelessness warring over the same ground. "Freja."

"Stop thinking so much," I say. Stop expecting so little. "What do you want?"

He smiles and his chin tips away like, *Can you believe this girl?* "I want to kiss you."

I reward him with a reproving frown. "Finally."

That's the last word I get before he pulls me to him, hands spanning my waist. His mouth covers mine, and I push my fingers through his hair, inhaling his scent. I expected something tentative and cautious. Something nice as he crossed this threshold.

This isn't nice. This is a wolf, I think as we ricochet slowly down the hall, searching for a place to forget that my security detail is waiting in a car on the street.

I touch his neck, feel the pulse race and his breath break in his lungs. It would be wise to withhold some portion of myself, setting it aside like a cookie folded into a napkin to be saved for later. But this isn't that kind of kiss.

Curling my fingers around his shirt, I tug him closer as he presses me against a wall. I feel a light scrape of facial hair and smile. We have found our place.

He lifts his head a fraction, his eyes tracing the lines of my face.

"What?" he asks, bracing his forearms on either side of my head.

"You've been thinking about doing that for a while."

He nuzzles my hair aside and kisses the spot under my ear. "How did you guess?"

A tremor runs along my veins, and I almost slide to the floor. "You're too good to have never given it any thought."

He shifts, pressing a soft kiss against the curve of my neck. I give a low laugh and he returns, eyes searching my face.

"We have to go on a date," he says. "An actual date. Not takeout in the studio."

The kiss was more momentous than a date, but this is a nod to conventions. We have to begin as others do.

I bite the smile spreading across my lips. "I'm booked up. It'll have to be after Christmas."

He nods, amused as I am by this conversation which has none of the tentative gestures between people who are at the beginning.

"After Christmas. Now, stop smiling. I can't kiss you until you do."

I rearrange my mouth. He leans forward, and there's a tap on the door.

Right against my lips, Oskar utters a beastly oath. He gives me a quick kiss. I repair my lipstick with the pad of my thumb, willing my heart to get out of my throat.

He opens the door, and I turn to look. It's Uncle Timo bearing a dish for Oskar's dinner with two oversized Christmas oven mitts, his face beaming. A more merry sight would be impossible to imagine. Who wouldn't want to see Uncle Timo?

Me. Right now, me.

"A guest," the old man beams. "Your Royal Highness, are you going to stay—?"

Having dinner across the table from Oskar without being able to touch? It would taste like sawdust. "No, no, I really must go. My security officer is waiting."

Uncle Timo gives me a brief bow, and Oskar catches my eyes above his head.

Later? A flash of a feral, wolfish smile.

Later. It's a promise.

I move quickly into the stairwell, fanning my warm cheeks. I cast a glance back toward the gleaming brass number and make another promise.

I'm going to marry that man.

32

A Sacrifice

FREJA

Despite wanting to cancel everything and take up a semi-permanent residence against the wall in Oskar's flat, the last Sunday before Christmas is busy. My mother's family has been arriving all weekend, bringing dogs and children, and the expectations of aristocrats used to being looked after by people paid to forget that the word "no" exists in any language.

I've managed to stay out of the melee with my work at the museum but am swept up on Sunday into a series of public-facing Christmas celebrations including a carol concert and a morning walk to the parish church, all of us bundled up in synthetic furs except for Tante Ann-Margrethe who refuses to wear polyester and smokes like a chimney. We're expected to ignore the crowd on the way into the church but have a brief walkabout afterward

The crowd, devoted royal watchers willing to stand in such weather, are delighted to see us, dipping into curtseys and nodding bows, teaching small children to do the same. We aren't to let it go to our heads, Mama taught. It's not us they're honoring. It's the nation, embodied by the royal family. That's well and good, but it doesn't stop signals of more particular affection.

Someone brought a pink flamingo balloon because they know Ella likes flamingos and she grips it in her gloved hand like a child at the zoo. Another person tells me they've been to the museum six times since October.

"I even saw you with him, once." Him. Oskar. She smiles brightly, unzipping her jacket (worrying Freddie briefly) to show me her #TeamOskar t-shirt. "My husband is Sondish but I'm from Motovia," she says. Something that might have been a non sequitur six months ago feels central now because an immigrant is commanding a large share of the national conversation.

"Thank you for coming. I'm glad you felt welcome," I say, fighting the wish to throw off the unnatural reserve of royalty by whispering, "Isn't Oskar the most delicious? He kissed me last night, you know."

I imagine Oskar at my side, learning to shake hands with strangers and be polite at all times. It's an odd picture until I remember how he was with Hafsa's school group as they toured his studio last week—patient and funny. He even prepared an amateur oil painting bought at a junk shop for the kids to "clean."

I move on, eyes watering from the biting chill, and see Caroline take another bouquet from my mother. Too bad. One of Caroline's gloves is missing and her fingers are red with cold, but we're in the middle of an engagement so she can't return to the church to grope under a pew for the missing article.

An uptick of excitement on my side of the pathway alerts me to my brother crossing over the gravel drive, warming the hearts of those who came for the man candy, I guess. Instead of going to the barricade, he bends—setting off another flutter—and collects something from the ground, then proceeds to Caroline. I should ignore it, but the young woman I've been shaking hands with has gone into a fugue state watching Noah, mouth slack, allowing me to give the byplay more attention than usual.

Caroline's face is carefully devoid of expression, and her hands are full of flowers. She stares at the proffered glove. She angles her hand, still securing the flowers, to take it. He shakes his head and scoops the flowers into his arms, handing off the glove, along with a low-voiced instruction. Why does she look so irritated?

Finally, Caroline fixes a sedate smile on her face, tugs the glove on, and reaches for the flowers. Noah, however, has moved ahead, handing the huge bouquet to his secretary and returning to the barricades.

"What was that?" The young woman has reanimated, echoing my own thoughts.

I smile and withdraw my hand. "Thank you for coming."

During the afternoon, I serve meals at a domestic abuse shelter with Alma, returning to the palace to be enveloped by dozens of guests hailing from every major area in northern Europe. We enjoy a cozy dinner, read Luke 2 by candlelight with my little cousins squished up next to us on the sofas, and play a rowdy game of charades.

When I make my excuses at the end of the night, Ella moans, "Tomorrow's Christmas Eve. You can't work."

"The Nat is open," I say. And Oskar will be there, I don't say.

I spend the night staring at my ceiling, fingers knitting an invisible scarf of worry, convincing myself that his silent declarations were no more than a bout of indigestion. Too much cheese. No, I decide when the sun comes. This is real. Like a spell, we only have to speak it into existence.

Over breakfast, as extended family members file in and out, I read the newspaper headlines. There's a significant feature about Oskar in *The Holy Pelican*—the most stodgy and mainline publication in all of Sondmark—detailing his contributions to The Nat, even going so far as to editorialize about the prime minister's proposals. "Things cannot remain as they are when Sondmark is perceived as closing its doors on its most dedicated and talented residents."

The prime minister is quoted too. "The path to citizenship is arduous, making it all the more valued when it is achieved. Our laws cannot bend, not even to Pixy dances and internet fangirls."

It's almost enough to put me off a full English breakfast.

Chewing away at the beans on toast, I see that Caroline, too, has made the cover of a few newspapers as a peripheral figure in the story about Noah's unexpected gallantry, her face obscured by flowers or her figure almost cropped out of the photos. "See," they seem to say, "he's perfect. He even treats completely ignorable people with consideration."

I meet Caroline on my way out of the Summer Palace and give her a sympathetic smile. "I'm sorry about the press," I say, tugging my gloves on.

She waves a hand. "It's part of the job. I can't take it personally." Her head straightens, and I recognize a shift into official mode. "Her Majesty is in a meeting with the prime minister and asked that you join them."

I check my watch. *Vede.* I wanted to be at The Nat first thing. I wanted Oskar to see me camping out by the door of his studio, ready to settle our future of getting to kiss each other whenever we have a mind to. "It's not the prime minister's day."

"It was an unscheduled visit," she says, leading me through the administrative wing at a brisk pace. She's smaller than I am, her strides shorter, but I have to work to keep up.

We fetch up outside my mother's official sitting room, the one that appears in portraits of new ambassadors and visiting envoys. Other prime ministers have been invited into Mama's inner sanctum—her office, two doors down—but not this one.

Caroline gives me a bracing smile and swings the door open. "Ma'am…"

I'm not sure why I have been summoned, and my suspicions are aroused when Mama offers me coffee and a cookie. She knows how weak I am for mid-morning snacks.

"*Neer* Torbald has an offer he'd like to discuss."

Prime Minister Torbald gives me a tight smile. "We've both won the match, Your Highness. The Nat of today is far more welcoming than The Nat of only three months ago. The galleries are filled with Sondish people rediscovering their heritage. The country is impressed, and so am I…even if you will fall short of the numbers we agreed upon." Amid so much magnanimity, there's a sting.

"We still have eight days until the new year."

"Can't count Christmas. And have you seen the forecast? A blizzard tonight. Our infrastructure will be snarled for days, and you still need thirty thousand visitors. It won't happen without a monumental exhibit, something on the order of Moses's original stone tablets signed by the Almighty, himself."

I open my mouth to reply, but Mama touches my arm. *Wait. Hear him out.*

Neer Torbald reaches for a cookie, takes a bite, and uses the rest as a pointer. "We'll ignore the deadline and the numbers—start with a blank slate. You had your heart set on the Romantics exhibit. The government will fully fund it, and you won't have to look for change in the sofa or beg for corporate sponsorship. We'll do an ad campaign, transportation vouchers to get the school kids in…whatever you need. I'll make the announcement today."

Mama takes a sip of coffee and flicks me a glance. "That's quite generous."

My midsection tightens with sudden awareness. Mama knows. She knows what comes next. I tend to be distracted and blind to things in front of my face, but I'm not her daughter for nothing. "What do you get in return?"

His smile brightens, and he shows too many teeth. It was this smile that got him elected. "A trifle. Instead of laying off a third of the museum staff, I'll take one dismissal as a token of your willingness to bear the consequences of failure. It'll be a quiet dismissal, only a small sacrifice."

My eyes narrow. "How small?"

The smile shifts into one edged with malice. "It's not a sacrifice if it doesn't hurt."

"Who?" I know who. I can feel it in the arches of my feet and the swimmy sensation in my stomach.

"Velasquez."

My mouth pinches and my nostrils flare. Only by imagining the possible headlines do I prevent myself from leaping across the table and smacking Oskar's name out of his mouth. Mama's hand covers my arm, but I'm shaking with rage, too far gone for discretion and meek acceptance. "What is this?"

Mama's grip tightens. "It's a deal," she explains. "The prime minister is offering excellent terms. You should think about it."

I don't have to think. "No. That condition is unacceptable."

Torbald's eyebrows lift. "One person. He's hardly worth triggering massive cuts over."

Spikes of pain and anger prickle my skin, but I see things clearly, now. Prime Minister Torbald has taken a beating in the press as stories frame him next to Oskar, the inconveniently telegenic immigrant whose ubiquity on social media has made it difficult to remind Sondmark's citizens that they need to hold the world at arm's length.

I see the consequences of this deal clearly, too. If Oskar loses his job, he won't be able to take his citizenship test. He'll be put on a repatriation program, and because he's become a minor celebrity, he won't slip through the cracks and disappear. We can't arrange for his paperwork to be lost. I bet the government will move with astonishing speed.

Mama is puzzled by my obstinance. "Freja, do consider—"

"No." I am unequivocal. "I won't take it. I won't make that deal."

The prime minister exhales gustily, crossing his leg, exposing a sock and three centimeters of hairy skin. "I've already given The Nat's temporary governing board my offer. Do you think they'll save him at the risk of losing their own jobs?" He sets the question between us like a dagger on the table. Who can we count on to stand with Oskar? Rik? Lynda? Agnes?

The prime minister leans back like this is his throne room. "I look forward to announcing your exhibit before the end of the day. Perhaps a line or two might be included in Her Majesty's Live Christmas message tomorrow?"

Mama smiles her diplomatic smile. "We won't keep you from more pressing matters," she says, rising. Prime Minister Torbald climbs to his feet and executes a careless bow. He received his education at an elite boarding school catering to European nobles. He knows how to do it properly. I want to trip him on the way out and shove him into a bramble patch with long, spiky thorns.

As soon as the door closes, Mama turns, her brows gathering. "Freja, explain yourself. The prime minister is poised to lose far more in this deal than you are. You should take it."

Tears crowd my throat. "No. I have to meet with the board, convince them—"

"Why? You won."

I bite my lip, my chin pulling with the effort of not weeping. "I lost. If he gets fired, the likelihood *Neer* Velasquez will be sent back to Pavieau is high."

Mama, utterly at sea, lifts her hands. I'm one of her easier children. I've never frustrated her like this. "Pavieau is on its way to becoming a thriving constitutional monarchy with the best weather in Europe. It's hardly banishment for a man who was born there."

Time slows and my sight seems to sharpen, bringing a host of things into deep focus. My gaze is level. "How can you say that? He came when he was five," I say. "He likes *Glogg*, for pity's sake."

Mama is puzzled by my anger. When she speaks again, she sounds tired. "Sometimes, Freja, leadership requires us to make hard choices. Sometimes it requires us to sacrifice the personal in favor of the political—to put aside the needs of the one for the needs of the many."

"Are we still talking about Oskar?"

Mama turns, her silhouette outlined against a steel-gray winter sky. I've seen her rigid control this past year, the way she watches her words among the family, the way her eyes follow Père from the room. My father left his family and his homeland to be her prince consort, and when there were sacrifices to be made, he made them.

Mama rests her hand lightly on a side table. "Your father understands the position I'm in."

"No, he doesn't." I see. For the first time, I see. "You didn't fight them about the funeral, Mama. He had to meet his family secretly," I breathe, the intensity of emotion rushing through me like a tide. "People can tell when they matter."

The surge of the ocean roars beyond the windows, the fire snaps in the hearth, and the bronze mantelpiece clock tick, tick, ticks. I think of Oskar's shy enjoyment of Sondish Christmas traditions and how he stands between his two cultures, a little outside both of them. The way he gripped my hand when he thought about his parents. The way we fit together.

Mama lifts her head like the dragon of Sondmark, loosed from her crest and shaking off droplets of rain. Whatever impression my words made, she's in control again. "Take the deal. Having this funding will benefit you, the entire staff, and the whole country."

"No." I don't budge. She can't move me. My spine is titanium. "When you decide you have to treat people like chess pieces to be manipulated around the board, it doesn't matter what the goal is. You've already lost the game. Oskar isn't a pawn the prime minister can discard because he wants to advance a policy."

"Oskar?" she repeats, her eyes narrowing. "What's going on, Freja? I thought your familiarity with him was an act for the cameras. I didn't say anything because I thought I could count on your discretion." There's an edge to her voice I've never been on the receiving end of. "Freja, he's Pavian."

"I don't need the reminder."

"Clearly you do. The royal house of Sondmark doesn't have parliamentary authorization to normalize relationships with Pavieau. You won't get what you want from the politicians, no matter how many likes *Neer* Velasquez gets on social media. If you expect to keep your place in the succession, any connection you form with this man can never be anything serious. I get no choice in the matter. You have to forget him."

There it is, the hard boundary—a thousand feet high, a thousand meters thick. Mama offers no help. Maybe she would sacrifice me for Sondmark, just as she sacrifices my father.

I have dipped countless curtsies to Queen Helena but in her role as my mother, I've only ever felt her hand on my back, lifting and supportive. I've lost that support, the suddenness of it like those first tentative steps on my own after surgery and the months afterward of learning to trust my body, learning to be strong. I did it then. I can do it now.

I gather my coat. "I have to go to The Nat and—"

"Would you do this for any provisional resident?"

I capture my lip in my teeth. "I don't know. I hope so," I say, imagining Oskar's hand in mine, giving it a squeeze to keep me from falling to pieces. "I won't let him think he doesn't matter."

Mama almost growls in frustration. "Of course, he matters, but we all have to come together to make a deal."

I shake my head. Will my family ever make sense? "You hold the sword and he lies at your feet, but the important thing to remember is that you were both at the massacre?"

This is fruitless. I won't change my mind. I cross to the door, reaching for the handle when Mama's voice arrests me.

"I suggest you take the deal, Freja. I mean it for your own good."

I train my eyes on the intricate paneling carved centuries ago, thinking of the men and women ushered into Mama's presence, bowing before her. Stronger people than I am. Better. Wiser. Many of them bent to her will.

I wish I could.

"I love him." A tear slips down my cheek, but she doesn't see it. "Whatever comes next, you need to know that."

33

IMPOSSIBLE SHOT

FREJA

Freddie tools the Mercedes through the heart of Handsel, and I peer up at the winter sky, keeping the ugly cry at bay. The snow is holding off, but the wind has picked up, rattling the windows. By this evening, we will be cloaked in snow, each household closed tightly against the storm.

My heart sinks when I enter the gallery. There are few visitors on Christmas Eve, and my presence is unnoticed as I skip up the administrative steps. The paper temperature gauge mocks me. Twenty-eight thousand, three hundred and fifty-seven visitors until our goal.

I put my head around the director's door. "Did the prime minister call?" I ask.

Marie, sitting at her desk, runs her ringed hands through her short crop of hair and looks up. "Yes. We'll meet at the end of the day to vote."

Not the answer I want to hear.

"So soon? Hold on to him until January. Surely—"

"The terms were crystal clear. With no fanfare, we are to push him out today—"

"Christmas Eve?"

"If we do it today," Marie repeats, "we move forward unscathed. If not—" She makes a face and exhales a great breath. "Can you believe I voted for that *vailys*? His office called. It wasn't even him but one of those chinless weasels he employs. He didn't even have the courage to knife Oskar in the back himself."

My mind replays the heated exchanges in our staff meetings. "Oskar will lose if you put it to a vote."

Marie lifts her shoulder. "Erik was ferocious when he heard. Said we'd be"—her fingers make air quotes—"'banana-crackers insane' to get rid of 'the best thing that's happened to Sondmark since the invention of plastic interlocking bricks.'"

As bad as things are, I smile. Erik is an unexpected treasure.

"Will Oskar make his case before the board?"

She shakes her head. "He's packing up."

I make a noise at the back of my throat and race out of the office and across the gallery, running so fast I almost fall through the door of the restoration studio. I skid to a stop to find Oskar filling a cardboard box with brushes and papers, each laid out meticulously on a worktable. His hand stills, and he holds my gaze. We were supposed to pick up where we left off on Saturday night, looking at each other past the turned figure of Uncle Timo.

He glances down, runs a tapping hand along a row of brushes, and crouches in front of a drawer, digging out a tool.

No. I can fix this. My heart is so high I can feel it pounding in my brain.

He straightens and I'm reminded of that first time I came here, hating him, hardly willing to acknowledge an attraction to a man I was certain would eat me alive if he got the chance. I liked his looks, against my better judgment. That's all I would admit. I like every part of him now.

His thumb flicks the bristles of the brush back and forth and then he sets it down with a snap, bracing his arms on two tables, bridging them.

"It's been good working with you," he says. Is this the opening line of a final goodbye? He lifts his head, half-smiling, eyes tracing the perimeter of the ceiling.

I'm too upset for politeness. "Do you think I made that deal with Torbald?"

His eyes travel over me–artist's eyes. He's seen every side of me in the last months. Can he see that I would never do this?

"No," he says, quiet, firm. "You wouldn't trade me."

Though the wind is whipping the trees beyond the window, within we are still.

I slot between the narrow channel of his worktables, relief squeezing out of me like glue from a canvas. I wouldn't trade him—not for all the art in Europe. Not for a thousand exhibits. Not for my mother's supporting hand.

"Never."

Though he says he knew it, he's pleased by my answer, his lower lip tightening a fraction.

"I'll have to take a raincheck for that date," he says.

I looked it up on my drive this morning. The process of repatriation away from Sondmark after a failed citizenship bid is theoretical until it suddenly and decisively isn't. In as little as two months, Oskar could find himself walking the streets of Gransoleil.

"A raincheck?" My tone is scornful as I lean against a table. A raincheck is what you get from the dentist when you develop a cold.

He rolls back to lean next to me, shirt stretched across his chest. I love him like this. He takes my hand, as he's done so often.

"Maybe when relations between Pavieau and Sondmark thaw," he says, "your family will send you on a delegation."

I blink heavily. It's silly to talk about his dismissal when the open question of when he's going to kiss me has yet to be answered. Warm sparks drift up from our lightly clasped hands.

"You could sneak away to meet that seedy art restorer you used to know," he bumps my shoulder with his. The contact is electric even if his words are light. He's trying to keep this from devolving into tragedy. "I'll find a job, get a flat—"

My free hand grips the table and I wonder for a fraught moment if I might overturn it like one of Ella's video game monsters. I'm mad and weepy and, somehow, very, very Pavian right now. "Don't you dare paint a picture that doesn't have me in it."

He exhales, hand tightening. "*Vede*, Freja, what am I supposed—"

"Oskar." His name is an oath. "You can't go. You speak in Sondish. You curse in Sondish. You love a Sondish princess."

He hasn't said any such thing, but I know. I know. I've merely dipped my ladle into the clear waters and drawn it up into the light.

The signs have been there from the beginning—most of which have been captured on camera and broadcast to the entire nation. The brush of our hands, the bracing intake of breath, how he was grumpy enough to cloak his feelings but never grumpy enough to drive me off entirely, the way he kisses. How he holds my hand and feeds me cookies from his desk drawer. How they never have raisins.

I dare him to deny it.

He takes a breath and turns, trapping me against the worktable, burying his head in my neck, lips against my skin, arms tight around my waist and back. I can't breathe, but I raise a hand to his hair with a small laugh. I knew it.

He raises his head, and the laugh dries up. At this moment, Oskar isn't Smit looking for a scratch behind his ears. His chin tips back, eyes filled with arrogance, and his hands settle on my waist. "What are you laughing for? You love me, too."

My throat hurts with the effort honesty demands. I nod.

He swallows and shakes his head. "How?"

"Like a fairy tale. You had me follow a trail of cookies to your door." I kiss him lightly, as though we've been kissing for years, but his gaze brushes my lips, warning me that I'm running a tab to be paid off later.

"What do we do?" he asks, abandoning gauzy fiction. "Meet in Switzerland?"

I make a noise. "Not that. Not Switzerland. My father meets his family in Switzerland, and they pretend it's enough. Switzerland is where long-distance relationships go to die." I tangle my fingers with his. "I have an idea. Come here."

I lead him to the sofa. This will require time and attention to explain. It will require the kind of clear-headedness not to be found when I'm pressed against him, his hands on my waist.

Though I imagined myself perched on my end of the sofa and him on the other, rational discourse filling the gap, Oskar allows no gap. He pulls me into his arms, and I try to remember the stakes. Deportation. Unemployment. Separation.

Do we have time for this? I run through the list of things I've planned for today, the logistics that keep filing into my brain like overeager queen's ministers. The letter I have to write. The emails I have to send. The treacherous interpersonal dynamics I have to avoid. Then his lips touch mine and I forget everything.

Some part of me must have understood, even in the beginning, that Oskar was dangerous to my future and my peace of mind. My only defenses were to avoid him like the plague and believe the worst of him. Such tissue-thin fortifications.

He lifts his head. "The timing is terrible," he says, short of breath, forehead resting against mine. "You might have discovered my merits three years ago."

"You might have been struck dumb by my beauty." I'm breathless, too.

"I *was* struck dumb," he says, leaning forward for another kiss. "Stupid. Idiotic."

I press a hand against his chest. "We have to talk."

He collapses against the back of the sofa, slides an arm around my shoulders, and pulls me close. Oskar doesn't feel an atom of apprehension that I'm about to break his heart, and I close my eyes against the brilliant light. This is trust. I'll need it.

"I'm listening," he says, bringing my palm to his mouth and kissing it, leaving behind the rasp of his chin and the vibration of his voice.

"I know what I'm supposed to say," I begin. "I'm supposed to say that we'll take it one day at a time, that we'll get to know each other, that we'll see how this develops."

"Mm." Oskar places my palm against his throat, the pulse beating under my hand, and pushes it around his neck.

"I'm supposed to go along with immigration law and sacrifice you to save the museum."

"Mm," he responds, slowly pulling me closer. Oskar has his own plans.

"I don't want to."

He curls me into his side, resting his chin on my hair. "What do you want?"

"Some version of this, forever and ever."

I feel a kiss on the top of my head. "I'm your willing servant."

I hold my breath and screw my eyes shut like a princess making a wish at an enchanted well. "Forever?"

It's too soon for that word. It should come after three years of dating, an exhaustive background check, a whole pro/con list drawn up by palace courtiers, and Mama's approval. My mother won't approve of this.

Oskar doesn't laugh, and he doesn't answer too quickly. When he does answer, I know he means it.

"Forever."

I twist so I can see his face. I know how he thinks. The precariousness of his future stops his words. He has nothing—no job, no home. He won't ask. He can't ask.

Only I can ask.

I take a breath, aiming my arrow at a target a thousand miles away. An impossible shot. The string strains as I pull it back. "Will you marry me?"

He breathes a laugh and kisses my mouth, adding to the tab. I can't be serious. "Next year at Roslav Cathedral, after we secure parliamentary approval?"

"Parliament won't ever approve."

The truth is too sad, so he kisses my mouth again.

Things won't be simple. I won't be able to follow a prescribed path. I might lose my place in the succession. My family will be furious.

It's not a sacrifice if it doesn't hurt. Damn Torbald for being right about something.

I can make peace with my sacrifices, but Oskar will have to sacrifice too.

"You'd be in the papers. They'll call you Pavi and worse." The thought of it twists my heart. I've never wanted to protect anyone as much as I want to protect him. "People will say you only married me for your citizenship or what my family could do for you."

His gaze is clear but he's silent. He kisses my mouth.

The arrow is still flying. "Could you do it, even with all that?"

He shifts, sitting up, and looks me square in the face. "Are you being serious?"

I nod.

It's outrageous what I'm asking. People don't do this. Princesses, especially, don't do this. But Oskar and I walk in and out of a building stuffed with ancient treasures every day. We breathe the dust of a dozen centuries and have learned how to recognize timeless things, lasting things. I should be more shocked at my words, but instead, I feel how solid and firm my foundations are as we lay the stones out one by one.

I tilt my chin. "Will you marry me?"

"I will."

"Today?"

He draws a breath. "How?"

"The Stranger's Parish. It would have to be just us."

Understanding dawns in his eyes, and he's silent for a long time, imagining how it would be. He touches my face. "You won't have Roslav Cathedral or a wedding dress."

My smile is as stupid as Clara's. Stupider, even. Oskar Velasquez loves me. "I'll wear your mother's if you'll allow me to borrow it."

He tips his head back to regard my face, his eyes bright. "Are you sacrificing yourself, saving me from the Dragon of Sondmark?"

I release a narrow breath—a scoffing, Pavian sound. "I decided to marry you days ago."

He grins. "Were you going to give me a choice in the matter?"

"I'll let you decide when."

Lacing our fingers together, his thumb traces the spot where my wedding ring will rest. The panic of the morning has given way to wonder.

"What about your family?"

I shake my head, firmly. "You were born in Pavieau. Even if it shouldn't be, it's complicated."

I pray my family will understand. My father is an immigrant who must see what Oskar is up against. My twin knows what it's like to feel the tight constraints of the monarchy. Clara is in love, and Alma is too busy worrying about her own engagement to worry about mine. Noah will be more upset about what it does to the reputation of the royal family than he will be about the fact he wasn't invited. My mother—I can't think about my mother. But they will understand. Though I can't have them come, I have to believe they'll understand.

"It'll be a proper elopement. The press will say and be the worst. You've seen how it's been with Clara and Alma," I remind him. "Their names are in the paper every day. People they've never met have opinions about the most intimate details of their lives. It's a lot. Even for those of us who are used to it, it's a lot."

I hold my breath. This is the animating worry of every Sondish princess. Who would choose this life if they didn't have to?

Oskar's thumb brushes my lips and comes to rest under my jaw. Then he pulls me to my feet. "Kiss me. We have a wedding to plan."

34

— • —

POCKET FULL OF HAIRPINS

FREJA

For something as stripped back to bare essentials as an elopement, we work hard through the afternoon to achieve it. Though the circle of those who know about it is necessarily small, there are still details to work out, people to contact, and letters to write. I hand my letters off to a courier, struck by how insufficient they are. One for Mama and Père to be read at once, the others for the rest of the family to be read much later tonight. The envelopes are too thin. They won't understand. I'll be banished to Switzerland.

I stare at the swinging door.

"I can chase him down," Oskar says, putting his arms around me. I settle back against his chest. "Cancel the church, ring up the photographer..." He kisses the scar at the base of my neck. I inhale the scent of his cologne.

In another world, I imagine a more conventional wedding day. The broadcast would begin from Roslav Cathedral, and a television presenter would name off Wolffe family guests, a titled network extending all over Europe and select enclaves of North America. The prime minister's wife might be mistaken for a distant cousin by the American press. Much would be made of the fact that Oskar's parents had the ill luck to be both Pavian and dead.

The date would have been chosen by a committee with optics in mind—a day with glorious weather, possibly meant to counteract a regrettable dip in the monarchy's popularity. We would have been buried under a mountain of logistics–the dress fittings and cake tastings, some details calibrated to reflect the interests of the public. There might even be a protest a few blocks away from the venue.

Who am I kidding? If I present Oskar as my future husband, we'd never arrive at an actual wedding day thanks to unending, parliamentary hissy fits.

"Don't you dare stop those letters," I reply.

He spins me around and his arms tighten. "What are the chances your mother will have me publicly murdered?"

"Very low. She'd do it quietly and pin it on a foreign government," I say between kisses that taste like ginger and cinnamon. It's a joke, but I fish the medallion of Santo Laurenzi from his shirt and hold it tight.

Oskar returns to his list, and I run up to meet with Marie. I return to find him striking lines through tasks accomplished with the same energy Caroline employs during a state visit.

Snow falls fitfully throughout the day, and the tufty flakes hardly accumulate. As the afternoon progresses, the wind picks up, pushing them into glittering whorls.

"We should go soon," I say.

Oskar checks his watch. "There's the board meeting."

I take his hand. "We don't need to go. You're staying in Sondmark no matter what."

He tugs me out the door. "I want to know if you'll be marrying the Head of Restoration at The Nat or running off with an unemployed artist." He smiles, but I feel his hand tighten as we draw near the conference room.

"We don't need him." Rik's voice carries into the hall. "Let's move forward."

The words send a sharp sense of betrayal through my chest. I had to listen to that man carry on about the Assyrian Empire under King Ashurbanipal for over an hour. He owes me.

Even though I said the vote didn't matter, my steps quicken. I'm ready to charge in there, bellowing like a Viking shield maiden and cleaving the conference table in two with a mighty swing of a sword. Oskar interrupts my progress, scooping me around the waist and depositing me into a cubicle. He puts a finger against my lips and leans against a desk. "I only want to know how the vote goes."

"Badly," I hiss. "Unless we get in there, it's going to go badly."

Someone raps their knuckles on the table. "Agree," Agnes says. "He belongs where he belongs. All of us want to go home."

I straighten and Oskar tugs the ties of my blouse until I'm level with him. He kisses me, which isn't fair at all.

"You have your ballots," Marie says. "Check one of the boxes and pass them forward. You know my thoughts, but I'll abide by the majority decision."

In the silence that follows, I hear Lynda's earrings play "Holy Night of Joy and Mercy" and the shuffling of pens and paper. Oskar puts his hands in his pockets, but I know better than to think he doesn't care about the outcome.

"All right," Marie says. "We have fifteen board members and eight is a majority. First vote...stay. Second...stay." Her voice gets more confident with each pass. Third, fourth, fifth, stay, stay, stay. "Eighth..." I hold my breath, hands wringing Oskar's arm. "Stay."

I shake his arm silently and am rewarded with the smallest smile.

"Count out the rest," Rik insists.

I straighten, ready for a fight, and Oskar tugs my ties again, the fabric slipping through the loops.

"You've undone me," I whisper, clutching the remnants of the bow. I put my hand up to fix them but freeze as the count continues in Oskar's favor. He only brushes my hands aside and does me up again.

"Thirteen...stay. Fourteen...stay. Fifteen..."

This will be Rik. It's a shame this will end on a sour note.

"Stay."

Oskar's hands drop to his side, and I blink several times.

"Rik, I thought you said we didn't need him," Marie says, absolutely incredulous.

"I meant for the meeting. He doesn't like meetings. But he's been front and center for The Nat over the last months, the least we can do is spare him having to be here. Somebody send him a text."

Oskar pulls me down to the entrance hall, opening and shutting his mouth several times. I stifle a laugh.

"They might be fired by the end of next week," he says.

"They know it."

We drive back to his flat together while the roads are passable. In the lobby he reaches into his pocket, giving me the key. "I rang up Uncle Timo and had him send my suit to be pressed. I'll dress at his place and let you know when I leave. Freddie dropped your bag earlier. He'll drive you to the church when you're ready."

A pang of guilt goes through me. Weddings aren't just for women. "You won't have Uncle Timo or any of your cousins."

"We'll have a party when the dust settles. Your family can squish in with mine," he says, painting a picture out of some absurdist night fever. "We'll dance on a tiny dancefloor and talk too loudly. I can push you into the kitchen again." He kisses my lips, the soft spot under my ear, my neck.

I shiver.

"Go," he says. I turn to the stairs and power off my phone. In his flat—our flat—I find the dress laid out on the bed, along with a note he sent on ahead.

"Uncle Timo had this pressed and several tucks let out in the hem. If my ancestors were not as clever as you thought, come in the clothes you're standing up in. I'll take you on any terms. Love."

I look out the window. The dark is broken by pools of lamplight as the outer band of snow begins to fall in earnest. We have an hour, no more, before the wise take refuge.

I shower and do my make-up from the bag I had Caroline put together. I dress, taking care not to smudge the fabric with lipstick as I work my way into it. I don't think about my sisters. I can't.

As expected, the ties at the waist give me a precise fit and accentuate the fullness of the skirts. The seamstress Uncle Timo found has done a masterful job unpicking the seams, carefully pressing them out, and finding the necessary length. Thank you, Oskar's mama for these warm petticoats. Thank you, Oskar's grandmama for this embroidery and these seams. I am a lone wolf, but, within this dress, I'm not alone.

I hear the turn of the lock of the outer door. "It's me," Oskar calls. "I have my eyes closed."

"Open them. I'm in your room," I answer.

"Our room," he corrects. My stomach dips as I press my ear and hand to the door.

I hear the scrape of his shoe on the other side. "Love, I'm going now," he says, voice muffled.

"Is that what you're going to call me?" I wish I had a picture of my face. If I sent it to my family, they'd understand everything.

"I'm trying it out. What do you think?"

I think I probably have enough time to fix my lipstick. I turn the handle, managing to get it open a crack before he grips it, halting me.

"*Elskede*, no," he scolds. "It's bad luck to see the bride, even in Pavieau."

I lace my fingers over his. "I like *elskede*, too."

"Freddie's worried about the snow. He wants you to go down in a quarter of an hour."

"You won't run away?"

His fingers tighten and I hear a smile in his voice. "Where would I run to? Home? You're home."

Another grain of rice added to an impossibly high mountain. "You'd best leave, Velasquez, before I break the door off its hinges."

"*Audicia*." He presses a kiss on my fingers, and when he's gone again, I look out the window for a long moment. I can't magic away the weather. I set aside the heels I had planned to wear and lace up a pair of sturdy boots, smoothing my skirts as I turn to the mirror.

An unconventional bride, but I want to remember this feeling if I'm ever missing the majesty of Roslav Cathedral, envious of what my sisters will have. I love my dress, the story of it woven before I was born. I love the man I'm going to marry. I love the life we'll make together, no matter where it happens.

Ten minutes later, Freddie hands me into the car, carefully lifting my skirts over the threshold. He expected a quiet Christmas Eve in the guardhouse.

"Are you shocked?" I ask.

He lifts a shoulder. "I've been your security officer for, what, six years, on and off? Each day planned to the last second—stand here, smile there—and then he comes along and—" Freddie gives a sharp die-away whistle, his lips twitching into a smile. "You're throwing your cap over the windmill, good and proper."

The ride is short, and when we arrive, Freddie helps me across the soft snow of the inner courtyard. On some level, I know it's bitterly cold, but I can't register it. The porch is illuminated, and I see a small wedding bouquet on the bench seat Oskar and I once occupied together, a posy of paperwhite narcissus tied up with a deep green ribbon. I recognize them as grown from a pot in Uncle Timo's kitchen window.

Freddie jogs ahead and brings it to me, pressing the posy into my hands with a bracing smile. His daughters are just about my age.

I swallow and try not to think of Père. "Are you going to scout the location for threats?" I ask. A reason to have him stay.

He smiles, seeing through my excuse. "And I'll tell *Neer* Velasquez you're on your way."

I nod, and then I'm alone in the courtyard. I take a breath and take a step.

"Ma'am," a voice calls, and I turn to see Caroline making her way across the snow with short, careful steps, carrying a couple of boxes.

My stomach lurches, and I measure the distance between me and the chapel. Is this Mama's objection? Has she managed a diplomatic miracle and suspended religious rites just for tonight? Can I make it and bar the door in time?

Before I lift my skirts and begin to sprint, the chapel door opens and Asger Hom steps out, wearing a puckish smile. A tuft of white hair sticks out of a knitted cap. "May I capture a few snaps out here?" he says, holding a complicated camera up to his eye. I nod.

Caroline fetches up in front of me, her breaths coming in small puffs. Her nose is rosy, and a thought intrudes. Noah wouldn't like her to be cold.

"Her Majesty sends her best wishes," she gasps, holding out the large box.

My heart beats hard in my chest, and I begin to feel the cold rushing in on me. "That's a tiara box."

"Yes, I have the veil, too, ma'am." She jiggles the other box. "And a pocket full of hairpins. If you'll get down a bit, I can have this secured in no time."

My heart has shifted to my throat and behind my eyes, but I do as she says. She puts the boxes in my hands and takes the tiara from its case. It's not my usual scrolling diamond bandeau but one of yellow gold and seed pearls. Floral motifs frame a series of soft carved cameos depicting the love story of Thora and Bjarke. Because of its high level of difficulty, no one has worn this tiara in more than a hundred years.

The veil? My fingers are shaking as I lift the lid, Asger slipping around me like a friendly ghost.

Vede. I can't cry. I'm ugly when I cry.

Five meters of Brussels lace, woven with the flowers of Sondmark along the scalloped edge. It was worn by six generations of Wolffe brides. Though she isn't here, my mother has sent every emblem she could collect in such a short amount of time.

"What does it mean?" I ask.

I don't blame my mother if it's a gambit to head off the bad press, a ploy to have royal approval stamped on the images which will arise from this day even if no such approval exists. Christmas is about grace and mercy. I will understand her. I'm determined to.

"People can tell when they matter." Caroline finishes with the bobby pins, collects the boxes, and assesses her work. "That's what your mother said."

I feel Mama's hand at my back, feel a stinging in my nose, and blot under my eyes with tapping fingers. "Tell them I'm happy."

She looks at me for a long moment. Every word and impression will be reported back to my parents within the hour.

"Yes," she decides. "Very happy. Best wishes, Your Royal Highness."

I hear the gentle strains of an organ, and Caroline stoops to adjust my veil so that with each step it unfurls. Wind gusts through the courtyard, Freddie opens the door, and I walk toward the blazing glow of candles.

This won't be hard. I only have to hold onto Oskar's hand.

35

HOME

FREJA

Snowflakes fall and swirl beyond the glass, muffling the roar of the wind. Nestled deep in a down comforter, I blink the sleep from my eyes. It's perfect weather for Christmas.

I stretch towards the ceiling, my fist finding its way from the too-long sleeve of the flannel pajama top, and feel for the other side of the bed. Finding nothing but cool linens, I sit up on my elbows and shake the hair out of my face, properly awake now.

I see the room with new eyes. There's the dress, draped carefully over an antique armchair. The desk and bookshelf have modern lines, but I recognize them as likely purchased in a flat pack from AKAE and put together in the front room along with indecipherable instructions and swearing. Original paintings hang over the bed. Otherwise, the space is empty.

The distant clinking of dishes is enough to tip me out of bed and onto my feet, bare against the cold floor. He's not in the sitting room, but he's been here before me, turning on the lights of the small Christmas tree to create a warm shield against the curtain of snow outside. I can't even see the palace. In any other circumstances, I would linger, tucking myself onto the sofa under a wooly blanket with one of those books from his well-filled shelves.

Such a thing would mark this as a different Christmas morning than any I've ever had. At the Summer Palace, the sound of bells would rouse me from sleep, and I would come down to breakfast to find a small pile of gifts next to my plate. Extended family visiting from France, Germany, or Tallinne would give the day a loud and festive air, and we would lapse into different languages as we tried to communicate. I wouldn't know a moment's peace until I climbed into bed sometime after midnight.

I rub my hands along my arms and pivot in this modest flat on the other side of the city, holding the contrast between this and the palace against my palms, trying to make them fit. Both places are part of me now.

My stomach shifts, an aftershock of yesterday's news no doubt still shaking the palace. I feel the dull ache of how things ought to have been and weren't, the weight of guilt. I feel, too, the kind of happiness that burrows into my bones, writing on my heart, fizzing like a bottle of sparkling water. These things are part of me now.

Another clink of dishes sends me running to the kitchen. I angle my head around the door and draw a breath. Oskar is wearing the bottom half of our pajamas, his arms braced against the counter, a wonder of human anatomy. The thin gold chain rolls lazily over the slope where his neck becomes shoulder.

My eyes close briefly. Merry Christmas to me.

Oskar reaches for the electric kettle, the muscles of his back shifting as he moves. He pours the contents over a filter, and I sniff, identifying the rich aroma of fresh ground coffee.

"French press?" I ask, and he turns, pushing his hair out of his face. The tiny medallion hitches on his skin, hanging off center. I have a good imagination, but after months of working with this man, side by side, I was not clever enough to imagine this.

I look and look and look. A blush warms my cheeks. He clears his throat, and my eyes return to his. For an anxious second, I look for signs of regret.

Then his gaze shifts over my bare legs and he grips the counter, turning his head to smile at the open shelves of crockery, at a houseplant in the window, at the refrigerator. He's self-conscious of the smile and of the way he can't seem to get rid of it. He nods several times—again at the crockery and houseplant—and bites his lip, an attempt to draw himself back into line.

No regret.

He sets a timer. "Like the view?" he prompts, his smile barely behaving.

I laugh, now unable to meet his eyes.

He opens his arms, and I walk into them, burrowing into his warmth, and wrap myself around him. His hands stroke my back, following the path of the long trailing scar.

He kisses the top of my head.

I press a kiss into his neck, the chain under my lips.

I look up and, as his mouth settles on mine, I'm dimly aware of the French press—of flyaway facts about how the coffee will be weak and sour if the steep time is too short, bitter if left too long. We wouldn't want weak coffee, I think, plowing my hand through his hair and working my way further into his arms.

Tick, tick, tick goes a timer, innocently counting off moments while my stomach coils tightly and the blush on my cheeks becomes a flush.

Ding.

It's a friendly sound, at odds with my overheated nerves. We draw back and I'm fighting to breathe properly. He's fighting too.

"Sit," he says, scooting me to the table. With great reluctance, I perch on a kitchen chair, watching him. He presses the coffee and pours out two mugs, setting them next to a tray of pastries.

I sniff appreciatively as he angles into the chair opposite me. "All this and a hot Danish, too?"

He leans against the wall, arms crossed over his chest. I used to think he was an unassailable monolith, reserving tender feelings for dead painters and good varnish. But now that I've assailed him, I know better.

He drinks from his cup and swallows. "The first rule of *Huis* Velasquez: Keep Freja fed."

I like that. *Huis* Velasquez. A Sondish word nestled against a Pavian name.

He looks at me, and his brows settle into goblin lines. He puts down his coffee with a grunt.

"What?" I ask, licking a crumb from the side of my lips.

He reaches his arm across the table and pulls me into his lap. Once upon a time I couldn't imagine him wearing anything but a waistcoat and tie–couldn't imagine his body relaxing around mine. He laces his fingers and rests them lightly on my hip, a thumb tracing the curve.

"Better?" I ask.

"Mm," he grunts, taking another swallow of coffee, setting the mug down, and holding me tightly. Already I have learned to interpret the unspoken communication of his breathing and his hands.

"I'm not going to stop eating," I warn.

"Heaven forbid." The words come with a smile, but he continues to hold me as I finish my breakfast, chin resting on my shoulder. Eventually, our breathing syncs up, a gentle and easy counterpoint to the howling wind.

My eyes drift to the window. The blizzard is a blessing. There won't be a soul in the streets today, giving us time to ourselves before a storm of another sort breaks.

I gather the air and breathe deeply. His hands tighten, comforting. He's learning me, too.

Absolute chaos has been left in our wake, but our worries can wait until tomorrow. Today belongs to us. I dust off my fingertips and wrap my arms around his neck, tracing the rim of his ear and liking the change I feel in the rhythm of his heart.

"I'm ready to be kissed."

He tips his head, saying against my lips, "Merry Christmas, wife."

36

·

Epilogue

FREJA

The press calls me The Winter Princess.

Asger Hom released a single image, snapped just as I was about to take my first steps toward the chapel, face and dress reflecting the glow of candlelight pouring from the doorway, the veil lifting gently with a gust of wind, snow falling around me. The photograph, along with a few, spare details of our elopement swallowed up every story across every Sondish news outlet and social media on Christmas morning.

I knew it would.

That already famous image has been reproduced on a massive scale behind me, covering an entire wall of the room that was once supposed to house the Romantics exhibit. It's New Year's Eve, and while The Nat has closed for the night, there's one last bit of business to conclude before we send everyone home for drunken karaoke and *oliebollen*.

I remove the cap from the marker, my heart beating out of time.

"Well?" I prompt Erik.

Though I sounded so certain when I put this idea to Marie on the day of my wedding, it's bound to be close. 28,000 guests in three days, just as the city was digging out of an enormous blizzard, was a lot to ask. As soon as the roads were clear they came in droves.

How many droves? I don't have an expression prepared if we don't reach our goal. Worry squeezes the air from my lungs. What if we've failed? The camera is going to catch me hauling a ceremonial axe from the wall and splitting the prime minister's skull.

"Twenty-" Erik begins, dragging the word out like his childhood, "nine thousand, six hundred and forty-nine!"

Though we're being filmed on Pixy, Oskar pulls me into his arms, lifting me off my feet. Lynda throws handfuls of shredded files like confetti and a cheer erupts in the gallery, an echo of riotous New Year's celebrations launching across Handsel in several hours. I bury my face in Oskar's tweed jacket as he spins around, and then lift my head. What do I care if Sondmark sees me kiss my husband?

"I'm shocked," Marie says, tipping her glass of champagne at us with a wicked smile. It's impossible to shock Marie. She knows more details than anyone, and when her ex-husband showed up on Christmas Eve with his tardy nut loaf and the juiciest gossip in northern Europe, I'm sure she pried every bit of information from him. The longshoreman was definitely a spy.

Oskar sets me down again, holding me steady against the jostling of the crowd piled into the gallery—every curator and restorer, every accountant and human resources officer, every janitor and lanyard-wearing volunteer has stayed long enough to hear the result. While I scribble out the white space at the top of the thermometer, someone pops a bottle of champagne and another sets up a portable speaker. An impromptu party breaks out.

I turn to the camera to sign off, but Prime Minister Torbald edges into the frame, hearty joviality on his face. "I knew you were capable of meeting my challenge," he says, calibrating his remarks for unseen constituencies on the other side of the screen. "I knew you could be roused from inaction and discover how to bring new patrons into The Nat."

He means none of it. After discovering I had given The Nat exclusive rights to stage a special exhibit about my elopement—complete with an array of hitherto unpublished Asger Hom images, a glass case Rik fabricated to hold my wedding gown, the veil and tiara borrowed from the royal collection, an illustration of the bride by her husband, and a supercut of Pixy feed highlights and raw video put together by Erik—he was livid.

He was also boxed neatly into a corner.

It was a foolish risk, bargaining with him in the first place. Museum staff gambled the future of The Nat and their careers on Oskar, refusing to dismiss him at the prime minister's request. I can sleep easy now, knowing we didn't send everyone to the unemployment office. I can sleep more easily knowing that they treated him as one of their own.

Mama protected me, too. On Christmas afternoon, Oskar and I watched her Address to the Nation, curled up on his sofa together after exchanging our gifts. He gave me the portrait I lent to the exhibit and a Waitrose Christmas sandwich brought over by a Pavian friend who came home for the holidays. I gave him a t-shirt, shipped from the Greybull Museum, which is a size too small or exactly right, depending on what your goals are.

"...Our own family shares the happy news that Her Royal Highness Princess Freja married *Neer* Oskar Velasquez in a private ceremony last night," Mama said, carefully avoiding the question of whether the family knew about it in advance. "Just as the family of Sondmark welcomes new citizens from every corner of the globe, our family welcomes a new member, eager to discover affinities and be invigorated by contrasts."

"Was that bit of backhanded rhetoric aimed at Torbald?" he asked.

I burrowed my cold feet under my new husband, adding a kiss. "You're catching on quickly."

The jostling crowd moves the prime minister out of the frame, and I squeeze Oskar's hand.

"Thank you for supporting The Nat," I say. "We couldn't have accomplished this without you. We hope you always feel at home here."

Erik signals that he's done with the Pixy feed, and Oskar gives Erik an avuncular nod of approval. Erik shoots us several finger hearts before melting away.

"Should I expect him to be godfather to our firstborn?"

I laugh but it was Erik who moved heaven and earth for Oskar—picking up the dry-cleaning on the wedding day, sourcing the candles and Christmas greenery, and pitching in as an organist when no one else could be found. Marie has offered him a permanent position when he's finished with university, and we'll be lucky to have him.

Oskar and I do the rounds, congratulating Roland on becoming a part-time contributor to a Sondish morning show. Agnes invites us to go boating when the weather improves. Finally, Oskar tugs me away from the party and to the outer rings where it's quiet.

It hasn't all been smooth going. Oskar and I have pushed Clara and Max out of the gossip columns for once. Questions have been raised about our relationship, as I predicted, and a small but vocal minority has called Oskar an opportunist and our marriage a citizenship scam. There have been calls for official investigations into the precise nature of our association—silly since the whole country watched me fall in love with Oskar on a live social media feed. Our honeymoon consisted of working flat out to get the exhibit up and running.

I smile primly. Not the whole honeymoon.

The press is mostly on our side, for now, inundating the country with write-ups like "Princess Freja's Fashion Diplomacy" and "10 Things Oskar Velasquez Might Eat for Breakfast," but the tide will turn one day.

"Worth it?" I ask.

"Mm." He murmurs, lacing our hands together. His thumb turns the simple gold band on my finger. He pauses by *The Battle of Durmstein*, tugging me to a halt. "You wanted to know what my favorite thing at the museum was."

"Ages ago, and you wouldn't tell me."

"I couldn't tell you." He nods at *The Winter Princess*. "I restored it last year. Do you know how much you look alike?"

We lean up against Director Knauss's hateful benches, due to be ripped out as soon as Rik gets the funding.

"People think he's rescuing her with that kiss," he says.

"He is. He woke her up."

Oskar shakes his head, pointing to the rim of gold on the horizon. "It's almost sunset. He would never have made it back to safety if she didn't rescue him back." He slides an arm around my waist and pulls me close.

"Are you going to ask?" he says at last.

"It doesn't matter if you didn't pass," I say. "You have your job. You're married to a citizen."

I see the corner of his smile and he reaches into his breast pocket, handing over a piece of paper. "I passed."

I exhale, and he leans over, lips pressing a lazy line of kisses against the side of my neck where he knows I like them. "I thought you said it didn't matter."

I plow my hand through his dark hair, reading off his results. "It's one less thing for my mother to fret about. Between me, Clara's lawsuit against the paparazzi, and Alma's broken engagement—"

He lifts his head. "What? Broken engagement?"

"You were studying, and I didn't want to distract you."

He frowns. "You've been distracting me all week."

I shouldn't smile at a time like this, but the way he says that makes me want to do unspeakable things.

"Pietor was caught...um...recycling plastics with an Italian bikini model. Alma seems to be taking it well but we're not supposed to say anything about it yet."

Oskar leans back, regarding me. "Lawsuits, elopements, broken engagements.... It's one thing right after another with you Wolffes."

I tug his tie, bringing his lips close to mine. "Welcome to the family."

Also By Keira Dominguez

The Magical Regency Series

Her Caprice

The Telling Touch

The Sweet Rowan

The Royals of Sondmark

The Impossible Princess

Acknowledgments

Dear Reader, thank you for coming with me on this journey. If I've happily distracted you from folding a laundry pile or writing a paper on the Punic Wars or taking a commute on public transit, please consider hopping over to Amazon or Goodreads and leaving a review. It is so helpful. If you'd also like to run rampant through the streets proclaiming your love for *The Winter Princess* at the top of your lungs, I won't stop you. I believe in freedom.

I like to have an idea of what my stories are going to turn into before I begin them, filling out beat sheets and outlines as I plan. For *The Winter Princess*, this process was almost useless. Oskar and Freja were both prickly introverts, unfolding themselves to me slowly and I met them on the page, as delighted to encounter them as any first-time reader. I love that one of her favorite things is when people bring her food and that she shows her affection to Oskar by bringing him food. I love that he's endlessly engrossed by her expressions and that he's also grossed out by her ancestor's heart-jars.

As I wrote, I leaned heavily on my first and most frequent beta reader, Debbie West. She's never chewed me out for asking her to reread chapter three to check for continuity issues or failed to respond when I needed to bounce ideas off her brain. ("Do you think I can get away with the northern European spelling for Oskar? Like, maybe his father thought he was being fancy? I need that *K*. I'm married to that *K*.") Stephanie McRae, Tia Hunsaker, and Kylene Grell were also invaluable beta readers, offering feedback and a second set of eyes I always rely on. When Kylene finished the manuscript, she left her house after 8 pm (bananas!) to knock on my door. When I threw it open, she whooped for joy and jumped into my arms. Get yourself friends like that, please. It will do you a world of good.

My critique partners, the incandescent Afton Nelson and the brilliant Christine Sandgren, are priceless when it comes to getting me to produce the best work I can. Time and again, they show up when I need them and I can't believe we've been together for eight years already. My books would be sad and boring without them.

Much of my research about art restoration came thanks to YouTube and Instagram. The account I found most fascinating and helpful was Baumgartner Fine Art Restoration. Julian Baumgartner produced content that aided me enormously when I was searching for ways to have Oskar—slightly taciturn and introverted—speak about his feelings without speaking about his feelings. Though I did a good deal of research, if you restore art and discover horrifying practices within these pages, please assume the mistakes are mine.

I'd like to thank my editor Emily Poole. I throw a lot of "foreign but not actually foreign" words at her, and the typos she catches are amazing. Also, she saved us all from a long and tortured metaphor about medieval paintings which was going nowhere. Thank you, Emily.

Leni Kauffman is my genius cover artist who read over my cover proposal and made magic happen. She took a 19th Century work of art (*The Painter's Honeymoon* by Frederic Leighton) and used it to convey a contemporary romance, all while keeping the quiet intimacy I loved about the inspiration piece in the first place. While the discourse about using AI for book covers rages, I'm more thankful than ever for the human artist who brought my vision to life.

Finally, I'd like to thank my husband who is not, nor ever could be, as grouchy as Oskar Velasquez—the man who stole my husband's eye and hair color. He is diligent and patient, does our taxes, tutors our son to figure out what a slope intercept even is, plans trips, hugs me when I need it, smudges my glasses when he kisses me properly, unloads lots of dishes, and squints in the darkness of the morning when I hold the phone up to his face and excitedly whisper, "Leni sent the new cover art!" We're coming up on 25 years of marriage this year and, while some of them have been hard, all of them have been happy. My husband believes in me and it's difficult to imagine that anything could ever make me richer than that.

ABOUT AUTHOR

Keira Dominguez grew up in Springfield, Oregon where she learned to refer to hazelnuts as filberts. She graduated from Brigham Young University with a B.A. in Random Historical Studies (Humanities) which would serve her well as a future novelist.

Though her personal style runs the gamut between "I'm definitely of wearing eyeliner" and "I'm driving the speed limit so no one catches me wearing pajamas to the school drop-off", Keira enjoys having opinions about award show fashions, scandalous historical drama, and dishy royal trivia. The heart wants what the heart wants.

Keira lives in Portland, Oregon, finding a lot of romantic inspiration in the way her husband maximizes deductions when doing the taxes, brings her Advil when she's sick, and unloads the dishwasher.